OUT OF THE DARK

COLLINS CHILLERS

· OUT OF ·
· THE DARK ·

TALES OF TERROR BY
ROBERT W. CHAMBERS

Edited, with an Introduction, by
HUGH LAMB

HarperCollins*Publishers*

HarperCollins*Publishers*
1 London Bridge Street
London SE1 9GF
www.harpercollins.co.uk

This edition 2018

First published in Canada in two volumes by Ash-Tree Press
1998, 1999

1

Selection, introduction and notes © Hugh Lamb 2018

A catalogue record for this book is available from the British Library

ISBN 978–0–00–826536–6

Typeset by Palimpsest Book Production Ltd, Falkirk, Stirlingshire

Printed and bound in Great Britain by CPI Group (UK) Ltd,
Croydon CR0 4YY

MIX
Paper from
responsible sources
FSC™ C007454

This book is produced from independently certified FSC™ paper
to ensure responsible forest management.

For more information visit: www.harpercollins.co.uk/green

*This collection of stories by a New York author
is dedicated, with great affection,
to another writer from that city –
my daughter-in-law,
Margaret Reyes Dempsey.*

PREFACE

Robert William Chambers, in his day one of America's most popular authors, was born in New York, 26 May 1865, the son of New York lawyer William P. Chambers. The family were of Scottish descent. He had an early interest in art, studying at the Art Students League in New York, and in 1886 he went to Paris where he studied at the Academie Julien for seven years. He was accompanied by Charles Dana Gibson, destined to become one of America's most celebrated portrait painters, who also illustrated some of Chambers's books in later life.

When Chambers and Gibson returned to America in 1893, it was Gibson who got the lucky break into an art career. Chambers turned to writing instead. His first book, *In the Quarter* (1894), was based on his experiences in France. It sold fairly well, enough to encourage him to try his hand at a second book based on his French sojourn. *The King in Yellow* (1895) turned out to be an instant success and set Chambers on a writing career that lasted forty years. It was also one of the most successful books of the macabre, a genre to which Chambers would return only occasionally during his life.

Out of the Dark contains the best of Chambers's work in this field, taken from books as far apart in publication as 1895 and 1920. By the time of his death on 16 December 1933, Robert W. Chambers had produced nearly 100 books (88 are listed in the British Library Catalogue in Britain alone). Sadly, only a very few dealt with the macabre.

CONTENTS

PART ONE

ORIGINS

1895–1899

INTRODUCTION

The tradition of the American in Paris – the expatriate enjoying himself in one of Europe's most appealing cities – goes back way beyond such luminaries as Henry Miller or Ernest Hemingway. So many Americans got to know the place as a result of the First World War that it was quite forgotten that others had been there before, under less trying circumstances.

When Robert Chambers and Charles Dana Gibson went there to study art in 1886, we must hope they had as good a time as Miller (while perhaps not so athletic). They stayed there for seven years, after all. What did come out of it was a book of tales of terror seldom surpassed in the genre, yet in its own way a very unsatisfying work, making the reader wish for more. Which statement just about sums up the writing career of Robert W. Chambers, as far as enthusiasts in this genre are concerned.

Chambers, despite displaying an early, unique talent for tales of terror, returned to them very seldom in later life. He was an astute writer, who knew what sold well, and produced the goods accordingly. Spy novels, adventure stories, society dramas, social comedies – if that's what the public wanted, then Chambers was happy to oblige.

He was one of the authors featured in 'How I "Broke into Print"', an article in the *Strand Magazine*'s November 1915 edition, and had this to say on his first major success:

My most important 'break into print' was with a collection of short stories of a weird and uncanny character, entitled *The King in Yellow*, which the public seemed to like. So flatteringly was it received, indeed, that it decided me to devote all my time to fiction, and so I have been writing ever since. I cannot say which of my books I prefer, because just as soon as I have finished a story I dislike it. I am continually trying to do something better, so that I presume my 'best' book will never be written.

The King in Yellow (1895) is at the same time one of the most enjoyable yet one of the most irritating books in the fantasy catalogue. At its best – as in 'The Yellow Sign' – it is genuinely scary, with original ideas seldom equalled. At its worst – as in 'The Prophets' Paradise' (not included here: think yourselves lucky) it is obscure, pompous, and overwritten.

The title refers to a play, rumoured to be so evil that it shatters lives and lays waste souls. We never get to see much of it; in fact, this much-vaunted evil work doesn't even appear in some of the stories. Where it does, as in 'The Yellow Sign' or 'The Mask', it adds untold atmosphere. Where it doesn't, as in 'The Street of the First Shell' (again not included), then the book is a distinct let-down. At times, it is hard to see what Chambers is intending with this erratic book. While it is an indispensable part of any self-respecting horror reader's library, I have to say that it does not live up to its reputation.

And yet, as strange as anything (and at a time when M.R. James was just starting his ghost story career), there comes a line in 'In the Court of the Dragon' which could not be more Jamesian:

> . . . I wondered idly . . . whether something not usually supposed to be at home in a Christian church, might have entered undetected, and taken possession of the west gallery.

'The Yellow Sign' is by far and away the most reprinted story from *The King in Yellow*, and earned the praise of H.P.

Lovecraft, among others. It very quickly conjures up an atmosphere of death and decay (count the words in this vein that appear in just the first few paragraphs) and, in the form of the church watchman, one of the genre's most disturbing figures.

'In the Court of the Dragon' and 'The Demoiselle D'Ys' are lesser items, though 'In the Court of the Dragon' has its own scary church figure. 'The Mask' limply trails its fingers in the waters of science fiction, like so many tales from the 1890s. (An odd fact: Chambers mentions Gounod's 'Sanctus' in 'The Mask', as a symbol of purity; Werner Herzog used the music over the closing credits of his film *Nosferatu* in 1979, a most un-pure film.)

While Chambers borrowed various things from Ambrose Bierce to embellish *The King in Yellow*, like the names Carcosa and Hastur, he has inspired precious few imitators himself. There may be one: Sidney Levett-Yeats, the British writer, introduces a book written by the devil (in his story 'The Devil's Manuscript' (1899)) which ruins lives when read. It is titled *The Yellow Dragon*.

As *The King in Yellow* proved to be a winner, Chambers turned to writing full-time, while still keeping up his artistic habits (though, oddly, he never seems to have illustrated any of his own books, Charles Dana Gibson certainly illustrated some for him). He supplied illustrations for magazines such as *Life*, *Truth*, and *Vogue*, and was photographed for *The King in Yellow*, palette in hand.

He married Elsa Vaughn Moller in 1898, and they spent their married life at Broadalbin, an 800 acre estate in the Sacandaga Valley, northern New York State. Broadalbin had been in the Chambers family since his grandfather William Chambers first settled there in the mid-1800s. This beautiful country estate in the Adirondacks included a game preserve (where it seems Chambers never shot) and a fishing lake.

Broadalbin House was remodelled by Chambers's architect brother, William Boughton Chambers, and was crammed with the family's and Chambers's collection of books, paintings, and

Oriental objets d'art. His collection of butterflies was said to be one of the most complete in America.

Chambers spent most of the year at Broadalbin, travelling into New York to work in an office which he kept secret from his family (so much so that they had trouble finding it when he died). His chauffeur would drop him off and pick him up again at a spot some distance from the office.

Chambers lavished much care and affection on Broadalbin, planting thousands of trees on the estate. When he died, he was buried under one of the oaks.

Not all his time at Broadalbin was contented. He saw 200 acres of the estate vanish under the waters of the Sacandaga Reservoir which now covers much of the valley. He would have been even more desolate at the fate of his carefully planted trees (see Part Two).

Though part of the house at Broadalbin was demolished, the building still stands, now owned by the Catholic Church. It was abandoned (literally overnight, on the death of Chambers's widow in 1938) for some years, and was vandalised terribly. It is reported that Chambers's papers were used by intruders and squatters to light fires.

Chambers loved the outdoor life: it shows up in his writing time and again, where his descriptions of nature, scenery and forests are superbly evocative. A keen hunter, shooter and fisher, his characters are so often engaged in these pursuits as to suggest Chambers himself at play. He could apparently call most kinds of birds and was well versed in Indian languages (see 'The Key to Grief').

He must have been the most fortunate of authors: successful, rich and surrounded by the life he loved and wrote about. It is easy to see why he was reported to be so popular with his estate workers and neighbours in this period of his life.

To follow up the success of *The King in Yellow*, Chambers published another book of short stories in 1896, *The Maker of Moons*.

The title story, included here, is in many ways a practice

run at his 1920 novel *The Slayer of Souls*. As in that book, we have ample helpings of the American secret service (fine men all), Oriental magic, and strange goings-on in the forest. It also shows how Chambers would finally drift away from the fantasy genre, into the world of espionage and adventure. 'The Maker of Moons' is nonetheless a superb fantasy, quite unlike anything else around at the time, and holds up well, even now.

From the same book comes 'A Pleasant Evening', another indication of the way Chambers would develop. Here, in a fairly traditional theme, he shows the skill that would lead to *The Tree of Heaven* (in Part Two) – the writing of neat and well crafted supernatural tales, not necessarily meant to frighten.

The next year, Chambers published *The Mystery of Choice*, a fine set of stories which was a series of vaguely connected tales, set mainly in France, but this time not in Paris. By far and away the most powerful of them was 'The Messenger'.

This is a long, sometimes rambling story that nevertheless guides the reader along to a most eerie conclusion. The setting – coastal Brittany – has seldom been used to such effect, and the historical tale behind the story's events has a grotesque ring of truth. This is one of Chambers's best stories, and its use of the traditional masked figure has never been bettered.

'Passeur' from the same book, is a much shorter, traditional ghost story, easily guessed by anyone familiar with the genre. But Chambers is too good to give it all away completely; relish the scenery he depicts in the closing paragraphs.

Sticking out like a sore thumb from the rest of the stories in the book, 'The Key to Grief' is set far away from France. Chambers might have borrowed the odd name or two from Bierce for *The King in Yellow*; here he all but ransacked Bierce's living-room. This is a shameless reworking of Bierce's 'An Occurrence at Owl Creek Bridge', which still has its own sense of the unknown, and is included here by virtue of its unusual location.

The Mystery of Choice contained a lot of what was to become the cardinal vice of Chambers's writing as time went by: an awful tendency to be rather soppy, especially in his romantic scenes. This style probably didn't read too well in the 1890s; nowadays it just grates alarmingly.

After 1900 Chambers moved steadily away from his roots in the fantasy genre, but still – though not often enough – popping back from time to time, as will be seen in Part Two.

Hugh Lamb
Sutton, Surrey
January 2018

THE YELLOW SIGN

'Let the red dawn surmise
What we shall do,
When this blue starlight dies
And all is through.'

I

There are so many things which are impossible to explain!
Why should certain chords in music make me think of the
brown and golden tints of autumn foliage? Why should the
Mass of Sainte Cécile send my thoughts wandering among
caverns whose walls blaze with ragged masses of virgin
silver? What was it in the roar and turmoil of Broadway at six
o'clock that flashed before my eyes the picture of a still
Breton forest where sunlight filtered through spring foliage
and Sylvia bent, half curiously, half tenderly, over a small
green lizard, murmuring: 'To think that this also is a little
ward of God'?

When I first saw the watchman his back was toward me.
I looked at him indifferently until he went into the church.
I paid no more attention to him than I had to any other
man who lounged through Washington Square that morning,
and when I shut my window and turned back into my studio
I had forgotten him. Late in the afternoon, the day being
warm, I raised the window again and leaned out to get a
sniff of air. A man was standing in the courtyard of the
church, and I noticed him again with as little interest as I
had that morning. I looked across the square to where the

fountain was playing and then, with my mind filled with vague impressions of trees, asphalt drives, and the moving groups of nursemaids and holiday-makers, I started to walk back to my easel. As I turned, my listless glance included the man below in the churchyard. His face was toward me now, and with a perfectly involuntary movement I bent to see it. At the same moment he raised his head and looked at me. Instantly I thought of a coffin-worm. Whatever it was about the man that repelled me I did not know, but the impression of a plump white grave-worm was so intense and nauseating that I must have shown it in my expression, for he turned his puffy face away with a movement which made me think of a disturbed grub in a chestnut.

I went back to my easel and motioned the model to resume her pose. After working awhile I was satisfied that I was spoiling what I had done as rapidly as possible, and I took up a palette knife and scraped the color out again. The flesh tones were sallow and unhealthy, and I did not understand how I could have painted such sickly color into a study which before that had glowed with healthy tones.

I looked at Tessie. She had not changed, and the clear flush of health dyed her neck and cheeks as I frowned.

'Is it something I've done?' she said.

'No – I've made a mess of this arm, and for the life of me I can't see how I came to paint such mud as that into the canvas,' I replied.

'Don't I pose well?' she insisted.

'Of course, perfectly.'

'Then it's not my fault?'

'No, it's my own.'

'I'm very sorry,' she said.

I told her she could rest while I applied rag and turpentine to the plague spot on my canvas, and she went off to smoke a cigarette and look over the illustrations in the *Courier Français*.

I did not know whether it was something in the turpentine or a defect in the canvas, but the more I scrubbed the more that gangrene seemed to spread. I worked like a beaver to get it out, and yet the disease appeared to creep from limb to limb of the study before me. Alarmed I strove to arrest it, but now the color on the breast changed and the whole figure seemed to absorb the infection as a sponge soaks up water. Vigorously I plied palette knife, turpentine, and scraper, thinking all the time what a séance I should hold with Duval who had sold me the canvas; but soon I noticed that it was not the canvas which was defective nor yet the colors of Edward. 'It must be the turpentine,' I thought angrily, 'or else my eyes have become so blurred and confused by the afternoon light that I can't see straight.' I called Tessie, the model. She came and leaned over my chair blowing rings of smoke into the air.

'What *have* you been doing to it?' she exclaimed.

'Nothing,' I growled, 'it must be this turpentine!'

'What a horrible color it is now,' she continued. 'Do you think my flesh resembles green cheese?'

'No, I don't,' I said angrily, 'did you ever know me to paint like that before?'

'No, indeed!'

'Well, then!'

'It must be the turpentine, or something,' she admitted.

She slipped on a Japanese robe and walked to the window. I scraped and rubbed until I was tired and finally picked up my brushes and hurled them through the canvas with a forcible expression, the tone alone of which reached Tessie's ears.

Nevertheless she promptly began: 'That's it! Swear and act silly and ruin your brushes! You have been three weeks on that study, and now look! What's the good of ripping the canvas? What creatures artists are!'

I felt about as much ashamed as I usually did after such an outbreak, and I turned the ruined canvas to the wall. Tessie helped me clean my brushes, and then danced away to dress. From the screen she regaled me with bits of advice concerning whole or partial loss of temper, until, thinking, perhaps, I had been tormented sufficiently, she came out to implore me to button her waist where she could not reach it on the shoulder.

'Everything went wrong from the time you came back from the window and talked about that horrid-looking man you saw in the churchyard,' she announced.

'Yes, he probably bewitched the picture,' I said yawning. I looked at my watch.

'It's after six, I know,' said Tessie, adjusting her hat before the mirror.

'Yes,' I replied, 'I didn't mean to keep you so long.' I leaned out of the window but recoiled with disgust, for the young man with the pasty face stood below in the church-yard. Tessie saw my gesture of disapproval and leaned from the window.

'Is that the man you don't like?' she whispered.

I nodded.

'I can't see his face, but he does look fat and soft. Someway or other,' she continued, turning to look at me, 'he reminds me of a dream – an awful dream I once had. Or,' she mused, looking down at her shapely shoes, 'was it a dream after all?'

'How should I know?' I smiled.

Tessie smiled in reply.

'You were in it,' she said, 'so perhaps you might know something about it.'

'Tessie! Tessie!' I protested, 'don't you dare flatter by saying that you dream about me!'

'But I did,' she insisted. 'Shall I tell you about it?'

'Go ahead,' I replied, lighting a cigarette.

Tessie leaned back on the open window-sill and began very seriously.

'One night last winter I was lying in bed thinking about nothing at all in particular. I had been posing for you and I was tired out, yet it seemed impossible for me to sleep. I heard the bells in the city ring, ten, eleven, and midnight. I must have fallen asleep about midnight because I don't remember hearing the bells after that. It seemed to me that I had scarcely closed my eyes when I dreamed that something impelled me to go to the window. I rose, and raising the sash leaned out. Twenty-fifth Street was deserted as far as I could see. I began to be afraid; everything outside seemed so – so black and uncomfortable. Then the sound of wheels in the distance came to my ears, and it seemed to me as though that was what I must wait for. Very slowly the wheels approached, and, finally, I could make out a vehicle moving along the street. It came nearer and nearer, and when it passed beneath my window I saw it was a hearse. Then, as I trembled with fear, the driver turned and looked straight at me. When I awoke I was standing by the open window shivering with cold, but the black-plumed hearse and the driver were gone. I dreamed this dream again in March last, and again awoke beside the open window. Last night the dream came again. You remember how it was raining; when I awoke, standing at the open window, my night-dress was soaked.'

'But where did I come into the dream?' I asked.

'You – you were in the coffin; but you were not dead.'

'In the coffin?'

'Yes.'

'How did you know? Could you see me?'

'No; I only knew you were there.'

'Had you been eating Welsh rarebits, or lobster salad?' I began laughing, but the girl interrupted me with a frightened cry.

'Hello! What's up?' I said, as she shrank into the embrasure by the window.

'The – the man below in the churchyard; he drove the hearse.'

'Nonsense,' I said, but Tessie's eyes were wide with terror. I went to the window and looked out. The man was gone. 'Come, Tessie,' I urged, 'don't be foolish. You have posed too long; you are nervous.'

'Do you think I could forget that face?' she murmured. 'Three times I saw the hearse pass below my window, and every time the driver turned and looked up at me. Oh, his face was so white and – and soft! It looked dead – it looked as if it had been dead a long time.'

I induced the girl to sit down and swallow a glass of Marsala. Then I sat down beside her, and tried to give her some advice.

'Look here, Tessie,' I said, 'you go to the country for a week or two, and you'll have no more dreams about hearses. You pose all day, and when night comes your nerves are upset. You can't keep this up. Then again, instead of going to bed when your day's work is done, you run off to picnics at Sulzer's Park, or go to the Eldorado or Coney Island, and when you come down here next morning you are fagged out. There was no real hearse. That was a soft-shell crab dream.'

She smiled faintly.

'What about the man in the churchyard?'

'Oh, he's only an ordinary unhealthy, everyday creature.'

'As true as my name is Tessie Rearden, I swear to you, Mr Scott, that the face of the man below in the churchyard is the face of the man who drove the hearse!'

'What of it?' I said. 'It's an honest trade.'

'Then you think I *did* see the hearse?'

'Oh, I said diplomatically, 'if you really did, it might not be unlikely that the man below drove it. There is nothing in that.'

Tessie rose, unrolled her scented handkerchief and taking a bit of gum from a knot in the hem, placed it in her mouth. Then drawing on her gloves she offered me her hand, with a frank, 'Good-night, Mr Scott,' and walked out.

II

The next morning, Thomas, the bellboy, brought me the *Herald* and a bit of news. The church next door had been sold. I thanked Heaven for it, not that I, being a Catholic, had any repugnance for the congregation next door, but because my nerves were shattered by a blatant exhorter, whose every word echoed through the aisle of the church as if it had been my own rooms, and who insisted on his *r*'s with a nasal persistence which revolted my every instinct. Then, too, there was a fiend in human shape, an organist, who reeled off some of the grand old hymns with an interpretation of his own, and I longed for the blood of a creature who could play the 'Doxology' with an amendment of minor chords which one hears only in a quartet of very young undergraduates. I believe the minister was a good man, but when he bellowed: 'And the Lorrrd said unto Moses, the Lorrrd is a man of war; the Lorrrd is my name. My wrath shall wax hot and I will kill you with my sworrrd!' I wondered how many centuries of purgatory it would take to atone for such a sin.

'Who bought the property?' I asked Thomas.

'Nobody that I knows, sir. They do say the gent wot owns this 'ere 'Amilton flats was lookin' at it. 'E might be a bildin' more studios.'

I walked to the window. The young man with the unhealthy face stood by the churchyard gate, and at the mere sight of him the same overwhelming repugnance took possession of me.

'By the way, Thomas,' I said, 'who is that fellow down there?'

Thomas sniffed. 'That there worm, sir? 'E's night-watchman of the church, sir. 'E maikes me tired-a-sittin' out all night on them steps and lookin' at you insultin' like. I'd a punched 'is 'ed, sir – beg pardon, sir—'

'Go on, Thomas.'

'One night a comin' 'ome with 'Arry, the other English boy, I sees 'im a sittin' there on them steps. We 'ad Molly and Jen with us, sir, the two girls on the tray service, an' 'e looks so insultin' at us that I up and sez: "Wat you looking hat, you fat slug?" – beg pardon, sir, but that's 'ow I sez, sir. Then 'e don't say nothin' and I sez: "Come out and I'll punch that puddin' 'ed." Then I hopens the gate and goes in, but 'e don't say nothin', only looks insultin' like. Then I 'its 'im one, but, ugh! 'is 'ed was that cold and mushy it ud sicken you to touch 'im.'

'What did he do then?' I asked, curiously.

''Im? Nawthin'.'

'And you, Thomas?'

The young fellow flushed with embarrassment and smiled uneasily.

'Mr Scott, sir, I ain't no coward an' I can't make it out at all why I run. I was in the 5th Lawncers, sir, bugler at Tel-el-Kebir, an' was shot by the wells.'

'You don't mean to say you ran away?'

'Yes, sir; I run.'

'Why?'

'That's just what I want to know, sir. I grabbed Molly an' run, an' the rest was as frightened as I.'

'But what were they frightened at?'

Thomas refused to answer for a while, but now my curiosity was aroused about the repulsive young man below and I pressed him. Three years' sojourn in America had not only modified Thomas's cockney dialect but had given him the American's fear of ridicule.

'You won't believe me, Mr Scott, sir?'

'Yes, I will.'

'You will lawf at me, sir?'

'Nonsense!'

He hesitated. 'Well, sir, it's Gawd's truth that when I 'it 'im 'e grabbed me wrists, sir, and when I twisted 'is soft, mushy fist one of 'is fingers come off in me 'and.'

The utter loathing and horror of Thomas's face must have been reflected in my own for he added:

'It's orful, an' now when I see 'im I just go away. 'E makes me hill.'

When Thomas had gone I went to the window. The man stood beside the church-railing with both hands on the gate, but I hastily retreated to my easel again, sickened and horrified, for I saw that the middle finger of his right hand was missing.

At nine o'clock Tessie appeared and vanished behind the screen with a merry 'Good morning, Mr Scott'. When she had reappeared and taken her pose upon the model-stand I started a new canvas much to her delight. She remained silent as long as I was on the drawing, but as soon as the scrape of the charcoal ceased and I took up my fixative she began to chatter.

'Oh, I had such a lovely time last night. We went to Tony Pastor's.'

'Who are "we"?' I demanded.

'Oh, Maggie, you know, Mr Whyte's model, and Pinkie McCormack – we call her Pinkie because she's got that beautiful red hair you artists like so much – and Lizzie Burke.'

I sent a shower of spray from the fixative over the canvas, and said: 'Well, go on.'

'We saw Kelly and Baby Barnes the skirt-dancer and – and all the rest. I made a mash.'

'Then you have gone back on me, Tessie?'

She laughed and shook her head.

'He's Lizzie Burke's brother, Ed. He's a perfect gen'l'man.'

I felt constrained to give her some parental advice concerning mashing, which she took with a bright smile.

'Oh, I can take care of a strange mash,' she said, examining her chewing gum, 'but Ed is different. Lizzie is my best friend.'

Then she related how Ed had come back from the stocking mill in Lowell, Massachusetts, to find her and Lizzie grown up – and what an accomplished young man he was – and how he thought nothing of squandering half a dollar for ice-cream and oysters to celebrate his entry as clerk into the woollen department of Macy's. Before she finished I began to paint, and she resumed the pose, smiling and chattering like a sparrow. By noon I had the study fairly well rubbed in and Tessie came to look at it.

'That's better,' she said.

I thought so too, and ate my lunch with a satisfied feeling that all was going well. Tessie spread her lunch on a drawing table opposite me and we drank our claret from the same bottle and lighted our cigarettes from the same match. I was very much attached to Tessie. I had watched her shoot up into a slender but exquisitely formed woman from a frail, awkward child. She had posed for me during the last three years, and among all my models she was my favorite. It would have troubled me very much indeed had she become 'tough' or 'fly', as the phrase goes, but I never noticed any deterioration of her manner, and felt at heart that she was all right. She and I never discussed morals at all, and I had no intention of doing so, partly because I had none myself, and partly because I knew she would do what she liked in spite of me. Still I did hope she would steer clear of complications, because I wished her well, and then also I had a selfish desire to retain the best model I had. I knew that mashing, as she termed it, had no significance with girls like Tessie, and that such things in America did not resemble in the least the same things in Paris. Yet having lived with my eyes open, I also knew that somebody would take Tessie away some day, in one manner or another, and though I professed to myself that marriage was nonsense, I sincerely hoped that, in this case, there would be a priest at the end of the vista. I am a Catholic. When I listen to high mass, when I sign myself, I feel that everything, including myself, is more cheerful, and when I confess, it does me good. A man who lives as much alone as I do, must confess to somebody. Then, again, Sylvia was Catholic, and it was reason enough for me. But I was speaking of Tessie, which is very different. Tessie also was Catholic and much more devout than I, so, taking it all in all, I had little fear for my pretty model until she should fall in love. But *then* I knew that fate alone would decide her future for her, and I prayed inwardly that fate would keep her away from men like me and throw into her path nothing but Ed Burkes and Jimmy McCormicks, bless her sweet face!

Tessie sat blowing rings of smoke up to the ceiling and tinkling the ice in her tumbler.

'Do you know that I also had a dream last night?' I observed.

'Not about that man?' she asked, laughing.

'Exactly. A dream similar to yours, only much worse.'

It was foolish and thoughtless of me to say this, but you know how little tact the average painter has.

'I must have fallen asleep about 10 o'clock,' I continued, 'and after a while I dreamt that I awoke. So plainly did I hear the midnight bells, the wind in the tree-branches, and the whistle of steamers from the bay, that even now I can scarcely believe I was not awake. I seemed to be lying in a box which had a glass cover. Dimly I saw the street lamps as I passed, for I must tell you, Tessie, the box in which I reclined appeared to lie in a cushioned wagon which jolted me over a stony pavement. After a while I became impatient and tried to move but the box was too narrow. My hands were crossed on my breast so I could not raise them to help myself. I listened and then tried to call. My voice was gone. I could hear the trample of the horses attached to the wagon and even the breathing of the driver. Then another sound broke upon my ears like the raising of a window sash. I managed to turn my head a little, and found I could look, not only through the glass cover of my box, but also through the glass panes in the side of the covered vehicle. I saw houses, empty and silent, with neither light nor life about any of them excepting one. In that house a window was open on the first floor and a figure all in white stood looking down into the street. It was you.'

Tessie had turned her face away from me and leaned on the table with her elbow.

'I could see your face,' I resumed, 'and it seemed to me to be very sorrowful. Then we passed on and turned into a narrow black lane. Presently the horses stopped. I waited and waited, closing my eyes with fear and impatience, but all was silent as the grave. After what seemed to me hours, I began to feel uncomfortable. A sense that somebody was close to me made me unclose my eyes. Then I saw the white face of the hearse-driver looking at me through the coffin lid—'

A sob from Tessie interrupted me. She was trembling like a leaf. I saw I had made an ass of myself and attempted to repair the damage.

'Why, Tess,' I said, 'I only told you this to show you what influence your story might have on another person's dreams. You don't suppose I really lay in a coffin, do you? What are you trembling for? Don't you see that your dream and my unreasonable dislike for that inoffensive watchman of the church simply set my brain working as soon as I fell asleep?'

She laid her head between her arms and sobbed as if her heart would break. What a precious triple donkey I had made of myself! But I was about to break my record. I went over and put my arm about her.

'Tessie, dear, forgive me,' I said; 'I had no business to frighten you with such nonsense. You are too sensible a girl, too good a Catholic to believe in dreams.'

Her hand tightened on mine and her head fell back upon my shoulder, but she still trembled and I petted her and comforted her.

'Come, Tess, open your eyes and smile.'

Her eyes opened with a slow languid movement and met mine, but their expression was so queer that I hastened to reassure her again.

'It's all humbug, Tessie. You surely are not afraid that any harm will come to you because of that?'

'No,' she said, but her scarlet lips quivered.

'Then what's the matter? Are you afraid?'

'Yes. Not for myself.'

'For me, then?' I demanded gayly.

'For you,' she murmured in a voice almost inaudible. 'I – I care for you.'

At first I started to laugh but when I understood her, a shock passed through me and I sat like one turned to stone. This was the crowning bit of idiocy I had committed. During the moment which elapsed between her reply and my answer

I thought of a thousand responses to that innocent confession. I could pass it by with a laugh. I could misunderstand her and reassure her as to my health. I could simply point out that it was impossible she could love me. But my reply was quicker than my thoughts, and I might think and think now when it was too late, for I had kissed her on the mouth.

That evening I took my usual walk in Washington Park, pondering over the occurrences of the day. I was thoroughly committed. There was no back-out now, and I stared the future straight in the face. I was not good, not even scrupulous, but I had no idea of deceiving either myself or Tessie. The one passion of my life lay buried in the sunlit forests of Brittany. Was it buried forever? Hope cried 'No!' For three years I had been listening to the voice of Hope, and for three years I had waited for a footstep on my threshold. Had Sylvia forgotten? 'No!' cried Hope.

I said that I was not good. That is true, but still I was not exactly a comic opera villain. I had led an easy-going reckless life, taking what invited me of pleasure, deploring and sometimes bitterly regretting consequences. In one thing alone, except my painting, was I serious, and that was something which lay hidden if not lost in the Breton forests.

It was too late now for me to regret what had occurred during the day. Whatever it had been, pity, a sudden tenderness for sorrow, or the more brutal instinct of gratified vanity, it was all the same now, and unless I wished to bruise an innocent heart my path lay marked before me. The fire and strength, the depth of passion of a love which I had never even suspected, with all my imagined experience in the world, left me no alternative but to respond or send her away. Whether because I am so cowardly about giving pain to others, or whether it was that I have little of the gloomy Puritan in me, I do not know, but I shrank from disclaiming responsibility for that thoughtless kiss, and in fact had no time to do so before the gates of her heart opened and the flood poured forth. Others who habitually do their duty and find a sullen satisfaction in making themselves and everybody else unhappy, might have withstood it. I did not. I dared not. After the storm had abated I did tell her that she might better have loved Ed Burke and worn a plain gold ring, but she would not hear of it, and I thought perhaps that as long as she had decided to love somebody she could not marry, it had better be me. I, at least, could treat her with an intelligent affection, and whenever she became tired of her infatuation she could go none the worse for it. For I was decided on that point although I knew how hard it would be. I remembered the usual termination of Platonic liaisons and thought how disgusted I had been whenever I heard of one. I knew I was undertaking a great deal for so unscrupulous a man as I was, and I dreaded the future, but never for one moment did I doubt that she was safe with me. Had it been anybody but Tessie I should not have bothered my head about scruples. For it did not occur to me to sacrifice Tessie as I would have sacrificed a woman of the world. I looked the future squarely in the face and saw the several probable endings to the affair. She would either tire of the whole thing, or become so unhappy that I should have either to marry her or go away. If I married her we would be unhappy. I with a wife unsuited to me, and she with a husband unsuitable for any woman. For my past life could scarcely entitle me to marry. If I went away she might either fall ill, recover, and marry some Eddie Burke, or she might recklessly or deliberately go and do something foolish. On the other hand if she tired of me, then her whole life would be before her with beautiful vistas of Eddie Burkes and marriage rings and twins and Harlem flats and Heaven knows what. As I strolled along through the trees by the Washington Arch, I decided that she should find a substantial friend in me anyway and the future could take care of itself. Then I went into the house and put on my evening dress, for the little faintly perfumed note on my dresser said, 'Have a cab at the stage door at eleven', and the note was signed 'Edith Carmichel, Metropolitan Theatre'.

I took supper that night, or rather we took supper, Miss Carmichel and I, at Solari's and the dawn was just beginning to gild the cross on the Memorial Church as I entered Washington Square after leaving Edith at the Brunswick. There was not a soul in the park as I passed among the trees and took the walk which leads from the Garibaldi statue to the Hamilton Apartment House, but as I passed the churchyard I saw a figure sitting on the stone steps. In spite of myself a chill crept over me at the sight of the white puffy face, and I hastened to pass. Then he said something which might have been addressed to me or might merely have been a mutter to himself, but a sudden furious anger flamed up within me that such a creature should address me. For an instant I felt like wheeling about and smashing my stick over his head, but I walked on, and entering the Hamilton went to my apartment. For some time I tossed about the bed trying to get the sound of his voice out of my ears, but could not. It filled my head, that muttering sound, like thick oily smoke from a fat-rendering vat or an odor of noisome decay. And as I lay and tossed about, the voice in my ears seemed more distinct, and I began to understand the words he had muttered. They came to me slowly as if I had forgotten them, and at last I could make some sense out of the sounds. It was this:

'Have you found the Yellow Sign?'

'Have you found the Yellow Sign?'

'Have you found the Yellow Sign?'

I was furious. What did he mean by that? Then with a curse upon him and his I rolled over and went to sleep, but when I awoke later I looked pale and haggard, for I had dreamed the dream of the night before and it troubled me more than I cared to think.

I dressed and went down into my studio. Tessie sat by the window, but as I came in she rose and put both arms around my neck for an innocent kiss. She looked so sweet and dainty that I kissed her again and then sat down before the easel.

'Hello! Where's the study I began yesterday?' I asked.

Tessie looked conscious, but did not answer. I began to

hunt among the piles of canvases, saying, 'Hurry up, Tess, and get ready; we must take advantage of the morning light.'

When at last I gave up the search among the other canvases and turned to look around the room for the missing study I noticed Tessie standing by the screen with her clothes still on.

'What's the matter,' I asked, 'don't you feel well?'

'Yes.'

'Then hurry.'

'Do you want me to pose as – as I have always posed?'

Then I understood. Here was a new complication. I had lost, of course, the best nude model I had ever seen. I looked at Tessie. Her face was scarlet. Alas! Alas! We had eaten of the tree of knowledge, and Eden and native innocence were dreams of the past – I mean for her.

I suppose she noticed the disappointment on my face, for she said: 'I will pose if you wish. The study is behind the screen here where I put it.'

'No,' I said, 'we will begin something new'; and I went into my wardrobe and picked out a Moorish costume which fairly blazed with tinsel. It was a genuine costume, and Tessie retired to the screen with it enchanted. When she came forth again I was astonished. Her long black hair was bound above her forehead with a circlet of turquoises, and the ends curled about her glittering girdle. Her feet were encased in the embroidered pointed slippers and the skirt of her costume, curiously wrought with arabesques in silver, fell to her ankles. The deep metallic blue vest embroidered with silver and the short Mauresque jacket spangled and sewn with turquoises became her wonderfully. She came up to me and held up her face smiling. I slipped my hand into my pocket and drawing out a gold chain with a cross attached, dropped it over her head.

'It's yours, Tessie.'

'Mine?' she faltered.

'Yours. Now go and pose.' Then with a radiant smile she

ran behind the screen and presently reappeared with a little box on which was written my name.

'I had intended to give it to you when I went home tonight,' she said, 'but I can't wait now.'

I opened the box. On the pink cotton inside lay a clasp of black onyx, on which was inlaid a curious symbol or letter in gold. It was neither Arabic nor Chinese, nor as I found afterwards did it belong to any human script.

'It's all I had to give you for a keepsake,' she said, timidly.

I was annoyed, but I told her how much I should prize it, and promised to wear it always. She fastened it on my coat beneath the lapel.

'How foolish, Tess, to go and buy me such a beautiful thing as this,' I said.

'I did not buy it,' she laughed.

'Then where did you get it?'

Then she told me how she had found it one day while coming from the Aquarium in the Battery, how she had advertised it and watched the papers, but at last gave up all hopes of finding the owner.

'That was last winter,' she said, 'the very day I had the first horrid dream about the hearse.'

I remembered my dream of the previous night but said nothing, and presently my charcoal was flying over a new canvas; and Tessie stood motionless on the model stand.

III

The day following was a disastrous one for me. While moving a framed canvas from one easel to another my foot slipped on the polished floor and I fell heavily on both wrists. They were so badly sprained that it was useless to attempt to hold a brush, and I was obliged to wander about the studio, glaring at unfinished drawings and sketches until despair seized me and I sat down to smoke and twiddle my thumbs with rage. The rain blew against the windows and rattled on the roof of the church, driving me into a nervous fit with its interminable patter. Tessie sat sewing by the window, and every now and then raised her head and looked at me with such innocent compassion that I began to feel ashamed of my irritation and looked about for something to occupy me. I had read all the papers and all the books in the library, but for the sake of something to do I went to the bookcases and shoved them open with my elbow. I knew every volume by its color and examined them all, passing slowly around the library and whistling to keep up my spirits. I was turning to go into the dining-room when my eye fell upon a book bound in serpent skin, standing in a corner of the top shelf of the last bookcase. I did not remember it and from the floor could not decipher the pale lettering on the back, so I went to the smoking-room and called Tessie. She came in from the studio and climbed up to reach the book.

'What is it?' I asked.

'"The King in Yellow".'

I was dumbfounded. Who had placed it there? How came it in my rooms? I had long ago decided that I should never open that book, and nothing on earth could have persuaded me to buy it. Fearful lest curiosity might tempt me to open it, I had never even looked at it in book-stores. If I ever had any curiosity to read it, the awful tragedy of young Castaigne, whom I knew, prevented me from exploring its wicked pages. I had always refused to listen to any description of it, and indeed, nobody ever ventured to discuss the second part aloud, so I had absolutely no knowledge of what those leaves might reveal. I stared at the poisonous mottled binding as I would at a snake.

'Don't touch it, Tessie,' I said; 'come down.'

Of course my admonition was enough to arouse her curiosity, and before I could prevent it she took the book and, laughing, danced off into the studio with it. I called to her but she slipped away with a tormenting smile at my helpless hands, and I followed her with some impatience.

'Tessie!' I cried, entering the library, 'listen, I am serious. Put that book away. I do not wish you to open it!' The library was empty. I went into both drawing-rooms, then into the bedrooms, laundry, kitchen, and finally returned to the library and began a systematic search. She had hidden herself so well that it was half an hour later when I discovered her crouching white and silent by the latticed window in the store-room above. At the first glance I saw she had been punished for her foolishness. 'The King in Yellow' lay at her feet, but the book was open at the second part. I looked at Tessie and saw it was too late. She had opened 'The King in Yellow'. Then I took her by the hand and led her into the studio. She seemed dazed, and when I told her to lie down on the sofa she obeyed me without a word. After a while she closed her eyes and her breathing became regular and deep, but I could not determine whether or not she slept. For a long while I sat silently beside her, but she neither stirred nor spoke, and at last I rose and entering the unused store-room took the book in my least injured hand. It seemed heavy as lead, but I carried it into the studio again, and sitting down on the rug beside the sofa, opened it and read it through from beginning to end.

When, faint with the excess of my emotions, I dropped the volume and leaned wearily back against the sofa, Tessie opened her eyes and looked at me.

We had been speaking for some time in a dull monotonous strain before I realized that we were discussing 'The King in Yellow'. Oh the sin of writing such words – words which are clear as crystal, limpid and musical as bubbling springs, words which sparkle and glow like the poisoned diamonds of the Medicis! Oh the wickedness, the hopeless damnation of a soul who could fascinate and paralyze human creatures with such words – words understood by the ignorant and wise alike, words which are more precious than jewels, more soothing than music, more awful than death!

We talked on, unmindful of the gathering shadows, and she was begging me to throw away the clasp of black onyx quaintly inlaid with what we now knew to be the Yellow Sign. I shall never know why I refused, though even at this hour, here in my bedroom as I write this confession, I should be glad to know *what* it was that prevented me from tearing the Yellow Sign from my breast and casting it into the fire. I am sure I wished to do so, and yet Tessie pleaded with me in vain. Night fell and hours dragged on, but still we murmured to each other of the King and the Pallid Mask, and midnight sounded from the misty spires in the fog-wrapped city. We spoke of Hastur and of Cassilda, while outside the fog rolled against the blank window-panes as the cloud waves roll and break on the shores of Hali.

The house was very silent now and not a sound came up from the misty streets. Tessie lay among the cushions, her face a gray blot in the gloom, but her hands were clasped in mine and I knew that she knew and read my thoughts as I read hers, for we had understood the mystery of the Hyades, and the Phantom of Truth was laid. Then as we answered each other, swiftly, silently, thought on thought, the shadows stirred in the gloom about us, and far in the distant streets we heard a sound. Nearer and nearer it came, the dull crunching of wheels, nearer and yet nearer, and now, outside before the door it ceased, and I dragged myself to the window and saw a black-plumed hearse. The gate below opened and shut, and I crept shaking to my door and bolted it, but I knew no bolts, no locks, could keep that creature out who was coming for the Yellow Sign. And now I heard him moving very softly along the hall. Now he was at the door, and the bolts rotted at his touch. Now he had entered. With eyes starting from my head I peered into the darkness, but when he came into the room I did not see him. It was only when I felt him envelop me in his cold soft grasp that I cried out and struggled with deadly fury, but my hands were useless and he tore the onyx clasp from my coat and struck me full in the face. Then, as I fell, I heard Tessie's soft cry and her spirit fled: and even while falling I longed to follow her, for I knew that the King in Yellow had opened his tattered mantle and there was only God to cry to now.

I could tell more, but I cannot see what help it will be to

the world. As for me I am past human help or hope. As I lie here, writing, careless even whether or not I die before I finish, I can see the doctor gathering up his powders and phials with a vague gesture to the good priest beside me, which I understand.

They will be very curious to know the tragedy – they of the outside world who write books and print millions of newspapers, but I shall write no more, and the father confessor will seal my last words with the seal of sanctity when his holy office is done. They of the outside world may send their creatures into wrecked homes and death-smitten firesides, and their newspapers will batten on blood and tears, but with me their spies must halt before the confessional. They know that Tessie is dead and that I am dying. They know how the people in the house, aroused by an infernal scream, rushed into my room and found one living and two dead, but they do not know what I shall tell them now; they do not know that the doctor said as he pointed to a horrible decomposed heap on the floor – the livid corpse of the watchman from the church: 'I have no theory, no explanation. That man must have been dead for months!'

I think I am dying. I wish the priest would—

A PLEASANT EVENING

'Et pis, doucett'ment on s'endort
On fait sa carne, on fait sa sorgue,
On ronfle, et, comme un tuyau d'orgue
L'tuyau s'met à ronfler plus fort . . .'

ARISTIDE BRUANT

I

As I stepped upon the platform of a Broadway cable-car at Forty-second Street, somebody said, 'Hello, Hilton, Jamison's looking for you.'

'Hello, Curtis,' I replied, 'what does Jamison want?'

'He wants to know what you've been doing all the week,' said Curtis, hanging desperately to the railing as the car lurched forward; 'he says you seem to think that the *Manhattan Illustrated Weekly* was created for the sole purpose of providing salary and vacations for you.'

'The shifty old tom-cat!' I said indignantly, 'he knows well enough where I've been. Vacation! Does he think the State Camp in June is a snap?'

'Oh,' said Curtis, 'you've been to Peekskill?'

'I should say so,' I replied, my wrath rising as I thought of my assignment.

'Hot?' inquired Curtis, dreamily.

'One hundred and three in the shade,' I answered. 'Jamison wanted three full pages and three half pages, all for process work, and a lot of line drawings into the bargain. I could have faked them – I wish I had. I was fool enough to hustle and break my neck to get some honest drawings, and that's the thanks I get!'

'Did you have a camera?'

'No. I will next time – I'll waste no more conscientious work on Jamison,' I said sulkily.

'It doesn't pay,' said Curtis. 'When I have military work assigned to me, I don't do the dashing sketch-artist act, you bet; I go to my studio, light my pipe, pull out a lot of old *Illustrated London News*, select several suitable battle scenes by Caton Woodville – and use 'em too.'

The car shot round the neck-breaking curve at Fourteenth Street.

'Yes,' continued Curtis, as the car stopped in front of the Morton House for a moment, then plunged forward again amid a furious clanging of gongs, 'it doesn't pay to do decent work for the fat-headed men who run the *Manhattan Illustrated*. They don't appreciate it.'

'I think the public does,' I said, 'but I'm sure Jamison doesn't. It would serve him right if I did what most of you fellows do – take a lot of Caton Woodville's and Thulstrup's drawings, change the uniforms, "chic" a figure or two, and turn in a drawing labelled "from life". I'm sick of this sort of thing anyway. Almost every day this week I've been chasing myself over that tropical camp, or galloping in the wake of those batteries. I've got a full page of the "camp by moonlight", full pages of "artillery drill" and "light battery in action", and a dozen smaller drawings that cost me more groans and perspiration than Jamison ever knew in all his lymphatic life!'

'Jamison's got wheels,' said Curtis, '—more wheels than there are bicycles in Harlem. He wants you to do a full page by Saturday.'

'A what?' I exclaimed, aghast.

'Yes he does – he was going to send Jim Crawford, but Jim expects to go to California for the winter fair, and you've got to do it.'

'What is it?' I demanded savagely.

'The animals in Central Park,' chuckled Curtis.

I was furious. The animals! Indeed! I'd show Jamison that I was entitled to some consideration! This was Thursday; that gave me a day and a half to finish a full-page drawing for the paper, and, after my work at the State Camp I felt that I was entitled to a little rest. Anyway I objected to the subject. I intended to tell Jamison so – I intended to tell him firmly. However, many of the things that we often intended to tell Jamison were never told. He was a peculiar man, fat-faced, thin-lipped, gentle-voiced, mild-mannered, and soft in his movements as a pussy cat. Just why our firmness should give way when we were actually in his presence, I have never quite been able to determine. He said very little – so did we, although we often entered his presence with other intentions.

The truth was that the *Manhattan Illustrated Weekly* was the best paying, best illustrated paper in America, and we young fellows were not anxious to be cast adrift. Jamison's knowledge of art was probably as extensive as the knowledge of any 'Art editor' in the city. Of course that was saying nothing, but the fact merited careful consideration on our part, and we gave it much consideration.

This time, however, I decided to let Jamison know that drawings are not produced by the yard, and that I was neither a floor-walker nor a hand-me-down. I would stand up for my rights; I'd tell old Jamison a few things to set the wheels under his silk hat spinning, and if he attempted any of his pussy-cat ways on me, I'd give him a few plain facts that would curl what hair he had left.

Glowing with a splendid indignation, I jumped off the car at the City Hall, followed by Curtis, and a few minutes later entered the office of the *Manhattan Illustrated News*.

'Mr Jamison would like to see you, sir,' said one of the compositors as I passed into the long hallway. I threw my drawings on the table and passed a handkerchief over my forehead.

'Mr Jamison would like to see you, sir,' said a small freckle-faced boy with a smudge of ink on his nose.

'I know it,' I said, and started to remove my gloves.

'Mr Jamison would like to see you, sir,' said a lank messenger who was carrying a bundle of proofs to the floor below.

'The deuce take Jamison,' I said to myself. I started toward the dark passage that leads to the abode of Jamison, running over in my mind the neat and sarcastic speech which I had been composing during the last ten minutes.

Jamison looked up and nodded softly as I entered the room. I forgot my speech.

'Mr Hilton,' he said, 'we want a full page of the Zoo before it is removed to Bronx Park. Saturday afternoon at three o'clock the drawing must be in the engraver's hands. Did you have a pleasant week in camp?'

'It was hot,' I muttered, furious to find that I could not remember my little speech.

'The weather,' said Jamison, with soft courtesy, 'is oppressive everywhere. Are your drawings in, Mr Hilton?'

'Yes. It was infernally hot and I worked like the devil—'

'I suppose you were quite overcome. Is that why you took a two days' trip to the Catskills? I trust the mountain air restored you – but – was it prudent to go to Cranston's for the cotillion Tuesday? Dancing in such uncomfortable weather is really unwise. Good-morning, Mr Hilton, remember the engraver should have your drawings on Saturday by three.'

I walked out, half hypnotized, half enraged. Curtis grinned at me as I passed – I could have boxed his ears.

'Why the mischief should I lose my tongue whenever that old tom-cat purrs!' I asked myself as I entered the elevator and was shot down to the first floor. 'I'll not put up with this sort of thing much longer – how in the name of all that's foxy did he know that I went to the mountains? I suppose he thinks I'm lazy because I don't wish to be boiled to death. How did he know about the dance at Cranston's? Old cat!'

The roar and turmoil of machinery and busy men filled my ears as I crossed the avenue and turned into the City Hall Park.

From the staff on the tower the flag drooped in the warm sunshine with scarcely a breeze to lift its crimson bars. Overhead stretched a splendid cloudless sky, deep, deep blue, thrilling, scintillating in the gemmed rays of the sun.

Pigeons wheeled and circled about the roof of the gray Post Office or dropped out of the blue above to flutter around the fountain in the square.

On the steps of the City Hall the unlovely politician lounged, exploring his heavy underjaw with wooden toothpick, twisting his drooping black moustache, or distributing tobacco juice over marble steps and close-clipped grass.

My eyes wandered from these human vermin to the calm scornful face of Nathan Hale, on his pedestal, and then to the gray-coated Park policeman whose occupation was to keep little children from the cool grass.

A young man with thin hands and blue circles under his eyes was slumbering on a bench by the fountain, and the policeman walked over to him and struck him on the soles of his shoes with a short club.

The young man rose mechanically, stared about, dazed by the sun, shivered, and limped away. I saw him sit down on the steps of the white marble building, and I went over and spoke to him. He neither looked at me, nor did he notice the coin I offered.

'You're sick,' I said, 'you had better go to the hospital.'

'Where?' he asked vacantly. 'I've been, but they wouldn't receive me.'

He stooped and tied the bit of string that held what remained of his shoe to his foot.

'You are French,' I said.

'Yes.'

'Have you no friends? Have you been to the French Consul?'

'The Consul!' he replied, 'no, I haven't been to the French Consul.'

After a moment I said, 'You speak like a gentleman.'

He rose to his feet and stood very straight, looking me, for the first time, directly in the eyes.

'Who are you?' I asked abruptly.

'An outcast,' he said, without emotion, and limped off thrusting his hands into his ragged pockets.

'Huh!' said the Park policeman who had come up behind me in time to hear my question and the vagabond's answer; 'don't you know who that hobo is? – An' you a newspaper man!'

'Who is he, Cusick?' I demanded, watching the thin shabby figure moving across Broadway toward the river.

'On the level you don't know, Mr Hilton?' repeated Cusick, suspiciously.

'No, I don't; I never before laid eyes on him.'

'Why,' said the sparrow policeman, 'that's "Soger Charlie"; – you remember – that French officer what sold secrets to the Dutch Emperor.'

'And was to have been shot? I remember now, four years ago – and he escaped – you mean to say that is the man?'

'Everybody knows it,' sniffed Cusick, 'I'd a-thought you newspaper gents would have knowed it first.'

'What was his name?' I asked after a moment's thought.

'Soger Charlie—'

'I mean his name at home.'

'Oh, some French dago name. No Frenchman will speak to him here; sometimes they curse him and kick him. I guess he's dyin' by inches.'

I remembered his case now. Two young French cavalry officers were arrested, charged with selling plans of fortifications and other military secrets to the Germans. On the eve of their conviction, one of them, Heaven only knows how, escaped and turned up in New York. The other was duly shot. The affair had made some noise, because both young men were of good families. It was a painful episode, and I had hastened to forget it. Now that it was recalled to my mind, I remembered the newspaper accounts of the case, but I had forgotten the names of the miserable young men.

'Sold his country,' observed Cusick, watching a group of children out of the corner of his eyes, '—you can't trust no Frenchman nor dagoes nor Dutchmen either. I guess Yankees are about the only white men.'

I looked at the noble face of Nathan Hale and nodded.

'Nothin' sneaky about us, eh, Mr Hilton?'

I thought of Benedict Arnold and looked at my boots.

Then the policeman said, 'Well, so long, Mr Hilton,' and went away to frighten a pasty-faced little girl who had climbed upon the railing and was leaning down to sniff the fragrant grass.

'Cheese it, de cop!' cried her shrill-voiced friends, and the whole bevy of small ragamuffins scuttled away across the square.

With a feeling of depression I turned and walked toward Broadway, where the long yellow cable-cars swept up and down, and the din of gongs and the deafening rumble of heavy trucks echoed from the marble walls of the Court House to the granite mass of the Post Office.

Throngs of hurrying busy people passed up town and down town, slim sober-faced clerks, trim cold-eyed brokers, here and there a red-necked politician linking arms with some favourite heeler, here and there a City Hall lawyer, sallow-faced and saturnine. Sometimes a fireman, in his severe blue uniform, passed through the crowd, sometimes a blue-coated policeman, mopping his clipped hair, holding his helmet in his white-gloved hand. There were women too, pale-faced shop girls with pretty eyes, tall blonde girls who might be typewriters and might not, and many, many older women whose business in that part of the city no human being could venture to guess, but who hurried up town and down town, all occupied with *something* that gave to the whole restless throng a common likeness – the expression of one who hastens toward a hopeless goal.

I knew some of those who passed me. There was little Jocelyn of the *Mail and Express*; there was Hood, who had more money than he wanted and was going to have less than he wanted when he left Wall Street; there was Colonel Tidmouse of the 45th Infantry, N.G.S.N.Y., probably coming from the office of the *Army and Navy Journal*, and there was Dick Harding who wrote the best stories of New York life that have been printed. People said that his hat no longer fitted – especially people who also wrote stories of New York life and whose hats threatened to fit as long as they lived.

I looked at the statue of Nathan Hale, then at the human stream that flowed around his pedestal.

'*Quand même*,' I muttered and walked into Broadway, signalling to the gripman of an uptown cable-car.

II

I passed into the Park by the Fifth Avenue and 59th Street gate; I could never bring myself to enter it through the gate that is guarded by the hideous pigmy statue of Thorwaldsen.

The afternoon sun poured into the windows of the New Netherlands Hotel, setting every orange-curtained pane a-glitter, and tipping the wings of the bronze dragons with flame.

Gorgeous masses of flowers blazed in the sunshine from the grey terraces of the Savoy, from the high grilled court of the Vanderbilt palace, and from the balconies of the Plaza opposite.

The white marble façade of the Metropolitan Club was a grateful relief in the universal glare, and I kept my eyes on it until I had crossed the dusty street and entered the shade of the trees.

Before I came to the Zoo I smelled it. Next week it was to be removed to the fresh cool woods and meadows in Bronx Park, far from the stifling air of the city, far from the infernal noise of the Fifth Avenue omnibuses.

A noble stag stared at me from his enclosure among the

trees as I passed down the winding asphalt walk. 'Never mind, old fellow,' said I, 'you will be splashing about in the Bronx River next week and cropping maple shoots to your heart's content.'

On I went, past herds of staring deer, past great lumbering elk, and moose, and long-faced African antelopes, until I came to the dens of the great carnivora.

The tigers sprawled in the sunshine, blinking and licking their paws; the lions slept in the shade or squatted on their haunches, yawning gravely. A slim panther travelled to and fro behind her barred cage, pausing at times to peer wistfully out into the free sunny world. My heart ached for caged wild things, and I walked on, glancing up now and then to encounter the blank stare of a tiger or the mean shifty eyes of some ill-smelling hyena.

Across the meadow I could see the elephants swaying and swinging their great heads, the sober bison solemnly slobbering over their cuds, the sarcastic countenances of camels, the wicked little zebras, and a lot more animals of the camel and llama tribe, all resembling each other, all equally ridiculous, stupid, deadly uninteresting.

Somewhere behind the old arsenal an eagle was screaming, probably a Yankee eagle; I heard the 'tchug! tchug!' of a blowing hippopotamus, the squeal of a falcon, and the snarling yap! of quarrelling wolves.

'A pleasant place for a hot day!' I pondered bitterly, and I thought some things about Jamison that I shall not insert in this volume. But I lighted a cigarette to deaden the aroma from the hyenas, unclasped my sketching block, sharpened my pencil, and fell to work on a family group of hippopotami.

They may have taken me for a photographer, for they all wore smiles as if 'welcoming a friend', and my sketch block presented a series of wide open jaws, behind which shapeless bulky bodies vanished in alarming perspective.

The alligators were easy; they looked to me as though they had not moved since the founding of the Zoo, but I had a bad time with the big bison, who persistently turned his tail to me, looking stolidly around his flank to see how I stood it. So I pretended to be absorbed in the antics of two bear cubs, and the dreary old bison fell into the trap, for I made some good sketches of him and laughed in his face as I closed the book.

There was a bench by the abode of the eagles, and I sat down on it to draw the vultures and condors, motionless as mummies among the piled rocks. Gradually I enlarged the sketch, bringing in the gravel plaza, the steps leading up to Fifth Avenue, the sleepy park policeman in front of the arsenal – and a slim, white-browed girl, dressed in shabby black, who stood silently in the shade of the willow trees.

After a while I found that the sketch, instead of being a study of the eagles, was in reality a composition in which the girl in black occupied the principal point of interest. Unwittingly I had subordinated everything else to her, the brooding vultures, the trees and walks, and the half indicated groups of sun-warmed loungers.

She stood very still, her pallid face bent, her thin white hands loosely clasped before her. 'Rather dejected reverie,' I thought, 'probably she's out of work.' Then I caught a glimpse of a sparkling diamond ring on the slender third finger of her left hand.

'She'll not starve with such a stone as that about her,' I said to myself, looking curiously at her dark eyes and sensitive mouth. They were both beautiful, eyes and mouth – beautiful, but touched with pain.

After a while I rose and walked back to make a sketch or two of the lions and tigers. I avoided the monkeys – I can't stand them, and they never seem funny to me, poor dwarfish, degraded caricatures of all that is ignoble in ourselves.

'I've enough now,' I thought; 'I'll go home and manufacture a full page that will probably please Jamison.' So I strapped the elastic band around my sketching block, replaced pencil and rubber in my waistcoat pocket, and strolled off toward the Mall to smoke a cigarette in the evening glow before going back to my studio to work until midnight, up to the chin in charcoal gray and Chinese white.

Across the long meadow I could see the roofs of the city faintly looming above the trees. A mist of amethyst, ever deepening, hung low on the horizon, and through it, steeple and dome, roof and tower, and the tall chimneys where thin fillets of smoke curled idly, were transformed into pinnacles of beryl and flaming minarets, swimming in filmy haze. Slowly the enchantment deepened; all that was ugly and shabby and mean had fallen away from the distant city, and now it towered into the evening sky, splendid, gilded, magnificent, purified in the fierce furnace of the setting sun.

The red disk was half hidden now; the tracery of trees, feathery willow and budding birch, darkened against the glow; the fiery rays shot far across the meadow, gilding the dead leaves, staining with soft crimson the dark moist tree trunks around me.

Far across the meadow a shepherd passed in the wake of a huddling flock, his dog at his heels, faint moving blots of gray.

A squirrel sat up on the gravel walk in front of me, ran a few feet, and sat up again, so close that I could see the palpitation of his sleek flanks.

Somewhere in the grass a hidden field insect was rehearsing last summer's solos; I heard the tap! tap! tat-tat-t-t-tat! of a woodpecker among the branches overhead and the querulous note of a sleepy robin.

The twilight deepened; out of the city the music of bells floated over wood and meadow; faint mellow whistles sounded from the river craft along the north shore, and the distant thunder of a gun announced the close of a June day.

The end of my cigarette began to glimmer with a redder light; shepherd and flock were blotted out in the dusk, and

I only knew they were still moving when the sheep bells tinkled faintly.

Then suddenly that strange uneasiness that all have known – that half-awakened sense of having seen it all before, of having been through it all, came over me, and I raised my head and slowly turned.

A figure was seated at my side. My mind was struggling with the instinct to remember. Something so vague and yet so familiar – something that eluded thought yet challenged it, something – God knows what! troubled me. And now, as I looked, without interest, at the dark figure beside me, an apprehension, totally involuntary, an impatience to *understand*, came upon me, and I sighed and turned restlessly again to the fading west.

I thought I heard my sigh re-echoed – but I scarcely heeded; and in a moment I sighed again, dropping my burned-out cigarette on the gravel beneath my feet.

'Did you speak to me?' said some one in a low voice, so close that I swung around rather sharply.

'No,' I said after a moment's silence.

It was a woman. I could not see her face clearly, but I saw on her clasped hands, which lay listlessly in her lap, the sparkle of a great diamond. I knew her at once. It did not need a glance at the shabby dress of black, the white face, a pallid spot in the twilight, to tell me that I had her picture in my sketch-book.

'Do – do you mind if I speak to you?' she asked timidly. The hopeless sadness in her voice touched me, and I said, 'Why, no, of course not. Can I do anything for you?'

'Yes,' she said, brightening a little, 'if you – you only would.'

'I will if I can,' said I cheerfully; 'what is it? Out of ready cash?'

'No, not that,' she said, shrinking back.

I begged her pardon, a little surprised, and withdrew my hand from my change pocket.

'It is only – only that I wish you to take these,' – she drew a thin packet from her breast – 'these two letters.'

'I?' I asked astonished.

'Yes, if you will.'

'But what am I to do with them?' I demanded.

'I can't tell you; I only know that I must give them to you. Will you take them?'

'Oh, yes, I'll take them,' I laughed, 'am I to read them?' I added to myself, 'It's some clever begging trick.'

'No,' she answered slowly, 'you are not to read them; you are to give them to somebody.'

'To whom? Anybody?'

'No, not to anybody. You will know whom to give them to when the time comes.'

'Then I am to keep them until further instructions?'

'Your own heart will instruct you,' she said, in a scarcely audible voice. She held the thin packet toward me, and to humor her I took it. It was wet.

'The letters fell into the sea,' she said. 'There was a photograph which should have gone with them but the salt water washed it blank. Will you care if I ask you something else?'

'I? Oh, no.'

'Then give me the picture that you made of me to-day.'

I laughed again, and demanded how she knew I had drawn her.

'Is it like me?' she said.

'I think it is very like you,' I answered truthfully.

'Will you not give it to me?'

Now it was on the tip of my tongue to refuse, but I reflected that I had enough sketches for a full page without that one, so I handed it to her, nodded that she was welcome, and stood up. She rose also, the diamond flashing on her finger.

'You are sure that you are not in want?' I asked, with a tinge of good-natured sarcasm.

'Hark!' she whispered; 'listen! – do you not hear the bells of the convent!'

I looked out into the misty night.

'There are no bells sounding,' I said, 'and anyway there

are no convent bells here. We are in New York, mademoiselle' – I had noticed her French accent – 'we are in Protestant
Yankee-land, and the bells that ring are much less mellow
than the bells of France.'

I turned pleasantly to say good-night. She was gone.

III

'Have you ever drawn a picture of a corpse?' inquired Jamison
next morning as I walked into his private room with a sketch
of the proposed full page of the Zoo.

'No, and I don't want to,' I replied, sullenly.

'Let me see your Central Park page,' said Jamison in his
gentle voice, and I displayed it. It was about worthless as an
artistic production, but it pleased Jamison, as I knew it would.

'Can you finish it by this afternoon?' he asked, looking
up at me with persuasive eyes.

'Oh, I suppose so,' I said, wearily; 'anything else, Mr
Jamison?'

'The corpse,' he replied, 'I want a sketch by tomorrow
– finished.'

'What corpse?' I demanded, controlling my indignation
as I met Jamison's soft eyes.

There was a mute duel of glances. Jamison passed his
hand across his forehead with a slight lifting of the eyebrows.

'I shall want it as soon as possible,' he said in his caressing
voice.

What I thought was, 'Damned purring pussy-cat!' What
I said was, 'Where is this corpse?'

'In the Morgue – have you read the morning papers? No?
Ah, – as you very rightly observe you are too busy to read
the morning papers. Young men must learn industry first,
of course, of course. What you are to do is this: the San
Francisco police have sent out an alarm regarding the disappearance of a Miss Tufft – the millionaire's daughter, you
know. Today a body was brought to the Morgue here in
New York, and it has been identified as the missing young

lady – by a diamond ring. Now I am convinced that it isn't, and I'll show you why, Mr Hilton.'

He picked up a pen and made a sketch of a ring on a margin of that morning's *Tribune*.

'That is the description of her ring as sent on from San Francisco. You notice the diamond is set in the centre of the ring where the two gold serpents' *tails* cross!

'Now the ring on the finger of the woman in the Morgue is like this,' and he rapidly sketched another ring where the diamond rested in the *fangs* of the two gold serpents.

'That is the difference,' he said in his pleasant, even voice.

'Rings like that are not uncommon,' said I, remembering that I had seen such a ring on the finger of the white-faced girl in the Park the evening before. Then a sudden thought took shape – perhaps that was the girl whose body lay in the Morgue!

'Well,' said Jamison, looking up at me, 'what are you thinking about?'

'Nothing,' I answered, but the whole scene was before my eyes, the vultures brooding among the rocks, the shabby black dress, and the pallid face – and the ring, glittering on that slim white hand!

'Nothing,' I repeated, 'when shall I go, Mr Jamison? Do you want a portrait – or what?'

'Portrait – careful drawing of the ring, and, er, a centre piece of the Morgue at night. Might as well give people the horrors while we're about it.'

'But,' said I, 'the policy of this paper—'

'Never mind, Mr Hilton,' purred Jamison, 'I am able to direct the policy of this paper.'

'I don't doubt you are,' I said angrily.

'I am,' he repeated, undisturbed and smiling; 'you see this Tufft case interests society. I am – er – also interested.'

He held out to me a morning paper and pointed to a heading.

I read: 'Miss Tufft Dead! Her Fiancé was Mr Jamison, the well known Editor'.

'What!' I cried in horrified amazement. But Jamison had left the room, and I heard him chatting and laughing softly with some visitors in the press-room outside.

I flung down the paper and walked out.

'The cold-blooded toad!' I exclaimed again and again; '—making capital out of his fiancée's disappearance! Well, I – I'm d—nd! I knew he was a bloodless, heartless, grippenny, but I never thought – I never imagined—' Words failed me.

Scarcely conscious of what I did I drew a *Herald* from my pocket and saw the column entitled: 'Miss Tufft Found! Identified by a Ring. Wild Grief of Mr Jamison, her Fiancé.'

That was enough. I went out into the street and sat down in City Hall Park. And, as I sat there, a terrible resolution came to me; I would draw the dead girl's face in such a way that it would chill Jamison's sluggish blood, I would crowd the black shadows of the Morgue with forms and ghastly faces, and every face should bear something in it of Jamison. Oh, I'd rouse him from his cold snaky apathy! I'd confront him with Death in such an awful form, that, passionless, base, inhuman as he was, he'd shrink from it as he would from a dagger thrust. Of course I'd lose my place, but that did not bother me, for I had decided to resign anyway, not having a taste for the society of human reptiles. And, as I sat there in the sunny park, furious, trying to plan a picture whose sombre horror should leave in his mind an ineffaceable scar, I suddenly thought of the pale black-robed girl in Central Park. Could it be her poor slender body that lay among the shadows of the grim Morgue! If ever brooding despair was stamped on any face, I had seen its print on hers when she spoke to me in the Park and gave me the letters. The letters! I had not thought of them since, but now I drew them from my pocket and looked at the addresses.

'Curious,' I thought, 'the letters are still damp; they smell of salt water too.'

I looked at the address again, written in the long fine

hand of an educated woman who had been bred in a French convent. Both letters bore the same address, in French:

CAPTAIN D'YNIOL
(Kindness of a Stranger.)

'Captain d'Yniol,' I repeated aloud, 'confound it, I've heard that name! Now, where the deuce – where in the name of all that's queer—' Somebody who had sat down on the bench beside me placed a heavy hand on my shoulder.

It was the Frenchman, 'Soger Charlie'.

'You spoke my name,' he said in apathetic tones.

'Your name!'

'Captain d'Yniol,' he repeated; 'it is my name.'

I recognized him in spite of the black goggles he was wearing, and, at the same moment it flashed into my mind that d'Yniol was the name of the traitor who had escaped. Ah, I remembered now!

'I am Captain d'Yniol,' he said again, and I saw his fingers closing on my coat sleeve.

It may have been my involuntary movement of recoil – I don't know – but the fellow dropped my coat and sat straight up on the bench.

'I am Captain d'Yniol,' he said for the third time, 'charged with treason and under sentence of death.'

'And innocent!' I muttered, before I was even conscious of having spoken. What was it that wrung those involuntary words from my lips, I shall never know, perhaps – but it was I, not he, who trembled, seized with a strange agitation, and it was I, not he, whose hand was stretched forth impulsively, touching his.

Without a tremor he took my hand, pressed it almost imperceptibly, and dropped it. Then I held both letters toward him, and, as he neither looked at them nor at me, I placed them in his hand. Then he started.

'Read them,' I said, 'they are for you.'

'Letters!' he gasped in a voice that sounded like nothing human.

'Yes, they are for you – I know it now—'

'Letters! – letters directed to *me*?'

'Can you not see?' I cried.

Then he raised one frail hand and drew the goggles from his eyes, and, as I looked I saw two tiny white specks exactly in the centre of both pupils.

'Blind!' I faltered.

'I have been unable to read for two years,' he said.

After a moment he placed the tip of one finger on the letters.

'They are wet,' I said; 'shall – would you like to have me read them?' For a long time he sat silently in the sunshine, fumbling with his cane, and I watched him without speaking. At last he said, 'Read, Monsieur,' and I took the letters and broke the seals.

The first letter contained a sheet of paper, damp and discolored, on which a few lines were written:

My darling, I knew you were innocent—

Here the writing ended, but, in the blur beneath, I read:

Paris shall know – France shall know, for at last I have the proofs and I am coming to find you, my soldier, and to place them in your own dear brave hands. They know, now, at the War Ministry – they have a copy of the traitor's confession – but they dare not make it public – they dare not withstand the popular astonishment and rage. Therefore I sail on Monday from Cherbourg by the Green Cross Line, to bring you back to your own again, where you will stand before all the world, without fear, without reproach.

ALINE.

'This – this is terrible!' I stammered; 'can God live and see such things done!'

But with his thin hand he gripped my arm again, bidding me read the other letter; and I shuddered at the menace in his voice.

Then, with his sightless eyes on me, I drew the other letter from the wet, stained envelope. And before I was aware – before I understood the purport of what I saw, I had read aloud these half effaced lines:

'The *Lorient* is sinking – an iceberg – mid-ocean – good-bye – you are innocent – I love—'

'The *Lorient*!' I cried; 'it was the French steamer that was never heard from – the *Lorient* of the Green Cross Line! I had forgotten – I—'

The loud crash of a revolver stunned me; my ears rang and ached with it as I shrank back from a ragged dusty figure that collapsed on the bench beside me, shuddered a moment, and tumbled to the asphalt at my feet.

The trampling of the eager hard-eyed crowd, the dust and taint of powder in the hot air, the harsh alarm of the ambulance clattering up Mail Street – these I remember, as I knelt there, helplessly holding the dead man's hands in mine.

'Soger Charlie,' mused the sparrow policeman, 'shot his-self, didn't he, Mr Hilton? You seen him, sir – blowed the top of his head off, didn't he, Mr Hilton?'

'Soger Charlie,' they repeated, 'a French dago what shot his-self'; and the words echoed in my ears long after the ambulance rattled away, and the increasing throng dispersed, sullenly, as a couple of policemen cleared a space around the pool of thick blood on the asphalt.

They wanted me as a witness, and I gave my card to one of the policemen who knew me. The rabble transferred its fascinated stare to me, and I turned away and pushed a path between frightened shop girls and ill-smelling loafers, until I lost myself in the human torrent of Broadway.

The torrent took me with it where it flowed – East? West? – I did not notice nor care, but I passed on through the throng, listless, deadly weary of attempting to solve God's justice – striving to understand His purpose – His laws – His judgments which are 'true and righteous altogether.'

IV

'More to be desired are they than gold, yea, than much fine gold. Sweeter also than honey and the honey-comb!'

I turned sharply toward the speaker who shambled at my elbow. His sunken eyes were dull and lustreless, his blood-less face gleamed pallid as a death mask above the blood-red jersey – the emblem of the soldiers of Christ.

I don't know why I stopped, lingering, but, as he passed, I said, 'Brother, I also was meditating upon God's wisdom and His testimonies.'

The pale fanatic shot a glance at me, hesitated, and fell into my own pace, walking by my side. Under the peak of his Salvation Army cap his eyes shone in the shadow with a strange light.

'Tell me more,' I said, sinking my voice below the roar of traffic, the clang! clang! of the cable-cars, and the noise of feet on the worn pavements – 'tell me of His testimonies.'

'Moreover by them is Thy servant warned and in keeping of them there is great reward. Who can understand His errors? Cleanse Thou me from secret faults. Keep back Thy servant also from presumptuous sins. Let them not have dominion over me. Then shall I be upright and I shall be innocent from the great transgression. Let the words of my mouth and the meditation of my heart be acceptable in Thy sight – O Lord! My strength and my Redeemer!'

'It is Holy Scripture that you quote,' I said; 'I also can read that when I choose. But it cannot clear for me the reasons – it cannot make me understand—'

'What?' he asked and muttered to himself.

'That, for instance,' I replied, pointing to a cripple, who had been *born* deaf and dumb and horridly misshapen – a wretched diseased lump on the sidewalk below St Paul's Churchyard

– a sore-eyed thing that mouthed and mowed and rattled pennies in a tin cup as though the sound of copper could stem the human pack that passed hot on the scent of gold.

Then the man who shambled beside me turned and looked long and earnestly into my eyes. And after a moment a dull recollection stirred within me – a vague something that seemed like the awakening memory of a past, long, long forgotten, dim, dark, too subtle, too frail, too indefinite – ah! the old feeling that all men have known – the old strange uneasiness, that useless struggle to remember when and where it all occurred before.

And the man's head sank on his crimson jersey, and he muttered, muttered to himself of God and love and compassion, until I saw that the fierce heat of the city had touched his brain, and I went away and left him prating of mysteries that none but such as he dare name.

So I passed on through dust and heat; and the hot breath of men touched my cheek and eager eyes looked into mine. Eyes, eyes, that met my own and looked through them, beyond – far beyond to where gold glittered amid the mirage of eternal hope. Gold! It was in the air where the soft sunlight gilded the floating motes, it was under foot in the dust that the sun made gilt, it glimmered from every window pane where the long red beams struck golden sparks above the gasping gold-hunting hordes of Wall Street.

High, high, in the deepening sky the tall buildings towered, and the breeze from the bay lifted the sun-dyed flags of commerce until they waved above the turmoil of the hives below – waved courage and hope and strength to those who lusted after gold.

The sun dipped low behind Castle William as I turned listlessly into the Battery, and the long straight shadows of the trees stretched away over greensward and asphalt walk.

Already the electric lights were glimmering among the foliage although the bay shimmered like polished brass and the topsails of the ships glowed with a deeper hue, where the red sun rays fall athwart the rigging.

Old men tottered along the sea-wall, tapping the asphalt with worn canes, old women crept to and fro in the coming twilight – old women who carried baskets that gaped for charity or bulged with moldy stuffs – food, clothing? – I could not tell; I did not care to know.

The heavy thunder from the parapets of Castle William died away over the placid bay, the last red arm of the sun shot up out of the sea, and wavered and faded into the sombre tones of the afterglow. Then came the night, timidly at first, touching sky and water with gray fingers, folding the foliage into soft massed shapes, creeping onward, onward, more swiftly now, until color and form had gone from all the earth and the world was a world of shadows.

And, as I sat there on the dusky sea-wall, gradually the bitter thoughts faded and I looked out into the calm night with something of that peace that comes to all when day is ended.

The death at my very elbow of the poor blind wretch in the Park had left a shock, but now my nerves relaxed their tension and I began to think about it all – about the letters and the strange woman who had given them to me. I wondered where she had found them – whether they really were carried by some vagrant current in to the shore from the wreck of the fated *Lorient*.

Nothing but these letters had human eyes encountered from the *Lorient*, although we believed that fire or berg had been her portion; for there had been no storms when the *Lorient* steamed away from Cherbourg.

And what of the pale-faced girl in black who had given these letters to me, saying that my own heart would teach me where to place them?

I felt in my pockets for the letters where I had thrust them all crumpled and wet. They were there, and I decided to turn them over to the police. Then I thought of Cusick and the City Hall Park and these set my mind running on Jamison and my own work – ah! I had forgotten that – I had forgotten that I had sworn to stir Jamison's cold, sluggish blood! Trading on his fiancée's reported suicide – or murder! True, he had told me that he was satisfied that the body at the Morgue was not Miss Tufft's because the ring did not correspond with his fiancée's ring. But what sort of man was that! – to go crawling and nosing about morgues and graves for a full-page illustration which might sell a few extra thousand papers. I had never known he was such a man. It was strange too – for that was not the sort of illustration that the *Weekly* used; it was against all precedent – against the whole policy of the paper. He would lose a hundred subscribers where he would gain one by such work.

'The callous brute!' I muttered to myself, 'I'll wake him up – I'll—'

I sat straight up on the bench and looked steadily at a figure which was moving toward me under the spluttering electric light.

It was the woman I had met in the Park.

She came straight up to me, her pale face gleaming like marble in the dark, her slim hands outstretched.

'I have been looking for you all day – all day,' she said, in the same low thrilling tones – 'I want the letters back; have you them here?'

'Yes,' I said, 'I have them here – take them in Heaven's name; they have done enough evil for one day!'

She took the letters from my hand; I saw the ring, made of the double serpents, flashing on her slim finger, and I stepped closer, and looked her in the eyes.

'Who are you?' I asked.

'I? My name is of no importance to you,' she answered.

'You are right,' I said, 'I do not care to know your name. That ring of yours—'

'What of my ring?' she murmured.

'Nothing – a dead woman lying in the Morgue wears such a ring. Do you know what your letters have done? No? Well I read them to a miserable wretch and he blew his brains out!'

'You read them to a man!'

'I did. He killed himself.'

'Who was that man?'

'Captain d'Yniol—'

With something between a sob and a laugh she seized my hand and covered it with kisses, and I, astonished and angry, pulled my hand away from her cold lips and sat down on the bench.

'You needn't thank me,' I said sharply; 'if I had known that – but no matter. Perhaps after all the poor devil is better off somewhere in other regions with his sweetheart who was drowned – yes, I imagine he is. He was blind and ill – and broken-hearted.'

'Blind?' she asked gently.

'Yes. Did you know him?'

'I knew him.'

'And his sweetheart, Aline?'

'Aline,' she repeated softly, '—she is dead. I come to thank you in her name.'

'For what? – for his death?'

'Ah, yes, for that.'

'Where did you get those letters?' I asked her, suddenly.

She did not answer, but stood fingering the wet letters.

Before I could speak again she moved away into the shadows of the trees, lightly, silently, and far down the dark walk I saw her diamond flashing.

Grimly brooding, I rose and passed through the Battery to the steps of the Elevated Road. These I climbed, bought my ticket, and stepped out to the damp platform. When a train came I crowded in with the rest, still pondering on my vengeance, feeling and believing that I was to scourge the conscience of the man who speculated on death.

At last the train stopped at 28th Street, and I hurried out and down the steps and away to the Morgue.

When I entered the Morgue, Skelton, the keeper, was standing before a slab that glistened faintly under the wretched gas jets. He heard my footsteps, and turned around to see who was coming. Then he nodded, saying, 'Mr Hilton, just take a look at this here stiff – I'll be back in a moment – this is the one that all the papers take to be Miss Tufft – but they're all off, because this stiff has been here now for two weeks.'

I drew out my sketching-block and pencils.

'Which is it, Skelton?' I asked, fumbling for my rubber.

'This one, Mr Hilton, the girl what's smilin'. Picked up off Sandy Hook, too. Looks as if she was asleep, eh?'

'What's she got in her hand – clenched tight? Oh, a letter. Turn up the gas, Skelton, I want to see her face.'

The old man turned up the gas jet, and the flame blazed and whistled in the damp, fetid air. Then suddenly my eyes fell on the dead.

Rigid, scarcely breathing, I stared at the ring, made of two twisted serpents set with a great diamond – I saw the wet letters crushed in her slender hand – I looked, and – God help me! – I looked upon the dead face of the girl with whom I had been speaking on the Battery!

'Dead for a month at least,' said Skelton, calmly.

Then, as I felt my senses leaving me, I screamed out, and at the same instant somebody from behind seized my shoulder and shook me savagely – shook me until I opened my eyes again and gasped and coughed.

'Now then, young feller!' said a Park policeman bending over me, 'if you go to sleep on a bench, somebody'll lift your watch!'

I turned, rubbing my eyes desperately.

Then it was all a dream – and no shrinking girl had come to me with damp letters – I had not gone to the office – there was no such person as Miss Tufft – Jamison was not an unfeeling villain – no, indeed! – he treated us all much better than we deserved, and he was kind and generous too. And the ghastly suicide! Thank God that also was a myth – and the Morgue and the Battery at night where that pale-faced girl had – ugh!

I felt for my sketch-block, found it; turned the pages of all the animals that I had sketched, the hippopotami, the buffalo, the tigers – ah! where was that sketch in which I had made the woman in shabby black the principal figure, with the brooding vultures all around and the crowd in the sunshine—? It was gone.

I hunted everywhere, in every pocket. It was gone.

At last I rose and moved along the narrow asphalt path in the falling twilight.

And as I turned into the broader walk, I was aware of a group, a policeman holding a lantern, some gardeners, and a knot of loungers gathered about something – a dark mass on the ground.

'Found 'em just so,' one of the gardeners was saying, 'better not touch 'em until the coroner comes.'

The policeman shifted his bull's-eye a little; the rays fell on two faces, on two bodies, half supported against a park bench. On the finger of the girl glittered a splendid diamond, set between the fangs of two gold serpents. The man had shot himself; he clasped two wet letters in his hand. The girl's clothing and hair were wringing wet, and her face was the face of a drowned person.

'Well, sir,' said the policeman, looking at me; 'you seem to know these two people – by your looks—'

'I never saw them before,' I gasped, and walked on, trembling in every nerve.

For among the folds of her shabby black dress I had noticed the end of a paper – my sketch that I had missed!

PASSEUR

When he had finished his pipe he tapped the brier bowl against the chimney until the ashes powdered the charred log smouldering across the andirons. Then he sat back in his chair, absently touched the hot pipe-bowl with the tip of each finger until it grew cool enough to be dropped into his coat pocket.

Twice he raised his eyes to the little American clock ticking upon the mantel. He had half an hour to wait.

The three candles that lighted the room might be trimmed to advantage; this would give him something to do. A pair of scissors lay open upon the bureau, and he rose and picked them up. For a while he stood dreamily shutting and opening the scissors, his eyes roaming about the room. There was an easel in the corner, and a pile of dusty canvases behind it; behind the canvases there was a shadow – that gray, menacing shadow that never moved.

When he had trimmed each candle he wiped the smoky scissors on a paint rag and flung them on the bureau again. The clock pointed to ten; he had been occupied exactly three minutes.

The bureau was littered with neckties, pipes, combs and brushes, matches, reels and fly-books, collars, shirt studs, a new pair of Scotch shooting stockings, and a woman's work-basket.

He picked out all the neckties, folded them once, and hung them over a bit of twine that stretched across the looking-glass; the shirt studs he shovelled into the top drawer along with brushes, combs, and stockings; the reels and fly-books he dusted with his handkerchief and placed methodically along the mantelshelf. Twice he stretched out his hand towards the woman's work-basket, but his hand fell to his side again, and he turned away into the room staring at the dying fire.

Outside the snow-sealed window a shutter broke loose and banged monotonously, until he flung open the panes and fastened it. The soft, wet snow, that had choked the window-panes all day, was frozen hard now, and he had to break the polished crust before he could find the rusty shutter hinge.

He leaned out for a moment, his numbed hands resting on the snow, the roar of a rising snow-squall in his ears; and out across the desolate garden and stark hedgerow he saw the flat black river spreading through the gloom.

A candle sputtered and snapped behind him; a sheet of drawing paper fluttered across the floor, and he closed the panes and turned back into the room, both hands in his worn pockets.

The little American clock on the mantel ticked and ticked, but the hands lagged, for he had not been occupied five minutes in all. He went up to the mantel and watched the hands of the clock. A minute – longer than a year to him – crept by.

Around the room the furniture stood ranged – a chair or two of yellow pine, a table, the easel, and in one corner the broad curtained bed; and behind each lay shadows, menacing shadows that never moved.

A little pale flame started up from the smoking log on the andirons; the room sang with the sudden hiss of escaping wood gases. After a little the back of the log caught fire; jets of blue flared up here and there with mellow sounds like the lighting of gas-burners in a row, and in a moment a thin sheet of yellow flame wrapped the whole charred log.

Then the shadows moved; not the shadows behind the

furniture – they never moved – but other shadows, thin, gray, confusing, that came and spread their slim patterns all around him, and trembled and trembled.

He dared not step or tread upon them, they were too real; they meshed the floor around his feet, they ensnared his knees, they fell across his breast like ropes. Some night, in the silence of the moors, when wind and river were still, he feared these strands of shadow might tighten – creep higher around his throat and tighten. But even then he knew that those other shadows would never move, those gray shapes that knelt crouching in every corner.

When he looked up at the clock again ten minutes had struggled past. Time was disturbed in the room; the strands of shadow seemed entangled among the hands of the clock, dragging them back from their rotation. He wondered if the shadows would strangle Time, some still night when the wind and the flat river were silent.

There grew a sudden chill across the floor; the cracks of the boards let it in. He leaned down and drew his sabots towards him from their place near the andirons, and slipped them over his chaussons; and as he straightened up, his eyes mechanically sought the mantel above, where in the dusk another pair of sabots stood, little slender, delicate sabots, carved from red beech. A year's dust grayed their surface; a year's rust dulled the silver band across the instep. He said this to himself aloud, knowing that it was within a few minutes of the year.

His own sabots came from Mort-Dieu; they were shaved square and banded with steel. But in days past he had thought that no sabot in Mort-Dieu was delicate enough to touch the instep of the Mort-Dieu passeur. So he sent to the shore light-house, and they sent to Lorient, where the women are coquettish and show their hair under the coiffe, and wear dainty sabots; and in this town, where vanity corrupts and there is much lace on coiffe and collarette, a pair of delicate sabots was found, banded with silver and chiselled in red beech. The sabots stood on the mantel above the fire now, dusty and tarnished.

There was a sound from the window, the soft murmur of snow blotting glass panes. The wind, too, muttered under the eaves. Presently it would begin to whisper to him from the chimney – he knew it – and he held his hands over his ears and stared at the clock.

In the hamlet of Mort-Dieu the panes sing all day of the sea secrets, but in the night the ghosts of little gray birds fill the branches, singing of the sunshine of past years. He heard the song as he sat, and he crushed his hands over his ears; but the gray birds joined with the wind in the chimney, and he heard all that he dared not hear, and he thought all that he dared not hope or think, and the swift tears scalded his eyes.

In Mort-Dieu the nights are longer than anywhere on earth; he knew it – why should he not know? This had been so for a year; it was different before. There were so many things different before; days and nights vanished like minutes then; the pines told no secrets of the sea, and the gray birds had not yet come to Mort-Dieu. Also, there was Jeanne, passeur at the Carmes.

When he first saw her she was poling the square, flat-bottomed ferry-skiff from the Carmes to Mort-Dieu, a red skirt fluttering just below her knees. The next time he saw her he had to call to her across the placid river, 'Ohé! Ohé! passeur!' She came, poling that flat skiff, her deep blue eyes fixed pensively on him, the scarlet skirt and kerchief idly flapping in the April wind. Then day followed day when the far call 'Passeur!' grew clearer and more joyous, and the faint answering cry, 'I come!' rippled across the water like music tinged with laughter. Then spring came, and with spring came love – love, carried free across the ferry from the Carmes to Mort-Dieu.

The flame above the charred log whistled, flickered, and went out in a jet of wood vapour, only to play like lightning above the gas and relight again. The clock ticked more loudly, and the song from the pines filled the room. But in his straining eyes a summer landscape was reflected, where white clouds sailed and white foam curled under the square bow of a little skiff. And he pressed his numbed hands tighter to his ears to drown the cry, 'Passeur! Passeur!'

And now for a moment the clock ceased ticking. It was time to go – who but he should know it, he who went out into the night swinging his lantern? And he went. He had gone each night from the first – from that first strange winter evening when a strange voice answered him across the river, the voice of the new passeur. He had never heard *her* voice again.

So he passed down the windy wooden stairs, lantern hanging lighted in his hand, and stepped out into the storm. Through sheets of drifting snow, over heaps of frozen seaweed and icy drift he moved, shifting his lantern right and left, until its glimmer on the water warned him. Then he called out into the night, 'Passeur!' The frozen spray spattered his face and crusted the lantern; he heard the distant boom of breakers beyond the bar, and the noise of mighty winds among the seaward cliffs.

'Passeur!'

Across the broad flat river, black as a sea of pitch, a tiny light sparkled a moment. Again he cried, 'Passeur!'

'I come!'

He turned ghastly white, for it was her voice – or was he crazy? – and he sprang waist deep into the icy current and cried out again, but his voice ended in a sob.

Slowly through the snow the flat skiff took shape, creeping nearer and nearer. But she was not at the pole – he saw that; there was a tall, thin man, shrouded to his eyes in oilskin; and he leaped into the boat and bade the ferryman hasten.

Halfway across he rose in the skiff, and called, 'Jeanne!' But the roar of the storm and the thrashing of the icy waves drowned his voice. Yet he heard her again, and she called to him by name.

When at last the boat grated upon the invisible shore, he

lifted his lantern, stumbling among the rocks, and calling to her, as though his voice could silence the voice that had spoken a year ago that night. And it could not. He sank shivering upon his knees, and looked out into the darkness, where an ocean rolled across a world. Then his stiff lips moved, and he repeated her name, but the hand of the ferryman fell gently upon his head.

And when he raised his eyes he saw that the ferryman was Death.

IN THE COURT OF THE DRAGON

'Oh Thou who burn'st in heart for those who burn
In Hell, whose fires thyself shall feed in turn;
How long be crying, "Mercy on them, God!"
Why, who are thou to teach and He to learn?'

In the Church of St Barnabé vespers were over; the clergy left the altar; the little choir-boys flocked across the chancel and settled in the stalls. A Suisse in rich uniform marched down the south aisle, sounding his staff at every fourth step on the stone pavement; behind him came that eloquent preacher and good man, Monseigneur C—.

My chair was near the chancel rail. I now turned toward the west end of the church. The other people between the altar and the pulpit turned too. There was a little scraping and rustling while the congregation seated itself again; the preacher mounted the pulpit stairs, and the organ voluntary ceased.

I had always found the organ-playing at St Barnabé highly interesting. Learned and scientific it was, too much so for my small knowledge, but expressing a vivid if cold intelligence. Moreover, it possessed the French quality of taste; taste reigned supreme, self-controlled, dignified and reticent.

Today, however, from the first choir I had felt a change for the worse, a sinister change. During vespers it had been chiefly the chancel organ which supported the beautiful choir, but now and again, quite wantonly as it seemed, from the west gallery where the great organ stands, a heavy hand had struck across the church, at the serene peace of those clear voices. It was something more than harsh and dissonant, and it betrayed no lack of skill. As it recurred again and again, it set me thinking of what my architect's books say about the custom in early times to consecrate the choir as soon as it was built, and that the nave, being finished sometimes half a century later, often did not get any blessing at all: I wondered idly if that had been the case at St Barnabé, and whether something not usually supposed to be at home in a Christian church, might have entered undetected, and taken possession of the west gallery. I had read of such things happening too, but not in works on architecture.

Then I remembered that St Barnabé was not much more than a hundred years old, and smiled at the incongruous association of mediaeval superstitions with that cheerful little piece of eighteenth century rococo.

But now vespers were over, and there should have followed a few quiet chords, fit to accompany meditation, while we waited for the sermon. Instead of that, the discord at the lower end of the church broke out with the departure of the clergy, as if now nothing could control it.

I belong to those children of an older and simpler generation, who do not love to seek for psychological subtleties in art; and I have ever refused to find in music anything more than melody and harmony, but I felt that in the labyrinth of sounds now issuing from that instrument there was something being hunted. Up and down the pedals chased him, while the manuals blared approval. Poor devil! whoever he was there seemed small hope of escape!

My nervous annoyance changed to anger. Who was doing this? How dare he play like that in the midst of divine service? I glanced at the people near me: not one appeared to be in the least disturbed. The placid brows of the kneeling nuns, still turned toward the altar, lost none of their devout abstraction, under the pale shadow of their white head-dress. The fashionable lady beside me was looking expectantly at

Monseigneur C—. For all her face betrayed, the organ might have been singing an Ave Maria.

But now, at last, the preacher had made the sign of the cross, and commanded silence. I turned to him gladly. Thus far I had not found the rest I had counted on, when I entered St Barnabé that afternoon.

I was worn out by three nights of physical suffering and mental trouble: the last had been the worst, and it was an exhausted body, and a mind benumbed and yet acutely sensitive, which I had brought to my favorite church for healing. For I had been reading 'The King in Yellow'.

'The sun ariseth; they gather themselves together and lay them down in their dens.' Monseigneur C – delivered his text in a calm voice, glancing quietly over the congregation. My eyes turned, I knew not why, toward the lower end of the church. The organist was coming from behind his pipes, and passing along the gallery on his way out, I saw him disappear by a small door that leads to some stone stairs which descend directly to the street. He was a slender man, and his face was as white as his coat was black. 'Good riddance!' I thought, 'with your wicked music! I hope your assistant will play the closing voluntary.'

With a feeling of relief, with a deep calm feeling of relief, I turned back to the mild face in the pulpit, and settled myself to listen. Here at last was the ease of mind I longed for.

'My children,' said the preacher, 'one truth the human soul finds hardest of all to learn; that it has nothing to fear. It can never be made to see that nothing can really harm it.'

'Curious doctrine!' I thought, 'for a Catholic priest. Let us see how he will reconcile that with the Fathers.'

'Nothing can really harm the soul,' he went on, in his coolest, clearest tones, 'because—'

But I never heard the rest; my eye left his face, I knew not for what reason, and sought the lower end of the church. The same man was coming out from behind the organ, and was passing along the gallery *the same way*. But there had not been time for him to return, and if he had returned, I must have seen him. I felt a faint chill, and my heart sank; and yet, his going and coming were no affair of mine. I looked at him: I could not look away from his black figure and his white face. When he was exactly opposite to me, he turned and sent across the church, straight into my eyes, a look of hate, intense and deadly: I have never seen any other like it; would to God I might never see it again! Then he disappeared by the same door through which I had watched him depart less than sixty seconds before.

I sat and tried to collect my thoughts. My first sensation was like that of a very young child badly hurt, when it catches its breath before crying out.

To suddenly find myself the object of such hatred was exquisitely painful: and this man was an utter stranger. Why should he hate me so? Me, whom he had never seen before? For the moment all other sensation was merged in this one pang; even fear was subordinate to grief, and for that moment I never doubted; but in the next I began to reason, and a sense of the incongruous came to my aid.

As I have said, St Barnabé is a modern church. It is small and well lighted; one sees all over it almost at a glance. The organ gallery gets a strong white light from a row of long windows in the clerestory, which have not even colored glass.

The pulpit being in the middle of the church, it followed that, when I was turned toward it, whatever moved at the west end could not fail to attract my eye. When the organist passed it was no wonder that I saw him; I had simply miscalculated the interval between his first and his second passing. He had come in that last time by the other side-door. As for the look which had so upset me, there had been no such thing, and I was a nervous fool.

I looked about. This was a likely place to harbor supernatural horrors! That clear-cut, reasonable face of Monseigneur

C—, his collected manner, and easy, graceful gestures, were they not just a little discouraging to the notion of a gruesome mystery? I glanced above his head, and almost laughed. That flyaway lady, supporting one corner of the pulpit canopy, which looked like a fringed damask table-cloth in a high wind, at the first attempt of a basilisk to pose up there in the organ loft, she would point her gold trumpet at him, and puff him out of existence! I laughed to myself over this conceit, which, at the time, I thought very amusing, and sat and chaffed myself and everything else, from the old harpy outside the railing, who had made me pay ten centimes for my chair, before she would let me in (she was more like a basilisk, I told myself, than was my organist with the anaemic complexion): from that grim old dame, to, yes, alas! to Monseigneur C— himself. For all devoutness had fled. I had never yet done such a thing in my life, but now I felt a desire to mock.

As for the sermon, I could not hear a word of it, for the jingle in my ears of

'The skirts of St Paul has reached.
Having preached us those six Lent lectures,
More unctuous than ever he preached:'

keeping time to the most fantastic and irreverent thoughts.

It was no use to sit there any longer: I must get out of doors and shake myself free from this hateful mood. I knew the rudeness I was committing but still I rose and left the church.

A spring sun was shining on the rue St Honoré, as I ran down the church steps. On one corner stood a barrow full of yellow jonquils, pale violets from the Riviera, dark Russian violets, and white Roman hyacinths in a golden cloud of mimosa. The street was full of Sunday pleasure-seekers. I swung my cane and laughed with the rest. Some one overtook and passed me. He never turned, but there was the same deadly malignity in his white profile that there had been in his eyes. I watched him as long as I could see him. His lithe back expressed the same menace; every step that carried him away from me seemed to bear him on some errand connected with my destruction.

I was creeping along, my feet almost refusing to move. There began to dawn in me a sense of responsibility for something long forgotten. It began to seem as if I deserved that which he threatened: it reached a long way back – a long, long way back. It had lain dormant all these years: it was there though, and presently it would rise and confront me. But I would try to escape; and I stumbled as best I could into the rue de Rivoli, across the Place de la Concorde and on to the Quai. I looked with sick eyes upon the sun, shining through the white foam of the fountain, pouring over the backs of the dusky bronze river-gods, on the far-away Arc, a structure of amethyst mist, on the countless vistas of gray stems and bare branches faintly green. Then I saw him again coming down one of the chestnut alleys of the Cours la Reine.

I left the river side, plunged blindly across to the Champs Elysées and turned toward the Arc. The setting sun was sending its rays along the green sward of the Rond-point: in the full glow he sat on a bench, children and young mothers all about him. He was nothing but a Sunday lounger, like the others, like myself. I said the words almost aloud, and all the while I gazed on the malignant hatred of his face. But he was not looking at me. I crept past and dragged my leaden feet up the Avenue. I knew that every time I met him brought him nearer to the accomplishment of his purpose and my fate. And still I tried to save myself.

The last rays of sunset were pouring through the great Arc. I passed under it, and met him face to face. I had left him far down the Champs Elysées, and yet he came in with a stream of people who were returning from the Bois de Boulogne. He came so close that he brushed me. His slender frame felt like iron inside its loose black covering. He showed no signs of haste, nor of fatigue, nor of any human feeling.

His whole being expressed but one thing: the will, and the power to work me evil.

In anguish I watched him, where he went down the broad crowded Avenue, that was all flashing with wheels and the trappings of horses, and the helmets of the Garde Republicaine.

He was soon lost to sight; then I turned and fled. Into the Bois, and far out beyond it – I know not where I went, but after a long while as it seemed to me, night had fallen, and I found myself sitting at a table before a small café. I had wandered back into the Bois. It was hours now since I had seen him. Physical fatigue, and mental suffering had left me no more power to think or feel. I was tired, so tired! I longed to hide away in my own den. I resolved to go home. But that was a long way off.

I live in the Court of the Dragon, a narrow passage that leads from the rue de Rennes to the rue du Dragon.

It is an 'Impasse', traversable only for foot passengers. Over the entrance on the rue de Rennes is a balcony, supported by an iron dragon. Within the court tall old houses rise on either side, and close the ends that give on the two streets. Huge gates, swung back during the day into the walls of the deep archways, close this court, after midnight, and one must enter then by ringing at certain small doors on the side. The sunken pavement collects unsavory pools. Steep stairways pitch down to doors that open on the court. The ground floors are occupied by shops of second-hand dealers, and by iron workers. All day long the place rings with the clink of hammers, and the clang of metal bars.

Unsavory as it is below, there is cheerfulness, and comfort, and hard, honest work above.

Five flights up are the ateliers of architects and painters, and the hiding-places of middle-aged students like myself who want to live alone. When I first came here to live I was young, and not alone.

I had to walk awhile before any conveyance appeared, but at last, when I had almost reached the Arc de Triomphe again, an empty cab came along and I took it.

From the Arc to the rue de Rennes is a drive of more than half an hour, especially when one is conveyed by a tired cab horse that has been at the mercy of Sunday fête makers.

There had been time before I passed under the Dragon's wings, to meet my enemy over and over again, but I never saw him once, now refuge was close at hand.

Before the wide gateway a small mob of children were playing. Our concierge and his wife walked about among them with their black poodle, keeping order; some couples were waltzing on the side-walk. I returned their greetings and hurried in.

All the inhabitants of the court had trooped out into the street. The place was quite deserted, lighted by a few lanterns hung high up, in which the gas burned dimly.

My apartment was at the top of a house, half way down the court, reached by a staircase that descended almost into the street, with only a bit of passage-way intervening. I set my foot on the threshold of the open door, the friendly, old ruinous stairs rose before me, leading up to rest and shelter. Looking back over my right shoulder, I saw *him*, ten paces off. He must have entered the court with me.

He was coming straight on, neither slowly, nor swiftly, but straight on to me. And now he was looking at me. For the first time since our eyes encountered across the church they met now again, and I knew that the time had come.

Retreating backward, down the court, I faced him. I meant to escape by the entrance on the rue du Dragon. His eyes told me that I never should escape.

It seemed ages while we were going, I retreating, he advancing, down the court in perfect silence; but at last I felt the shadow of the archway, and the next step brought me within it. I had meant to turn here and spring through into the street. But the shadow was not that of an archway; it was that of a vault. The great doors on the rue du Dragon were closed. I felt this by the blackness which surrounded me, and at the same instant I read it in his face. How his face gleamed in the darkness, drawing swiftly nearer! The deep vaults, the huge closed doors, their cold iron clamps were all on his side. The thing which he had threatened had arrived: it gathered and bore down on me from the fathomless shadows; the point from which it would strike was his infernal eyes. Hopeless, I set my back against the barred doors and defied him.

There was a scraping of chairs on the stone floor, and a rustling as the congregation rose. I could hear the Suisse's staff in the south aisle, preceding Monseigneur C— to the sacristy.

The kneeling nuns, roused from their devout abstraction, made their reverence and went away. The fashionable lady, my neighbor, rose also, with graceful reserve. As she departed her glance just flitted over my face in disapproval.

Half dead, or so it seemed to me, yet intensely alive to every trifle, I sat among the leisurely moving crowd, then rose too and went toward the door.

I had slept through the sermon. Had I slept through the sermon? I looked up and saw him passing along the gallery to his place. Only his side I saw; the thin bent arm in its black covering looked like one of those devilish, nameless instruments which lie in the disused torture chambers of mediaeval castles.

But I had escaped him, though his eyes had said I should not. *Had* I escaped? That which gave him the power over me came back out of oblivion, where I had hoped to keep it. For I knew him now. Death and the awful abode of lost souls, whither my weakness long ago had sent him – they had changed him for every other eye, but not for mine. I had recognized him almost from the first; I had never doubted what he was come to do; and now I knew that while my body sat safe in the cheerful little church, he had been hunting my soul in the Court of the Dragon.

I crept to the door; the organ broke out overhead with a blare. A dazzling light filled the church, blotting the altar from my eyes. The people faded away, the arches, the vaulted roof vanished. I raised my seared eyes to the fathomless glare, and I saw the black stars hanging in the heavens; and the wet winds from the Lake of Hali chilled my face.

And now, far away, over leagues of tossing cloud-waves, I saw the moon dripping with spray; and beyond, the towers of Carcosa rose behind the moon.

Death and the awful abode of lost souls, whither my weakness long ago had sent him, had changed him for every other eye but mine. And now I heard *his voice*, rising, swelling, thundering through the flaring light, and as I fell, the radiance increasing, increasing, poured over me in waves of flame. Then I sank into the depths, and I heard the King in Yellow whispering to my soul: 'It is a fearful thing to fall into the hands of the living God!'

THE MAKER OF MOONS

'I have heard what the Talkers were talking – the talk
Of the beginning and the end;
But I do not talk of the beginning or the end.'

I

Concerning Yue-Laou and the Xin I know nothing more than you shall know. I am miserably anxious to clear the matter up. Perhaps what I write may save the United States Government money and lives, perhaps it may arouse the scientific world to action; at any rate it will put an end to the terrible suspense of two people. Certainty is better than suspense.

If the Government dares to disregard this warning and refuses to send a thoroughly equipped expedition at once, the people of the State may take swift vengeance on the whole region and leave a blackened devastated waste where today forest and flowering meadowland border the lake in the Cardinal Woods.

You already know part of the story; the New York papers have been full of alleged details. This much is true: Barris caught the 'Shiner' red-handed, or rather yellow-handed, for his pockets and boots and dirty fists were stuffed with lumps of gold. I say gold, advisedly. You may call it what you please. You also know how Barris was – but unless I begin at the beginning of my own experiences you will be none the wiser after all.

On the third of August of this present year I was standing in Tiffany's, chatting with George Godfrey of the designing department. On the glass counter between us lay a coiled serpent, an exquisite specimen of chiseled gold.

'No,' replied Godfrey to my question, 'it isn't my work; I wish it was. Why, man, it's a masterpiece!'

'Whose?' I asked.

'Now I should be very glad to know also,' said Godfrey. 'We bought it from an old jay who says he lives in the country somewhere about the Cardinal Woods. That's near Starlit Lake, I believe—'

'Lake of the Stars?' I suggested.

'Some call it Starlit Lake – it's all the same. Well, my rustic Reuben says that he represents the sculptor of this snake for all practical and business purposes. He got his price too. We hope he'll bring us something more. We have sold this already to the Metropolitan Museum.'

I was leaning idly on the glass case, watching the keen eyes of the artist in precious metals as he stooped over the gold serpent.

'A masterpiece!' he muttered to himself, fondling the glittering coil, 'look at the texture! whew!' But I was not looking at the serpent. Something was moving – crawling out of Godfrey's coat pocket – the pocket nearest me – something soft and yellow with crablike legs all covered with coarse yellow hair.

'What in Heaven's name,' said I, 'have you got in your pocket? It's crawling out – it's trying to creep up your coat, Godfrey!'

He turned quickly and dragged the creature out with his left hand.

I shrank back as he held the repulsive object dangling before me, and he laughed and placed it on the counter.

'Did you ever see anything like that?' he demanded.

'No,' said I truthfully, 'and I hope I never shall again. What is it?'

'I don't know. Ask them at the Natural History Museum

– they can't tell you. The Smithsonian is all at sea too. It is, I believe, the connecting link between a sea urchin, a spider, and the devil. It looks venomous but I can't find either fangs or mouth. Is it blind? These things may be eyes but they looks as if they were painted. A Japanese sculptor might have produced such an impossible beast, but it is hard to believe that God did. It looks unfinished too. I have a mad idea that this creature is only one of the parts of some larger and more grotesque organism – it looks so lonely, so hopelessly dependent, so cursedly unfinished. I'm going to use it as a model. If I don't out-Japanese the Japs my name isn't Godfrey.'

The creature was moving slowly across the glass case towards me. I drew back.

'Godfrey,' I said, 'I would execute a man who executed any such work as you propose. What do you want to perpetuate such a reptile for? I can stand the Japanese grotesque but I can't stand that – spider—'

'It's a crab.'

'Crab or spider or blindworm – ugh! What do you want to do it for? It's a nightmare – it's unclean!'

I hated the thing. It was the first living creature that I had ever hated.

For some time I had noticed a damp acrid odor in the air, and Godfrey said it came from the reptile.

'Then kill it and bury it,' I said, 'and by the way, where did it come from?'

'I don't know that either,' laughed Godfrey. 'I found it clinging to the box that this gold serpent was brought in. I suppose my old Reuben is responsible.'

'If the Cardinal Woods are the lurking places for things like this,' said I, 'I am sorry that I am going to the Cardinal Woods.'

'Are you?' asked Godfrey; 'for the shooting?'

'Yes, with Barris and Pierpont. Why don't you kill that creature?'

'Go off on your shooting trip, and let me alone,' laughed Godfrey.

I shuddered at the 'crab', and bade Godfrey good-bye until December.

That night, Pierpont, Barris, and I sat chatting in the smoking car of the Quebec Express when the long train pulled out of the Grand Central Depot. Old David had gone forward with the dogs; poor things, they hated to ride in the baggage car, but the Quebec and Northern road provides no sportsman's cars, and David and the three Gordon setters were in for an uncomfortable night.

Except for Pierpont, Barris, and myself, the car was empty. Barris, trim, stout, ruddy, and bronzed, sat drumming on the window ledge, puffing a short fragrant pipe. His gun case lay beside him on the floor.

'When *I* have white hair and years of discretion,' said Pierpont languidly, 'I'll not flirt with pretty serving maids; will you, Roy?'

'No,' said I, looking at Barris.

'You mean the maid with the cap in the Pullman car?' asked Barris.

'Yes,' said Pierpont.

I smiled, for I had seen it also.

Barris twisted his crisp gray moustache, and yawned.

'You children had better be toddling off to bed,' he said. 'That lady's-maid is a member of the Secret Service.'

'Oh,' said Pierpont, 'one of your colleagues?'

'You might present us, you know,' I said; 'the journey is monotonous.'

Barris had drawn a telegram from his pocket, and as he sat turning it over and over between his fingers he smiled. After a moment or two he handed it to Pierpont who read it with slightly raised eyebrows.

'It's rot – I suppose it's cipher,' he said. 'I see it's signed by General Drummond—'

'Drummond, Chief of the Government Secret Service,' said Barris.

'Something interesting?' I enquired, lighting a cigarette.

'Something so interesting,' replied Barris, 'that I'm going to look into it myself—'

'And break up our shooting trio—'

'No. Do you want to hear about it? Do you, Billy Pierpont?'

'Yes,' replied that immaculate young man.

Barris rubbed the amber mouthpiece of his pipe on his handkerchief, cleared the stem with a bit of wire, puffed once or twice, and leaned back in his chair.

'Pierpont,' he said, 'do you remember that evening at the United States Club when General Miles, General Drummond, and I were examining that gold nugget that Captain Mahan had? You examined it also, I believe.'

'I did,' said Pierpont.

'Was it gold?' asked Barris, drumming on the window.

'It was,' replied Pierpont.

'I saw it too,' said I; 'of course, it was gold.'

'Professor La Grange saw it also,' said Barris; 'he said it was gold.'

'Well?' said Pierpont.

'Well,' said Barris, 'it was not gold.'

After a silence Pierpont asked what tests had been made.

'The usual tests,' replied Barris. 'The United States Mint is satisfied that it is gold, so is every jeweller who has seen it. But it is not gold – and yet – it is gold.'

Pierpont and I exchanged glances.

'Now,' said I, 'for Barris' usual *coup-de-théâtre*: what was the nugget?'

'Practically it was pure gold; but,' said Barris, enjoying the situation intensely, 'really it was not gold. Pierpont, what is gold?'

'Gold's an element, a metal—'

'Wrong! Billy Pierpont,' said Barris coolly.

'Gold was an element when I went to school,' said I.

'It has not been an element for two weeks,' said Barris; 'and, except General Drummond, Professor La Grange, and myself, you two youngsters are the only people, except one, in the world who know it – or have known it.'

'Do you mean to say that gold is a composite metal?' said Pierpont slowly.

'I do. La Grange has made it. He produced a scale of pure gold day before yesterday. That nugget was manufactured gold.'

Could Barris be joking? Was this a colossal hoax? I looked at Pierpont. He muttered something about that settling the silver question, and turned his head to Barris, but there was that in Barris' face which forbade jesting, and Pierpont and I sat silently pondering.

'Don't ask me how it's made,' said Barris, quietly; 'I don't know. But I do know that somewhere in the region of the Cardinal Woods there is a gang of people who do know how gold is made, and who make it. You understand the danger this is to every civilized nation. It's got to be stopped of course. Drummond and I have decided that I am the man to stop it. Wherever and whoever these people are – these gold makers – they must be caught, every one of them – caught or shot.'

'Or shot,' repeated Pierpont, who was owner of the Cross-Cut Gold Mine and found his income too small; 'Professor La Grange will of course be prudent – science need not know things that would upset the world!'

'Little Willy,' said Barris laughing, 'your income is safe.'

'I suppose,' said I, 'some flaw in the nugget gave Professor La Grange the tip.'

'Exactly. He cut the flaw out before sending the nugget to be tested. He worked on the flaw and separated gold into its three elements.'

'He is a great man,' said Pierpont, 'but he will be the greatest man in the world if he can keep his discovery to himself.'

'Who?' said Barris.

'Professor La Grange.'

'Professor La Grange was shot through the heart two hours ago,' replied Barris slowly.

II

We had been at the shooting box in the Cardinal Woods five days when a telegram was brought to Barris by a mounted messenger from the nearest telegraph station, Cardinal Springs, a hamlet on the lumber railroad which joins the Quebec and Northern at Three Rivers Junction, thirty miles below.

Pierpont and I were sitting out under the trees, loading some special shells as experiments; Barris stood beside us, bronzed, erect, holding his pipe carefully so that no sparks should drift into our powder box. The beat of hoofs over the grass aroused us, and when the lank messenger drew bridle before the door, Barris stepped forward and took the sealed telegram. When he had torn it open he went into the house and presently reappeared, reading something that he had written.

'This should go at once,' he said, looking the messenger full in the face.

'At once, Colonel Barris,' replied the shabby countryman.

Pierpont glanced up and I smiled at the messenger who was gathering his bridle and settling himself in his stirrups. Barris handed him the written reply and nodded good-bye: there was a thud of hoofs on the greensward, a jingle of bit and spur across the gravel, and the messenger was gone. Barris' pipe went out and he stepped to windward to relight it.

'It is queer,' said I, 'that your messenger – a battered native – should speak like a Harvard man.'

'He is a Harvard man,' said Barris.

'And the plot thickens,' said Pierpont; 'are the Cardinal Woods full of your Secret Service men, Barris?'

'No,' replied Barris, 'but the telegraph stations are. How many ounces of shot are you using, Roy?'

I told him, holding up the adjustable steel measuring cup. He nodded. After a moment or two he sat down on a camp stool beside us and picked up a crimper.

'That telegram was from Drummond,' he said; 'the messenger was one of my men as you two bright little boys divined. Pooh! If he had spoken the Cardinal County dialect you wouldn't have known.'

'His make-up was good,' said Pierpont.

Barris twirled the crimper and looked at the pile of loaded shells. Then he picked up one and crimped it.

'Let 'em alone,' said Pierpont, 'you crimp too tight.'

'Does his little gun kick when the shells are crimped too tight?' enquired Barris tenderly; 'well, he shall crimp his own shells then – where's his little man?'

'His little man,' was a weird English importation, stiff, very carefully scrubbed, tangled in his aspirates, named Howlett. As valet, gilly, gunbearer, and crimper, he aided Pierpont to endure the ennui of existence, by doing for him everything except breathing. Lately, however, Barris' taunts had driven Pierpont to do a few things for himself. To his astonishment he found that cleaning his own gun was not a bore, so he timidly loaded a shell or two, was much pleased with himself, loaded some more, crimped them, and went to breakfast with an appetite. So when Barris asked where 'his little man' was, Pierpont did not reply but dug a cupful of shot from the bag and poured it solemnly into the half filled shell.

Old David came out with the dogs and of course there was a powwow when Voyou, my Gordon, wagged his splendid tail across the loading table and sent a dozen unstopped cartridges rolling over the grass, vomiting powder and shot.

'Give the dogs a mile or two,' said I; 'we will shoot over the Sweet Fern Covert about four o'clock, David.'

'Two guns, David,' added Barris.

'Are you not going?' asked Pierpont, looking up, as David disappeared with the dogs.

'Bigger game,' said Barris shortly. He picked up a mug of ale from the tray which Howlett had just set down beside us and took a long pull. We did the same, silently. Pierpont set his mug on the turf beside him and returned to his loading.

We spoke of the murder of Professor La Grange, of how it had been concealed by the authorities in New York at

Drummond's request, of the certainty that it was one of the gang of gold-makers who had done it, and of the possible alertness of the gang.

'Oh, they know that Drummond will be after them sooner or later,' said Barris, 'but they don't know that the mills of the gods have already begun to grind. Those smart New York papers built better than they knew when their ferret-eyed reporter poked his red nose into the house on 58th Street and sneaked off with a column on his cuffs about the "suicide" of Professor La Grange. Bill Pierpont, my revolver is hanging in your room; I'll take yours too—'

'Help yourself,' said Pierpont.

'I shall be gone over night,' continued Barris; 'my poncho and some bread and meat are all I shall take except the "barkers".'

'Will they bark tonight?' I asked.

'No, I trust not for several weeks yet. I shall nose about a bit. Roy, did it ever strike you how queer it is that this wonderfully beautiful country should contain no inhabitants?'

'It's like those splendid stretches of pools and rapids which one finds on every trout river and in which one never finds a fish,' suggested Pierpont.

'Exactly – and Heaven alone knows why;' said Barris; 'I suppose this country is shunned by human beings for the same mysterious reasons.'

'The shooting is the better for it,' I observed.

'The shooting is good,' said Barris, 'have you noticed the snipe on the meadow by the lake? Why it's brown with them! That's a wonderful meadow.'

'It's a natural one,' said Pierpont, 'no human being ever cleared that land.'

'Then it's supernatural,' said Barris; 'Pierpont, do you want to come with me?'

Pierpont's handsome face flushed as he answered slowly, 'It's awfully good of you – if I may.'

'Bosh,' said I, piqued because he had asked Pierpont, 'what use is little Willy without his man?'

'True,' said Barris gravely, 'you can't take Howlett you know.'

Pierpont muttered something which ended in 'd—n'.

'Then,' said I, 'there will be but one gun on the Sweet Fern Covert this afternoon. Very well, I wish you joy of your cold supper and cold bed. Take your nightgown, Willy, and don't sleep on the damp ground.'

'Let Pierpont alone,' retorted Barris, 'you shall go next time, Roy.'

'Oh, all right – you mean when there's shooting going on?'

'And I?' demanded Pierpont grieved.

'You too, my son; stop quarrelling! Will you ask Howlett to pack our kits – lightly mind you – no bottles – they clink.'

'My flask doesn't,' said Pierpont, and went off to get ready for a night's stalking of dangerous men.

'It is strange,' said I, 'that nobody ever settles in this region. How many people live in Cardinal Springs, Barris?'

'Twenty counting the telegraph operator and not counting the lumbermen; they are always changing and shifting. I have six men among them.'

'Where have you no men? In the Four Hundred?'

'I have men there also – chums of Billy's only he doesn't know it. David tells me that there was a strong flight of woodcock last night. You ought to pick up some this afternoon.'

Then we chatted about alder-cover and swamp until Pierpont came out of the house and it was time to part.

'Au revoir,' said Barris, buckling on his kit, 'come along, Pierpont, and don't walk in the damp grass.'

'If you are not back by tomorrow noon,' said I, 'I will take Howlett and David and hunt you up. You say your course is due north?'

'Due north,' replied Barris, consulting his compass.

'There is a trail for two miles and a spotted lead for two more,' said Pierpont.

'Which we won't use for various reasons,' added Barris

pleasantly; 'don't worry, Roy, and keep your confounded expedition out of the way; there's no danger.'

He knew, of course, what he was talking about and I held my peace.

When the tip end of Pierpont's shooting coat had disappeared in the Long Covert, I found myself standing alone with Howlett. He bore my gaze for a moment and then politely lowered his eyes.

'Howlett,' said I, 'take these shells and implements to the gun room, and drop nothing. Did Voyou come to any harm in the briers this morning?'

'No 'arm, Mr Cardenhe, sir,' said Howlett.

'Then be careful not to drop anything else,' said I, and walked away leaving him decorously puzzled. For he had dropped no cartridges. Poor Howlett!

III

About four o'clock that afternoon I met David and the dogs at the spinney which leads into Sweet Fern Covert. The three setters, Voyou, Gamin, and Mioche were in fine feather – David had killed a woodcock and a brace of grouse over them that morning – and they were thrashing about the spinney at short range when I came up, gun under arm and pipe lighted.

'What's the prospect, David,' I asked, trying to keep my feet in the tangle of wagging, whining dogs; 'hello, what's amiss with Mioche?'

'A brier in his foot sir; I drew it and stopped the wound but I guess the gravel's got in. If you have no objection, sir, I might take him back with me.'

'It's safer,' I said; 'take Gamin too, I only want one dog this afternoon. What is the situation?'

'Fair sir; the grouse lie within a quarter of a mile of the oak second growth. The woodcock are mostly on the alders. I saw any number of snipe in the meadows. There's something else in by the lake – I can't just tell what, but the woodduck set up a clatter when I was in the thicket and they come dashing through the wood as if a dozen foxes was snappin' at their tail feathers.'

'Probably a fox,' I said; 'leash those dogs – they must learn to stand it. I'll be back by dinner time.'

'There is one more thing sir,' said David, lingering with his gun under his arm.

'Well,' said I.

'I saw a man in the woods by the Oak Covert – at least I think I did.'

'A lumberman?'

'I think not sir – at least – do they have Chinamen among them?'

'Chinese? No. You didn't see a Chinaman in the woods here?'

'I – I think I did sir – I can't say positively. He was gone when I ran into the covert.'

'Did the dogs notice it?'

'I can't say – exactly. They acted queer like. Gamin here lay down and whined – it may have been colic – and Mioche whimpered – perhaps it was the brier.'

'And Voyou?'

'Voyou, he was most remarkable sir, and the hair on his back stood up. I did see a groundhog makin' for a tree near by.'

'Then no wonder Voyou bristled. David, your Chinaman was a stump or tussock. Take the dogs now.'

'I guess it was sir; good afternoon sir,' said David, and walked away with the Gordons leaving me alone with Voyou in the spinney.

I looked at the dog and he looked at me.

'Voyou!'

The dog sat down and danced with his fore feet, his beautiful brown eyes sparkling.

'You're a fraud,' I said; 'which shall it be, the alders or the upland? Upland? Good! – now for the grouse – heel, my friend, and show your miraculous self-restraint.'

Voyou wheeled into my tracks and followed closely, nobly refusing to notice the impudent chipmunks and the thousand

and one alluring and important smells which an ordinary dog would have lost no time in investigating.

The brown and yellow autumn woods were crisp with drifting heaps of leaves and twigs that crackled under foot as we turned from the spinney into the forest. Every silent little stream, hurrying toward the lake, was gay with painted leaves afloat, scarlet maple or yellow oak. Spots of sunlight fell upon the pools, searching the brown depths, illuminating the gravel bottom where shoals of minnows swam to and fro, and to and fro again, busy with the purpose of their little lives. The crickets were chirping in the long brittle grass on the edge of the woods, but we left them far behind in the silence of the deeper forest.

'Now!' said I to Voyou.

The dog sprang to the front, circled once, zigzagged through the ferns around us and, all in a moment, stiffened stock still, rigid as sculptured bronze. I stepped forward, raising my gun, two paces, three paces, ten perhaps, before a great cock grouse blundered up from the brake and burst through the thicket fringe toward the deeper growth. There was a flash and puff from my gun, a crash of echoes among the low wooded cliffs, and through the faint veil of smoke something dark dropped from mid-air amid a cloud of feathers, brown as the brown leaves under foot.

'Fetch!'

Up from the ground sprang Voyou, and in a moment he came galloping back, neck arched, tail stiff but waving, holding tenderly in his pink mouth a mass of mottled bronzed feathers. Very gravely he laid the bird at my feet and crouched beside it, his silky ears across his paws, his muzzle on the ground.

I dropped the grouse into my pocket, held for a moment a silent caressing communion with Voyou, then swung my gun under my arm and motioned the dog on.

It must have been five o'clock when I walked into a little opening in the woods and sat down to breathe. Voyou came and sat down in front of me.

'Well?' I enquired.

Voyou gravely presented one paw which I took.

'We will never get back in time for dinner,' said I, 'so we might as well take it easy. It's all your fault, you know. Is there a brier in your foot? – let's see – there! it's out my friend and you are free to nose about and lick it. If you loll your tongue out you'll get it all over twigs and moss. Can't you lie down and try to pant less? No, there is no use in sniffing and looking at that fern patch, for we are going to smoke a little, doze a little, and go home by moonlight. Think what a big dinner we will have! Think of Howlett's despair when we are not in time! Think of all the stories you will have to tell to Gamin and Mioche! Think what a good dog you have been! There – you are tired old chap; take forty winks with me.'

Voyou was tired. He stretched out on the leaves at my feet but whether or not he really slept I could not be certain, until his hind legs twitched and I knew he was dreaming of mighty deeds.

Now I may have taken forty winks, but the sun seemed to be no lower when I sat up and unclosed my lids. Voyou raised his head, saw in my eyes that I was not going yet, thumped his tail half a dozen times on the dried leaves, and settled back with a sigh.

I looked lazily around, and for the first time noticed what a wonderfully beautiful spot I had chosen for a nap. It was an oval glade in the heart of the forest, level and carpeted with green grass. The trees that surrounded it were gigantic; they formed one towering circular wall of verdure, blotting out all except the turquoise blue of the sky-oval above. And now I noticed that in the center of the greensward lay a pool of water, crystal clear, glimmering like a mirror in the meadow grass, beside a block of granite. It scarcely seemed possible that the symmetry of tree and lawn and lucent pool could have been one of nature's accidents. I had never before seen this glade nor had I ever heard it spoken of by either Pierpont or Barris. It was a marvel, this diamond-clear basin, regular and graceful as a Roman fountain, set in the gem of turf. And these great trees – they also belonged, not in America but in some legend-haunted forest of France, where moss-grown marbles stand neglected in dim glades, and the twilight of the forest shelters fairies and slender shapes from shadow-land.

I lay and watched the sunlight showering the tangled thicket where masses of crimson cardinal flowers glowed, or where one long dusty sunbeam tipped the edge of the floating leaves in the pool, turning them to palest gilt. There were birds too, passing through the dim avenues of trees like jets of flame – the gorgeous cardinal bird in his deep stained crimson robe – the bird that gave to the woods, to the village fifteen miles away, to the whole country, the name of Cardinal.

I rolled over on my back and looked up at the sky. How pale – paler than a robin's egg – it was. I seemed to be lying at the bottom of a well, walled with verdure, high towering on every side. And, as I lay, all about me the air became sweet scented. Sweeter and sweeter and more penetrating grew the perfume, and I wondered what stray breeze, blowing over acres of lilies could have brought it. But there was no breeze; the air was still. A gilded fly alighted on my hand – a honey fly. It was as troubled as I by the scented silence.

Then, behind me, my dog growled.

I sat quite still at first, hardly breathing, but my eyes were fixed on a shape that moved along the edge of the pool among the meadow grasses. The dog had ceased growling and was now staring, alert and trembling.

At last I rose and walked rapidly down to the pool, my dog following close to heel.

The figure, a woman's, turned slowly toward us.

IV

She was standing still when I approached the pool. The forest around us was so silent that when I spoke the sound of my own voice startled me.

'No,' she said – and her voice was smooth as flowing

water, 'I have not lost my way. Will he come to me, your beautiful dog?'

Before I could speak, Voyou crept to her and laid his silky head against her knees.

'But surely,' said I, 'you did not come here alone.'

'Alone? I did come alone.'

'But the nearest settlement is in Cardinal, probably nineteen miles from where we are standing.'

'I do not know Cardinal,' she said.

'Ste. Croix in Canada is forty miles at least – how did you come into the Cardinal Woods?' I asked amazed.

'Into the woods?' she repeated a little impatiently.

'Yes.'

She did not answer at first but stood caressing Voyou with gentle phrase and gesture.

'Your beautiful dog I am fond of, but I am not fond of being questioned,' she said quietly. 'My name is Ysonde and I came to the fountain here to see your dog.'

I was properly quenched. After a moment or two I did say that in another hour it would be growing dusky, but she neither replied nor looked at me.

'This,' I ventured, 'is a beautiful pool – you call it a fountain – a delicious fountain: I have never before seen it. It is hard to imagine that nature did all this.'

'Is it?' she said.

'Don't you think so?' I asked.

'I haven't thought; I wish when you go you would leave me your dog.'

'My – my dog?'

'If you don't mind,' she said sweetly, and looked at me for the first time in the face.

For an instant our glances met, then she grew grave, and I saw that her eyes were fixed on my forehead. Suddenly she rose and drew nearer, looking intently at my forehead. There was a faint mark there, a tiny crescent, just over my eyebrow. It was a birthmark.

'Is that a scar?' she demanded drawing nearer.

'That crescent-shaped mark? No.'

'No? Are you sure?' she insisted.

'Perfectly,' I replied, astonished.

'A—a birthmark?'

'Yes – may I ask why?'

As she drew away from me, I saw that the color had fled from her cheeks. For a second she clasped both hands over her eyes as if to shut out my face, then slowly dropping her hands, she sat down on a long square block of stone which half encircled the basin, and on which to my amazement I saw carving. Voyou went to her again and laid his head in her lap.

'What is your name?' she asked at length.

'Roy Cardenhe.'

'Mine is Ysonde. I carved these dragonflies on the stone, these fishes and shells and butterflies you see.'

'You! They are wonderfully delicate – but those are not American dragonflies—'

'No – they are more beautiful. See, I have my hammer and chisel with me.'

She drew from a queer pouch at her side a small hammer and chisel and held them toward me.

'You are very talented,' I said, 'where did you study?'

'I? I never studied – I knew how. I saw things and cut them out of stone. Do you like them? Some time I will show you other things that I have done. If I had a great lump of bronze I could make your dog, beautiful as he is.'

Her hammer fell into the fountain and I leaned over and plunged my arm into the water to find it.

'It is there, shining on the sand,' she said, leaning over the pool with me.

'Where,' said I, looking at our reflected faces in the water. For it was only in the water that I had dared, as yet, to look her long in the face.

The pool mirrored the exquisite oval of her head, the heavy hair, the eyes. I heard the silken rustle of her girdle, I caught the flash of a white arm, and the hammer was drawn up dripping with spray.

The troubled surface of the pool grew calm and again I saw her eyes reflected.

'Listen,' she said in a low voice, 'do you think you will come again to my fountain?'

'I will come,' I said. My voice was dull; the noise of water filled my ears.

Then a swift shadow sped across the pool; I rubbed my eyes. Where her reflected face had bent beside mine there was nothing mirrored but the rosy evening sky with one pale star glimmering. I drew myself up and turned. She was gone. I saw the faint star twinkling above me in the afterglow, I saw the tall trees motionless in the still evening air, I saw my dog slumbering at my feet.

The sweet scent in the air had faded, leaving in my nostrils the heavy odor of fern and forest mould. A blind fear seized me, and I caught up my gun and sprang into the darkening woods. The dog followed me, crashing through the undergrowth at my side. Duller and duller grew the light, but I strode on, the sweat pouring from my face and hair, my mind a chaos. How I reached the spinney I can hardly tell. As I turned up the path I caught a glimpse of a human face peering at me from the darkening thicket – a horrible human face, yellow and drawn with high-boned cheeks and narrow eyes.

Involuntarily I halted; the dog at my heels snarled. Then I sprang straight at it, floundering blindly through the thicket, but the night had fallen swiftly and I found myself panting and struggling in a maze of twisted shrubbery and twining vines, unable to see the very undergrowth that ensnared me.

It was a pale face, and a scratched one that I carried to a late dinner that night. Howlett served me, dumb reproach in his eyes, for the soup had been standing and the grouse was juiceless.

David brought the dogs in after they had had their supper, and I drew my chair before the blaze and set my ale on a table beside me. The dogs curled up at my feet, blinking gravely at the sparks that snapped and flew in eddying showers from the heavy birch logs.

'David,' said I, 'did you say you saw a Chinaman today?'

'I did sir.'

'What do you think about it now?'

'I may have been mistaken sir—'

'But you think not. What sort of whiskey did you put in my flask today?'

'The usual sir.'

'Is there much gone?'

'About three swallows sir, as usual.'

'You don't suppose there could have been any mistake about that whiskey – no medicine could have gotten into it for instance.'

David smiled and said, 'No sir.'

'Well,' said I, 'I have had an extraordinary dream.'

When I said 'dream', I felt comforted and reassured. I had scarcely dared to say it before, even to myself.

'An extraordinary dream,' I repeated; 'I fell asleep in the woods about five o'clock, in that pretty glade where the fountain – I mean the pool is. You know the place?'

'I do not sir.'

I described it minutely, twice, but David shook his head.

'Carved stone did you say sir? I never chanced on it. You don't mean the New Spring—'

'No, no! This glade is way beyond that. Is it possible that any people inhabit the forest between here and the Canada line?'

'Nobody short of Ste. Croix; at least I have no knowledge of any.'

'Of course,' said I, 'when I thought I saw a Chinaman, it was imagination. Of course I had been more impressed than I was aware of by your adventure. Of course you saw no Chinaman, David.'

'Probably not sir,' replied David dubiously.

I sent him off to bed, saying I should keep the dogs with me all night; and when he was gone, I took a good long draught of ale, 'just to shame the devil', as Pierpont said, and lighted a cigar. Then I thought of Barris and Pierpont, and their cold bed, for I knew they would not dare build a fire, and, in spite of the hot chimney corner and the crackling blaze, I shivered in sympathy.

'I'll tell Barris and Pierpont the whole story and take them to see the carved stone and the fountain,' I thought to myself; what a marvelous dream it was – Ysonde – if it was a dream.

Then I went to the mirror and examined the faint white mark above my eyebrow.

V

About eight o'clock next morning, as I sat listlessly eyeing my coffee cup which Howlett was filling, Gamin and Mioche set up a howl, and in a moment more I heard Barris' step on the porch.

'Hello, Roy,' said Pierpont, stamping into the dining room, 'I want my breakfast by jingo! Where's Howlett – none of your *café au lait* for me – I want a chop and some eggs. Look at that dog, he'll wag the hinge off his tail in a moment—'

'Pierpont,' said I, 'this loquacity is astonishing but welcome. Where's Barris? You are soaked from neck to ankle.'

Pierpont sat down and tore off his stiff muddy leggings.

'Barris is telephoning to Cardinal Springs – I believe he wants some of his men – down! Gamin, you idiot! Howlett, three eggs poached and more toast – what was I saying? Oh, about Barris; he's struck something or other which he hopes will locate these gold-making fellows. I had a jolly time – he'll tell you about it.'

'Billy! Billy!' I said in pleased amazement, 'you are learning to talk! Dear me! You load your shells and you carry your own gun and you fire it yourself – hello! here's Barris all over mud. You fellows really ought to change your rig – whew! what a frightful odor!'

'It's probably this,' said Barris tossing something onto the hearth where it shuddered for a moment and then began to writhe; 'I found it in the woods by the lake. Do you know what it can be, Roy?'

To my disgust I saw it was another of those spidery wormy crablike creatures that Godfrey had in Tiffany's.

'I thought I recognized that acrid odor,' I said; 'for the love of the Saints take it away from the breakfast table, Barris!'

'But what is it?' he persisted, unslinging his field-glasses and revolver.

'I'll tell you what I know after breakfast,' I replied firmly, 'Howlett, get a broom and sweep that thing into the road – what are you laughing at, Pierpont?'

Howlett swept the repulsive creature out and Barris and Pierpont went to change their dew-soaked clothes for dryer raiment. David came to take the dogs for an airing and in a few minutes Barris reappeared and sat down in his place at the head of the table.

'Well,' said I, 'is there a story to tell?'

'Yes, not much. They are near the lake on the other side of the woods – I mean these gold-makers. I shall collar one of them this evening. I haven't located the main gang with any certainty – shove the toast rack this way will you, Roy – no, I am not at all certain, but I've nailed one anyway. Pierpont was a great help, really – and, what do you think, Roy? He wants to join the Secret Service!'

'Little Willy!'

'Exactly. Oh, I'll dissuade him. What sort of reptile was it that I brought in? Did Howlett sweep it away?'

'He can sweep it back again for all I care,' I said indifferently, 'I've finished my breakfast.'

'No,' said Barris, hastily swallowing his coffee, 'it's of no importance; you can tell me about the beast—'

'Serve you right if I had it brought in on toast,' I returned.

Pierpont came in radiant, fresh from the bath.

'Go on with your story, Roy,' he said; and I told them about Godfrey and his reptile pet.

'Now what in the name of common sense can Godfrey

find interesting in that creature?' I ended, tossing my cigarette into the fireplace.

'It's Japanese, don't you think?' said Pierpont.

'No,' said Barris, 'it is not artistically grotesque, it's vulgar
and horrible – it looks cheap and unfinished—'

'Unfinished – exactly,' said I, 'like an American humorist—'

'Yes,' said Pierpont, 'cheap. What about that gold serpent?'

'Oh, the Metropolitan Museum bought it; you must see
it, it's marvelous.'

Barris and Pierpont had lighted their cigarettes and, after
a moment, we all rose and strolled out to the lawn, where
chairs and hammocks were placed under the maple trees.

David passed, gun under arm, dogs heeling.

'Three guns on the meadows at four this afternoon,' said
Pierpont.

'Roy,' said Barris as David bowed and started on, 'what
did you do yesterday?'

This was the question that I had been expecting. All night
long I had dreamed of Ysonde and the glade in the woods,
where, at the bottom of the crystal fountain, I saw the
reflection of her eyes. All the morning while bathing and
dressing I had been persuading myself that the dream was
not worth recounting and that a search for the glade and
the imaginary stone carving would be ridiculous. But now,
as Barris asked the question, I suddenly decided to tell him
the whole story.

'See here, you fellows,' I said abruptly, 'I am going to tell
you something queer. You can laugh as much as you please
to, but first I want to ask Barris a question or two. You have
been in China, Barris?'

'Yes,' said Barris, looking straight into my eyes.

'Would a Chinaman be likely to turn lumberman?'

'Have you seen a Chinaman?' he asked in a quiet voice.

'I don't know; David and I both imagined we did.'

Barris and Pierpont exchanged glances.

'Have you seen one also?' I demanded, turning to include
Pierpont.

'No,' said Barris slowly; 'but I know that there is, or has been, a Chinaman in these woods.'

'The devil!' said I.

'Yes,' said Barris gravely; 'the devil, if you like – a devil – a member of the Kuen-Yuin.'

I drew my chair close to the hammock where Pierpont lay at full length, holding out to me a ball of pure gold.

'Well?' said I, examining the engraving on its surface, which represented a mass of twisted creatures – dragons, I supposed.

'Well,' repeated Barris, extending his hand to take the golden ball, 'this globe of gold engraved with reptiles and Chinese hieroglyphics is the symbol of the Kuen-Yuin.'

'Where did you get it?' I asked, feeling that something startling was impending.

'Pierpont found it by the lake at sunrise this morning. It is the symbol of the Kuen-Yuin,' he repeated, 'the terrible Kuen-Yuin, the sorcerers of China, and the most murderously diabolical sect on earth.'

We puffed our cigarettes in silence until Barris rose, and began to pace backward and forward among the trees, twisting his gray moustache.

'The Kuen-Yuin are sorcerers,' he said, pausing before the hammock where Pierpont lay watching him; 'I mean exactly what I say – sorcerers. I've seen them – I've seen them at their devilish business, and I repeat to you solemnly, that as there are angels above, there is a race of devils on earth and they are sorcerers. Bah!' he cried, 'talk to me of Indian magic and Yogis and all that clap-trap! Why, Roy, I tell you that the Kuen-Yuin have absolute control of a hundred millions of people, mind and body, body and soul. Do you know what goes on in the interior of China? Does Europe know – could any human being conceive of the condition of that gigantic hellpit? You read the papers, you hear diplomatic twaddle about Li Hung Chang and the Emperor, you see accounts of battles on sea and land, and you know that Japan has raised a toy tempest along the jagged edge of the great unknown. But you never before heard of the Kuen-Yuin; no, nor has any European except a stray missionary or two, and yet I tell you that when the fires from this pit of hell have eaten through the continent to the coast, the explosion will inundate half a world – and God help the other half.'

Pierpont's cigarette went out; he lighted another, and looked hard at Barris.

'But,' resumed Barris quietly, '"sufficient unto the day", you know – I didn't intend to say as much as I did – it would do no good – even you and Pierpont will forget it – it seems so impossible and so far away – like the burning out of the sun. What I want to discuss is the possibility or probability of a Chinaman – a member of the Kuen-Yuin, being here, at this moment, in the forest.'

'If he is,' said Pierpont, 'possibly the gold-makers owe their discovery to him.'

'I do not doubt it for a second,' said Barris earnestly.

I took the little golden globe in my hand, and examined the characters engraved upon it.

'Barris,' said Pierpont, 'I can't believe in sorcery while I am wearing one of Sanford's shooting suits in the pocket of which rests an uncut volume of the "Duchess".'

'Neither can I,' I said, 'for I read the *Evening Post*, and I know Mr Godkin would not allow it. Hello! What's the matter with this gold ball?'

'What is the matter?' said Barris grimly.

'Why – why – it's changing color – purple, no, crimson – no, it's green I mean – good Heavens! these dragons are twisting under my fingers—'

'Impossible!' muttered Pierpont, leaning over me; 'those are not dragons—'

'No!' I cried excitedly; 'they are pictures of that reptile that Barris brought back – see – see – how they crawl and turn—'

'Drop it!' commanded Barris; and I threw the ball on the turf. In an instant we had all knelt down on the grass beside it, but the globe was again golden, grotesquely wrought with dragons and strange signs.

Pierpont, a little red in the face, picked it up, and handed it to Barris. He placed it on a chair, and sat down beside me.

'Whew!' said I, wiping the perspiration from my face, 'how did you play us that trick, Barris?'

'Trick?' said Barris contemptuously.

I looked at Pierpont, and my heart sank. If this was not a trick, what was it? Pierpont returned my glance and colored, but all he said was, 'It's devilish queer,' and Barris answered, 'Yes, devilish'. Then Barris asked me again to tell my story, and I did, beginning from the time I met David in the spinney to the moment when I sprang into the darkening thicket where that yellow mask had grinned like a phantom skull.

'Shall we try to find the fountain?' I asked after a pause.

'Yes – and – er – the lady,' suggested Pierpont vaguely.

'Don't be an ass,' I said a little impatiently, 'you need not come, you know.'

'Oh, I'll come,' said Pierpont, 'unless you think I am indiscreet—'

'Shut up, Pierpont,' said Barris, 'this thing is serious; I never heard of such a glade or such a fountain, but it's true that nobody knows this forest thoroughly. It's worthwhile trying for; Roy, can you find your way back to it?'

'Easily,' I answered; 'when shall we go?'

'It will knock our snipe shooting on the head,' said Pierpont, 'but when one has the opportunity of finding a live dream-lady—'

I rose, deeply offended, but Pierpont was not very penitent and his laughter was irresistible.

'The lady's yours by right of discovery,' he said, 'I'll promise not to infringe on your dreams – I'll dream about other ladies—'

'Come, come,' said I, 'I'll have Howlett put you to bed in a minute. Barris, if you are ready – we can get back to dinner—'

Barris had risen and was gazing at me earnestly.

'What's the matter?' I asked nervously, for I saw that his eyes were fixed on my forehead, and I thought of Ysonde and the white crescent scar.

'Is that a birthmark?' said Barris.

'Yes – why, Barris?'

'Nothing – an interesting coincidence—'

'What! – for Heaven's sake!'

'The scar – or rather the birthmark. It is the print of the dragon's claw – the crescent symbol of Yue-Laou—'

'And who the devil is Yue-Laou?' I said crossly.

'Yue-Laou – the Moon Maker, Dzil-Nbu of the Kuen-Yuin – it's Chinese Mythology, but it is believed that Yue-Laou has returned to rule the Kuen-Yuin—'

'The conversation,' interrupted Pierpont, 'smacks of peacocks' feathers and yellow-jackets. The chicken pox has left its card on Roy, and Barris is guying us. Come on, you fellows, and make your call on the dream-lady. Barris, I hear galloping; here come your men.'

Two mud-splashed riders clattered up to the porch and dismounted at a motion from Barris. I noticed that both of them carried repeating rifles and heavy Colt revolvers.

They followed Barris, deferentially, into the dining room, and presently we heard the tinkle of plates and bottles and the low hum of Barris' musical voice.

Half an hour later they came out again, saluted Pierpont and me, and galloped away in the direction of the Canadian frontier. Ten minutes passed, and, as Barris did not appear, we rose and went into the house, to find him. He was sitting silently before the table, watching the small golden globe, now glowing with scarlet and orange fire, brilliant as a live coal. Howlett, mouth ajar, and eyes starting from the sockets, stood petrified behind him.

'Are you coming,' asked Pierpont, a little startled. Barris did not answer. The globe slowly turned to pale gold again – but the face that Barris raised to ours was white as a sheet. Then he stood up, and smiled with an effort which was painful to us all.

'Give me a pencil and a bit of paper,' he said.

Howlett brought it. Barris went to the window and wrote rapidly. He folded the paper, placed it in the top drawer of his desk, locked the drawer, handed me the key, and motioned us to precede him.

When we again stood under the maples, he turned to me with an impenetrable expression. 'You will know when to use the key,' he said; 'Come, Pierpont, we must try to find Roy's fountain.'

VI

At two o'clock that afternoon, at Barris' suggestion, we gave up the search for the fountain in the glade and cut across the forest to the spinney where David and Howlett were waiting with our guns and the three dogs.

Pierpont guyed me unmercifully about the 'dream-lady' as he called her, and, but for the significant coincidence of Ysonde's and Barris' questions concerning the white scar on my forehead, I should long ago have been perfectly persuaded that I had dreamed the whole thing. As it was, I had no explanation to offer. We had not been able to find the glade although fifty times I came to landmarks which convinced me that we were just about to enter it. Barris was quiet, scarcely uttering a word to either of us during the entire search. I had never before seen him depressed in spirits. However, when we came in sight of the spinney where a cold bit of grouse and a bottle of Burgundy awaited each, Barris seemed to recover his habitual good humor.

'Here's to the dream-lady!' said Pierpont, raising his glass and standing up.

I did not like it. Even if she was only a dream, it irritated me to hear Pierpont's mocking voice. Perhaps Barris understood – I don't know, but he bade Pierpont drink his wine without further noise, and that young man obeyed with a childlike confidence which almost made Barris smile.

'What about the snipe, David,' I asked; 'the meadows should be in good condition.'

'There is not a snipe on the meadows, sir,' said David solemnly.

'Impossible,' exclaimed Barris, 'they can't have left.'

'They have, sir,' said David in a sepulchral voice which I hardly recognized.

We all three looked at the old man curiously, waiting for his explanation of this disappointing but sensational report.

David looked at Howlett and Howlett examined the sky.

'I was going,' began the old man, with his eyes fastened on Howlett, 'I was going along by the spinney with the dogs when I heard a noise in the covert and I seen Howlett come walkin' very fast toward me. In fact,' continued David, 'I may say he was runnin'. Was you runnin', Howlett?'

Howlett said 'Yes', with a decorous cough.

'I beg pardon,' said David, 'but I'd rather Howlett told the rest. He saw things which I did not.'

'Go on, Howlett,' commanded Pierpont, much interested.

Howlett coughed again behind his large red hand.

'What David says is true sir,' he began; 'I h'observed the dogs at a distance 'ow they was a workin' sir, and David stood a lightin' of 's pipe be'ind the spotted beech when I see a 'ead pop up in the covert 'oldin' a stick like 'e was h'aimin' at the dogs sir—'

'A head holding a stick?' said Pierpont severely.

'The 'ead 'ad 'ands, sir,' explained Howlett, ''ands that 'eld a painted stick – like that, sir. 'Owlett, thinks I to myself, this 'ere's queer, so I jumps in an' runs, but the beggar 'e seen me an' w'en I comes alongside of David 'e was gone. "'Ello 'Owlett," sez David, "what the 'ell" – I beg pardon, sir – "'ow did you come 'ere," sez 'e very loud. "Run!" sez I, "the Chinaman is harryin' the dawgs!" "For Gawd's sake wot Chinaman?" sez David, h'aimin' 'is gun at every bush. Then I thinks I see 'im an' we run an' run, the dawgs a boundin' close to heel sir, but we don't see no Chinaman.'

'I'll tell the rest,' said David, as Howlett coughed and stepped in a modest corner behind the dogs.

'Go on,' said Barris in a strange voice.

'Well sir, when Howlett and I stopped chasin', we was on the cliff overlooking the south meadow. I noticed that there was hundreds of birds there, mostly yellowlegs and plover, and Howlett seen them too. Then before I could say a word to Howlett, something out in the lake gave a splash – a splash as if the whole cliff had fallen into the water. I was that scared that I jumped straight into the bush and Howlett he sat down quick, and all those snipe wheeled up – there was hundreds – all asquealin' with fright, and the woodduck came bowlin' over the meadows as if the old Nick was behind.'

David paused and glanced meditatively at the dogs.

'Go on,' said Barris in the same strained voice.

'Nothing more sir. The snipe did not come back.'

'But that splash in the lake?'

'I don't know what it was sir.'

'A salmon? A salmon couldn't have frightened the duck and the snipe that way?'

'No – oh no, sir. If fifty salmon had jumped they couldn't have made that splash. Couldn't they, Howlett?'

'No 'ow,' said Howlett.

'Roy,' said Barris at length, 'what David tells us settles the snipe shooting for today. I am going to take Pierpont up to the house. Howlett and David will follow with the dogs – I have something to say to them. If you care to come, come along; if not, go and shoot a brace of grouse for dinner and be back by eight if you want to see what Pierpont and I discovered last night.'

David whistled Gamin and Mioche to heel and followed Howlett and his hamper toward the house. I called Voyou to my side, picked up my gun and turned to Barris.

'I will be back by eight,' I said; 'you are expecting to catch one of the gold-makers are you not?'

'Yes,' said Barris listlessly.

Pierpont began to speak about the Chinaman but Barris motioned him to follow, and, nodding to me, took the path that Howlett and David had followed toward the house.

When they disappeared I tucked my gun under my arm and turned sharply into the forest, Voyou trotting close to my heels.

In spite of myself the continued apparition of the Chinaman made me nervous. If he troubled me again I had fully decided to get the drop on him and find out what he was doing in the Cardinal Woods. If he could give no satisfactory account of himself I would march him in to Barris as a gold-making suspect – I would march him in anyway, I thought, and rid the forest of his ugly face. I wondered what it was that David had heard in the lake. It must have been a big fish, a salmon, I thought; probably David's and Howlett's nerves were overwrought after their Celestial chase.

A whine from the dog broke the thread of my meditation and I raised my head. Then I stopped short in my tracks.

The lost glade lay straight before me.

Already the dog had bounded into it, across the velvet turf to the carved stone where a slim figure sat. I saw my dog lay his silky head lovingly against her silken kirtle; I saw her face bend above him, and I caught my breath and slowly entered the sunlit glade.

Half timidly she held out one white hand.

'Now that you have come,' she said, 'I can show you more of my work. I told you that I could do other things besides these dragonflies and moths carved here in stone. Why do you stare at me so? Are you ill?'

'Ysonde,' I stammered.

'Yes,' she said, with a faint color under her eyes.

'I – I never expected to see you again,' I blurted out, '—you – I – I – thought I had dreamed—'

'Dreamed, of me? Perhaps you did, is that strange?'

'Strange? N—no – but – where did you go when – when we were leaning over the fountain together? I saw your face – your face reflected beside mine and then – then suddenly I saw the blue sky and only a star twinkling.'

'It was because you fell asleep,' she said, 'was it not?'

'I – asleep?'

'You slept – I thought you were very tired and I went back—'

'Back? – where?'

'Back to my home where I carve my beautiful images; see, here is one I brought to show you today.'

I took the sculptured creature that she held toward me, a massive golden lizard with frail claw-spread wings of gold so thin that the sunlight burned through and fell on the ground in flaming gilded patches.

'Good Heavens!' I exclaimed, 'this is astounding! Where did you learn to do such work? Ysonde, such a thing is beyond price!'

'Oh, I hope so,' she said earnestly, 'I can't bear to sell my work, but my step-father takes it and sends it away. This is the second thing I have done and yesterday he said I must give it to him. I suppose he is poor.'

'I don't see how he can be poor if he gives you gold to model in,' I said, astonished.

'Gold!' she exclaimed, 'gold! He has a room full of gold! He makes it.'

I sat down on the turf at her feet completely unnerved.

'Why do you look at me so?' she asked, a little troubled.

'Where does your step-father live?' I said at last.

'Here.'

'Here!'

'In the woods near the lake. You could never find our house.'

'A house!'

'Of course. Did you think I lived in a tree? How silly. I live with my step-father in a beautiful house – a small house, but very beautiful. He makes his gold there but the men who carry it away never come to the house, for they don't know where it is and if they did they could not get in. My step-father carries the gold in lumps to a canvas satchel. When the satchel is full he takes it out into the woods where the men live and I don't know what they do with it. I wish he could sell the gold and become rich for then I could go back to Yian where all the gardens are sweet and the river flows under the thousand bridges.'

'Where is this city?' I asked faintly.

'Yian? I don't know. It is sweet with perfume and the sound of silver bells all day long. Yesterday I carried a blossom of dried lotus buds from Yian, in my breast, and all the woods were fragrant. Did you smell it?'

'Yes.'

'I wondered last night whether you did. How beautiful your dog is; I love him. Yesterday I thought most about your dog but last night—'

'Last night,' I repeated below my breath.

'I thought of you. Why do you wear the dragon claw?'

I raised my hand impulsively to my forehead, covering the scar.

'What do you know of the dragon claw?' I muttered.

'It is the symbol of Ye-Laou, and Ye-Laou rules the Kuen-Yuin, my step-father says. My step-father tells me everything that I know. We lived in Yian until I was sixteen years old. I am eighteen now; that is two years we have lived in the forest. Look! – see those scarlet birds! What are they? There are birds of the same color in Yian.'

'Where is Yian, Ysonde?' I asked with deadly calmness.

'Yian? I don't know.'

'But you have lived there?'

'Yes, a very long time.'

'Is it across the ocean, Ysonde?'

'It is across seven oceans and the great river which is longer than from the earth to the moon.'

'Who told you that?'

'Who? My step-father; he tells me everything.'

'Will you tell me his name, Ysonde?'

'I don't know it, he is my step-father, that is all.'

'And what is your name?'

'You know it, Ysonde.'

'Yes, but what other name?'

'That is all, Ysonde. Have you two names? Why do you look at me so impatiently?'

'Does your step-father make gold? Have you seen him make it?'

'Oh yes. He made it also in Yian and I loved to watch the sparks at night whirling like golden bees. Yian is lovely – if it is all like our garden and the gardens around. I can see the thousand bridges from my garden and the white mountain beyond—'

'And the people – tell me of the people, Ysonde!' I urged gently.

'The people of Yian? I could see them in swarms like ants – oh! many, many millions crossing and recrossing the thousand bridges.'

'But how did they look? Did they dress as I do?'

'I don't know. They were very far away, moving specks on the thousand bridges. For sixteen years I saw them every day from my garden but I never went out of my garden into the streets of Yian, for my step-father forbade me.'

'You never saw a living creature nearby in Yian?' I asked in despair.

'My birds, oh such tall, wise-looking birds, all over gray and rose color.'

She leaned over the gleaming water and drew her polished hand across the surface.

'Why do you ask me these questions,' she murmured; 'are you displeased?'

'Tell me about your step-father,' I insisted. 'Does he look as I do? Does he dress, does he speak as I do? Is he American?'

'American? I don't know. He does not dress as you do and he does not look as you do. He is old, very, very old. He speaks sometimes as you do, sometimes as they do in Yian. I speak also in both manners.'

'Then speak as they do in Yian,' I urged impatiently, 'speak as – why, Ysonde! why are you crying? Have I hurt you? – I did not intend – I did not dream of your caring! There

Ysonde, forgive me – see, I beg you on my knees here at your feet.'

I stopped, my eyes fastened on a small golden ball which hung from her waist by a golden chain. I saw it trembling against her thigh, I saw it change color, now crimson, now purple, now flaming scarlet. It was the symbol of the Kuen-Yuin.

She bent over me and laid her fingers gently on my arm.

'Why do you ask me such things?' she said, while the tears glistened on her lashes. 'It hurts me here—' she pressed her hand to her breast – 'it pains – I don't know why. Ah, now your eyes are hard and cold again; you are looking at the golden globe which hangs from my waist. Do you wish to know also what that is?'

'Yes,' I muttered, my eyes fixed on the infernal colored flames which subsided as I spoke, leaving the ball a pale gilt again.

'It is the symbol of the Kuen-Yuin,' she said in a trembling voice; 'why do you ask?'

'Is it yours?'

'Y – yes.'

'Where did you get it?' I cried harshly.

'My – my step-fa—'

Then she pushed me away from her with all the strength of her slender wrists and covered her face.

If I slipped my arm about her and drew her to me – if I kissed away the tears that fell slowly between her fingers – if I told her how I loved her – how it cut me to the heart to see her unhappy – after all that is my own business. When she smiled through her tears, the pure love and sweetness in her eyes lifted my soul higher than the high moon vaguely glimmering through the sunlit blue above. My happiness was so sudden, so fierce and overwhelming that I only knelt there, her fingers clasped in mine, my eyes raised to the blue vault and the glimmering moon. Then something in the long grass beside me moved close to my knees and a damp acrid odor filled my nostrils.

'Ysonde!' I cried, but the touch of her hand was already gone and my two clenched fists were cold and damp with dew.

'Ysonde!' I called again, my tongue stiff with fright – but I called as one awakening from a dream – a horrid dream, for my nostrils quivered with the damp acrid odor and I felt the crab-reptile clinging to my knee. Why had the night fallen so swiftly – and where was I – where? – stiff, chilled, torn, and bleeding, lying flung like a corpse over my own threshold with Voyou licking my face and Barris stooping above me in the light of a lamp that flared and smoked in the night breeze like a torch. Faugh! the choking stench of the lamp aroused me and I cried out:

'Ysonde!'

'What the devil's the matter with him?' muttered Pierpont, lifting me in his arms like a child, 'has he been stabbed, Barris?'

VII

In a few minutes I was able to stand and walk stiffly into my bedroom where Howlett had a hot bath ready and a hotter tumbler of Scotch. Pierpont sponged the blood from my throat where it had coagulated. The cut was slight, almost invisible, a mere puncture from a thorn. A shampoo cleared my mind, and a cold plunge and alcohol friction did the rest.

'Now,' said Pierpont, 'swallow your hot Scotch and lie down. Do you want a broiled woodcock? Good, I fancy you are coming about.'

Barris and Pierpont watched me as I sat on the edge of the bed, solemnly chewing on the woodcock's wishbone and sipping my Bordeaux, very much at my ease.

Pierpont sighed his relief.

'So,' he said pleasantly, 'it was a mere case of ten dollars or ten days. I thought you had been stabbed—'

'I was not intoxicated,' I replied, serenely picking up a bit of celery.

'Only jagged?' enquired Pierpont, full of sympathy.

'Nonsense,' said Barris, 'let him alone. Want some more celery, Roy? – it will make you sleep.'

'I don't want to sleep,' I answered; 'when are you and Pierpont going to catch your gold-maker?'

Barris looked at his watch and closed it with a snap.

'In an hour; you don't propose to go with us?'

'But I do – toss me a cup of coffee, Pierpont, will you – that's just what I propose to do. Howlett, bring the new box of Panatella's – the mild imported – and leave the decanter. Now Barris, I'll be dressing, and you and Pierpont keep still and listen to what I have to say. Is that door shut tight?'

Barris locked it and sat down.

'Thanks,' said I, 'Barris, where is the city of Yian?'

An expression akin to terror flashed into Barris' eyes and I saw him stop breathing for a moment.

'There is no such city,' he said at length, 'have I been talking in my sleep?'

'It is a city,' I continued, calmly, 'where the river winds under the thousand bridges, where the gardens are sweetly scented and the air is filled with the music of silver bells—'

'Stop!' gasped Barris, and rose trembling from his chair. He had grown ten years older.

'Roy,' interposed Pierpont coolly, 'what the deuce are you harrying Barris for?'

I looked at Barris and he looked at me. After a second or two he sat down again.

'Go on, Roy,' he said.

'I must,' I answered, 'for now I am certain that I have not dreamed.'

I told them everything; but, even as I told it, the whole thing seemed so vague, so unreal, that at times I stopped with the hot blood tingling in my ears, for it seemed impossible that sensible men, in the year of our Lord 1896 could seriously discuss such matters.

I feared Pierpont, but he did not even smile. As for Barris, he sat with his handsome head sunk on his breast, his unlighted pipe clasped tight in both hands.

When I had finished, Pierpont turned slowly and looked at Barris. Twice he moved his lips as if about to ask something and then remained mute.

'Yian is a city,' said Barris, speaking dreamily; 'was that what you wished to know, Pierpont?'

We nodded silently.

'Yian is a city,' repeated Barris, 'where the great river winds under the thousand bridges – where the gardens are sweet scented, and the air is filled with the music of silver bells.'

My lips formed the question, 'Where is this city?'

'It lies,' said Barris, almost querulously, 'across the seven oceans and the river which is longer than from the earth to the moon.'

'What do you mean?' said Pierpont.

'Ah,' said Barris, rousing himself with an effort and raising his sunken eyes, 'I am using the allegories of another land; let it pass. Have I not told you of the Kuen-Yuin? Yian is the center of the Kuen-Yuin. It lies hidden in that gigantic shadow called China, vague and vast as the midnight Heavens – a continent unknown, impenetrable.'

'Impenetrable,' repeated Pierpont below his breath.

'I have seen it,' said Barris dreamily. 'I have seen the dead plains of Black Cathay and I have crossed the mountains of Death, whose summits are above the atmosphere. I have seen the shadow of Xangi cast across Abaddon. Better to die a million miles from Yezd and Ater Quedah than to have seen the white water lotus close in the shadow of Xangi! I have slept among the ruins of Xaindu where the winds never cease and the Wulwulleh is wailed by the dead.'

'And Yian,' I urged gently.

There was an unearthly look on his face as he turned slowly toward me.

'Yian – I have lived there – and loved there. When the breath of my body shall cease, when the dragon's claw shall fade from my arm' – he tore up his sleeve, and we saw a white crescent shining above his elbow – 'when the light of my eyes has faded forever, then, even then I shall not forget the city of Yian. Why, it is my home – mine! The river and the thousand bridges, the white peak beyond, the sweet-scented gardens, the lilies, the pleasant noise of the summer wind laden with bee music and the music of bells – all these are mine. Do you think because the Kuen-Yuin feared the dragon's claw on my arm that my work with them is ended? Do you think that because Yue-Laou could give, that I acknowledge his right to take away? Is he Xangi in whose shadow the white water lotus dares not raise its head? No! No!' he cried violently, 'it was not from Yue-Laou, the sorcerer, the Maker of Moons, that my happiness came! It was real, it was not a shadow to vanish like a tinted bubble! Can a sorcerer create and give a man the woman he loves? Is Yue-Laou as great as Xangi then? Xangi is God. In His own time, in His infinite goodness and mercy He will bring me again to the woman I love. And I know she waits for me at God's feet.'

In the strained silence that followed I could hear my heart's double beat and I saw Pierpont's face, blanched and pitiful. Barris shook himself and raised his head. The change in his ruddy face frightened me.

'Heed!' he said, with a terrible glance at me; 'the print of the dragon's claw is on your forehead and Yue-Laou knows it. If you must love, then love like a man, for you will suffer like a soul in hell, in the end. What is her name again?'

'Ysonde,' I answered simply.

VIII

At nine o'clock that night we caught one of the gold-makers. I do not know how Barris had laid his trap; all I saw of the affair can be told in a minute or two.

We were posted on the Cardinal road about a mile below the house, Pierpont and I with drawn revolvers on one side, under a butternut tree, Barris on the other, a Winchester across his knees.

I had just asked Pierpont the hour, and he was feeling for his watch when far up the road we heard the sound of a galloping horse, nearer, nearer, clattering, thundering past. Then Barris' rifle spat flame and the dark mass, horse and rider, crashed into the dust. Pierpont had the half-stunned horseman by the collar in a second – the horse was stone dead – and, as we lighted a pine knot to examine the fellow, Barris' two riders galloped up and drew bridle beside us.

'Hm!' said Barris with a scowl, 'it's the "Shiner", or I'm a moonshiner.'

We crowded curiously around to see the 'Shiner'. He was red-headed, fat and filthy, and his little red eyes burned in his head like the eyes of an angry pig.

Barris went through his pockets methodically while Pierpont held him and I held the torch. The Shiner was a gold mine; pockets, shirt, bootlegs, hat, even his dirty fists, clutched tight and bleeding, were bursting with lumps of soft yellow gold. Barris dropped this 'moonshine gold', as we had come to call it, into the pockets of his shooting coat, and withdrew to question the prisoner. He came back again in a few minutes and motioned his mounted men to take the Shiner in charge. We watched them, rifle on thigh, walking their horses slowly away into the darkness, the Shiner, tightly bound, shuffling sullenly between them.

'Who is the Shiner?' asked Pierpont, slipping the revolver into his pocket again.

'A moonshiner, counterfeiter, forger, and highwayman,' said Barris, 'and probably a murderer. Drummond will be glad to see him, and I think it likely he will be persuaded to confess to him what he refuses to confess to me.'

'Wouldn't he talk?' I asked.

'Not a syllable. Pierpont, there is nothing more for you to do.'

'For me to do? Are you not coming back with us, Barris?'

'No,' said Barris.

We walked along the dark road in silence for a while, I wondering what Barris intended to do, but he said nothing more until we reached our own verandah. Here he held out his hand, first to Pierpont, then to me, saying good-bye as though he were going on a long journey.

'How soon will you be back?' I called out to him as he turned away toward the gate. He came across the lawn again and again took our hands with a quiet affection that I had never imagined him capable of.

'I am going,' he said, 'to put an end to this gold-making tonight. I know that you fellows have never suspected what I was about on my little solitary evening strolls after dinner. I will tell you. Already I have unobtrusively killed four of these gold-makers – my men put them under ground just below the new washout at the four-mile stone. There are three left alive – the Shiner, whom we have, another criminal named "Yellow", or "Yaller" in the vernacular, and the third—'

'The third,' repeated Pierpont, excitedly.

'The third I have never yet seen. But I know who and what he is – I know; and if he is of human flesh and blood, his blood will flow tonight.'

As he spoke a slight noise across the turf attracted my attention. A mounted man was advancing silently in the starlight over the spongy meadowland. When he came nearer Barris struck a match, and we saw that he bore a corpse across his saddle bow.

'Yaller, Colonel Barris,' said the man, touching his slouched hat in salute.

This grim introduction to the corpse made me shudder, and, after a moment's examination of the stiff, wide-eyed dead man, I drew back.

'Identified,' said Barris, 'take him to the four-mile post and carry his effects to Washington – under seal, mind, Johnstone.'

Away cantered the rider with his ghastly burden, and Barris took our hands once more for the last time. Then he went away, gaily, with a jest on his lips, and Pierpont and I turned back into the house.

For an hour we sat moodily smoking in the hall before the fire, saying little until Pierpont burst out with: 'I wish Barris had taken one of us with him tonight!'

The same thought had been running in my mind, but I said: 'Barris knows what he's about.'

This observation neither comforted us nor opened the lane to further conversation, and after a few minutes Pierpont said good night and called for Howlett and hot water. When he had been warmly tucked away by Howlett, I turned out all but one lamp, sent the dogs away with David and dismissed Howlett for the night.

I was not inclined to retire for I knew I could not sleep. There was a book lying open on the table beside the fire and I opened it and read a page or two, but my mind was fixed on other things.

The window shades were raised and I looked out at the star-set firmament. There was no moon that night but the sky was dusted all over with sparkling stars and a pale radiance, brighter even than moonlight, fell over meadow and wood. Far away in the forest I heard the voice of the wind, a soft warm wind that whispered a name, Ysonde.

'Listen,' sighed the voice of the wind, and 'listen' echoed the swaying trees with every little leaf aquiver. I listened.

Where the long grasses trembled with the cricket's cadence I heard her name, Ysonde; I heard it in the rustling woodbine where gray moths hovered; I heard it in the drip, drip, drip of the dew from the porch. The silent meadow brook whispered her name, the rippling woodland streams repeated it, Ysonde, Ysonde, until all earth and sky were filled with the soft thrill, Ysonde, Ysonde, Ysonde.

A night thrush sang in a thicket by the porch and I stole to the verandah to listen. After a while it began again, a little further on. I ventured out into the road. Again I heard it far away in the forest and I followed it, for I knew it was singing of Ysonde.

When I came to the path that leaves the main road and enters the Sweet Fern Covert below the spinney, I hesitated; but the beauty of the night lured me on and the night thrushes called me from every thicket. In the starry radiance, shrubs, grasses, field flowers, stood out distinctly, for there was no moon to cast shadows. Meadow and brook, grove and stream, were illuminated by the pale glow. Like great lamps lighted the planets hung from the high-domed sky and through their mysterious rays the fixed stars, calm, serene, stared from the heavens like eyes.

I waded on waist deep through fields of dewy golden-rod, through late clover and wild-oat wastes, through crimson-fruited sweetbrier, blueberry, and wild plum, until the low whisper of the Weir Brook warned me that the path had ended.

But I would not stop, for the night air was heavy with the perfume of water lilies and far away, across the low wooded cliffs and the wet meadowland beyond, there was a distant gleam of silver, and I heard the murmur of sleepy waterfowl. I would go to the lake. The way was clear except for the dense young growth and the snares of the moosebush.

The night thrushes had ceased but I did not want for the company of living creatures. Slender, quick darting forms crossed my path at intervals, sleek mink, that fled like shadows at my step, wiry weasels and fat muskrats, hurrying onward to some tryst or killing.

I never had seen so many little woodland creatures on the move at night. I began to wonder where they all were going so fast, why they all hurried on in the same direction. Now I passed a hare hopping through the brushwood, now a rabbit scurrying by, flag hoisted. As I entered the beech second-growth two foxes glided by me; a little further on a doe crashed out of the underbrush, and close behind her stole a lynx, eyes shining like coals.

He neither paid attention to the doe nor to me, but loped away toward the north.

The lynx was in flight.

'From what?' I asked myself, wondering. There was no forest fire, no cyclone, no flood.

If Barris had passed that way could he have stirred up this sudden exodus? Impossible; even a regiment in the forest could scarcely have put to rout these frightened creatures.

'What on earth,' thought I, turning to watch the headlong flight of a fisher cat, 'what on earth has started the beasts out at this time of night.'

I looked up into the sky. The placid glow of the fixed stars comforted me and I stepped on through the narrow spruce belt that leads down to the borders of the Lake of the Stars.

Wild cranberry and moosebush entwined my feet, dewy branches spattered me with moisture, and the thick spruce needles scraped my face as I threaded my way over mossy logs and deep spongy tussocks down to the level gravel of the lake shore.

Although there was no wind the little waves were hurrying in from the lake and I heard them splashing among the pebbles. In the pale star glow thousands of water lilies lifted their half-closed chalices toward the sky.

I threw myself full length upon the shore, and, chin on hand, looked out across the lake.

Splash, splash, came the waves along the shore, higher, nearer, until a film of water, thin and glittering as a knife blade, crept up to my elbows. I could not understand it; the lake was rising, but there had been no rain. All along the shore the water was running up; I heard the waves among the sedge grass; the weeds at my side were awash in the ripples. The lilies rocked on the tiny waves, every wet pad rising on the swells, sinking, rising again until the whole lake was glimmering with undulating blossoms. How sweet and deep was the fragrance from the lilies. And now the water was ebbing, slowly, and the waves receded, shrinking from the shore rim until the white pebbles appeared again, shining like froth on a brimming glass.

No animal swimming out in the darkness along the shore, no heavy salmon surging, could have set the whole shore aflood as though the wash from a great boat were rolling in. Could it have been the overflow, through the Weir Brook, of some cloudburst far back in the forest? This was the only way I could account for it, and yet when I had crossed the Weir Brook I had not noticed that it was swollen.

And as I lay there thinking, a faint breeze sprang up and I saw the surface of the lake whiten with lifted lily pads.

All around me the alders were sighing; I heard the forest behind me stir; the crossed branches rubbing softly, bark against bark. Something – it may have been an owl – sailed out of the night, dipped, soared, and was again engulfed, and far across the water I heard its faint cry, Ysonde.

Then first, for my heart was full, I cast myself down upon my face, calling on her name. My eyes were wet when I raised my head – for the spray from the shore was drifting in again – and my heart beat heavily; 'No more, no more.' But my heart lied, for even as I raised my face to the calm stars, I saw her standing still, close beside me; and very gently I spoke her name, Ysonde. She held out both hands.

'I was lonely,' she said, 'and I went to the glade, but the forest is full of frightened creatures and they frightened me. Has anything happened in the woods? The deer are running toward the heights.'

Her hand still lay in mine as we moved along the shore, and the lapping of the water on rock and shallow was no lower than our voices.

'Why did you leave me without a word, there at the fountain in the glade?' she said.

'I leave you!—'

'Indeed you did, running swiftly with your dog, plunging through thickets and brush – oh – you frightened me.'

'Did I leave you so?'

'Yes – after—'

'After?'

'You had kissed me—'

Then we leaned down together and looked into the black

water set with stars, just as we had bent together over the fountain in the glade.

'Do you remember?' I asked.

'Yes. See, the water is inlaid with silver stars – everywhere white lilies floating and the stars below, deep, deep down.'

'What is the flower you hold in your hand?'

'White water lotus.'

'Tell me about Yue-Laou, Dzil Nbu of the Kuen-Yuin,' I whispered, lifting her head so I could see her eyes.

'Would it please you to hear?'

'Yes, Ysonde.'

'All that I know is yours, now, as I am yours, all that I am. Bend closer. Is it of Yue-Laou you would know? Yue-Laou is Dzil-Nbu of the Kuen-Yuin. He lived in the Moon. He is old – very, very old, and once, before he came to rule the Kuen-Yuin, he was the old man who unites with a silken cord all predestined couples, after which nothing can prevent their union. But all that is changed since he came to rule the Kuen-Yin. Now he has perverted the Xin – the good genii of China – and has fashioned from their warped bodies a monster which he calls the Xin. This monster is horrible, for it not only lives in its own body, but it has thousand of loathsome satellites – living creatures without mouths, blind, that move when the Xin moves, like a mandarin and his escort. They are part of the Xin although they are not attached. Yet if one of these satellites is injured the Xin writhes with agony. It is fearful – this huge living bulk and these creatures spread out like severed fingers that wriggle around a hideous hand.'

'Who told you this?'

'My step-father.'

'Do you believe it?'

'Yes. I have seen one of the Xin's creatures.'

'Where, Ysonde?'

'Here in these woods.'

'Then you believe there is a Xin here?'

'There must be – perhaps in the lake—'

'Oh, Xins inhabit lakes?'

'Yes, and the seven seas. I am not afraid here.'

'Why?'

'Because I wear the symbol of the Kuen-Yuin.'

'Then I am not safe,' I smiled.

'Yes you are, for I hold you in my arms. Shall I tell you more about the Xin? When the Xin is about to do to death a man, the Yeth-hounds gallop through the night—'

'What are the Yeth-hounds, Ysonde?'

'The Yeth-hounds are dogs without heads. They are the spirits of murdered children, which pass through the woods at night, making a wailing noise.'

'Do you believe this?

'Yes, for I have worn the yellow lotus—'

'The yellow lotus—'

'Yellow is the symbol of faith—'

'Where?'

'In Yian,' she said faintly.

After a while I said, 'Ysonde, you know there is a God?'

'God and Xangi are one.'

'Have you ever heard of Christ?'

'No,' she answered softly.

The wind began again among the tree tops. I felt her hands closing in mine.

'Ysonde,' I asked again, 'do you believe in sorcerers?'

'Yes, the Kuen-Yuin are sorcerers; Yue-Laou is a sorcerer.'

'Have you seen sorcery?'

'Yes, the reptile satellite of the Xin—'

'Anything else?'

'My charm – the golden ball, the symbol of the Kuen-Yuin. Have you seen it change – have you seen the reptiles writhe—?'

'Yes,' said I shortly, and then remained silent, for a sudden shiver of apprehension had seized me. Barris also had spoken gravely, ominously of the sorcerers, the Kuen-Yuin, and I had seen with my own eyes the graven reptiles turning and twisting on the glowing globe.

'Still,' said I aloud, 'God lives and sorcery is but a name.'

'Ah,' murmured Ysonde, drawing closer to me, 'they say, in Yian, the Kuen-Yuin live; God is but a name.'

'They lie,' I whispered fiercely.

'Be careful,' she pleased, 'they may hear you. Remember that you have the mark of the dragon's claw on your brow.'

'What of it?' I asked, thinking also of the white mark on Barris' arm.

'Ah, don't you know that those who are marked with the dragon's claws are followed by Yue-Laou, for good or for evil – and the evil means death if you offend him?'

'Do you believe that!' I asked impatiently.

'I know it,' she sighed.

'Who told you all this? Your step-father? What in Heaven's name is he then – a Chinaman!'

'I don't know; he is not like you.'

'Have – have you told him anything about me?'

'He knows about you – no, I have told him nothing – ah, what is this – see – it is a cord, a cord of silk about your neck – and about mine!'

'Where did it come from?' I asked astonished.

'It must be – it must be Yue-Laou who binds me to you – it is as my step-father said – he said Yue-Laou would bind us—'

'Nonsense,' I said almost roughly, and seized the silken cord, but to my amazement it melted in my hand like smoke.

'What is all this damnable jugglery!' I whispered angrily, but my anger vanished as the words were spoken, and a convulsive shudder shook me to the feet. Standing on the shore of the lake, a stone's throw away, was a figure, twisted and bent – a little old man, blowing sparks from a live coal which he held in his naked hand. The coal glowed with increasing radiance, lighting up the skull-like face above it, and threw a red glow over the sands at his feet. But the face! – the ghastly Chinese face on which the light flickered – and the snaky slitted eyes, sparkling as the coal glowed hotter. Coal! It was not a coal but a golden globe staining the night with crimson flames – it was the symbol of the Kuen-Yuin.

'See! See!' gasped Ysonde, trembling violently, 'see the moon rising from between his fingers! Oh I thought it was my step-father and it is Yue-Laou the Maker of Moons – no! no! it is my step-father – ah God! they are the same!'

Frozen with terror I stumbled to my knees, groping for my revolver which bulged in my coat pocket; but something held me – something which bound me like a web in a thousand strong silky meshes. I struggled and turned but the web grew tighter; it was over us – all around us, drawing, pressing us into each other's arms until we lay side by side, bound hand and body and foot, palpitating, panting like a pair of netted pigeons.

And the creature on the shore below! What was my horror to see a moon, huge, silvery, rise like a bubble from between his fingers, mount higher, higher into the still air and hang aloft in the midnight sky, while another moon rose from his fingers, and another and yet another until the vast span of Heaven was set with moons and the earth sparkled like a diamond in the white glare.

A great wind began to blow from the east and it bore to our ears a long mournful howl – a cry so unearthly that for a moment our hearts stopped.

'The Yeth-hounds!' sobbed Ysonde, 'do you hear! – they are passing through the forest! The Xin is near!'

Then all around us in the dry sedge grasses came a rustle as if some small animals were creeping, and a damp acrid odor filled the air. I knew the smell, I saw the spidery crab-like creatures swarm out around me and drag their soft yellow hairy bodies across the shrinking grasses. They passed, hundreds of them, poisoning the air, tumbling, writhing, crawling with their blind mouthless heads raised. Birds, half asleep and confused by the darkness fluttered away before them in helpless fright, rabbits sprang from their forms, weasels glided away like flying shadows. What remained of the forest creatures rose and fled from the loathsome invasion; I heard the squeak of a terrified hare, the snort of stampeding deer, and the lumbering gallop of a bear; and all the time I was choking, half suffocated by the poisoned air.

Then, as I struggled to free myself from the silken snare about me, I cast a glance of deadly fear at the sorcerer below, and at the same moment I saw him turn in his tracks.

'Halt!' cried a voice from the bushes.

'Barris!' I shouted, half leaping up in my agony.

I saw the sorcerer spring forward, I heard the bang! bang! bang! of a revolver, and, as the sorcerer fell on the water's edge, I saw Barris jump out into the white glare and fire again, once, twice, three times, into the writhing figure at his feet.

Then an awful thing occurred. Up out of the black lake reared a shadow, a nameless shapeless mass, headless, sightless, gigantic, gaping from end to end.

A great wave struck Barris and he fell, another washed him up on the pebbles, another whirled him back into the water and then – and then the thing fell over him – and I fainted.

This, then, is all that I know concerning Yue-Laou and the Xin. I do not fear the ridicule of scientists or of the press for I have told the truth. Barris is gone and the thing that killed him is alive today in the Lake of the Stars while the spiderlike satellites roam through the Cardinal Woods. The game has fled, the forests around the lake are empty of any living creatures save the reptiles that creep when the Xin moves in the depths of the lake.

General Drummond knows what he has lost in Barris, and we, Pierpont and I, know what we have lost also. His will we found in the drawer, the key of which he had handed me. It was wrapped in a bit of paper on which was written:

'Yue-Laou the sorcerer is here in the Cardinal Woods. I must kill him or he will kill me. He made and gave to me the woman I love – he made her – I saw him – he made her out of a white water-lotus bud. When our child was born, he came again before me and demanded from me the woman I loved. Then, when I refused, he went away, and that night my wife and child vanished from my side, and I found upon her pillow a white lotus bud. Roy, the woman of your dream, Ysonde, may be my child. God help you if you love her for Yue-Laou will give – and take away, as though he were Xangi, which is God. I will kill Yue-Laou before I leave this forest – or he will kill me.

                                        'FRANKLYN BARRIS.'

Now the world knows what Barris thought of the Kuen-Yuin and of Yue-Laou. I see that the newspapers are just becoming excited over the glimpses that Li-Hung-Chang has afforded them of Black Cathay and the demons of the Kuen-Yuin. The Kuen-Yuin are on the move.

Pierpont and I have dismantled the shooting box in the Cardinal Woods. We hold ourselves ready at a moment's notice to join and lead the first Government party to drag the Lake of the Stars and cleanse the forest of the crab reptiles. But it will be necessary that a large force assembles, a well-armed force, for we have never found the body of Yue-Laou, and, living or dead, I fear him. Is he living?

Pierpont, who found Ysonde and myself lying unconscious on the lake shore, the morning after, saw no trace of corpse or blood on the sands. He may have fallen into the lake, but I fear and Ysonde fears that he is still alive. We never were able to find either her dwelling place or the glade and the fountain again. The only thing that remains to her of her former life is the gold serpent in the Metropolitan Museum and her golden globe, the symbol of the Kuen-Yuin; but the latter no longer changes color.

THE MASK

CAMILLA: You sir, should unmask.
STRANGER: Indeed?
CASSILDA: Indeed it's time. We all have laid aside disguise
            but you.
STRANGER: I wear no mask.
CAMILLA: (Terrified, aside to Cassilda.) No mask? No
            mask!
                        THE KING IN YELLOW: Act I – Scene 2d

I

Although I knew nothing of chemistry, I listened fascinated.
He picked up an Easter lily which Geneviève had brought
that morning from Notre Dame and dropped it into the
basin. Instantly the liquid lost its crystalline clearness. For
a second the lily was enveloped in a milk-white foam,
which disappeared, leaving the fluid opalescent. Changing
tints of orange and crimson played over the surface, and
then what seemed to be a ray of pure sunlight struck
through from the bottom where the lily was resting. At
the same instant he plunged his hand into the basin and
drew out the flower. 'There is no danger,' he explained,
'if you choose the right moment. That golden ray is the
signal.'

He held the lily toward me and I took it in my hand. It
had turned to stone, to the purest marble.

'You see,' he said, 'it is without a flaw. What sculptor could reproduce it?'

The marble was white as snow, but in its depths the veins of the lily were tinged with palest azure, and a faint flush lingered deep in its heart.

'Don't ask me the reason of that,' he smiled, noticing my wonder. 'I have no idea why the veins and the heart are tinted, but they always are. Yesterday I tried one of Geneviève's gold fish – there it is.'

The fish looked as if sculptured in marble. But if you held it to the light the stone was beautifully veined with a faint blue, and from somewhere within came a rosy light like the tint which slumbers in an opal. I looked into the basin. Once more it seemed filled with clearest crystal.

'If I should touch it now?' I demanded.

'I don't know,' he replied, 'but you had better not try.'

'There is one thing I'm curious about,' I said, 'and that is where the ray of sunlight came from.'

'It looked like a sunbeam, true enough,' he said. 'I don't know, it always comes when I immerse any living thing. Perhaps,' he continued smiling, 'perhaps it is the vital spark of the creature escaping to the source from whence it came.'

I saw he was mocking and threatened him with a mahl-stick, but he only laughed and changed the subject.

'Stay to lunch. Geneviève will be here directly.'

'I saw her going to early mass,' I said, 'and she looked as fresh and sweet as that lily – before you destroyed it.'

'Do you think I destroyed it?' said Boris gravely.

'Destroyed, preserved, how can we tell?'

We sat in the corner of a studio near his unfinished group of 'The Fates'. He leaned back on the sofa, twirling a sculptor's chisel and squinting at his work.

'By the way, I have finished pointing up that old academic "Ariadne" and I suppose it will have to go to the Salon. It's all I have ready this year, but after the success the "Madonna" brought me I feel ashamed to send a thing like that.'

The 'Madonna', an exquisite marble for which Geneviève had sat, had been the sensation of last year's Salon. I looked at the 'Ariadne'. It was a magnificent piece of technical work, but I agreed with Boris that the world would expect something better of him than that. Still it was impossible now to think of finishing in time for the Salon, that splendid terrible group half shrouded in the marble behind me. 'The Fates' would have to wait.

We were proud of Boris Yvain. We claimed him and he claimed us on the strength of his having been born in America, although his father was French and his mother was a Russian. Every one in the Beaux Arts called him Boris. And yet there were only two of us whom he addressed in the same familiar way – Jack Scott and myself.

Perhaps my being in love with Geneviève had something to do with his affection for me. Not that it had ever been acknowledged between us. But after all was settled, and she had told me with tears in her eyes that it was Boris whom she loved, I went over to his house and congratulated him. The perfect cordiality of that interview did not deceive either of us, I always believed, although to one at least it was a great comfort. I do not think he and Geneviève ever spoke of the matter together, but Boris knew.

Geneviève was lovely. The Madonna-like purity of her face might have been inspired by the 'Sanctus' in Gounod's Mass. But I was always glad when she changed that mood for what we called her 'April Manoeuvres'. She was often as variable as an April day. In the morning grave, dignified and sweet; at noon laughing, capricious; at evening whatever one least expected. I preferred her so rather than in that Madonna-like tranquility which stirred the depths of my heart. I was dreaming of Geneviève when he spoke again.

'What do you think of my discovery, Alec?'

'I think it wonderful.'

'I shall make no use of it, you know, beyond satisfying my own curiosity so far as may be and the secret will die with me.'

'It would be rather a blow to sculpture, would it not? We painters lose more than we ever gain by photography.'

Boris nodded, playing with the edge of the chisel.

'This new vicious discovery would corrupt the world of art. No, I shall never confide the secret to any one,' he said slowly.

It would be hard to find any one less informed about such phenomena than myself; but of course I had heard of mineral springs so saturated with silica that the leaves and twigs which fell into them were turned to stone after a time. I dimly comprehended the process, how the silica replaced the vegetable matter, atom by atom, and the result was a duplicate of the object in stone. This I confess had never interested me greatly, and as for the ancient fossils thus produced, they disgusted me. Boris, it appeared, feeling curiosity instead of repugnance, had investigated the subject, and had accidentally stumbled on a solution which, attacking the immersed object with a ferocity unheard of, in a second did the work of years. This was all I could make out of the strange story he had just been telling. He spoke again after a long silence.

'I am almost frightened when I think what I have found. Scientists would go mad over the discovery. It was so simple too; it discovered itself. When I think of that formula, and that new element precipitated in metallic scales—'

'What new element?'

'Oh, I haven't thought of naming it, and I don't believe I ever shall. There are enough precious metals now in the world to cut throats over.'

I pricked up my ears. 'Have you struck gold, Boris?'

'No, better; but see here, Alec!' he laughed, starting up. 'You and I have all we need in this world. Ah! how sinister and covetous you look already!' I laughed too, and told him I was devoured by the desire for gold, and we had better talk of something else; so when Geneviève came in shortly after, we had turned our backs on alchemy.

Geneviève was dressed in silvery gray from head to foot.

The light glinted along the soft curves of her fair hair as she turned her cheek to Boris; then she saw me and returned my greeting. She had never before failed to blow me a kiss from the tips of her white fingers, and I promptly complained of the omission. She smiled and held out her hand which dropped almost before it had touched mine; then she said, looking at Boris: 'You must ask Alec to stay for luncheon.'

This also was something new. She had always asked me herself until today.

'I did,' said Boris shortly.

'And you said yes, I hope,' she turned to me with a charming conventional smile. I might have been an acquaintance of the day before yesterday. I made her a low bow. *'J'avais bien l'honneur, madame,'* but refusing to take up our usual bantering tone she murmured a hospitable commonplace and disappeared. Boris and I looked at one another.

'I had better go home, don't you think?' I asked.

'Hanged if I know,' he replied frankly.

While we were discussing the advisability of my departure Geneviève reappeared in the doorway without her bonnet. She was wonderfully beautiful, but her color was too deep and her lovely eyes were too bright. She came straight up to me and took my arm.

'Luncheon is ready. Was I cross, Alec? I thought I had a headache but I haven't. Come here, Boris,' and she slipped her other arm through his. 'Alec knows that after you there is no one in the world whom I like as well as I like him, so if he sometimes feels snubbed it won't hurt him.'

'À la bonheur!' I cried, 'who says there are no thunderstorms in April?'

'Are you ready?' chanted Boris. 'Aye ready'; and arm in arm we raced into the dining-room scandalizing the servants. After all we were not so much to blame; Geneviève was eighteen, Boris was twenty-three and I not quite twenty-one.

II

Some work that I was doing about this time on the decorations for Geneviève's boudoir kept me constantly at the quaint little hotel in the rue Sainte-Cécile. Boris and I in those days labored hard but as we pleased, which was fitfully, and we all three, with Jack Scott, idled a great deal together.

One quiet afternoon I had been wandering alone over the house examining curios, prying into odd corners, bringing out sweetmeats and cigars from strange hiding-places, and at last I stopped in the bathing-room. Boris, all over clay, stood there washing his hands.

The room was built of rose-colored marble excepting the floor which was tessellated in rose and gray. In the centre was a square pool sunken below the surface of the floor; steps led down into it, sculptured pillars supported a frescoed ceiling. A delicious marble Cupid appeared to have just alighted on his pedestal at the upper end of the room. The whole interior was Boris' work and mine. Boris, in his working clothes of white canvas, scraped the traces of clay and red modelling wax from his handsome hands, and coquetted over his shoulder with the Cupid.

'I see you,' he insisted, 'don't try to look the other way and pretend not to see me. You know who made you, little humbug!'

It was always my rôle to interpret Cupid's sentiments in these conversations, and when my turn came I responded in such a manner, that Boris seized my arm and dragged me toward the pool, declaring he would duck me. Next instant he dropped my arm and turned pale. 'Good God!' he said, 'I forgot the pool is full of the solution!'

I shivered a little, and drily advised him to remember better where he had stored the precious liquid.

'In Heaven's name why do you keep a small lake of that gruesome stuff here of all places?' I asked.

'I want to experiment on something large,' he replied.

'On me, for instance!'

'Ah! that came too close for jesting; but I do want to watch the action of that solution on a more highly organized living body; there is that big white rabbit,' he said, following me into the studio.

Jack Scott, wearing a paint-stained jacket, came wandering in, appropriated all the Oriental sweetmeats he could lay his hand on, looted the cigarette case, and finally he and Boris disappeared together to visit the Luxembourg gallery, where a new silver bronze by Rodin and a landscape of Monet's were claiming the exclusive attention of artistic France. I went back to the studio, and resumed my work. It was a Renaissance screen, which Boris wanted me to paint for Geneviève's boudoir. But the small boy who was unwillingly dawdling through a series of poses for it, today refused all bribes to be good. He never rested an instant in the same position, and inside of five minutes, I had as many different outlines of the little beggar.

'Are you posing, or are you executing a song and dance, my friend?' I inquired.

'Whichever monsieur pleases,' he replied with an angelic smile.

Of course I dismissed him for the day, and of course I paid him for the full time, that being the way we spoil our models.

After the young imp had gone, I made a few perfunctory daubs at my work, but was so thoroughly out of humor, that it took me the rest of the afternoon to undo the damage I had done, so at last I scraped my palette, stuck my brushes in a bowl of black soap, and strolled into the smoking-room. I really believe that, excepting Geneviève's apartments, no room in the house was so free from the perfume of tobacco as this one. It was a queer chaos of odds and ends hung with threadbare tapestry. A sweet-toned old spinet in good repair stood by the window. There were stands of weapons, some old and dull, others bright and modern, festoons of Indian and Turkish armor over the mantel, two or three good pictures, and a pipe-rack. It was here that we used to come for new sensations in smoking. I doubt if any type of pipe ever existed which was not represented in that rack. When we had selected one, we immediately carried it somewhere else and smoked it; for the place was, on the whole, more gloomy and less inviting than any in the house. But this afternoon, the twilight was very soothing, the rugs and skins on the floor looked brown and soft and drowsy; the big couch was piled with cushions.

I found my pipe and curled up there for an unaccustomed smoke in the smoking-room. I had chosen one with a long flexible stem, and lighting it fell to dreaming. After a while it went out, but I did not stir. I dreamed on and presently fell asleep.

I awoke to the saddest music I had ever heard. The room was quite dark, I had no idea what time it was. A ray of moonlight silvered one edge of the old spinet, and the polished wood seemed to exhale the sounds as perfume floats above a box of sandal wood. Someone rose in the darkness, and came away weeping quietly, and I was fool enough to cry out 'Geneviève!'

She dropped at my voice, and I had time to curse myself while I made a light and tried to raise her from the floor. She shrank away with a murmur of pain. She was very quiet, and asked for Boris. I carried her to the divan, and went to look for him, but he was not in the house, and the servants were gone to bed. Perplexed and anxious, I hurried back to Geneviève. She lay where I left her, looking very white.

'I can't find Boris nor any of the servants,' I said.

'I know,' she answered faintly, 'Boris has gone to Ept with Mr Scott. I did not remember when I sent you for him just now.'

'But he can't get back in that case before tomorrow afternoon, and – are you hurt? Did I frighten you into falling? What an awful fool I am, but I was only half awake.'

'Boris thought you had gone home before dinner. Do please excuse us for letting you stay here all this time.'

'I have had a long nap,' I laughed, 'so sound that I did not know whether I was still asleep or not when I found myself staring at a figure that was moving toward me, and called out your name. Have you been trying the old spinet? You must have played very softly.'

I would tell a thousand more lies worse than that one to see the look of relief that came into her face. She smiled adorably and said in her natural voice: 'Alec, I tripped on that wolf's head, and I think my ankle is sprained. Please call Marie and then go home.'

I did as she bade me and left her there when the maid came in.

III

At noon next day when I called, I found Boris walking restlessly about his studio.

'Geneviève is asleep just now,' he told me, 'the sprain is nothing, but why should she have such a high fever? The doctor can't account for it; or else he will not,' he muttered.

'Geneviève has a fever?' I asked.

'I should say so, and has actually been a little light-headed at intervals all night. The idea! gay little Geneviève, without a care in the world – and she keeps saying her heart's broken, and she wants to die!'

My own heart stood still.

Boris leaned against the door of his studio, looking down, his hands in his pockets, his kind, keen eyes clouded, a new line of trouble drawn 'over the mouth's good mark, that made the smile'. The maid had orders to summon him the instant Geneviève opened her eyes. We waited and waited, and Boris growing restless wandered about, fussing with modelling wax and red clay. Suddenly he started for the next room. 'Come and see my rose-colored bath full of death,' he cried.

'Is it death?' I asked to humor his mood.

'You are not prepared to call it life, I suppose,' he answered.

As he spoke he plucked a solitary gold fish squirming and twisting out of its globe. 'We'll send this one after the other – wherever that is,' he said. There was feverish excitement in his voice. A dull weight of fever lay on my limbs and on my brain as I followed him to the fair crystal pool with its pink-tinted sides; and he dropped the creature in. Falling, its scales flashed with a hot orange gleam in its angry twistings and contortions; the moment it struck the liquid it became rigid and sank heavily to the bottom. Then came the milky foam, the splendid hues radiating on the surface and then the shaft of pure serene light broke through from seemingly infinite depths. Boris plunged in his hand and drew out an exquisite marble thing, blue-veined, rose-tinted and glistening with opalescent drops.

'Child's play,' he muttered, and looked wearily, longingly at me – as if I could answer such questions! But Jack Scott came in and entered into the 'game' as he called it with ardor. Nothing would do but to try the experiment on the white rabbit then and there. I was willing that Boris should find distraction from his cares, but I hated to see the life go out of a warm, living creature and I declined to be present.

Picking up a book at random I sat down in the studio to read. Alas, I had found 'The King in Yellow'. After a few moments which seemed ages, I was putting it away with a nervous shudder, when Boris and Jack came in bringing their marble rabbit. At the same time the bell rang above and a cry came from the sick room. Boris was gone like a flash, and the next moment he called, 'Jack, run for the doctor; bring him back with you. Alec, come here.'

I went and stood at her door. A frightened maid came out in haste and ran away to fetch some remedy. Geneviève sitting bolt upright, with crimson cheeks and glittering eyes, babbled incessantly and resisted Boris' gentle restraint. He called me to help. At my first touch she sighed and sank back, closing her eyes, and then – then – as we still bent above her, she opened them again, looked straight into Boris' face, poor fever-crazed girl, and told her secret. At the same instant, our three lives turned into new channels; the bond that had held us so long together snapped forever and a new bond was forged in its place, for she had spoken my name, and as the fever tortured her, her heart poured out its load of hidden sorrow. Amazed and dumb I bowed my head, while my face burned like a live coal, and the blood surged in my ears, stupefying me with its clamor. Incapable of movement, incapable of speech, I listened to her feverish words in an agony of shame and sorrow. I could not silence her, I could not look at Boris. Then I felt an arm upon my shoulder, and Boris turned a bloodless face to mine.

'It is not your fault, Alec, don't grieve so if she loves you—' but he could not finish; and as the doctor stepped swiftly into the room saying – 'Ah, the fever!' I seized Jack Scott and hurried him to the street saying, 'Boris would rather be alone.' We crossed the street to our own apartment and that night, seeing I was going to be ill too, he went for the doctor again. The last thing I recollect with any distinctness was hearing Jack say, 'For Heaven's sake, doctor, what ails him, to wear a face like that?' and I thought of 'The King in Yellow' and the Pallid Mask.

I was very ill, for the strain of two years which I had endured since that fatal May morning when Geneviève murmured, 'I love you, but I think I love Boris best' told on me at last. I had never imagined that it could become more than I could endure. Outwardly tranquil, I had deceived myself. Although the inward battle raged night after night, and, I, lying alone in my room, cursed myself for rebellious thoughts unloyal to Boris and unworthy of Geneviève, the morning always brought relief, and I returned to Geneviève and to my dear Boris with a heart washed clean by the tempests of the night.

Never in word or deed or thought while with them had I betrayed my sorrow even to myself.

The mask of self-deception was no longer a mask for me, it was a part of me. Night lifted it, laying bare the stifled truth below; but there was no one to see except myself, and when day broke the mask fell back again of its own accord. These thoughts passed through my troubled mind as I lay sick, but they were hopelessly entangled with visions of white creatures, heavy as stone, crawling about in Boris' basin – of the wolf's head on the rug, foaming and snapping at Geneviève, who lay smiling beside it. I thought, too, of The King in Yellow wrapt in the fantastic colors of his tattered mantle, and that bitter cry of Cassilda, 'Not upon us, O King, not upon us!' Feverishly I struggled to put it from me, but I saw the lake of Hali, thin and blank, without a ripple or wind to stir it, and I saw the towers of Carcosa behind the moon. Aldebaran, the Hyades, Alar, Hastur, glided through the cloud rifts which fluttered and flapped as they passed like the scalloped tatters of The King in Yellow. Among all these, one sane thought persisted. It never wavered, no matter what else was going on in my disordered mind, that my chief reason for existing, was to meet some requirement of Boris and Geneviève. What this obligation was, its nature, was never clear; sometimes it seemed to be protection, sometimes support, through a great crisis. Whatever it seemed to be for the time, its weight rested only on me, and I was never so ill or so weak that I did not respond with my whole soul. There were always crowds of faces about me, mostly strange, but a few I recognized, Boris among them. Afterward they told me that this could not have been, but I know that once at least he bent over me. It was only a touch, a faint echo of his voice, then the clouds settled back on my senses, and I lost him, but he *did* stand there and bend over me *once* at least.

At last, one morning I awoke to find the sunlight falling across my bed, and Jack Scott reading beside me. I had not strength enough to speak aloud, neither could I think, much less remember, but I could smile feebly, as Jack's eyes met mine, and when he jumped up and asked eagerly if I wanted anything, I could whisper, 'Yes, Boris'. Jack moved to the head of my bed, and leaned down to arrange my pillow; I did not see his face, but he answered heartily, 'You must wait Alec, you are too weak to see even Boris.'

I waited and I grew strong; in a few days I was able to see whom I would, but meanwhile I had thought and remembered. From the moment when all the past grew clear again in my mind, I never doubted what I should do when the time came, and I felt sure that Boris would have resolved upon the same course so far as he was concerned; as for what pertained to me alone, I knew he would see that also as I did. I no longer asked for any one. I never inquired why no message came from them; why during the week I lay there, waiting and growing stronger, I never heard their name spoken. Preoccupied with my own searchings for the right way, and with my feeble but determined fight against despair, I simply acquiesced in Jack's reticence, taking for granted that he was afraid to speak of them, lest I should turn unruly and insist on seeing them.

Meanwhile I said over and over to myself, how it would be when life began again for us all. We would take up our relations exactly as they were before Geneviève fell ill. Boris and I would look into each other's eyes and there would be no rancor nor cowardice nor mistrust in that glance. I would be with them again for a little while in the dear intimacy of their home, and then, without pretext or explanation, I would disappear from their lives forever. Boris would know, Geneviève – the only comfort was that she would never know. It seemed, as I thought it over, that I had found the meaning of that sense of obligation which had persisted all through my delirium, and the only possible answer to it. So, when I was quite ready, I beckoned Jack to me one day, and said, 'Jack, I want Boris at once; and take my dearest greeting to Geneviève . . .'

When at last he made me understand that they were both dead, I fell into a wild rage that tore all my little convalescent strength to atoms. I raved and cursed myself into a relapse, from which I crawled forth some weeks afterward a boy of twenty-one who believed that his youth was gone forever. I seemed to be past the capability of further suffering, and one day when Jack handed me a letter and the keys to Boris' house, I took them without a tremor and asked him to tell me all. It was cruel of me to ask him, but there was no help for it, and he leaned wearily on his thin hands to reopen the wound which could never entirely heal. He began very quietly.

'Alec, unless you have a clue that I know nothing about, you will not be able to explain any more than I, what has happened. I suspect that you would rather not hear these details, but you must learn them, else I would spare you the relation. God knows I wish I could be spared the telling. I shall use few words.

'That day when I left you in the doctor's care and came back to Boris, I found him working on the "Fates". Geneviève, he said, was sleeping under the influence of drugs. She had been quite out of her mind, he said. He kept on working, not talking any more, and I watched him. Before long, I saw that the third figure of the group – the one looking straight ahead, out over the world – bore his face; not as you ever saw it, but as it looked then and to the end. This is one thing for which I should like to find an explanation, but I never shall.

'Well, he worked and I watched him in silence, and we went on that way until nearly midnight. Then we heard a door open and shut sharply, and a swift rush in the next room. Boris sprang through the doorway and I followed; but we were too late. She lay at the bottom of the pool, her hands across her breast. Then Boris shot himself through the heart.'

Jack stopped speaking, drops of sweat stood under his eyes, and his thin cheeks twitched. 'I carried Boris to his room. Then I went back and let that hellish fluid out of the pool, and turning on all the water, washed the marble clean of every drop. When at length I dared descend the steps, I found her lying there as white as snow. At last, when I had decided what was best to do, I went into the laboratory, and first emptied the solution in the basin into the waste-pipe; then I poured the contents of every jar and bottle after it. There was wood in the fireplace, so I built a fire, and breaking the locks of Boris' cabinet I burnt every paper, notebook and letter that I found there. With a mallet from the studio I smashed to pieces all the empty bottles, then loading them into a coal scuttle, I carried them to the cellar and threw them over the red-hot bed of the furnace.

'Six times I made the journey, and at last, not a vestige remained of anything which might again aid in seeking for the formula which Boris had found. Then at last I dared call the doctor. He is a good man, and together we struggled to keep it from the public. Without him I never could have succeeded. At last we got the servants paid and sent away into the country, where old Rosier keeps them quiet with stories of Boris' and Genevieve's travels in distant lands, from whence they will not return for years. We buried Boris in the little cemetery of Sèvres. The doctor is a good creature and knows when to pity a man who can bear no more. He gave his certificate of heart disease and asked no questions of me.'

Then lifting his head from his hands, he said, 'Open the letter, Alec; it is for us both'.

I tore it open. It was Boris' will dated a year before. He left everything to Geneviève, and in the case of her dying childless, I was to take control of the house in the rue Sainte-Cécile, and Jack Scott, the management at Ept. On our deaths the property reverted to his mother's family in Russia, with the exception of the sculptured marbles executed by himself. These he left to me.

The page blurred under our eyes, and Jack got up and walked to the window. Presently he returned and sat down again. I dreaded to hear what he was going to say, but he spoke with the same simplicity and gentleness.

'Geneviève lies before the "Madonna" in the marble room. The "Madonna" bends tenderly above her, and Geneviève smiles back into that calm face that never would have been except for her.'

His voice broke, but he grasped my hand, saying, 'Courage, Alec.' Next morning he left for Ept to fulfil his trust.

IV

The same evening I took the keys and went into the house I had known so well. Everything was in order, but the silence was terrible. Though I went twice to the door of the marble room, I could not force myself to enter. It was beyond my strength. I went into the smoking-room and sat down before the spinet. A small lace handkerchief lay on the keys, and I turned away, choking. It was plain I could not stay, so I locked every door, every window, and the three front and back gates, and went away. Next morning Alcide packed my valise, and leaving him in charge of my apartments I took the Orient express for Constantinople. During the two years that I wandered through the East, at first, in our letters, we never mentioned Geneviève and Boris, but gradually their names crept in. I recollect a passage in one of Jack's letters replying to one of mine:

'What you tell me of seeing Boris bending over you while you lay ill, and feeling his touch on your face, and hearing his voice of course troubles me. This that you describe must have happened a fortnight after he died. I say to myself that you were dreaming, that it was part of your delirium, but the explanation does not satisfy me, nor would it you.'

Toward the end of the second year a letter came from Jack to me in India so unlike anything that I had ever known of him that I decided to return at once to Paris. He wrote, 'I am well and sell all my pictures as artists do, who have no need of money. I have not a care of my own, but I am more restless than if I had. I am unable to shake off a strange anxiety about you. It is not apprehension, it is rather a breathless expectancy – of what, God knows! I can only say it is wearing me out. Nights I dream always of you and Boris. I can never recall anything afterward, but I wake in the morning with my heart beating, and all day the excitement increases until I fall asleep at night to recall the same experience. I am quite exhausted by it, and have determined to break up this morbid condition. I must see you. Shall I go to Bombay or will you come to Paris?'

I telegraphed him to expect me by the next steamer.

When we met I thought he had changed very little; I, he insisted, looked in splendid health. It was good to hear his voice again, and as we sat and chatted about what life still held for us, we felt that it was pleasant to be alive in the bright spring weather.

We stayed in Paris together a week, and then I went for a week to Ept with him, but first of all we went to the cemetery at Sèvres, where Boris lay.

'Shall we place the "Fates" in the little grove above him?' Jack asked, and I answered.

'I think only the "Madonna" should watch over Boris' grave.' But Jack was none the better for my home-coming. The dreams of which he could not retain even the least definite outline continued, and he said that at times the sense of breathless expectancy was suffocating.

You see I do you harm and not good,' I said. 'Try a change without me.' So he started alone for a ramble among the Channel Islands and I went back to Paris. I had not yet entered Boris' house, now mine, since my return, but I knew it must be done. It had been kept in order by Jack; there were servants there, so I gave up my own apartment and went there to live. Instead of the agitation I had feared, I found myself able to paint there tranquilly. I visited all the rooms – all but one. I could not bring myself to enter the marble room where Geneviève lay, and yet I felt the longing growing daily to look upon her face, to kneel beside her.

One April afternoon, I lay dreaming in the smoking-room, just as I had lain two years before, and mechanically I looked among the tawny Eastern rugs for the wolf-skin. At last I distinguished the pointed ears and the flat cruel head, and I thought of my dream where I saw Geneviève lying beside it. The helmets still hung against the threadbare tapestry, among them the old Spanish morion which I remembered Geneviève had once put on when we were amusing ourselves with the ancient bits of mail. I turned my eyes to the spinet; every yellow key seemed eloquent of her caressing hand,

and I rose, drawn by the strength of my life's passion to the sealed door of the marble room. The heavy doors swung inward under my trembling hands. Sunlight poured through the window, tipping with gold the wings of Cupid, and lingered like a nimbus over the brows of the 'Madonna'. Her tender face bent in compassion over a marble form so exquisitely pure that I knelt and signed myself. Geneviève lay in the shadow under the 'Madonna', and yet, through her white arms, I saw the pale azure vein, and beneath her softly clasped hands the folds of her dress were tinged with rose, as if from some faint warm light within her breast.

Bending, with a breaking heart, I touched the marble drapery with my lips, then crept back into the silent house.

A maid came and brought me a letter, and I sat down in the little conservatory to read it; but as I was about to break the seal, seeing the girl lingering, I asked her what she wanted.

She stammered something about a white rabbit that had been caught in the house and asked what should be done with it. I told her to let it loose in the walled garden behind the house and opened my letter. It was from Jack, but so incoherent that I thought he must have lost his reason. It was nothing but a series of prayers to me not to leave the house until he could get back; he could not tell me why, there were the dreams, he said – he could explain nothing, but he was sure that I must not leave the house in the rue Sainte-Cécile.

As I finished reading I raised my eyes and saw the same maid-servant standing in the doorway holding a glass dish in which two gold fish were swimming: 'Put them back into the tank and tell me what you mean by interrupting me,' I said.

With a half suppressed whimper she emptied water and fish into an aquarium at the end of the conservatory, and turning to me asked my permission to leave my service. She said people were playing tricks on her, evidently with a design of getting her into trouble; the marble rabbit had been stolen and a live one had been brought into the house; the two beautiful marble fish were gone and she had just found those common live things flopping on the dining-room floor. I reassured her and sent her away saying I would look about myself. I went into the studio; there was nothing there but my canvasses and some casts, except the marble of the Easter Lily. I saw it on a table across the room. Then I strode angrily over to it. But the flower I lifted from the table was fresh and fragile and filled the air with perfume.

Then suddenly I comprehended and sprang through the hall-way to the marble room. The doors flew open, the sunlight streamed into my face and through it, in a heavenly glory, the 'Madonna' smiled, as Geneviève lifted her flushed face from her marble couch, and opened her sleepy eyes.

THE DEMOISELLE D'YS

'Mais je croy que je
Suis descendu on puiz
Tenebreux onquel disoit
Heraclytus estre Verité cachée.'

'There be three things which are too wonderful for me,
yea, four which I know not:
'The way of an eagle in the air; the way of a serpent
upon a rock; the way of a ship in the midst of the sea;
and the way of a man with a maid.'

I

The utter desolation of the scene began to have its effect; I sat
down to face the situation and, if possible, recall to mind
some landmark which might aid me in extricating myself
from my present position. If I could only find the ocean again
all would clear, for I knew one could see the island of Groix
from the cliffs.

I laid down my gun, and kneeling behind a rock lighted
a pipe. Then I looked at my watch. It was nearly four o'clock.
I might have wandered from Kerselec since day-break.

Standing the day before on the cliffs below Kerselec with
Goulven, looking out over the sombre moors among which
I had now lost my way, these downs had appeared to me

level as a meadow, stretching to the horizon, and although I knew how deceptive is distance, I could not realize that what from Kerselec seemed to be mere grassy hollows were great valleys covered with gorse and heather, and what looked like scattered boulders were in reality enormous cliffs of granite.

'It's a bad place for a stranger,' old Goulven had said; 'you'd better take a guide,' and I had replied, 'I shall not lose myself.' Now I knew that I had lost myself, as I sat there smoking, with the sea-wind blowing in my face. On every side stretched the moorland, covered with flowering gorse and heath and granite boulders. There was not a tree in sight, much less a house. After a while, I picked up the gun, and turning my back on the sun tramped on again.

There was little use in following any of the brawling streams which every now and then crossed my path, for instead of flowing into the sea, they ran inland to reedy pools in the hollows of the moors. I had followed several, but they all led me to swamps or silent little ponds from which the snipe rose peeping and wheeled away in an ecstasy of fright. I began to feel fatigued, and the gun galled my shoulder in spite of the double pads. The sun sank lower and lower, shining level across yellow gorse and the moorland pools.

As I walked my own gigantic shadow led me on, seeming to lengthen at every step. The gorse scraped against my leggings, crackled beneath my feet, showering the brown earth with blossoms, and the brake bowed and billowed along my path. From tufts of heath rabbits scurried away through the bracken, and among the swamp grass I heard the wild duck's drowsy quack. Once a fox stole across my path, and again, as I stooped to drink at a hurrying rill, a heron flapped heavily from the reeds beside me. I turned to look at the sun. It seemed to touch the edges of the plain. When at last I decided that it was useless to go on, and that I must make up my mind to spend at least one night on the moors, I threw myself down thoroughly fagged out. The evening sunlight slanted warm across my body, but the sea-winds began to rise, and I felt a chill strike through me from my wet shooting boots. High overhead gulls were wheeling and tossing like bits of white paper; from some distant marsh a solitary curlew called. Little by little the sun sank into the plain, and the zenith flushed with the afterglow. I watched the sky change from palest gold to pink and then to smouldering fire. Clouds of midges danced above me, and high in the calm air a bat dipped and soared. My eyelids began to droop. Then as I shook off the drowsiness a sudden crash among the bracken roused me. I raised my eyes. A great bird hung quivering in the air above my face. For an instant I stared, incapable of motion; then something leaped past me in the ferns and the bird rose, wheeled, and pitched headlong into the brake.

I was on my feet in an instant peering through the gorse. There came the sound of a struggle from a bunch of heather close by, and then all was quiet. I stepped forward, my gun poised, but when I came to the heather the gun fell under my arm again, and I stood motionless in silent astonishment. A dead hare lay on the ground, and on the hare stood a magnificent falcon, one talon buried in the creature's neck, the other planted firmly on its limp flank. But what astonished me, was not the mere sight of a falcon sitting upon its prey. I had seen that more than once. It was that the falcon was fitted with a sort of leash about both talons, and from the leash hung a round bit of metal like a sleigh-bell. The bird turned its fierce yellow eyes on me, and then stooped and struck its curved beak into the quarry. At the same instant hurried steps sounded among the heather, and a girl sprang into the covert in front. Without a glance at me she walked up to the falcon, and passing her gloved hand under its breast, raised it from the quarry. Then she deftly slipped a small hood over the bird's head, and holding it out on her gauntlet, stooped and picked up the hare.

She passed a cord about the animal's legs and fastened

the end of the thong to her girdle. Then she started to retrace her steps through the covert. As she passed me I raised my cap and she acknowledged my presence with a scarcely perceptible inclination. I had been so astonished, so lost in admiration of the scene before my eyes, that it had not occurred to me that here was my salvation. But as she moved away I recollected that unless I wanted to sleep on a windy moor that night I had better recover my speech without delay. At my first word she hesitated, and as I stepped before her I thought a look of fear came into her beautiful eyes. But as I humbly explained my unpleasant plight, her face flushed and she looked at me in wonder.

'Surely you did not come from Kerselec!' she repeated.

Her sweet voice had no trace of the Breton accent nor of any accent which I knew, and yet there was something in it I seemed to have heard before, something quaint and indefinable, like the theme of an old song.

I explained that I was an American, unacquainted with Finistèrre, shooting there for my own amusement.

'An American,' she repeated in the same quaint musical tones. 'I have never before seen an American.'

For a moment she stood silent, then looking at me she said: 'If you should walk all night you could not reach Kerselec now, even if you had a guide'.

This was pleasant news.

'But,' I began, 'if I could only find a peasant's hut where I might get something to eat, and shelter.'

The falcon on her wrist fluttered and shook its head. The girl smoothed its glossy back and glanced at me.

'Look around,' she said gently. 'Can you see the end of these moors? Look, north, south, east, west. Can you see anything but moorland and bracken?'

'No,' I said.

'The moor is wild and desolate. It is easy to enter, but sometimes they who enter never leave it. There are no peasants' huts here.'

'Well,' I said, 'if you will tell me in which direction Kerselec lies, tomorrow it will take me no longer to go back than it has to come.'

She looked at me again with an expression almost like pity.

'Ah,' she said, 'to come is easy and takes hours; to go is different – and may take centuries.'

I stared at her in amazement but decided that I had misunderstood her. Then before I had time to speak she drew a whistle from her belt and sounded it.

'Sit down and rest,' she said to me; 'you have come a long distance and are tired.'

She gathered up her pleated skirts and motioning me to follow picked her dainty way through the gorse to a flat rock among the ferns.

'They will be here directly,' she said, and taking a seat at one end of the rock invited me to sit down on the other edge. The after-glow was beginning to fade in the sky and a single star twinkled faintly through the rosy haze. A long wavering triangle of water-fowl drifted southward over our heads and from the swamps around plover were calling.

'They are very beautiful – these moors,' she said quietly.

'Beautiful, but cruel to strangers,' I answered.

'Beautiful and cruel,' she repeated dreamily, 'beautiful and cruel.'

'Like a woman,' I said stupidly.

'Oh,' she cried with a little catch in her breath and looked at me. Her dark eyes met mine and I thought she seemed angry or frightened.

'Like a woman,' she repeated under her breath, 'how cruel to say so!' Then after a pause, as though speaking aloud to herself, 'How cruel for him to say that.'

I don't know what sort of an apology I offered for my inane, though harmless speech, but I know that she seemed so troubled about it that I began to think I had said something very dreadful without knowing it, and remembered with horror the pitfalls and snares which the French language sets for foreigners. While I was trying to imagine what I might have said, a sound of voices came across the moor and the girl rose to her feet.

'No,' she said, with a trace of a smile on her pale face, 'I will not accept your apologies, Monsieur, but I must prove you wrong and that shall be my revenge. Look. Here come Hastur and Raoul.'

Two men loomed up in the twilight. One had a sack across his shoulders and the other carried a hoop before him as a waiter carries a tray. The hoop was fastened with straps to his shoulders and around the edge of the circlet sat three hooded falcons fitted with tinkling bells. The girl stepped up to the falconer, and with a quick turn of her wrist transferred her falcon to the hoop where it quickly sidled off and nestled among its mates who shook their hooded heads and ruffled their feathers till the belled jesses tinkled again. The other man stepped forward and bowing respectfully took up the hare and dropped it into the game-sack.

'These are my piqueurs,' said the girl turning to me with a gentle dignity. 'Raoul is a good fauconnier and I shall some day make him grand veneur. Hastur is incomparable.'

The two silent men saluted me respectfully.

'Did I not tell you, Monsieur, that I should prove you wrong?' she continued. 'This then is my revenge, that you do me the courtesy of accepting food and shelter at my own house.'

Before I could answer she spoke to the falconers who started instantly across the heath, and with a gracious gesture to me she followed. I don't know whether I made her understand how profoundly grateful I felt, but she seemed pleased to listen, as we walked over the dewy heather.

'Are you not very tired?' she asked.

I had clean forgotten my fatigue in her presence and I told her so.

'Don't you think your gallantry is a little old-fashioned?' she said; and when I looked confused and humbled, she added quietly, 'Oh, I like it, I like everything old-fashioned, and it is delightful to hear you say such pretty things.'

The moorland around us was very still now under its ghostly sheet of mist. The plover had ceased their calling; the crickets and all the little creatures of the fields were silent as we passed, yet it seemed to me as if I could hear them beginning again far behind us. Well in advance the two tall falconers strode across the heather and the faint jingling of the hawk's bells came to our ears in distant murmuring chimes.

Suddenly a splendid hound dashed out of the mist in front, followed by another and another until half a dozen or more were bounding and leaping around the girl beside me. She caressed and quieted them with her gloved hand, speaking to them in quaint terms which I remembered to have seen in old French manuscripts.

Then the falcons on the circlet borne by the falconer ahead began to beat their wings and scream, and from somewhere out of sight the notes of a hunting-horn floated across the moor. The hounds sprang away before us and vanished in the twilight, the falcons flapped and squealed upon their perch and the girl taking up the song of the horn began to hum. Clear and mellow her voice sounded in the night air.

'Chasseur, chasseur, chassez encore,
Quittez Rosette et Jeanneton,
Tonton, tonton, tontaine, tonton,
Ou, pour, rabattre dès l'aurore,
Que les Amours soient de planton,
Tonton, tontaine, tonton.'

As I listened to her lovely voice a gray mass which rapidly grew more distinct loomed up in front, and the horn rang out joyously through the tumult of the hounds and falcons. A torch glimmered at a gate, a light streamed through an opening door, and we stepped upon a wooden bridge which trembled under our feet and rose creaking and straining behind us as we passed over the moat and into a small stone court, walled on every side. From an open doorway a man came and bending in salutation presented a cup to the girl beside me. She took the cup and touched it with her lips, then lowering it turned to me and said in a low voice, 'I bid you welcome'.

At that moment one of the falconers came with another cup, but before handing it to me, presented it to the girl, who tasted it. The falconer made a gesture to receive it, but she hesitated for a moment and then stepping forward offered me the cup with her own hands. I felt this to be an act of extraordinary graciousness, but hardly knew what was expected of me, and did not raise it to my lips at once. The girl flushed crimson. I saw that I must act quickly.

'Mademoiselle,' I faltered, 'a stranger whom you have saved from dangers he may never realize, empties this cup to the gentlest and loveliest hostess of France.'

'In His name,' she murmured, crossing herself as I drained the cup. Then stepping into the doorway she turned to me with a pretty gesture and taking my hand in hers, led me into the house saying again and again: 'You are very welcome, indeed you are welcome to the Château d'Ys.'

II

I awoke next morning with the music of the horn in my ears, and leaping out of the ancient bed, went to a curtained window where the sunlight filtered through little deep-set panes. The horn ceased as I looked into the court below.

A man who might have been brother to the two falconers of the night before stood in the midst of a pack of hounds. A curved horn was strapped over his back, and in his hand he held a long-lashed whip. The dogs whined and yelped, dancing around him in anticipation; there was the stamp of horses too in the walled yard.

'Mount!' cried a voice in Breton, and with a clatter of hoofs the two falconers, with falcons upon their wrists, rode into the courtyard among the hounds. Then I heard another voice which sent the blood throbbing through my heart:

'Piriou Louis, hunt the hounds well and spare neither spur nor whip. Thou Raoul and thou Gaston, see that the *épervier* does not prove himself *niais*, and if it be best in your judgment, *faites courtoisie à l'oiseau. Fardiner un oiseau* like the *mué* there on Hastur's wrist is not difficult, but thou, Raoul mayest not find it so simple to govern that *hagard*. Twice last week he foamed *au vif* and lost the *beccade* although he is used to the *leurre*. The bird acts like a stupid *branchier. Paitre un hagard n'est pas si facile*.'

Was I dreaming? The old language of falconry which I had read in yellow manuscripts – the old forgotten French of the middle ages was sounding in my ears while the hounds bayed and the hawk's bells tinkled accompaniment to the stamping horses. She spoke again in the sweet forgotten language:

'If you would rather attach the *longe* and leave thy *hagard au bloc*, Raoul, I shall say nothing; for it were a pity to spoil so fair a day's sport with an ill-trained *sors. Essimer abaisser* – it is possibly the best way. *Ca lui donnera des reins*. I was perhaps hasty with the bird. It takes time to pass *à la filière* and the exercises *d'escap*.'

Then the falconer Raoul bowed in his stirrups and replied: 'If it be the pleasure of Mademoiselle, I shall keep the hawk'.

'It is my wish,' she answered. 'Falconry I know, but you have yet to give me many a lesson in *Autourserie*, my poor Raoul. Sieur Piriou Louis, mount!'

The huntsman sprang into an archway and in an instant returned, mounted upon a strong black horse, followed by a piqueur also mounted.

'Ah!' she cried joyously, 'speed Glemarec René! speed! speed all! Sound thy horn Sieur Piriou!'

The silvery music of the hunting-horn filled the courtyard, the hounds sprang through the gateway and galloping hoof-beats plunged out of the paved court; loud on the drawbridge, suddenly muffled, then lost in the heather and bracken of the moors. Distant and more distant sounded the horn, until it became so faint that the sudden carol of a soaring lark drowned it in my ears. I heard the voice below responding to some call from within the house.

'I do not regret the chase, I will go another time. Courtesy to the stranger, Pelagie, remember!'

And a feeble voice came quavering from within the house, '*Courtoisie*'.

I stripped, and rubbed myself from head to foot in the huge earthen basin of icy water which stood upon the stone floor at the foot of my bed. Then I looked about for my clothes. They were gone, but on a settle near the door lay a heap of garments which I inspected with astonishment. As my clothes had vanished I was compelled to attire myself in the costume which had evidently been placed there for me to wear while my own clothes dried. Everything was there, cap, shoes, and hunting doublet of silvery gray homespun; but the close-fitting costume and seamless shoes belonged to another century, and I remembered the strange costumes of the three falconers in the courtyard. I was sure that it was not the modern dress of any portion of France or Brittany; but not until I was dressed and stood before a mirror between the windows did I realize that I was clothed much more like a young huntsman of the middle ages than like a Breton of that day. I hesitated and picked up the cap. Should I go down and present myself in that strange guise? There seemed to be no help for it, my own clothes were gone and there was no bell in the ancient chamber to call a servant, so I contented myself with removing a short hawk's feather from the cap, and opening the door went downstairs.

By the fireplace in the large room at the foot of the stairs an old Breton woman sat spinning with a distaff. She looked up at me when I appeared, and, smiling frankly, wished me health in the Breton language, to which I laughingly replied in French. At the same moment my hostess appeared and returned my salutation with a grace and dignity that sent a thrill to my heart. Her lovely head with its dark curly hair was crowned with a head-dress which set all doubts as to the epoch of my own costume at rest. Her slender figure was exquisitely set off in the homespun hunting-gown edged with silver, and on her gauntlet-covered wrist she bore one of her petted hawks. With perfect simplicity she took my hand and led me into the garden in the court, and seating herself before a table invited me very sweetly to sit beside her. Then she asked me in her soft quaint accent how I had passed the night and whether I was very much inconvenienced by wearing the clothes which old Pelagie had put there for me while I slept. I looked at my own clothes and shoes, drying in the sun by the garden-wall, and hated them. What horrors they were compared with the graceful costume which I now wore! I told her this laughing, but she agreed with me very seriously.

'We will throw them away,' she said in a quiet voice. In my astonishment I attempted to explain that I not only could not think of accepting clothes from anybody, although for all I knew it might be the custom of hospitality in that part of the country, but that I should cut an impossible figure if I returned to France clothed as I was then.

She laughed and tossed her pretty head, saying something in old French which I did not understand, and then Pelagie trotted out with a tray on which stood two bowls of milk, a loaf of white bread; fruit, a platter of honey-comb, and a flagon of deep red wine. 'You see I have not yet broken my fast because I wished you to eat with me. But I am very hungry,' she smiled.

'I would rather die than forget one word of what you have said!' I blurted out while my cheeks burned. 'She will think me mad,' I added to myself, but she turned to me with sparkling eyes.

'Ah!' she murmured. 'Then Monsieur knows all that there is of chivalry—'

She crossed herself and broke bread – I sat and watched her white hands, not daring to raise my eyes to hers.

'Will you not eat,' she asked; 'why do you look so troubled?'

Ah, why? I knew it now. I knew I would give my life to

touch with my lips those rosy palms – I understood now that from the moment when I looked into her dark eyes there on the moor last night I had loved her. My great and sudden passion held me speechless.

'Are you ill at ease?' she asked again.

Then like a man who pronounces his own doom I answered in a low voice: 'Yes, I am ill at ease for love of you.' And as she did not stir nor answer, the same power moved my lips in spite of me and I said, 'I, who am unworthy of the lightest of your thoughts, I who abuse hospitality and repay your gentle courtesy with bold presumption, I love you.'

She leaned her head upon her hands, and answered softly, 'I love you. Your words are very dear to me. I love you.'

'Then I shall win you.'

'Win me,' she replied.

But all the time I had been sitting silent, my face turned toward her. She also silent, her sweet face resting on her upturned palm, sat facing me, and as her eyes looked into mine, I knew that neither she nor I had spoken human speech; but I knew that her soul had answered mine, and I drew myself up feeling youth and joyous love coursing through every vein. She, with a bright color in her lovely face, seemed as one awakened from a dream, and her eyes sought mine with a questioning glance which made me tremble with delight. We broke our fast, speaking of ourselves. I told her my name and she told me hers, the Demoiselle Jeanne d'Ys.

She spoke of her father and mother's death, and how the nineteen of her years had been passed in the little fortified farm alone with her nurse Pelagie, Glemarec René the piqueur, and the four falconers, Raoul, Gaston, Hastur, and the Sieur Piriou Louis, who had served her father. She had never been outside the moorland – never even had seen a human soul before, except the falconers and Pelagie. She did not know how she had heard of Kerselec; perhaps the falconers had spoken of it. She knew the legends of Loup

Garou and Jeanne la Flamme from her nurse Pelagie. She embroidered and spun flax. Her hawks and hounds were her only distraction. When she had met me there on the moor she had been so frightened that she almost dropped at the sound of my voice. She had, it was true, seen ships at sea from the cliffs, but as far as the eye could reach the moors over which she galloped were destitute of any sign of human life. There was a legend which old Pelagie told, how anybody once lost in the unexplored moorland might never return, because the moors were enchanted. She did not know whether it was true, she never had thought about it until she met me. She did not know whether the falconers had even been outside or whether they could go if they would. The books in the house which Pelagie the nurse had taught her to read were hundreds of years old.

All this she told me with a sweet seriousness seldom seen in any one but children. My own name she found easy to pronounce and insisted, because my first name was Philip, I must have French blood in me. She did not seem curious to learn anything about the outside world, and I thought perhaps she considered it had forfeited her interest and respect from the stories of her nurse.

We were still sitting at the table and she was throwing grapes to the small field birds which came fearlessly to our very feet.

I began to speak in a vague way of going, but she would not hear of it, and before I knew it I had promised to stay a week and hunt with hawk and hound in their company. I also obtained permission to come again from Kerselec and visit her after my return.

'Why,' she said innocently, 'I do not know what I should do if you never came back'; and I, knowing that I had no right to awaken her with the sudden shock which the avowal of my own love would bring to her, sat silent, hardly daring to breathe.

'You will come very often?' she said.

'Very often,' I said.

'Every day?'

'Every day.'

'Oh,' she sighed, 'I am very happy – come and see my hawks.'

She rose and took my hand again with a childlike innocence of possession, and we walked through the garden and fruit trees to a grassy lawn which was bordered by a brook. Over the lawn were scattered fifteen or twenty stumps of trees – partially imbedded in the grass – and upon all of these except two sat falcons. They were attached to the stumps by thongs which were in turn fastened with still rivets to their legs just above the talons. A little stream of pure spring water flowed in a winding course within easy distance of each perch.

The birds set up a clamor when the girl appeared, but she went from one to another caressing some, taking others for an instant upon her wrist, or stooping to adjust their jesses.

'Are they not pretty?' she said. 'See, here is a falcon-gentil. We call it "ignoble", because it takes the quarry in direct chase. This is a blue falcon. In falconry we call it "noble" because it rises over the quarry, and wheeling, drops upon it from above. This white bird is a gerfalcon from the north. It is also "noble"! Here is a merlin, and this tiercelet is a falcon-heroner.'

I asked her how she had learned the old language of falconry. She did not remember, but thought her father must have taught it to her when she was very young.

Then she led me away and showed me the young falcons still in the nest. 'They are termed *niais* in falconry,' she explained. 'A *branchier* is the young bird which is just able to leave the nest and hop from branch to branch. A young bird which has not yet moulted is called a *sors*, and a *mué* is a hawk which has moulted in captivity. When we catch a wild falcon which has changed its plumage we term it a *hagard*. Raoul first taught me to dress a falcon. Shall I teach you how it is done?'

She seated herself on the bank of the stream among the falcons and I threw myself at her feet to listen.

Then the Demoiselle d'Ys held up one rosy-tipped finger and began very gravely.

'First one must catch the falcon.'

'I am caught,' I answered.

She laughed very prettily and told me my *dressage* would perhaps be difficult as I was noble.

'I am already tamed,' I replied; 'jessed and belled.'

She laughed, delighted. 'Oh, my brave falcon; then you will return at my call?'

'I am yours,' I answered gravely.

She sat silent for a moment. Then the color heightened in her cheeks and she held up a finger again saying,'Listen; I wish to speak of falconry—'

'I listen, Countess Jeanne d'Ys.'

But again she fell into the reverie, and her eyes seemed fixed on something beyond the summer clouds.

'Philip,' she said at last.

'Jeanne,' I whispered.

'That is all – that is what I wished,' she sighed – 'Philip and Jeanne.'

She held her hand toward me and I touched it with my lips.

'Win me,' she said, but this time it was the body and soul which spoke in unison.

After a while she began again: 'Let us speak of falconry'.

'Begin,' I replied; 'we have caught the falcon.'

Then Jeanne d'Ys took my hand in both of hers and told me how with infinite patience the young falcon was taught to perch upon the wrist, how little by little it became used to the belled jesses and the *chaperon à cornette*.

'They must first have a good appetite,' she said, 'then little by little I reduce their nourishment which in falconry we call *pât*. When after many nights passed *au bloc* as these birds are now, I prevail upon the *hagard* to stay quietly on the wrist, then the bird is ready to be taught to come for its food. I fix the *pât* to the end of a thong or *leurre*, and teach the bird to come to me as soon as I begin to whirl the cord in circles about my head. At first I drop the *pât* when the falcon comes, and he eats the food on the ground. After a little he will learn to seize the *leurre* in motion as I whirl it around my head, or drag it over the ground. After that it is easy to teach the falcon to strike at game, always remembering to *faire courtoisie à l'oiseau,* that is, to allow the bird to taste the quarry.'

A squeal from one of the falcons interrupted her, and she arose to adjust the *longe* which had become whipped about the *bloc*, but the bird still flapped its wings and screamed.

'What *is* the matter?' she said; 'Philip, can you see?'

I looked around and at first saw nothing to cause the commotion which was now heightened by the screams and flappings of all the birds. Then my eye fell upon the flat rock beside the stream from which the girl had risen. A gray serpent was moving slowly across the surface of the boulder, and the eyes in its flat triangular head sparkled like jet.

'A couleuvre,' she said quickly.

'It is harmless, is it not?' I asked.

She pointed to the black V-shaped figure on the neck.

'It is certain death,' she said; 'it is a viper.'

We watched the reptile moving slowly over the smooth rock to where the sunlight fell in a broad warm patch.

I started forward to examine it, but she clung to my arm crying, 'Don't, Philip, I am afraid.'

'For me?'

'For you, Philip – I love you.'

Then I took her in my arms and kissed her on the lips, but all I could say was: 'Jeanne, Jeanne, Jeanne'. And as she lay trembling on my breast, something struck my foot in the grass below, but I did not heed it. Then again something struck my ankle, and a sharp pain shot through me. I looked into the sweet face of Jeanne d'Ys and kissed her, and with all my strength lifted her in my arms and flung her from me. Then bending, I tore the viper from my ankle, and set my heel upon its head. I remember feeling weak and numb – I remember falling to the ground. Through my slowly glazing eyes I saw Jeanne's white face bending close to mine, and when the light in my eyes went out I still felt her arms about my neck, and her soft cheek against my drawn lips.

When I opened my eyes, I looked around in terror. Jeanne was gone. I saw the stream and the flat rock; I saw the crushed viper in the grass beside me, but the hawks and the *blocs* had disappeared. I sprang to my feet. The garden, the fruit trees, the drawbridge and the walled court were gone. I stared stupidly at a heap of crumbling ruins, ivy-covered and gray, through which great trees had pushed their way. I crept forward, dragging my numbed foot, and as I moved, a falcon sailed from the tree-tops among the ruins and soaring, mounting in narrowing circles, faded and vanished in the clouds above.

'Jeanne, Jeanne,' I cried, but my voice died on my lips and I fell on my knees among the weeds. And as God willed it, I, not knowing, had fallen kneeling before a crumbling shrine carved in stone for our Mother of Sorrows. I saw the sad face of the Virgin wrought in the cold stone. I saw the cross and thorns at her feet, and beneath it I read:

'PRAY FOR THE SOUL OF THE
DEMOISELLE JEANNE D'YS,
WHO DIED
IN HER YOUTH FOR LOVE OF
PHILIP, A STRANGER.
A.D. 1573.'

But upon the icy slab lay a woman's glove still warm and fragrant.

THE KEY TO GRIEF

'The wild hawk to the wind-swept sky
The deer to the wholesome wold,
And the heart of a man to the heart of a maid,
As it was in the days of old.'

KIPLING

I

They were doing their work very badly. They got the rope around his neck, and tied his wrists with moose-bush withes, but again he fell, sprawling, turning, twisting over the leaves, tearing up everything around him like a trapped panther.

He got the rope away from them; he clung to it with bleeding fists; he set his white teeth in it, until the jute strands relaxed, unravelled, and snapped, gnawed through by his white teeth.

Twice Tully struck him with a gum hook. The dull blows fell on flesh rigid as stone.

Panting, foul with forest mold and rotten leaves, hands and face smeared with blood, he sat up on the ground, glaring at the circle of men around him.

'Shoot him!' gasped Tully, dashing the sweat from his bronzed brow; and Bates, breathing heavily, sat down on a log and dragged a revolver from his rear pocket. The man on the ground watched him; there was froth in the corners of his mouth.

'Git back!' whispered Bates, but his voice and hand trembled. 'Kent,' he stammered, 'won't ye hang?'

The man on the ground glared.

'Ye've got to die, Kent,' he urged; 'they all say so. Ask Lefty Sawyer; ask Dyce; ask Carrots – He's got to swing fur it – ain't he, Tully? – Kent, fur God's sake, swing fur these here gents!'

The man on the ground panted; his bright eyes never moved.

After a moment Tully sprang on him again. There was a flurry of leaves, a crackle, a gasp and a grunt, then the thumping and thrashing of two bodies writhing in the brush. Dyce and Carrots jumped on the prostrate men. Lefty Sawyer caught the rope again, but the jute strands gave way and he stumbled. Tully began to scream, 'He's chokin' me!' Dyce staggered out into the open, moaning over a broken wrist.

'Shoot!' shouted Lefty Sawyer, and dragged Tully aside. 'Shoot, Jim Bates! Shoot straight, b'God!'

'Git back!' gasped Bates, rising from the fallen log.

The crowd parted right and left; a quick report rang out – another – another. Then from the whirl of smoke a tall form staggered, dealing blows – blows that sounded sharp as the crack of a whip.

'He's off! Shoot straight!' they cried.

There was a gallop of heavy boots in the woods. Bates, faint and dazed, turned his head.

'Shoot!' shrieked Tully.

But Bates was sick; his smoking revolver fell to the ground; his white face and pale eyes contracted. It lasted only a moment; he started after the others, plunging, wallowing through thickets of osier and hemlock underbrush.

Far ahead he heard Kent crashing on like a young moose in November, and he knew he was making for the shore. The others knew too. Already the gray gleam of the sea cut a straight line along the forest edge; already the soft clash of the surf on the rocks broke faintly through the forest silence.

'He's got a canoe there!' bawled Tully. 'He'll be into it!'

And he was into it, kneeling in the bow, driving his paddle to the handle. The rising sun gleamed like red lightning on the flashing blade; the canoe shot to the crest of a wave, hung, bows dripping in the wind, dropped into the depths, glided, tipped, rolled, shot up again, staggered, and plunged on.

Tully ran straight out into the cove surf; the water broke against his chest, bare and wet with sweat. Bates sat down on a worn black rock and watched the canoe listlessly.

The canoe dwindled to a speck of gray and silver; and when Carrots, who had run back to the gum camp for a rifle, returned, the speck on the water might have been easier to hit than a loon's head at twilight. So Carrots, being thrifty by nature, fired once, and was satisfied to save the other cartridges. The canoe was still visible, making for the open sea. Somewhere beyond the horizon lay the keys, a string of rocks bare as skulls, black and slimy where the sea cut their base, white on the crests with the excrement of sea birds.

'He's makin' fur the Key to Grief!' whispered Bates to Dyce.

Dyce, moaning, and nursing his broken wrist, turned a sick face out to sea.

The last rock seaward was the Key to Grief, a splintered pinnacle polished by the sea. From the Key to Grief, seaward a day's paddle, if a man dared, lay the long wooded island in the ocean known as Grief on the charts of the bleak coast.

In the history of the coast, two men had made the voyage to the Key to Grief, and from there to the island. One of these was a rum-crazed pelt hunter, who lived to come back; the other was a college youth; they found his battered canoe at sea, and a day later his battered body was flung up in the cove.

So, when Bates whispered to Dyce, and when Dyce called to the others, they knew that the end was not far off for Kent and his canoe; and they turned away into the forest, sullen, but satisfied that Kent would get his dues when the devil got his.

Lefty spoke vaguely of the wages of sin. Carrots, with an eye to thrift, suggested a plan for an equitable division of Kent's property.

When they reached the gum camp they piled Kent's personal effects on a blanket.

Carrots took the inventory: a revolver, two gum hooks, a fur cap, a nickel-plated watch, a pipe, a pack of new cards, a gum sack, forty pounds of spruce gum, and a frying pan.

Carrots shuffled the cards, picked out the joker, and flipped it pensively into the fire. Then he dealt cold decks all around.

When the goods and chattels of their late companion had been divided by chance – for there was no chance to cheat – somebody remembered Tully.

'He's down there on the coast, starin' after the canoe,' said Bates huskily.

He rose and walked toward a heap on the ground covered by a blanket. He started to lift the blanket, hesitated, and finally turned away. Under the blanket lay Tully's brother, shot the night before by Kent.

'Guess we'd better wait till Tully comes,' said Carrots uneasily. Bates and Kent had been campmates. An hour later Tully walked into camp.

He spoke to no one that day. In the morning Bates found him down on the coast digging, and said: 'Hello, Tully! Guess we ain't much hell on lynchin'!'

'Naw,' said Tully. 'Git a spade.'

'Goin' to plant him there?'

'Yep.'

'Where he kin hear them waves?'

'Yep.'

'Purty spot.'

'Yep.'

'Which way will he face?'

'Where he kin watch fur that damned canoe!' cried Tully fiercely.

'He – he can't see,' ventured Bates uneasily. 'He's dead, ain't he?'

'He'll heave up that there sand when the canoe comes back! An' it's a-comin'! An' Bud Kent'll be in it, dead or alive! Git a spade!'

The pale light of superstition flickered in Bates' eyes. He hesitated.

'The – the dead can't see,' he began; 'kin they?'

Tully turned a distorted face toward him.

'Yer lie!' he roared. 'My brother kin see, dead or livin'! An' he'll see the hangin' of Bud Kent! An' he'll git up outer the grave fur to see it, Bill Bates! I'm tellin' ye! I'm tellin' ye! Deep as I'll plant him, he'll heave that there sand and call to me, when the canoe comes in! I'll hear him; I'll be here! An' we'll live to see the hangin' of Bud Kent!'

About sundown they planted Tully's brother, face to the sea.

II

On the Key to Grief the green waves rub all day. White at the summit, black at the base, the shafted rocks rear splintered pinnacles, slanting like channel buoys. On the polished pillars sea birds brood – white-winged, bright-eyed sea birds, that nestle and preen and flap and clatter their orange-coloured beaks when the sifted spray drives and drifts across the reef.

As the sun rose, painting crimson streaks criss-cross over the waters, the sea birds sidled together, huddling row on row, steeped in downy drowse.

Where the sun of noon burnished the sea, an opal wave washed, listless, noiseless; a sea bird stretched one listless wing.

And into the silence of the waters a canoe glided, bronzed by the sunlight, jewelled by the salt drops stringing from prow to thwart, seaweed a-trail in the diamond-flashing wake, and in the bow a man dripping with sweat.

Up rose the gulls, sweeping in circles, turning, turning over rock and sea, and their clamor filled the sky, starting little rippling echoes among the rocks.

The canoe grated on a shelf of ebony; the seaweed rocked and washed; the little sea crabs sheered sideways, down, down into limpid depths of greenest shadows. Such was the coming of Bud Kent to the Key to Grief.

He drew the canoe halfway up the shelf of rock and sat down, breathing heavily, one brown arm across the bow. For an hour he sat there. The sweat dried under his eyes. The sea birds came back, filling the air with soft querulous notes.

There was a livid mark around his neck, a red, raw circle. The salt wind stung it; the sun burned it into his flesh like a collar of red-hot steel. He touched it at times; once he washed it with cold salt water.

Far in the north a curtain of mist hung on the sea, dense, motionless as the fog on the Grand Banks. He never moved his eyes from it; he knew what it was. Behind it lay the Island of Grief.

All the year round the Island of Grief is hidden by the banks of mist, ramparts of dead white fog encircling it on every side. Ships give it wide berth. Some speak of warm springs on the island whose waters flow far out to sea, rising in steam eternally.

The pelt hunter had come back with tales of forests and deer and flowers everywhere; but he had been drinking much, and much was forgiven him.

The body of the college youth tossed up in the cove on the mainland was battered out of recognition, but some said, when found, one hand clutched a crimson blossom half wilted, but broad as a sap pan.

So Kent lay motionless beside his canoe, burned with

thirst, every nerve vibrating, thinking of all these things. It was not fear that whitened the firm flesh under the tan; it was the fear of fear. He must not think – he must throttle dread; his eyes must never falter, his head never turn from that wall of mist across the sea. With set teeth he crushed back terror; with glittering eyes he looked into the hollow eyes of fright. And so he conquered fear.

He rose. The sea birds whirled up into the sky, pitching, tossing, screaming, till the sharp flapping of their pinions set the snapping echoes flying among the rocks.

Under the canoe's sharp prow the kelp bobbed and dipped and parted; the sunlit waves ran out ahead, glittering, dancing. Splash! splash! bow and stern! And now he knelt again, and the polished paddle swung and dipped, and swept and swung and dipped again.

Far behind, the clamour of the sea birds lingered in his ears, till the mellow dip of the paddle drowned all sound and the sea was a sea of silence.

No wind came to cool the hot sweat on cheek and breast. The sun blazed a path of flame before him, and he followed out into the waste of waters. The still ocean divided under the bows and rippled innocently away on either side, tinkling, foaming, sparkling like the current in a woodland brook. He looked around at the world of flattened water, and the fear of fear rose up and gripped his throat again. Then he lowered his head, like a tortured bull, and shook the fear of fear from his throat, and drove the paddle into the sea as a butcher stabs, to the hilt.

So at last he came to the wall of mist. It was thin at first, thin and cool, but it thickened and grew warmer, and the fear of fear dragged at his head, but he would not look behind.

Into the fog the canoe shot; the gray water ran by, high as the gunwales, oily, silent. Shapes flickered across the bows, pillars of mist that rode the waters, robed in films of tattered shadows. Gigantic forms towered to dizzy heights above him, shaking out shredded shrouds of cloud. The vast draperies of the fog swayed and hung and trembled as he brushed them; the white twilight deepened to a sombre gloom. And now it grew thinner; the fog became a mist, and the mist a haze, and the haze floated away and vanished into the blue of the heavens.

All around lay a sea of pearl and sapphire, lapping, lapping on a silver shoal.

So he came to the Island of Grief.

III

On the silver shoal the waves washed and washed, breaking like crushed opals where the sands sang with the humming froth.

Troops of little shore birds, wading on the shoal, tossed their sun-tipped wings and scuttled inland, where, dappled with shadow from the fringing forest, the white beach of the island stretched.

The water all around was shallow, limpid as crystal, and he saw the ribbed sand shining on the bottom, where purple seaweed floated, and delicate sea creatures darted and swarmed and scattered again at the dip of his paddle.

Like velvet rubbed on velvet the canoe brushed across the sand. He staggered to his feet, stumbled out, dragged the canoe high up under the trees, turned it bottom upward, and sank beside it, face downward in the sand. Sleep came to drive away the fear of fear, but hunger, thirst, and fever fought with sleep, and he dreamed – dreamed of a rope that sawed his neck, of the fight in the woods, and the shots. He dreamed, too, of the camp, of his forty pounds of spruce gum, of Tully, and of Bates. He dreamed of the fire and the smoke-scorched kettle, of the foul odor of musty bedding, of the greasy cards, and of his own new pack, hoarded for weeks to please the others. All this he dreamed, lying there face downward in the sand; but he did not dream of the face of the dead.

The shadows of the leaves moved on his blond head, crisp

with clipped curls. A butterfly flitted around him, alighting now on his legs, now on the back of his bronzed hands. All the afternoon the bees hung droning among the wildwood blossoms; the leaves above scarcely rustled; the shore birds brooded along the water's edge; the thin tide, sleeping on the sand, mirrored the sky.

Twilight paled the zenith; a breeze moved in the deeper woods; a star glimmered, went out, glimmered again, faded, and glimmered.

Night came. A moth darted to and fro under the trees; a beetle hummed around a heap of seaweed and fell scrambling in the sand. Somewhere among the trees a sound had become distinct, the song of a little brook, melodious, interminable. He heard it in his dream; it threaded all his dreams like a needle of silver, and like a needle it pricked him – pricked his dry throat and cracked lips. It could not awake him; the cool night swathed him head and foot.

Toward dawn a bird woke up and piped. Other birds stirred, restless, half awakened; a gull spread a cramped wing on the shore, preened its feathers, scratched its tufted neck, and took two drowsy steps toward the sea.

The sea breeze stirred out behind the mist bank; it raised the feathers on the sleeping gulls; it set the leaves whispering. A twig snapped, broke off, and fell. Kent stirred, sighed, trembled, and awoke.

The first thing he heard was the song of the brook, and he stumbled straight into the woods. There it lay, a thin, deep stream in the gray morning light, and he stretched himself beside it and laid his cheek in it. A bird drank in the pool, too – a little fluffy bird, bright-eyed and fearless.

His knees were firmer when at last he rose, heedless of the drops that beaded lips and chin. With his knife he dug and scraped at some white roots that hung half meshed in the bank of the brook, and when he had cleaned them in the pool he ate them.

The sun stained the sky when he went down to the canoe,

but the eternal curtain of fog, far out at sea, hid it as yet from sight.

He lifted the canoe, bottom upwards, to his head, and, paddle and pole in either hand, carried it into the forest.

After he had set it down he stood a moment, opening and shutting his knife. Then he looked up into the trees. There were birds there, if he could get at them. He looked at the brook. There were prints of his fingers in the sand; there, too, was the print of something else – a deer's pointed hoof.

He had nothing but his knife. He opened it again and looked at it.

That day he dug for clams and ate them raw. He waded out into the shallows, too, and jabbed at fish with his setting pole, but hit nothing except a yellow crab.

Fire was what he wanted. He hacked and chipped at flinty-looking pebbles, and scraped tinder from a stick of sun-dried driftwood. His knuckles bled, but no fire came.

That night he heard deer in the woods, and could not sleep for thinking, until the dawn came up behind the wall of mist, and he rose with it to drink his fill at the brook and tear raw clams with his white teeth. Again he fought for fire, craving it as he had never craved water, but his knuckles bled, and the knife scraped on the flint in vain.

His mind, perhaps, had suffered somewhat. The white beach seemed to rise and fall like a white carpet on a gusty hearth. The birds, too, that ran along the sand, seemed big and juicy, like partridges; and he chased them, hurling shells and bits of driftwood at them till he could scarcely keep his feet for the rising, plunging beach – or carpet, whichever it was. That night the deer aroused him at intervals. He heard them splashing and grunting and crackling along the brook. Once he arose and stole after them, knife in hand, till a false step into the brook awoke him to his folly, and he felt his way back to the canoe, trembling.

Morning came, and again he drank at the brook, lying on the sand where countless heart-shaped hoofs had passed leaving clean imprints; and again he ripped the raw clams from their shells and swallowed them, whimpering.

All day long the white beach rose and fell and heaved and flattened under his bright dry eyes. He chased the shore birds at times, till the unsteady beach tripped him up and he fell full length in the sand. Then he would rise moaning, and creep into the shadow of the wood, and watch the little song-birds in the branches, moaning, always moaning.

His hands, sticky with blood, hacked steel and flint together, but so feebly that now even the cold sparks no longer came.

He began to fear the advancing night; he dreaded to hear the big warm deer among the thickets. Fear clutched him suddenly, and he lowered his head and set his teeth and shook fear from his throat again.

Then he started aimlessly into the woods, crowding past bushes, scraping trees, treading on moss and twig and mouldy stump, his bruised hands swinging, always swinging.

The sun set in the mist as he came out of the woods on to another beach – a warm, soft beach, crimsoned by the glow in the evening clouds.

And on the sand at his feet lay a young girl asleep, swathed in the silken garment of her own black hair, round limbed, brown, smooth as the bloom on the tawny beach.

A gull flapped overhead, screaming. Her eyes, deeper than night, unclosed. Then her lips parted in a cry, soft with sleep, 'Ihó!'

She rose, rubbing her velvet eyes. 'Ihó!' she cried in wonder; 'Inâh!'

The gilded sand settled around her little feet. Her cheeks crimsoned. 'E-hó! E-hó!' she whispered, and hid her face in her hair.

IV

The bridge of the stars spans the sky seas; the sun and the moon are the travellers who pass over it. This was also known in the lodges of the Isantee, hundreds of years ago. Chaské told it to Hârpam, and when Hârpam knew he told it to Hapéda; and so the knowledge spread to Hârka, and from Winona to Wehârka, up and down, across and ever across, woof and web, until it came to the Island of Grief. And how? God knows!

Weharka, prattling in the tules, may have told Ne-kâ; and Ne-kâ, high in the November clouds, may have told Kay-óshk, who told it to Shinge-bis, who told it to Skeé-skah, who told it to Sé-só-Kah.

Ihó! Inâh! Behold the wonder of it! And this is the fate of all knowledge that comes to the Island of Grief.

As the red glow died in the sky, and the sand swam in shadows, the girl parted the silken curtains of her hair and looked at him.

'Ehó!" she whispered again in soft delight.

For now it was plain to her that he was the sun! He had crossed the bridge of stars in the blue twilight; he had come!

'E-tó!'

She stepped nearer, shivering, faint with the ecstasy of this holy miracle wrought before her.

He was the Sun! His blood streaked the sky at dawn; his blood stained the clouds at even. In his eyes the blue of the sky still lingered, smothering two blue stars; and his body was as white as the breast of the Moon.

She opened both arms, hands timidly stretched, palm upward. Her face was raised to his, her eyes slowly closed; the deep-fringed lids trembled.

Like a young priestess she stood, motionless save for the sudden quiver of a limb, a quick pulse-flutter in the rounded throat. And so she worshipped, naked and unashamed, even after he, reeling, fell heavily forward on his face; even when the evening breeze stealing over the sands stirred the hair on his head, as winds stir the fur of a dead animal in the dust.

When the morning sun peered over the wall of mist, and she saw it was the sun, and she saw him, flung on the sand at her feet, then she knew that he was a man, only a man, pallid as death and smeared with blood.

And yet – miracle of miracles! – the divine wonder in her eyes deepened, and her body seemed to swoon, and fall a-trembling, and swoon again.

For, although it was but a man who lay at her feet, it had been easier for her to look upon a god.

He dreamed that he breathed fire – fire, that he craved as he had never craved water. Mad with delirium, he knelt before the flames, rubbing his torn hands, washing them in the crimson-scented flames. He had water, too, cool scented water, that sprayed his burning flesh, that washed in his eyes, his hair, his throat. After that came hunger, a fierce rending agony, that scorched and clutched and tore at his entrails; but that, too, died away, and he dreamed that he had eaten and all his flesh was warm. Then he dreamed that he slept; and when he slept he dreamed no more.

One day he awoke and found her stretched beside him, soft palms tightly closed, smiling, asleep.

V

Now the days began to run more swiftly than the tide along the tawny beach; and the nights, star-dusted and blue, came and vanished and returned, only to exhale at dawn like perfume from a violet.

They counted hours as they counted the golden bubbles, winking with a million eyes along the foam-flecked shore; and the hours ended, and began, and glimmered, iridescent, and ended as bubbles end in a tiny rainbow haze.

There was still fire in the world; it flashed up at her touch and where she chose. A bow strung with the silk of her own hair, an arrow winged like a sea bird and tipped with shell, a line from the silver tendon of a deer, a hook of polished bone – these were the mysteries he learned, and learned them laughing, her silken head bent close to his.

The first night that the bow was wrought and the glossy string attuned, she stole into the moonlit forest to the brook; and there they stood, whispering, listening, and whispering, though neither understood the voice they loved.

In the deeper woods, Kaug, the porcupine, scraped and snuffed. They heard Wabóse, the rabbit, pit-a-pat, pit-a-pat, loping across dead leaves in the moonlight. Skeé-skah, the wood-duck, sailed past, noiseless, gorgeous as a floating blossom.

Out on the ocean's placid silver, Shinge-bis, the diver, shook the scented silence with his idle laughter, till Kay-óshk, the gray gull, stirred in his slumber. There came a sudden ripple in the stream, a mellow splash, a soft sound on the sand.

'Ihó! Behold!'

'I see nothing.'

The beloved voice was only a wordless melody to her.

'Ihó! Ta-hinca, the red deer! E-hó! The buck will follow!'

'Ta-hinca,' he repeated, notching the arrow.

'E-tó! Ta-mdóka!'

So he drew the arrow to the head, and the gray gull feathers brushed his ear, and the darkness hummed with the harmony of the singing string.

Thus died Ta-mdóka, the buck deer of seven prongs.

VI

As an apple tossed spinning into the air, so spun the world above the hand that tossed it into space.

And one day in early spring, Sé-só-Kah, the robin, awoke at dawn, and saw a girl at the foot of the blossoming tree holding a babe cradled in the silken sheets of her hair.

At its feeble cry, Kaug, the porcupine, raised his quilled head. Wabóse, the rabbit, sat still with palpitating sides. Kay-óshk, the gray gull, tiptoed along the beach.

Kent knelt with one bronzed arm around them both.

'Ihó! Inâh!' whispered the girl, and held the babe up in the rosy flames of dawn.

But Kent trembled as he looked, and his eyes filled. On the pale green moss their shadows lay – three shadows. But the shadow of the babe was white as froth.

Because it was the firstborn son, they named it Chaské; and the girl sang as she cradled it there in the silken vestments of her hair; all day long in the sunshine she sang:

Wâ-wa, wâ-wa, wâ-we – yeá;
Kah-wéen, nee-zhéka Ke-diaus-âi,
Ke-gâh nau-wâi, ne-mé-go S'weén,
Ne-bâun, ne-bâun, ne-dâun-is âis.
E-we wâ-wa, wâ-we – yeá;
E-we wâ-wa, wâ-we – yeá.

Out in the calm ocean, Shinge-bis, the diver, listened, preening his satin breast in silence. In the forest, Ta-hinca, the red deer, turned her delicate head to the wind.

That night Kent thought of the dead, for the first time since he had come to the Key of Grief.

'Aké-u! aké-u!' chirped Sé-só-Kah, the robin. But the dead never come again.

'Beloved, sit close to us,' whispered the girl, watching his troubled eyes. 'Ma-cânte maséca.'

But he looked at the babe and its white shadow on the moss, and he only sighed: 'Ma-cânte maséca, beloved! Death sits watching us across the sea.'

Now for the first time he knew more than the fear of fear; he knew fear. And with fear came grief.

He never before knew that grief lay hidden there in the forest. Now he knew it. Still, that happiness, eternally reborn when two small hands reached up around his neck, when feeble fingers clutched his hand – that happiness that Sé-só-Kah understood, chirping to his brooding mate – that Ta-mdóka knew, licking his dappled fawns – that happiness gave him heart to meet grief calmly, in dreams or in the forest depths, and it helped him to look into the hollow eyes of fear.

He often thought of the camp now; of Bates, his blanket mate; of Dyce, whose wrist he had broken with a blow; of Tully, whose brother he had shot. He even seemed to hear the shot, the sudden report among the hemlocks; again he saw the haze of smoke, he caught a glimpse of a tall form falling through the bushes.

He remembered every minute incident of the trial: Bates's hand laid on his shoulder; Tully, red-bearded and wild-eyed, demanding his death; while Dyce spat and spat and smoked and kicked at the blackened log-ends projecting from the fire. He remembered, too, the verdict, and Tully's terrible laugh; and the new jute rope that they stripped off the market-sealed gum packs.

He thought of these things, sometimes wading out on the shoals, shell-tipped fish spear poised: at such times he would miss his fish. He thought of it sometimes when he knelt by the forest stream listening for Ta-hinca's splash among the cresses: at such moments the feathered shaft whistled far from the mark, and Ta-mdóka stamped and snorted till even the white fisher, stretched on a rotting log, flattened his whiskers and stole away into the forest's blackest depths.

When the child was a year old, hour for hour notched at sunset and sunrise, it prattled with the birds, and called to Ne-Kâ, the wild goose, who called again to the child from the sky: 'Northward! northward, beloved!'

When winter came – there is no frost on the Island of Grief – Ne-Kâ, the wild goose, passing high in the clouds, called: 'Southward! southward, beloved!' And the child answered in a soft whisper of an unknown tongue, till the mother shivered, and covered it with her silken hair.

'O beloved!' said the girl, 'Chaské calls to all things living – to Kaug, the porcupine, to Wabóse, to Kay-óshk, the gray gull – he calls, and they understand.'

Kent bent and looked into her eyes.

'Hush, beloved; it is not *that* I fear.'

'Then what, beloved?'

'His shadow. It is white as surf foam. And at night – I – I have seen—'

'Oh, what?'

'The air about him aglow like a pale rose.'

'Ma cânté maséca. The earth alone lasts. I speak as one dying – I know, O beloved!'

Her voice died away like a summer wind.

'Beloved!' he cried.

But there before him she was changing; the air grew misty, and her hair wavered like shreds of fog, and her slender form swayed, and faded, and swerved, like the mist above a pond.

In her arms the babe was a figure of mist, rosy, vague as a breath on a mirror.

'The earth alone lasts. Inâh! It is the end, O beloved!'

The words came from the mist – a mist as formless as the ether – a mist that drove in and crowded him, that came from the sea, from the clouds from the earth at his feet. Faint with terror, he staggered forward calling, 'Beloved! And thou, Chaské, O beloved! Aké u! Aké u!'

Far out at sea a rosy star glimmered an instant in the mist and went out.

A sea bird screamed, soaring over the waste of fog-smothered waters. Again he saw the rosy star; it came nearer; its reflection glimmered in the water.

'Chaské!' he cried.

He heard a voice, dull in the choking mist.

'O beloved, I am here!' he called again.

There was a sound on the shoal, a flicker in the fog, the flare of a torch, a face white, livid, terrible – the face of the dead.

He fell upon his knees; he closed his eyes and opened them. Tully stood beside him with a coil of rope.

Ihó! Behold the end! The earth alone lasts. The sand, the

opal wave on the golden beach, the sea of sapphire, the dusted starlight, the wind, and love, shall die. Death also shall die, and lie on the shores of the skies like the bleached skull there on the Key to Grief, polished, empty, with, its teeth embedded in the sand.

THE MESSENGER

I

'The bullet entered here,' said Max Fortin, and he placed his middle finger over a smooth hole exactly in the centre of the forehead.

I sat down upon a mound of dry seaweed and unslung my fowling piece.

The little chemist cautiously felt the edges of the shot-hole, first with his middle finger, then with his thumb.

'Let me see the skull again,' said I.

Max Fortin picked it up from the sod. 'It's like all the others,' he observed. I nodded, without offering to take it from him. After a moment he thoughtfully replaced it upon the grass at my feet.

'It's like all the others,' he repeated, wiping his glasses on his handkerchief. 'I thought you might care to see one of the skulls, so I brought this over from the gravel pit. The men from Bannalec are digging yet. They ought to stop.'

'How many skulls are there altogether?' I inquired.

'They found thirty-eight skulls; there are thirty-nine noted in the list. They lie piled up in the gravel pit on the edge of Le Bihan's wheat field. The men are at work yet. Le Bihan is going to stop them.'

'Let's go over,' said I; and I picked up my gun and started across the cliffs, Fortin on one side, Mome on the other.

'Who has the list?' I asked, lighting my pipe. 'You say there is a list?'

'The list was found rolled up in a brass cylinder,' said the little chemist. He added, 'You should not smoke here. You know that if a single spark drifted into the wheat—'

'Ah, but I have a cover to my pipe,' said I, smiling.

Fortin watched me as I closed the pepper-box arrangement over the glowing bowl of the pipe. And then he continued:

'The list was made out on thick yellow paper; the brass tube has preserved it. It is as fresh today as it was in 1760. You shall see it.'

'Is that the date?'

'The list is dated "April, 1760". The Brigadier Durand has it. It is not written in French.'

'Not written in French!' I exclaimed.

'No,' replied Fortin solemnly, 'it is written in Breton.'

'But,' I protested, 'the Breton language was never written or printed in 1760.'

'Except by priests,' said the chemist.

'I have heard of but one priest who ever wrote the Breton language,' I began.

Fortin stole a glance at my face.

'You mean – the Black Priest?' he asked.

I nodded.

Fortin opened his mouth to speak again, hesitated, and finally shut his teeth obstinately over the wheat stem that he was chewing.

'And the Black Priest?' I suggested encouragingly. But I knew it was useless; for it is easier to move the stars from their courses than to make an obstinate Breton talk. We walked on for a minute or two in silence.

'Where is the Brigadier Durand?' I asked, motioning Mome to come out of the wheat, which he was trampling as though it was heather. As I spoke we came in sight of the farther edge of the wheat field and the dark, wet mass of cliffs beyond.

'Durand is down there – you can see him; he stands just behind the Mayor of St Gildas.'

'I see,' said I; and we struck straight down, following a sun-baked cattle path across the heather.

When we reached the edge of the wheat field, Le Bihan, the Mayor of St Gildas, called to me, and I tucked my gun under my arm and skirted the wheat to where he stood.

'Thirty-eight skulls,' he said in his thin, high-pitched voice; 'there is but one more, and I am opposed to further search. I suppose Fortin told you?'

I shook hands with him, and returned the salute of the Brigadier Durand.

'I am opposed to further search,' repeated Le Bihan, nervously picking at the mass of silver buttons which covered the front of his velvet and broadcloth jacket like a breastplate of scale armor.

Durand pursed up his lips, twisted his tremendous moustache, and hooked his thumbs in his sabre belt.

'As for me,' he said, 'I am in favour of further search.'

'Further search for what – for the thirty-ninth skull?' I asked.

Le Bihan nodded. Durand frowned at the sunlit sea, rocking like a bowl of molten gold from the cliffs to the horizon. I followed his eyes. On the dark glistening cliffs, silhouetted against the glare of the sea, sat a cormorant, black, motionless, its horrible head raised towards heaven.

'Where is that list, Durand?' I asked.

The gendarme rummaged in his despatch pouch and produced a brass cylinder about a foot long. Very gravely he unscrewed the head and dumped out a scroll of thick yellow paper closely covered with writing on both sides. At a nod from Le Bihan he handed me the scroll. But I could make nothing of the coarse writing, now faded to a dull brown.

'Come, come, Le Bihan,' I said impatiently, 'translate it, won't you? You and Max Fortin make a lot of mystery out of nothing, it seems.'

Le Bihan went to the edge of the pit where the three Bannalec men were digging, gave an order or two in Breton, and turned to me.

As I came to the edge of the pit the Bannalec men were removing a square piece of sail-cloth from what appeared to be a pile of cobblestones.

'Look!' said Le Bihan shrilly. I looked. The pile below was a heap of skulls. After a moment I clambered down the gravel sides of the pit and walked over to the men of Bannalec. They saluted me gravely, leaning on their picks and shovels, and wiping their sweating faces with sunburned hands.

'How many?' said I in Breton.

'Thirty-eight,' they replied.

I glanced around. Beyond the heap of skulls lay two piles of human bones. Beside these was a mound of broken, rusted bits of iron and steel. Looking closer, I saw that this mound was composed of rusty bayonets, sabre blades, scythe blades, with here and there a tarnished buckle attached to a bit of leather as hard as iron.

I picked up a couple of buttons and a belt plate. The buttons bore the royal arms of England; the belt plate was emblazoned with the English arms, and also with the number '27'.

'I have heard my grandfather speak of the terrible English regiment, the 27th Foot, which landed and stormed the fort up there,' said one of the Bannalec men.

'Oh!' said I; 'then these are the bones of English soldiers?'

'Yes,' said the men of Bannalec.

Le Bihan was calling to me from the edge of the pit above, and I handed the belt plate and buttons to the men and climbed the side of the excavation.

'Well,' said I, trying to prevent Mome from leaping up and licking my face as I emerged from the pit, 'I suppose you know what these bones are. What are you going to do with them?'

'There was a man,' said Le Bihan angrily, 'an Englishman, who passed here in a dogcart on his way to Quimper about an hour ago, and what do you suppose he wished to do?'

'Buy the relics?' I asked, smiling.

'Exactly – the pig!' piped the Mayor of St Gildas. 'Jean Marie Tregunc, who found the bones, was standing there where Max Fortin stands, and do you know what he answered? He spat upon the ground, and said, "Pig of an Englishman, do you take me for a desecrator of graves?"'

I knew Tregunc, a sober, blue-eyed Breton, who lived from one year's end to the other without being able to afford a single bit of meat for a meal.

'How much did the Englishman offer Tregunc?' I asked.

'Two hundred francs for the skulls alone.'

I thought of the relic hunters and the relic buyers on the battlefields of our civil war.

'Seventeen hundred and sixty is long ago,' I said.

'Respect for the dead can never die,' said Fortin.

'And the English soldiers came here to kill your fathers and burn your homes,' I continued.

'They were murderers and thieves, but – they are dead,' said Tregunc, coming up from the beach below, his long sea rake balanced on his dripping jersey.

'How much do you earn every year, Jean Marie?' I asked, turning to shake hands with him.

'Two hundred and twenty francs, monsieur.'

'Forty-five dollars a year,' I said. 'Bah! You are worth more, Jean. Will you take care of my garden for me? My wife wished me to ask you. I think it would be worth one hundred francs a month to you and to me. Come on, Le Bihan – come along, Fortin – and you, Durand. I want somebody to translate that list into French for me.'

Tregunc stood gazing at me, his blue eyes dilated.

'You may begin at once,' I said, smiling, 'if the salary suits you?'

'It suits,' said Tregunc, fumbling for his pipe in a silly way that annoyed Le Bihan.

'Then go and begin your work,' cried the mayor impatiently; and Tregunc started across the moors towards St Gildas, taking off his velvet-ribboned cap to me and gripping his sea rake very hard.

'You offer him more than my salary,' said the mayor, after a moment's contemplation of his silver buttons.

'Pooh!' said I, 'what do you do for your salary except play dominoes with Max Fortin at the Groix Inn?'

Le Bihan turned red, but Durand rattled his sabre and winked at Max Fortin, and I slipped my arm through the arm of the sulky magistrate, laughing.

'There's a shady spot under the cliff,' I said; 'come on, Le Bihan, and read me what is in the scroll.'

In a few moments we reached the shadow of the cliff, and I threw myself upon the turf, chin on hand, to listen.

The gendarme, Durand, also sat down, twisting his moustache into needlelike points. Fortin leaned against the cliff, polishing his glasses and examining us with vague, near-sighted eyes; and Le Bihan, the mayor, planted himself in our midst, rolling up the scroll and tucking it under his arm.

'First of all,' he began in a shrill voice, 'I am going to light my pipe, and while lighting it I shall tell you what I have heard about the attack on the fort yonder. My father told me; his father told him.'

He jerked his head in the direction of the ruined fort, a small, square stone structure on the sea cliff, now nothing but crumbling walls. Then he slowly produced a tobacco pouch, a bit of flint and tinder, and a long-stemmed pipe fitted with a microscopical bowl of baked clay. To fill such a pipe requires ten minutes' close attention. To smoke it to a finish takes but four puffs. It is very Breton, this Breton pipe. It is the crystallization of everything Breton.

'Go on,' said I, lighting a cigarette.

'The fort,' said the mayor, 'was built by Louis XIV, and was dismantled twice by the English. Louis XV restored it in 1739. In 1760 it was carried by assault by the English. They came across from the island of Groix – three shiploads – and they stormed the fort and sacked St Julien yonder, and they started to burn St Gildas – you can see the marks

of their bullets on my house yet; but the men of Bannalec
and the men of Lorient fell upon them with pike and scythe
and blunderbuss, and those who did not run away lie there
below in the gravel pit now – thirty-eight of them.'

'And the thirty-ninth skull?' I asked, finishing my cigarette.

The mayor succeeded in filling his pipe, and now he began
to put his tobacco pouch away.

'The thirty-ninth skull,' he mumbled, holding the pipestem
between his defective teeth – 'the thirty-ninth skull is no
business of mine. I have told the Bannalec men to cease
digging.'

'But what is – whose is the missing skull?' I persisted
curiously.

The mayor was busy trying to strike a spark to his tinder.
Presently he set it aglow, applied it to his pipe, took the
prescribed four puffs, knocked the ashes out of the bowl,
and gravely replaced the pipe in his pocket.

'The missing skull?' he asked.

'Yes,' said I, impatiently.

The mayor slowly unrolled the scroll and began to translate the Breton into French. And this is what he read:

> 'On the Cliffs of St Gildas.
> 'April 13, 1760.

> 'On this day, by order of the Count of Soisic, general
> in chief of the Breton forces now lying in Kerselec
> Forest, the bodies of thirty-eight English soldiers of the
> 27th, 50th, and 72nd regiments of Foot were buried
> in this spot, together with their arms and equipments.'

The mayor paused and glanced at me reflectively.

'Go on, Le Bihan,' I said.

'With them,' continued the mayor, turning the scroll and
reading on the other side,

'was buried the body of that vile traitor who betrayed the fort to the English. The manner of his death was as follows: By order of the most noble Count of Soisic, the traitor was first branded upon the forehead with the brand of the arrowhead. The iron burned through the flesh, and was pressed heavily so that the brand should even burn into the bone of the skull. The traitor was then led out and bidden to kneel. He admitted having guided the English from the island of Groix. Although a priest and a Frenchman, he had violated his priestly office to aid him in discovering the password to the fort. This password he extorted during confession from a young Breton girl who was in the habit of rowing across from the island of Groix to visit her husband in the fort. When the fort fell, this young girl, crazed by the death of her husband, sought the Count of Soisic and told how the priest had forced her to confess to him all she knew about the fort. The priest was arrested at St Gildas as he was about to cross the river to Lorient. When arrested he cursed the girl, Marie Trevec—'

'What!' I exclaimed, 'Marie Trevec!'
'Marie Trevec,' repeated Le Bihan:

'the priest cursed Marie Trevec, and all her family and descendants. He was shot as he knelt, having a mask of leather over his face, because the Bretons who composed the squad of execution refused to fire at a priest unless his face was concealed. The priest was l'Abbé Sorgue, commonly known as the Black Priest on account of his dark face and swarthy eyebrows. He was buried with a stake through his heart.'

Le Bihan paused, hesitated, looked at me, and handed the manuscript back to Durand. The gendarme took it and slipped it into the brass cylinder.

'So,' I said, 'the thirty-ninth skull is the skull of the Black Priest.'

'Yes,' said Fortin. 'I hope they won't find it.'

'I have forbidden them to proceed,' said the mayor querulously. 'You heard me, Max Fortin.'

I rose and picked up my gun. Mome came and pushed his head into my hand.

'That's a fine dog,' observed Durand, also rising.

'Why don't you wish to find his skull?' I asked Le Bihan. 'It would be curious to see whether the arrow brand really burned into the bone.'

'There is something in that scroll that I didn't read to you,' said the mayor grimly. 'Do you wish to know what it is?'

'Of course,' I replied in surprise.

'Give me the scroll again, Durand,' he said; then he read from the bottom:

'I, l'Abbé Sorgue, forced to write the above by my executioners, have written it in my own blood; and with it I leave my curse. My curse on St Gildas, on Marie Trevec, and on her descendants. I will come back to St Gildas when my remains are disturbed. Woe to that Englishman whom my branded skull shall touch!'

'What rot!' I said. 'Do you believe it was really written in his own blood?'

'I am going to test it,' said Fortin, 'at the request of Monsieur le Maire. I am not anxious for the job, however.'

'See,' said Le Bihan, holding out the scroll to me, 'it is signed, "l'Abbé Sorgue".'

I glanced curiously over the paper.

'It must be the Black Priest,' I said. 'He was the only man who wrote in the Breton language. This is a wonderfully interesting discovery, for now, at last, the mystery of the Black Priest's disappearance is cleared up. You will, of course, send this scroll to Paris, Le Bihan?'

'No,' said the mayor obstinately, 'it shall be buried in the pit below where the rest of the Black Priest lies.'

I looked at him and recognized that argument would be useless. But still I said, 'It will be a loss to history, Monsieur Le Bihan.'

'All the worse for history, then,' said the enlightened Mayor of St Gildas.

We had sauntered back to the gravel pit while speaking. The men of Bannalec were carrying the bones of the English soldiers towards the St Gildas cemetery, on the cliffs to the east, where already a knot of white-coiffed women stood in attitudes of prayer; and I saw the sombre robe of a priest among the crosses of the little graveyard.

'They were thieves and assassins; they are dead now,' muttered Max Fortin.

'Respect the dead,' repeated the Mayor of St Gildas, looking after the Bannalec men.

'It was written in that scroll that Marie Trevec, of Groix Island, was cursed by the priest – she and her descendants,' I said, touching Le Bihan on the arm. 'There was a Marie Trevec who married an Yves Trevec of St Gildas—'

'It is the same,' said Le Bihan, looking at me obliquely.

'Oh!' said I; 'then they were ancestors of my wife.'

'Do you fear the curse?' asked Le Bihan.

'What?' I laughed.

'There was the case of the Purple Emperor,' said Max Fortin timidly.

Startled for a moment, I faced him, then shrugged my shoulders and kicked at a smooth bit of rock which lay near the edge of the pit, almost embedded in gravel.

'Do you suppose the Purple Emperor drank himself crazy because he was descended from Marie Trevec?' I asked contemptuously.

'Of course not,' said Max Fortin hastily.

'Of course not,' piped the mayor. 'I only – Hello! what's that you're kicking?'

'What?' said I, glancing down, at the same time involuntarily giving another kick. The smooth bit of rock dislodged itself and rolled out of the loosened gravel at my feet.

'The thirty-ninth skull!' I exclaimed. 'By jingo, it's the noddle of the Black Priest! See! There is the arrowhead branded on the front!'

The mayor stepped back. Max Fortin also retreated. There was a pause, during which I looked at them, and they looked anywhere but at me.

'I don't like it,' said the mayor at last, in a husky, high voice. 'I don't like it! The scroll says he will come back to St Gildas when his remains are disturbed. I – I don't like it, Monsieur Darrel—'

'Bosh!' said I; 'the poor wicked devil is where he can't get out. For Heaven's sake, Le Bihan, what is this stuff you are talking in the year of grace 1896?'

The mayor gave me a look.

'And he says "Englishman". You are an Englishman, Monsieur Darrel,' he announced.

'You know better. You know I'm an American.'

'It's all the same,' said the Mayor of St Gildas, obstinately.

'No, it isn't!' I answered, much exasperated, and deliberately pushed the skull till it rolled into the bottom of the gravel pit below.

'Cover it up,' said I; 'bury the scroll with it too, if you insist, but I think you ought to send it to Paris. Don't look so gloomy, Fortin, unless you believe in were-wolves and ghosts. Hey! what the – what the devil's the matter with you, anyway? What are you staring at, Le Bihan?'

'Come, come,' muttered the mayor in a low, tremulous voice, 'it's time we got out of this. Did you see? Did you see, Fortin?'

'I saw,' whispered Max Fortin, pallid with fright.

The two men were almost running across the sunny pasture now, and I hastened after them, demanding to know what was the matter.

'Matter!' chattered the mayor, gasping with exasperation

and terror. 'The skull is rolling uphill again!' and he burst
into a terrific gallop. Max Fortin followed close behind.

I watched them stampeding across the pasture, then
turned towards the gravel pit, mystified, incredulous. The
skull was lying on the edge of the pit, exactly where it had
been before I pushed it over the edge. For a second I stared
at it; a singular chilly feeling crept up my spinal column,
and I turned and walked away, sweat starting from the root
of every hair on my head. Before I had gone twenty paces
the absurdity of the whole thing struck me. I halted, hot
with shame and annoyance, and retraced my steps.

There lay the skull.

'I rolled a stone down instead of the skull,' I muttered to
myself. Then with the butt of my gun I pushed the skull
over the edge of the pit and watched it roll to the bottom;
and as it struck the bottom of the pit, Mome, my dog,
suddenly whipped his tail between his legs, whimpered, and
made off across the moor.

'Mome!' I shouted, angry and astonished; but the dog
only fled the faster, and I ceased calling from sheer surprise.

'What the mischief is the matter with that dog?' I thought.
He had never before played me such a trick.

Mechanically I glanced into the pit, but I could not see
the skull. I looked down. The skull lay at my feet again,
touching them.

'Good heavens!' I stammered, and struck at it blindly
with my gunstock. The ghastly thing flew into the air,
whirling over and over, and rolled down the sides of the
pit to the bottom. Breathlessly I stared at it, then confused
and scarcely comprehending, I stepped back from the pit,
still facing it, one, ten, twenty paces, my eyes almost starting
from my head, as though I expected to see the thing roll
up from the bottom of the pit under my very gaze. At last
I turned my back to the pit and strode out across the
gorse-covered moorland towards my home. As I reached
the road that winds from St Gildas to St Julien I gave one
hasty glance at the pit over my shoulder. The sun shone

hot on the sod about the excavation. There was something white and bare and round on the turf at the edge of the pit. It might have been a stone; there were plenty of them lying about.

II

When I entered my garden I saw Mome sprawling on the stone doorstep. He eyed me sideways and flopped his tail.

'Are you not mortified, you idiot dog?' I said, looking about the upper windows for Lys.

Mome rolled over on his back and raised one deprecating forepaw, as though to ward off calamity.

'Don't act as though I was in the habit of beating you to death,' I said, disgusted. I had never in my life raised whip to the brute. 'But you are a fool dog,' I continued. 'No, you needn't come to be babied and wept over; Lys can do that, if she insists, but I am ashamed of you, and you can go to the devil.'

Mome slunk off into the house, and I followed, mounting directly to my wife's boudoir. It was empty.

'Where has she gone?' I said, looking hard at Mome, who had followed me. 'Oh! I see you don't know. Don't pretend you do. Come off that lounge! Do you think Lys wants tan-coloured hairs all over her lounge?'

I rang the bell for Catherine and 'Fine, but they didn't know where 'madame' had gone, so I went into my room, bathed, exchanged my somewhat grimy shooting clothes for a suit of warm, soft knickerbockers, and, after lingering for some extra moments over my toilet – for I was particular, now that I had married Lys – I went down to the garden and took a chair out under the fig-trees.

'Where can she be?' I wondered. Mome came sneaking out to be comforted, and I forgave him for Lys's sake, where-upon he frisked.

'You bounding cur,' said I, 'now what on earth started you off across the moor? If you do it again I'll push you along with a charge of dust shot.'

As yet I had scarcely dared think about the ghastly hallucination of which I had been a victim, but now I faced it squarely, flushing a little with mortification at the thought of my hasty retreat from the gravel pit.

'To think,' I said aloud, 'that those old woman's tales of Max Fortin and Le Bihan should have actually made me see what didn't exist at all! I lost my nerve like a schoolboy in a dark bedroom.' For I knew now that I had mistaken a round stone for a skull each time, and had pushed a couple of big pebbles into the pit instead of the skull itself.

'By jingo!' said I, 'I'm nervous; my liver must be in a devil of a condition if I see such things when I'm awake! Lys will know what to give me.'

I felt mortified and irritated and sulky, and thought disgustedly of Le Bihan and Max Fortin.

But after a while I ceased speculating, dismissed the mayor, the chemist, and the skull from my mind, and smoked pensively, watching the sun low dipping in the western ocean and moorland; a wistful, restless happiness filled my heart, the happiness that all men know – all men who have loved.

Slowly the purple mist crept out over the sea; the cliffs darkened; the forest was shrouded.

Suddenly the sky above burned with the afterglow, and the world was alight again.

Cloud after cloud caught the rose dye; the cliffs were tinted with it; moor and pasture, heather and forest burned and pulsated with the gentle flush. I saw the gulls turning and tossing above the sand bar, their snowy wings tipped with pink; I saw the sea swallows sheering the surface of the still river, stained to its placid depths with warm reflections of the clouds. The twitter of drowsy hedge birds broke out in the stillness; a salmon rolled its shining side above tide-water.

The interminable monotone of the ocean intensified the silence. I sat motionless, holding my breath as one who listens to the first low rumble of an organ. All at once the pure whistle of a nightingale cut the silence, and the first moonbeam silvered the wastes of mist-hung waters.

I raised my head.

Lys stood before me in the garden.

When we had kissed each other, we linked arms and moved up and down the gravel walks, watching the moonbeams sparkle on the sand bar as the tide ebbed and ebbed. The broad beds of white pinks about us were atremble with hovering white moths; the October roses hung all abloom, perfuming the salt wind.

'Sweetheart,' I said, 'where is Yvonne? Has she promised to spend Christmas with us?'

'Yes, Dick; she drove me down from Plougat this afternoon. She sent her love to you. I am not jealous. What did you shoot?'

'A hare and four partridges. They are in the gun room. I told Catherine not to touch them until you had seen them.'

Now I suppose I knew that Lys could not be particularly enthusiastic over game or guns; but she pretended she was, and always scornfully denied that it was for my sake and not for the pure love of sport. So she dragged me off to inspect the rather meagre game bag, and she paid me pretty compliments and gave a little cry of delight and pity as I lifted the enormous hare out of the sack by his ears.

'He'll eat no more of our lettuce,' I said, attempting to justify the assassination.

'Unhappy little bunny – and what a beauty! O Dick, you are a splendid shot, are you not?'

I evaded the question and hauled out a partridge.

'Poor little dead things!' said Lys in a whisper; 'it seems a pity doesn't it, Dick? But then you are so clever—'

'We'll have them broiled,' I said guardedly; 'tell Catherine.'

Catherine came in to take away the game, and presently 'Fine Lelocard, Lys's maid, announced dinner, and Lys tripped away to her boudoir.

I stood an instant contemplating her blissfully, thinking, 'My boy, you're the happiest fellow in the world – you're in love with your wife!'

I walked into the dining-room, beamed at the plates, walked

out again; met Tregunc in the hallway, beamed on him; glanced into the kitchen, beamed at Catherine, and went upstairs, still beaming.

Before I could knock at Lys's door it opened, and Lys came hastily out. When she saw me she gave a little cry of relief, and nestled close to my breast.

'There is something peering in at my window,' she said.

'What!' I cried angrily.

'A man, I think, disguised as a priest, and he has a mask on. He must have climbed up by the bay tree.'

I was down the stairs and out of doors in no time. The moonlit garden was absolutely deserted. Tregunc came up, and together we searched the hedge and shrubbery around the house and out to the road.

'Jean Marie,' said I at length, 'loose my bulldog – he knows you – and take your supper on the porch where you can watch. My wife says the fellow is disguised as a priest, and wears a mask.'

Tregunc showed his white teeth in a smile. 'He will not care to venture in here again, I think, Monsieur Darrel.'

I went back and found Lys seated quietly at the table.

'The soup is ready, dear,' she said. 'Don't worry; it was only some foolish lout from Bannalec. No one in St Gildas or St Julien would do such a thing.'

I was too exasperated to reply at first, but Lys treated it as a stupid joke, and after a while I began to look at it in that light.

Lys told me about Yvonne, and reminded me of my promise to have Herbert Stuart down to meet her.

'You wicked diplomat!' I protested. 'Herbert is in Paris, and hard at work for the Salon.'

'Don't you think he might spare a week to flirt with the prettiest girl in Finisterre?' inquired Lys innocently.

'Prettiest girl! Not much!' I said.

'Who is, then?' urged Lys.

I laughed a trifle sheepishly.

'I suppose you mean me, Dick,' said Lys, colouring up.

'Now I bore you, don't I?'

'Bore me? Ah, no, Dick.'

After coffee and cigarettes were served I spoke about Tregunc, and Lys approved.

'Poor Jean! He will be glad, won't he? What a dear fellow you are!'

'Nonsense,' said I; 'we need a gardener; you said so yourself, Lys.'

But Lys leaned over and kissed me, and then bent down and hugged Mome, who whistled through his nose in sentimental appreciation.

'I am a very happy woman,' said Lys.

'Mome was a very bad dog today,' I observed.

'Poor Mome!' said Lys, smiling.

When dinner was over and Mome lay snoring before the blaze – for the October nights are often chilly in Finisterre – Lys curled up in the chimney corner with her embroidery, and gave me a swift glance from under her drooping lashes.

'You look like a schoolgirl, Lys,' I said teasingly. 'I don't believe you are sixteen yet.'

She pushed back her heavy burnished hair thoughtfully. Her wrist was as white as surf foam.

'Have you been married four years? I don't believe it,' I said.

She gave me another swift glance and touched the embroidery on her knee, smiling faintly.

'I see,' said I, also smiling at the embroidered garment. 'Do you think it will fit?'

'Fit?' repeated Lys. Then she laughed.

'And,' I persisted, 'are you perfectly sure that you – er – we shall need it?'

'Perfectly,' said Lys. A delicate colour touched her cheeks and neck. She held up the little garment, all fluffy with misty lace and wrought with quaint embroidery.

'It is very gorgeous,' said I; 'don't use your eyes too much, dearest. May I smoke a pipe?'

'Of course,' she said, selecting a skein of pale blue silk.

For a while I sat and smoked in silence, watching her slender fingers among the tinted silks and thread of gold.

Presently she spoke. 'What did you say your crest is, Dick?'

'My crest? Oh, something or other rampant on a something or other—'

'Dick!'

'Dearest?'

'Don't be flippant.'

'But I really forget. It's an ordinary crest; everybody in New York has them. No family should be without 'em.'

'You are disagreeable, Dick. Send Josephine upstairs for my album.'

'Are you going to put that crest on the – the – whatever it is?'

'I am; and my own crest, too.'

I thought of the Purple Emperor and wondered a little.

'You didn't know I had one, did you?' she smiled.

'What is it?' I replied evasively.

'You shall see. Ring for Josephine.'

I rang, and, when 'Fine appeared, Lys gave her some orders in a low voice, and Josephine trotted away, bobbing her white-coiffed head with a *'Bien, madame!'*

After a few minutes she returned, bearing a tattered, musty volume, from which the gold and blue had mostly disappeared.

I took the book in my hands and examined the ancient emblazoned covers.

'Lilies!' I exclaimed.

'Fleur-de-lis,' said my wife demurely.

'Oh,' said I, astonished, and opened the book.

'You have never before seen this book?' asked Lys, with a touch of malice in her eyes.

'You know I haven't. Hello! what's this? Oho! So there should be a *de* before Trevec? Lys de Trevec? Then why in the world did the Purple Emperor—'

'Dick!' cried Lys.

'All right,' said I. 'Shall I read about the Sieur de Trevec who rode to Saladin's tent alone to seek for medicine for St Louis? Or shall I read about – what is it? Oh, here it is, all down in black and white – about the Marquis de Trevec who drowned himself before Alva's eyes rather than surrender the banner of the fleur-de-lis to Spain? It's all written here. But, dear, how about that soldier named Trevec, who was killed in the old fort on the cliff yonder?'

'He dropped the *de*, and the Trevecs since then have been Republicans,' said Lys – 'all except me.'

'That's quite right,' said I; 'it is time that we Republicans should agree upon some feudal system. My dear, I drink to the king!' and I raised my wine-glass and looked at Lys.

'To the king,' said Lys, flushing. She smoothed out the tiny garment on her knees, she touched the glass with her lips; her eyes were very sweet. I drained the glass to the king.

After a silence, I said, 'I will tell the king stories. His Majesty shall be amused.'

'His Majesty,' repeated Lys softly.

'Or hers,' I laughed. 'Who knows?'

'Who knows?' murmured Lys, with a gentle sigh.

'I know some stories about Jack the Giant-Killer,' I announced. 'Do you, Lys?'

'I? No, not about a giant-killer, but I know all about the were-wolf, and Jeanne-la-Flamme, and the Man in Purple Tatters, and – O dear me! I know lots more.'

'You are very wise,' said I. 'I shall teach his Majesty English.'

'And I Breton,' cried Lys jealously.

'I shall bring playthings to the king,' said I – 'big green lizards from the gorge, little grey mullets to swim in glass globes, baby rabbits from the forest of Kerselec—'

'And I,' said Lys, 'will bring the first primrose, the first branch of aubepine, the first jonquil, to the king – my king.'

'Our king,' said I; and there was peace in Finisterre.

I lay back, idly turning the leaves of the curious old volume.

'I am looking,' said I, 'for the crest.'

'The crest, dear? It is a priest's head with an arrow-shaped mark on the forehead, on a field—'

I sat up and stared at my wife.

'Dick, whatever is the matter?' she smiled. 'The story is there in that book. Do you care to read it? No? Shall I tell it to you? Well, then; it happened in the third crusade. There was a monk whom men called the Black Priest. He turned apostate, and sold himself to the enemies of Christ. A Sieur de Trevec burst into the Saracen camp, at the head of only one hundred lances, and carried the Black Priest away out of the very midst of their army.'

'So that is how you came by the crest,' I said quietly; but I thought of the branded skull in the gravel pit, and wondered.

'Yes,' said Lys. 'The Sieur de Trevec cut the Black Priest's head off, but first he branded him with an arrow mark on the forehead. The book says it was a pious action, and the Sieur de Trevec got great merit by it. But I think it was cruel, the branding,' she sighed.

'Did you ever hear of any other Black Priest?'

'Yes. There was one in the last century, here in St Gildas. He cast a white shadow in the sun. He wrote in the Breton language. Chronicles, too, I believe. I never saw them. His name was the same as that of the old chronicler, and of the other priest, Jacques Sorgue. Some said he was a lineal descendant of the traitor. Of course the first Black Priest was bad enough for anything. But if he did have a child, it need not have been the ancestor of the last Jacques Sorgue. They say this one was a holy man. They say he was so good he was not allowed to die, but was caught up to heaven one day,' added Lys, with believing eyes.

I smiled.

'But he disappeared,' persisted Lys.

'I'm afraid his journey was in another direction,' I said jestingly, and thoughtlessly told her the story of the morning. I had utterly forgotten the masked man at her window, but before I finished I remembered him fast enough, and realized what I had done as I saw her face whiten.

'Lys,' I urged tenderly, 'that was only some clumsy clown's trick. You said so yourself. You are not superstitious, my dear?'

Her eyes were on mine. She slowly drew the little gold cross from her bosom and kissed it. But her lips trembled as they pressed the symbol of faith.

III

About nine o'clock the next morning, I walked into the Groix Inn and sat down at the long discolored oaken table, nodding good-day to Marianne Brupère, who in turn bobbed her white coiffe at me.

'My clever Bannalec maid,' I said, 'what is good for a stirrup-cup at the Groix Inn?'

'*Schist*?' she inquired in Breton.

'With a dash of red wine, then,' I replied.

She brought the delicious Quimperle cider, and I poured a little Bordeaux into it. Marianne watched me with laughing black eyes.

'What makes your cheeks so red, Marianne?' I asked. 'Has Jean Marie been here?'

'We are to be married, Monsieur Darrel.' She laughed.

'Ah! Since when has Jean Marie Tregunc lost his head?'

'His head? Oh, Monsieur Darrel – his heart, you mean!'

'So I do,' said I. 'Jean Marie is a practical fellow.'

'It is all due to your kindness—' began the girl, but I raised my hand and held up the glass.

'It's due to himself. To your happiness, Marianne,' and I took a hearty draught of the *schist*. 'Now,' said I, 'tell me where I can find Le Bihan and Max Fortin.'

'Monsieur Le Bihan and Monsieur Fortin are above in the broad room. I believe they are examining the Red Admiral's effects.'

'To send them to Paris? Oh, I know. May I go up, Marianne?'

'And God go with you.' The girl smiled.

When I knocked at the door of the broad room above, little Max Fortin opened it. Dust covered his spectacles and nose; his hat, with the tiny velvet ribbons fluttering, was all awry.

'Come in, Monsieur Darrel,' he said; 'the mayor and I are packing up the effects of the Purple Emperor and of the poor Red Admiral.'

'The collection?' I asked, entering the room. 'You must be very careful in packing those butterfly cases; the slightest jar might break wings and antennae, you know.'

Le Bihan shook hands with me and pointed to the great pile of boxes.

'They're all cork lined,' he said, 'but Fortin and I are putting felt around each box. The Entomological Society of Paris pays the freight.'

The combined collections of the Red Admiral and the Purple Emperor made a magnificent display.

I lifted and inspected case after case set with gorgeous butterflies and moths, each specimen carefully labelled with the name in Latin. There were cases filled with crimson tiger moths all aflame with color; cases devoted to the common yellow butterflies; symphonies in orange and pale yellow; cases of soft grey and dun-colored sphinx moths; and cases of garish nettlebred butterflies of the numerous family of *Vanessa*.

All alone in a great case by itself was pinned the purple emperor, the Apatura Iris, that fatal specimen that had given the Purple Emperor his name and quietus.

I remembered the butterfly, and stood looking at it with bent eyebrows.

Le Bihan glanced up from the floor where he was nailing down the lid of a box full of cases.

'It is settled then,' said he, 'that madame, your wife, gives the Purple Emperor's entire collection to the city of Paris?'

I nodded.

'Without accepting anything for it?'

'It is a gift,' I said.

'Including the purple emperor there in the case? That butterfly is worth a great deal of money,' persisted Le Bihan.

'You don't suppose that we would wish to sell that specimen, do you?' I answered a trifle sharply.

'If I were you I should destroy it,' said the mayor in his high-pitched voice.

'That would be nonsense,' said I – 'like your burying the brass cylinder and scroll yesterday.'

I looked at Max Fortin, who immediately avoided my eyes.

'You are a pair of superstitious old women,' said I, digging my hands into my pockets; 'you swallow every nursery tale that is invented.'

'What of it?' said Le Bihan sulkily; 'there's more truth than lies in most of 'em.'

'Oh!' I sneered. 'Does the Mayor of St Gildas and St Julien believe in the Loup-garou?'

'No, not in the Loup-garou.'

'In what, then – Jeanne-la-Flamme?'

'That,' said Le Bihan with conviction, 'is history.'

'The devil it is!' said I; 'and perhaps, monsieur the mayor, your faith in giants is unimpaired?'

'There were giants – everyone knows it,' growled Max Fortin.

'And you a chemist!' I observed scornfully.

'Listen, Monsieur Darrel,' squeaked Le Bihan; 'you know yourself that the Purple Emperor was a scientific man. Now suppose I should tell you that he always refused to include in his collection a Death's Messenger?'

'A what?' I exclaimed.

'You know what I mean – that moth that flies by night; some calls it the Death's Head, but in St Gildas we call it "Death's Messenger".'

'Oh!' said I, 'you mean that big sphinx moth that is commonly called the "death's-head moth". Why the mischief should the people here call it death's messenger?'

'For hundreds of years it has been known as dea..
messenger in St Gildas,' said Max Fortin. 'Even Froissan
speaks of it in his commentaries on Jacques Sorgue's
Chronicles. The book is in your library.'

'Sorgue? And who is Jacques Sorgue? I never read his book.'

'Jacques Sorgue was the son of some unfrocked priest – I
forget. It was during the crusades.'

'Good heavens!' I burst out. 'I've been hearing of nothing
but crusades and priests and death and sorcery ever since I
kicked that skull into the gravel pit, and I am tired of it, I
tell you frankly. One would think we lived in the dark ages.
Do you know what year of our Lord it is, Le Bihan?'

'Eighteen hundred and ninety-six,' replied the mayor.

'And yet you two hulking men are afraid of a death's-
head moth.'

'I don't care to have one fly into the window,' said Max
Fortin; 'it means evil to the house and the people in it.'

'God alone knows why he marked one of His creatures
with a yellow death's head on the back,' observed Le Bihan
piously, 'but I take it that He meant it as a warning; and I
propose to profit by it,' he added triumphantly.

'See here, Le Bihan,' I said; 'by a stretch of imagination
one can make out a skull on the thorax of a certain big
sphinx moth. What of it?'

'It is a bad thing to touch,' said the mayor, wagging his
head.

'It squeaks when handled,' added Max Fortin.

'Some creatures squeak all the time,' I observed, looking
hard at Le Bihan.

'Pigs,' added the mayor.

'Yes, and asses,' I replied. 'Listen, Le Bihan: do you mean
to tell me that you saw that skull roll uphill yesterday?'

The mayor shut his mouth tightly and picked up his
hammer.

'Don't be obstinate,' I said; 'I asked you a question.'

'And I refuse to answer,' snapped Le Bihan. 'Fortin saw
what I saw; let him talk about it.'

I looked searchingly at the little chemist.

'I don't say that I saw it actually roll up out of the pit, all by itself,' said Fortin with a shiver, 'but – but then, how did it come up out of the pit, if it didn't roll up all by itself?'

'It didn't come up at all; that was a yellow cobblestone that you mistook for the skull again,' I replied. 'You are nervous, Max.'

'A – a very curious cobblestone, Monsieur Darrel,' said Fortin.

'I also was a victim of the same hallucination,' I continued, 'and I regret to say that I took the trouble to roll two innocent cobblestones into the gravel pit, imagining each time that it was the skull I was rolling.'

'It was,' observed Le Bihan with a morose shrug.

'It just shows,' said I, ignoring the mayor's remark, 'how easy it is to fix up a train of coincidences so that the result seems to savor of the supernatural. Now, last night my wife imagined that she saw a priest in a mask peer in at her window—'

Fortin and Le Bihan scrambled hastily from their knees, dropping hammer and nails.

'W-h-a-t – what's that?' demanded the mayor.

I repeated what I had said. Max Fortin turned livid.

'My God!' muttered Le Bihan, 'the Black Priest is in St Gildas!'

'D-don't you – you know the old prophecy?' stammered Fortin; 'Froissart quotes it from Jacques Sorgue:

'"When the Black Priest rises from the dead,
St Gildas folk shall shriek in bed;
When the Black Priest rises from his grave,
May the good God St Gildas save!"'

'Aristide Le Bihan,' I said angrily, 'and you, Max Fortin, I've got enough of this nonsense! Some foolish lout from Bannalec has been in St Gildas playing tricks to frighten old fools like you. If you have nothing better to talk about than nursery legends I'll wait until you come to your senses. Good morning.' And I walked out, more disturbed than I cared to acknowledge to myself.

The day had become misty and overcast. Heavy, wet clouds hung in the east. I heard the surf thundering against the cliffs, and the gray gulls squealed as they tossed and turned high in the sky. The tide was creeping across the river sands, higher, higher, and I saw the seaweed floating on the beach, and the *lançons* springing from the foam, silvery threadlike flashes in the gloom. Curlew were flying up the river in twos and threes; the timid sea swallows skimmed across the moors towards some quiet, lonely pool, safe from the coming tempest. In every hedge field birds were gathering, huddling together, twittering restlessly.

When I reached the cliffs I sat down, resting my chin on my clenched hands. Already a vast curtain of rain, sweeping across the ocean miles away, hid the island of Groix. To the east, behind the white semaphore on the hills, black clouds crowded up over the horizon. After a little thunder boomed, dull, distant, and slender skeins of lightning unravelled across the crest of the coming storm. Under the cliff at my feet the surf rushed foaming over the shore, and the *lançons* jumped and skipped and quivered until they seemed to be but the reflections of the meshed lightning.

I turned to the east. It was raining now at the semaphore. High in the storm whirl a few gulls pitched; a nearer cloud trailed veils of rain in its wake; the sky was spattered with lightning; the thunder boomed.

As I rose to go, a cold raindrop fell upon the back of my hand, and another, and yet another on my face. I gave a last glance at the sea, where the waves were bursting into strange white shapes that seemed to fling out menacing arms towards me. Then something moved on the cliff, something black as the black rock it clutched – a filthy cormorant, craning its hideous head at the sky.

Slowly I plodded homeward across the sombre moorland, where the gorse stems glimmered with a dull metallic green, and the heather, no longer violet and purple, hung drenched and dun-coloured among the dreary rocks. The wet turf creaked under my heavy boots, the black-thorn scraped and grated against my knee and elbow. Over all lay a strange light, pallid, ghastly, where the sea spray whirled across the landscape and drove into my face until it grew numb with the cold. In broad bands, rank after rank, billow on billow, the rain burst out across the endless moors, and yet there was no wind to drive it at such a pace.

Lys stood at the door as I turned into the garden, motioning me to hasten: and then for the first time I became conscious that I was soaked to the skin.

'However in the world did you come to stay out when such a storm threatened?' she said. 'Oh, you are dripping! Go quickly and change; I have laid your warm underwear on the bed, Dick.'

I kissed my wife, and went upstairs to change my dripping clothes for something more comfortable.

When I returned to the morning room there was a drift-wood fire on the hearth, and Lys sat in the chimney corner embroidering.

'Catherine tells me that the fishing fleet from Lorient is out. Do you think they are in danger, dear?' asked Lys, raising her blue eyes to mine as I entered.

'There is no wind, and there will be no sea,' said I, looking out of the window. Far across the moor I could see the black cliffs looming in the mist.

'How it rains!' murmured Lys; 'come to the fire, Dick.'

I threw myself on the fur rug, my hands in my pockets, my head on Lys's knees.

'Tell me a story,' I said. 'I feel like a boy of ten.'

Lys raised a finger to her scarlet lips. I always waited for her to do that.

'Will you be very still, then?' she said.

'Still as death.'

'Death,' echoed a voice very softly.

'Did you speak, Lys?' I asked, turning so that I could see her face.

'No; did you, Dick?'

'Who said "death"?' I asked, startled.

'Death,' echoed a voice, softly.

I sprang up and looked around. Lys rose too, her needles and embroidery falling to the floor. She seemed about to faint, leaning heavily on me, and I led her to the window and opened it a little way to give her air. As I did so the chain lightning split the zenith, the thunder crashed, and a sheet of rain swept into the room, driving with it something that fluttered – something that flapped, and squeaked and beat upon the rug with soft, moist wings.

We bent over it together, Lys clinging to me, and we saw that it was a death's-head moth drenched with rain.

The dark day passed slowly as we sat beside the fire, hand in hand, her head against my breast, speaking of sorrow and mystery and death. For Lys believed that there were things on earth that none might understand, things that must be nameless forever and ever, until God rolls up the scroll of life and all is ended. We spoke of hope and fear and faith, and the mystery of the saints; we spoke of the beginning and the end, of the shadow of sin, of omens, and of love. The moth still lay on the floor, quivering its sombre wings in the warmth of the fire, the skull and the ribs clearly etched upon its neck and body.

'If it is a messenger of death to this house,' I said, 'why should we fear, Lys?'

'Death should be welcome to those who love God,' murmured Lys, and she drew the cross from her breast and kissed it.

'The moth might die if I threw it out into the storm,' I said after a silence.

'Let it remain,' sighed Lys.

Late that night my wife lay sleeping, and I sat beside her bed and read in the Chronicle of Jacques Sorgue. I shaded the candle, but Lys grew restless, and finally I took the book down into the morning room, where the ashes of the fire rustled and whitened on the hearth.

The death's-head moth lay on the rug before the fire where I had left it. At first I thought it was dead, but, when I looked closer I saw a lambent fire in its amber eyes. The straight white shadow it cast across the floor wavered as the candle flickered.

The pages of the Chronicle of Jacques Sorgue were damp and sticky; the illuminated gold and blue initials left flakes of azure and gilt where my hand brushed them.

'It is not paper at all; it is thin parchment,' I said to myself; and I held the discolored page close to the candle flame and read, translating laboriously:

'I, Jacques Sorgue, saw all these things. And I saw the Black Mass celebrated in the chapel of St Gildas-on-the-Cliff. And it was said by the Abbé Sorgue, my kinsman: for which deadly sin the apostate priest was seized by the most noble Marquis of Plougastel and by him condemned to be burned with hot irons, until his seared soul quit its body and fly to its master the devil. But when the Black Priest lay in the crypt of Plougastel, his master Satan came at night and set him free, and carried him across land and sea to Mahmoud, which is Soldan or Saladin. And I, Jacques Sorgue, travelling afterward by sea, beheld with my own eyes my kinsman, the Black Priest of St Gildas, borne along in the air upon a vast black wing, which was the wing of his master Satan. And this was seen also by two men of the crew.'

I turned the page. The wings of the moth on the floor began to quiver. I read on and on, my eyes blurring under the shifting candle flame. I read of battles and of saints, and I learned how the great Soldan made his pact with Satan, and then I came to the Sieur de Trevec, and read how he seized the Black Priest in the midst of Saladin's tents and carried him away and cut off his head, first branding him on the forehead. 'And before he suffered,' said the Chronicle, 'he cursed the Sieur de Trevec and his descendants, and he said he would surely return to St Gildas. "For the violence you do to me, I will do violence to you. For the evil I suffer at your hands, I will work evil on you and your descendants. Woe to your children, Sieur de Trevec!" There was a whirr, a beating of strong wings, and my candle flashed up as in a sudden breeze. A humming filled the room; the great moth darted hither and thither, beating, buzzing, on ceiling and wall. I flung down my book and stepped forward. Now it lay fluttering upon the window sill, and for a moment I had it under my hand, but the thing squeaked and I shrank back. Then suddenly it darted across the candle flame; the light flared and went out, and at the same moment a shadow moved in the darkness outside. I raised my eyes to the window. A masked face was peering in at me.

Quick as thought I whipped out my revolver and fired every cartridge, but the face advanced beyond the window, the glass melting away before it like mist, and through the smoke of my revolver I saw something creep swiftly into the room. Then I tried to cry out, but the thing was at my throat, and I fell backward among the ashes of the hearth.

When my eyes unclosed I was lying on the hearth, my head among the cold ashes. Slowly I got on my knees, rose painfully, and groped my way to a chair. On the floor lay my revolver, shining in the pale light of early morning. My mind clearing by degrees, I looked, shuddering, at the window. The glass was unbroken. I stooped stiffly, picked up my revolver and opened the cylinder. Every cartridge had been fired. Mechanically I closed the cylinder and placed the revolver in my pocket. The book, the Chronicles of Jacques Sorgue, lay on the table beside me, and as I started to close it I glanced at the page. It was all splashed with rain, and the lettering had run, so that the page was merely a confused blur of gold and red and black. As I stumbled towards the door I cast a fearful glance over my shoulder. The death's-head moth crawled shivering on the rug.

IV

The sun was about three hours high. I must have slept, for I was aroused by the sudden gallop of horses under our window. People were shouting and calling in the road. I sprang up and opened the sash. Le Bihan was there, an image of helplessness, and Max Fortin stood beside him, polishing his glasses. Some gendarmes had just arrived from Quimperle, and I could hear them around the corner of the house, stamping, and rattling their sabres and carbines, as they led their horses into my stable.

Lys sat up, murmuring half-sleepy, half-anxious questions.

'I don't know,' I answered. 'I am going out to see what it means.'

'It is like the day they came to arrest you,' Lys said, giving me a troubled look. But I kissed her, and laughed at her until she smiled too. Then I flung on coat and cap, and hurried down the stairs.

The first person I saw standing in the road was the Brigadier Durand.

'Hello!' said I, 'have you come to arrest me again? What the devil is all this fuss about, anyway?'

'We were telegraphed for an hour ago,' said Durand briskly, 'and for sufficient reason, I think. Look here, Monsieur Darrel!'

He pointed to the ground almost under my feet.

'Good Heavens!' I cried, 'where did that puddle of blood come from?'

'That's what I want to know, Monsieur Darrel. Max Fortin found it at daybreak. See, it's splashed all over the grass, too. A trail of it leads into your garden, across the flower beds to your very window, the one that opens from the morning room. There is another trail leading from this spot across the road to the cliffs, then to the gravel pit, and thence across the moor to the forest of Kerselec. We are going to mount in a minute and search the bosquets. Will you join us? *Bon Dieu!* but the fellow bled like an ox. Max Fortin says it's human blood, or I should not have believed it.'

The little chemist of Quimperle came up at that moment, rubbing his glasses with a coloured handkerchief.

'Yes, it is human blood,' he said, 'but one thing puzzles me: the corpuscles are yellow. I never saw any human blood before with yellow corpuscles. But your English Doctor Thompson asserts that he has—'

'Well, it's human blood, anyway – isn't it?' insisted Durand impatiently.

'Ye-es,' admitted Max Fortin.

'Then it's my business to trail it,' said the big gendarme, and he called his men and gave the order to mount.

'Did you hear anything last night?' asked Durand of me.

'I heard the rain. I wonder the rain did not wash away these traces.'

'They must have come after the rain ceased. See this thick splash, how it lies over and weighs down the wet grass blades. Pah!'

It was a heavy, evil-looking clot, and I stepped back from it, my throat closing in disgust.

'My theory,' said the brigadier, 'is this: Some of those Biribi fishermen, probably the Icelanders, got an extra glass of cognac into their hides and quarrelled on the road. Some of them were slashed, and staggered to your house. But there is only one trail – and yet, and yet, how could all that blood come from only one person? Well, the wounded man, let us say, staggered first to your house and then back here, and he wandered off, drunk and dying, God knows where. That's my theory.'

'A very good one,' said I calmly. 'And you are going to trail him?'

'Yes.'

'When?'

'At once. Will you come?'

'Not now. I'll gallop over bye-and-bye. You are going to the edge of the Kerselec forest?'

'Yes; you will hear us calling. Are you coming, Max Fortin? And you, Le Bihan? Good; take the dog-cart.'

The big gendarme tramped around the corner to the stable and presently returned mounted on a strong grey horse; his sabre shone on his saddle; his pale yellow and white facings were spotless. The little crowd of white-coiffed women with their children fell back, as Durand touched spurs and clattered away followed by his two troopers. Soon after Le Bihan and Max Fortin also departed in the mayor's dingy dog-cart.

'Are you coming?' piped Le Bihan shrilly.

'In a quarter of an hour,' I replied, and went back to the house.

When I opened the door of the morning room the death's-head moth was beating its strong wings against the window. For a second I hesitated, then walked over and opened the sash. The creature fluttered out, whirred over the flower beds a moment, then darted across the moorland toward the sea. I called the servants together and questioned them. Josephine, Catherine, Jean Marie Tregunc, not one of them had heard the slightest disturbance during the night. Then I told Jean Marie to saddle my horse, and while I was speaking Lys came down.

'Dearest,' I began, going to her.

'You must tell me everything you know, Dick,' she interrupted, looking me earnestly in the face.

'But there is nothing to tell – only a drunken brawl, and someone wounded.'

'And you are going to ride – where, Dick?'

'Well, over the edge of Kerselec forest. Durand and the mayor, and Max Fortin, have gone on, following a – a trail.'

'What trail?'

'Some blood.'

'Where did they find it?'

'Out in the road there.'

Lys crossed herself.

'Does it come near our house?'

'Yes.'

'How near?'

'It comes up to the morning-room window,' said I, giving in.

Her hand on my arm grew heavy. 'I dreamed last night—'

'So did I—' but I thought of the empty cartridges in my revolver, and stopped suddenly.

'I dreamed that you were in great danger, and I could not move hand or foot to save you; but you had your revolver, and I called out to you to fire—'

'I did fire!' I cried excitedly.

'You – you fired?'

I took her in my arms. 'My darling,' I said, 'something strange has happened – something that I cannot understand as yet. But, of course, there is an explanation. Last night I thought I fired at the Black Priest.'

'Ah!' gasped Lys.

'Is that what you dreamed?'

'Yes, yes that was it! I begged you to fire—'

'And I did.'

Her heart was beating against my breast. I held her close in silence.

'Dick,' she said at length, 'perhaps you killed the – the thing.'

'If it was human I did not miss,' I answered grimly. 'And it was human,' I went on, pulling myself together, ashamed of having so nearly gone to pieces. 'Of course, it was human; the whole affair is plain enough. Not a drunken brawl, as Durand thinks; it was a drunken lout's practical joke, for which he has suffered. I suppose I must have filled him pretty full of bullets, and he has crawled away to die in Kerselec forest. It's a terrible affair; I'm sorry I fired so hastily; but that idiot Le Bihan and Max Fortin have been working on my nerves till I am as hysterical as a schoolgirl,' I ended angrily.

'You fired – but the window glass was not shattered,' said Lys in a low voice.

'Well, the window was open, then. And as for the – the rest – I've got nervous indigestion, and a doctor will settle the Black Priest for me, Lys.'

I glanced out of the window at Tregunc waiting with my horse at the gate.

'Dearest, I think I had better go to join Durand and the others.'

'I will go too.'

'Oh, no!'

'Yes, Dick.'

'Don't, Lys.'

'I shall suffer every moment you are away.'

'The ride is too fatiguing, and we can't tell what unpleasant sight you may come upon. Lys, you don't really think there is anything supernatural in this affair?'

'Dick,' she answered gently, 'I am a Bretonne.' With both arms around my neck, my wife said, 'Death is the gift of God. I do not fear it when we are together. But alone – oh, my husband, I should fear a God who could take you away from me!'

We kissed each other soberly, simply, like two children. Then Lys hurried away to change her gown, and I paced up and down the garden waiting for her.

She came, drawing her slender gauntlets on. I swung her into the saddle, gave a hasty order to Jean Marie, and mounted.

Now, to quail under thoughts of terror on a morning like this, with Lys in the saddle beside me, no matter what had happened or might happen, was impossible. Moreover, Mome came sneaking after us. I asked Tregunc to catch him, for I was afraid he might be brained by our horses' hoofs if he followed, but the wily puppy dodged and bolted after Lys, who was trotting along the high-road. 'Never mind,' I thought; 'if he's hit he'll live, for he has no brains to lose.'

Lys was waiting for me in the road beside the Shrine of Our Lady of St Gildas when I joined her. She crossed herself, I doffed my cap, then we shook out our bridles and galloped toward the forest of Kerselec.

We said very little as we rode. I always loved to watch Lys in the saddle. Her exquisite figure and lovely face were the incarnation of youth and grace; her curling hair glistened like threaded gold.

Out of the corner of my eye I saw the spoiled puppy

Mome come bounding cheerfully alongside, oblivious of our horses' heels. Our road swung close to the cliffs. A filthy cormorant rose from the black rocks and flapped heavily across our path. Lys's horse reared, but she pulled him down, and pointed at the bird with her riding crop.

'I see,' said I; 'it seems to be going our way. Curious to see a cormorant in a forest, isn't it?'

'It is a bad sign,' said Lys. 'You know the Morbihan proverb: "When the cormorant turns from the sea, Death laughs in the forest, and wise woodsmen build boats".'

'I wish,' said I sincerely, 'that there were fewer proverbs in Brittany.'

We were in sight of the forest now; across the gorse I could see the sparkle of the gendarmes' trappings, and the glitter of Le Bihan's silver-buttoned jacket. The hedge was low and we took it without difficulty, and trotted across the moor to where Le Bihan and Durand stood gesticulating.

They bowed ceremoniously to Lys as we rode up.

'The trail is horrible – it is a river,' said the mayor in his squeaky voice. 'Monsieur Darrel, I think perhaps madame would scarcely care to come any nearer.'

Lys drew bridle and looked at me.

'It is horrible!' said Durand, walking up beside me; 'it looks as though a bleeding regiment had passed this way. The trail winds about there in the thickets; we lose it at times, but we always find it again. I can't understand how one man – no, nor twenty – could bleed like that!'

A halloo, answered by another, sounded from the depths of the forest.

'It's my men; they are following the trail,' muttered the brigadier. 'God alone knows what is at the end!'

'Shall we gallop back, Lys?' I asked.

'No; let us ride along the western edge of the woods and dismount. The sun is so hot now, and I should like to rest for a moment,' she said.

'The western forest is clear of anything disagreeable,' said Durand.

'Very well,' I answered; 'call me, Le Bihan, if you find anything.'

Lys wheeled her mare, and I followed across the springy heather, Mome trotting cheerfully in the rear.

We entered the sunny woods about a quarter of a kilometre from where we left Durand. I took Lys from her horse, flung both bridles over a limb, and giving my wife my arm, aided her to a flat mossy rock which overhung a shallow brook gurgling among the beech trees. Lys sat down and drew off her gauntlets. Mome pushed his head into her lap, received an undeserved caress, and came doubtfully towards me. I was weak enough to condone his offence, but I made him lie down at my feet, greatly to his disgust.

I rested my head on Lys's knees looking up at the sky through the crossed branches of the trees.

'I suppose I have killed him,' I said. 'It shocks me terribly, Lys.'

'You could not have known, dear. He may have been a robber, and – if – not – Dick – have you ever fired your revolver since that day four years ago, when the Red Admiral's son tried to kill you? But I know you have not.'

'No,' said I, wondering. 'It's a fact, I have not. Why?'

'And don't you remember that I asked you to let me load it for you the day when Yves went away, swearing to kill you and his father?'

'Yes, I do remember. Well?'

'Well, I – I took the cartridges first to St Gildas chapel and dipped them in holy water. You must not laugh, Dick,' said Lys gently, laying her cool hands on my lips.

'Laugh, my darling!'

Overhead the October sky was pale amethyst, and the sunlight burned like orange flame through the yellow leaves of beech and oak. Gnats and midges danced and wavered overhead; a spider dropped from a twig half-way to the ground and hung suspended on the end of his gossamer thread.

'Are you sleepy, dear?' asked Lys, bending over me.

'I am – a little; I scarcely slept two hours last night,' I answered.

'You may sleep, if you wish,' said Lys, and touched my eyes caressingly.

'Is my head heavy on your knees?' I asked.

'No, Dick.'

I was already in a half doze; still I heard the brook babbling under the beeches and the humming of forest flies overhead. Presently even these were stilled.

The next thing I knew I was sitting bolt upright, my ears ringing with a scream, and I saw Lys cowering beside me, covering her white, set face with both hands.

As I sprang to my feet she cried again and clung to my knees. I saw my dog rush growling into the thicket, then I heard him whimper, and he came backing out, whining, ears flat, tail down. I stooped and disengaged Lys's hand.

'Don't go, Dick!' she cried. 'O God, it's the Black Priest!'

In a moment I had leaped across the brook and pushed my way into the thicket. It was empty. I stared about me; I scanned every tree trunk, every bush. Suddenly I saw him. He was seated on a fallen log, his head resting in his hands, his rusty black robe gathered around him. For a moment my hair stirred under my cap; then I recovered my reason, and understood that the man was human and was probably wounded to death. Ay, to death; for there, at my feet, lay the wet trail of blood, over leaves and stone, down into the little hollow, across to the figure in black resting silently under the dark trees.

I saw that he could not escape even if he had the strength, for before him, almost at his very feet, lay a deep, shining swamp.

As I stepped onward my foot broke a twig.

At the sound the figure started a little, then its head fell forward again. Its face was masked. Walking up to the man, I bade him tell where he was wounded.

Durand and the others broke through the thicket at the same moment and hurried to my side.

'Who are you who hide a masked face in a priest's robe?' said the gendarme loudly.

There was no answer.

'See – see the stiff blood all over his robe!' muttered Le Bihan to Fortin.

'He will not speak,' said I.

'He may be too badly wounded,' whispered Le Bihan.

'I saw him raise his head,' I said; 'my wife saw him creep up here.'

Durand stepped forward and touched the figure.

'Speak!' he said.

'Speak!' quavered Fortin.

Durand waited a moment, then with a sudden upward movement he stripped off the mask and threw the man's head back. We were looking into the eye sockets of a skull.

Durand stood rigid and the mayor shrieked. The skeleton burst out from its rotting robes and collapsed on the ground before us. From between the staring ribs and the grinning teeth spurted a torrent of black blood, showering and shrinking grasses; then the thing shuddered, and fell over into the black ooze of the bog. Little bubbles of iridescent air appeared from the mud; the bones were slowly engulfed, and, as the last fragments sank out of sight, up from the depths and along the bank crept a creature, shiny, shivering, quivering its wings.

It was a death's-head moth.

PART TWO

DIVERSIONS

1900–1938

INTRODUCTION

'They call him the most popular writer in America.'

By 1911, Robert W. Chambers had progressed to the stage where *Cosmopolitan* magazine could describe him in those words. Not bad for a man who had hoped to be a professional artist but who had found, almost by accident, that he could write.

And write Chambers did. He treated writing as a business, and worked at it in a very professional manner. He had his office in New York, kept secret from his family, and he worked a strict number of hours a day. No sitting waiting for inspiration for him! He had the journalist's knack of starting to write as soon as he sat down.

Out flowed short stories, essays, verse, plays, articles and novels. He is reported to have written an opera, just for good measure. Between the publication of *The Mystery of Choice* (1896) and his next title in this genre, *In Search of the Unknown* (1904), he published thirteen novels. In all, he would publish nearly a hundred books before his death. He must have worked like a demon: among modern authors, Stephen King comes to mind as a comparable writing machine. Like King, Chambers not only wrote a good many novels, he also wrote very long novels – most of his books are around the four hundred page mark.

All this writing industry translated into lots of money, and Chambers lived very well. Broadalbin, his estate in the

Adirondacks, was kept up and improved where necessary. When not writing, he shot, fished, and hunted, and kept up his painting skills. He belonged to the National Institute of Arts and Letters and was a member of various clubs, like the Century Club, the Authors Club and the Saratoga Golf Club (yet another passion).

It is certain that the first twenty years or so of the century saw Chambers as a happy and fulfilled man, doing the job he loved, living the life he enjoyed, and being accorded vast public admiration. What demons he had stayed well hidden. But this was not to last.

There are conflicting stories about Chambers's only son, Robert Junior. One local legend in the Broadalbin area is that in later life Robert Jr. was mentally unsound and was put in a home; another version is that he was not institutionalised but lived on in the Chambers mansion after the death of his parents, being taken roundly to the cleaners by his wife, who ended up with all his money. Whatever the truth of the matter, Robert W. Chambers had at least one cross to bear in his family; such stories do not appear from nowhere.

While he was certainly well liked in the area in the early part of the century, it does seem that for some reason Chambers grew increasingly unpopular with his neighbours towards the end of his life. He is reported to have kept to himself more and more, a situation occasioned, perhaps, by his losing a large amount of money during the 1929 Stock Market crash.

Money may have become a problem in other ways. After 1920, Chambers's output went down to one or two books per year. There may be two reasons for this. The first one, quite possibly, is that either he did not need to write so much to keep up his finances, or that he found it harder to keep up his output as he grew older. A second, and very plausible, reason may be that Chambers had started to go out of fashion. His brand of thriller and social comedy, drama and fashion, had its roots in the 1900s, and it showed more and more as time went by. He was moving into the era of the hard-boiled detective story, with people like Raymond Chandler and Dashiell Hammett looming up on the horizon; and the market would change drastically from 1930 onwards.

The real tragedy of Chambers's life was the fate of Broadalbin. This estate and house, which he had cherished all his life, hardly survived him. Chambers died on 16 December 1933, after a long illness. He was buried under one of his beloved oak trees on the estate, but his body was later moved to the Chambers family vault in Broadalbin Cemetery. His wife, Elsa, lived on in the house until her death in 1938. The house was abandoned (this seems to be true, casting doubt on the story of his son living there) literally overnight, with everything in it. Local children would break in and make fires of Chambers's papers, and there are reports of the house being used as a brothel at one time. Half the estate had already gone under the encroaching waters of the Sacandaga Reservoir; the house itself, now owned by the Roman Catholic church, was remodelled to form a rectory, losing a third of its original structure. Chambers's carefully planted trees were cut down for timber in the 1970s. It is not difficult to be glad that Chambers never saw any of this happen.

Robert W. Chambers's fortunes were based on his ability to write what the public wanted to read, at least for the first twenty-five years of his career. He wrote and sold popular fiction, making no attempt to sell more 'literary' works (one wonders if he ever wrote such things). There is no shame in that: if you want to make a living as a writer, people have to buy your works. What is regrettable is that Chambers so seldom returned to the genre in which he had made his first reputation – the tale of terror. Of the seventy-five or more books he wrote from 1900 onwards, only a scant half-dozen qualify for inclusion in the genre, though one was to be his finest work.

The first such book was *In Search of the Unknown* (1904), a collection of magazine tales featuring Mr Smith, the expert who scours the world for strange animals on behalf of the Bronx Park Zoological Gardens. The same character was to reappear in a subsequent book, *Police!!!* (1915). Written with style and good humour, the stories from *In Search of the Unknown* are Chambers at his best, eminently readable. I have selected two from the book (both are untitled in the original, and the titles given them in this volume are mine). 'In Search of the Great Auk' sees our hero on the trail of the extinct bird, but finding something altogether different, while 'In Search of the Mammoth' speaks for itself. Chambers supplied a tongue-in-cheek introduction to the book, writing in the guise of the narrator, and hoped it would 'inspire enthusiasm for natural and scientific research, and inculcate a passion for accurate observation among the young'. The young would be hard pressed to fail to observe Chambers's glorious creations in these stories.

The author's next foray into weird fiction was in a much gentler, more relaxed vein. *The Tracer of Lost Persons* (1906) recounts the exploits of Westrel Keen, the eponymous investigator of missing people. Keen is a mysterious figure who runs an agency 'prepared to locate the whereabouts of anybody on earth', as his advertising claims, and in a series of loosely-connected tales proceeds to do just that. The only other connecting character in the stories is Tommy Kerns, who introduces his friends to Westrel Keen. In the two extracts included here (again, the titles are mine), we see both Keen's prowess with various arcane subjects and his seemingly limitless range of contacts. A man falls in love with a vision in 'The Seal of Solomon', who turns out to be nearer home than he thought; while Jack Burke in 'Samaris' falls in love with a four thousand year old woman (later in the book he marries her, which is taking a taste for the older woman a bit far). The exploits of Westrel Keen have been oddly neglected in the various revivals of Chambers's work, though they do seem rather old-fashioned now.

The Tree of Heaven (1907) remains a very distinctive book in Robert W. Chambers's diversions into the supernatural genre. The stories seem to be the final form of the kind of tale that Chambers first attempted in 'A Pleasant Evening' in Part One: low-key, well written essays into the ghost story, reminiscent of the kind of material Algernon Blackwood did so well. There is a tantalising possibility that Blackwood and Chambers met. Blackwood was in New York in the 1890s, knew Chambers's friend Charles Dana Gibson, and sat for him. It is not over-fanciful to wonder if some of Blackwood's style rubbed off on Chambers. Certainly, 'Out of the Depths' explores the same territory as Blackwood's 'Keeping His Promise'. The other stories are small gems, well worth reviving. There is also that touch of spirituality so characteristic of Blackwood, especially in 'The Case of Mr Helmer'.

In *Police!!!* (1915; the exclamation marks are all Chambers's), he returned to the free and easy style of *In Search of the Unknown*, collecting together more adventures of the man from the Bronx Park Zoological Gardens. There are two stories from the collection included here. 'Un Peu D'Amour' is an amusing tale of the problems an artist has with a moving landscape, while 'The Third Eye' has nothing to do with Eastern mysticism, but is set in the Florida everglades. They may not be the best stories Chambers ever wrote, and some of the romantic interludes are a bit toe-curling, but I find the stories from *Police!!!* and *In Search of the Unknown* to be the author at his most readable and enjoyable.

Five years after *Police!!!*, Chambers published his last major work in this genre, the novel *The Slayer of Souls* (1920). (A later novel, *The Talkers* (1925), is not half as good.) Originally written as a magazine serialisation (evident from the plot summaries at the start of some of the chapters), *The Slayer of Souls* saw Chambers returning to the vein he had explored in *The Maker of Moons*. This time, however, he had a new angle.

The novel tells of an unholy alliance between the Bolsheviks and the most sinister kind of Oriental magic. Aimed at the West, and particularly America, the threat seems almost unstoppable. Our gallant friends, the U.S. secret service, find their only weapon in the form of Tressa Norne, a young American girl kidnapped by the Yezidee, the oriental sect behind it all. Trained in their magic, she is rescued by the Japanese and returns to America. Only she can fight the Yezidee on their own terms, and secret service agent Victor Cleves is assigned to help her.

Chambers wrote the book in a glow of anti-Bolshevik feeling common in America at the time. The Bolsheviks are the devil incarnate in this book – 'that sexless monster born of hell and called the Bolshevik!' – and they join up with the Yezidee, anarchists, Germans: all the usual suspects. This was America in the 1920s, of course, and Chambers was only echoing a nationwide surge of antipathy and prejudice towards anyone, particularly foreigners, of even vaguely left-wing politics. This wave of prejudice reached its dismal peak with the disgraceful execution in 1927 of the two Italian Communists, Sacco and Vanzetti, after an unfair trial for robbery and murder in 1922. Diplomatic recognition of the USSR by America only happened when Franklin Roosevelt was elected President in 1933, not long before Chambers died.

Yet Chambers, like so many, got it wrong. He saw the Bolsheviks and the Chinese as the next enemy, while the Japanese are the 'good guys' in his book, rescuing Tressa Norne. The irony is that his own government, with that of Britain, were already working on the assumption that their next enemy in the Pacific would be Japan, despite their alliance with Japan in the First World War. And the Japanese in the next war behaved far worse than even Chambers could describe the Bolsheviks as acting.

The book romps along with hardly a dull page (though with a fair bit of Chambers's customary soppiness in the love scenes). Our old friends the Xin, from *The Maker of Moons*, get a mention, as does Arthur Conan Doyle, called in for psychic help when things get bad. *The Slayer of Souls* himself is Sanang, the chief Yezidee assassin and man of magic, who fancies Tressa no end. Chambers really goes back to his roots in chapter eleven, where we find the line, 'It is a fearful thing to fall into the hands of the living God!' (quoted verbatim from 'In the Court of the Dragon' in *The King in Yellow*).

There is a splendid touch of Charles Fort in the book. Tressa outlines a rare old theory that the demons and evil come from a dark planet close to Earth, called Yrimid – 'a planet wrapped in darkness – a black star' – which is less than a hundred miles away (!) and is responsible for all strange phenomena which science cannot explain. 'All new and sudden pestilences; all convulsions of nature; the newly noticed radio disturbances; the new, so-called interplanetary signals – all have their hidden causes within that black and demon-haunted planet'. It really did sound a job for Flash Gordon.

I have included three chapters in this book, and given each a title either already in the text or springing from the subject matter. In the last two, it is evident that Chambers had not lost his touch for real horror in his writing. There are few jokes in *The Slayer of Souls*, and it stands as his finest work in the genre, despite his prejudices and political short sight.

After his death, Chambers passed into the shadows fairly quickly. His widow published some of his works posthumously, until she died in 1938. There were reprints from time to time, in Britain and America. For some reason there was an odd flurry of interest in Chambers during the Second World War, when the London firm Mellifont Press brought out abridged editions of some of his books, produced in Dublin. *The King in Yellow* enjoyed a paperback revival in the 1960s, and the British reprint firm Tom Stacey produced an edition of *The Slayer of Souls* in 1972. But Chambers has really lived on only in the fantasy genre, which has kept his name alive for 85 years.

I have always rated Chambers among the best dozen or so authors in this field, based on a childhood acquaintance with *The Slayer of Souls*. When you start tracking down what else he produced, you quickly realise the variety of styles he had at his disposal, more than most of his contemporaries. It makes his neglect of the supernatural genre all the more lamentable.

The final words should belong to Rupert Hughes, a friend of the author, as he wrote in his foreword to the 1938 edition of *The King in Yellow*:

> Bob Chambers was, for all his fame and success, the shyest, simplest author I ever knew. He was modest, lovable, devoted to his beautiful and devoted wife, and he died slowly in heroic patience. He had his ideals and he lived up to them. He strove for charm, action, and character . . . he was a teller of stories, and to tell a good story well is a high and difficult art.

It speaks well of an author that he should engender such affection after his death. I hope *Out of the Dark* will help to keep Robert W. Chambers, that most professional of writers, alive in the genre where he did his best work.

Hugh Lamb
Sutton, Surrey
January 2018

OUT OF THE DEPTHS

Dust and wind had subsided; there seemed to be a hint of rain in the starless west.

Because the August evening had become oppressive, the club windows stood wide open as though gaping for the outer air. Rugs and curtains had been removed; an incandescent light or two accentuated the emptiness of the rooms; here and there shadowy servants prowled, gilt buttons sparkling through the obscurity, their footsteps on the bare floor intensifying the heavy quiet.

Into this week's-end void wandered young Shannon, drifting aimlessly from library to corridor, finally entering the long room where the portraits of dead governors smirked through the windows at the deserted avenue.

As his steps echoed on the rugless floor, a shadowy something detached itself from the depths of a padded armchair by the corner window, and a voice he recognized greeted him by name.

'You are here, Harrod!' he exclaimed. 'Thought you were at Bar Harbor.'

'I was. I had business in town.'

'Do you stay here long?'

'Not long,' said Harrod slowly.

Shannon dropped into a chair with a yawn which ended in a groan.

'Of all God-forsaken places,' he began, 'a New York club in August.'

Harrod touched an electric button, but no servant answered the call; and presently Shannon, sprawling in his chair, jabbed the button with the ferrule of his walking stick, and a servant took the order, repeating as though he had not understood: 'Did you say two, sir?'

'With olives, dry,' nodded Shannon irritably. They sat there in silence until the tinkle of ice aroused them, and—

'Double luck to you,' muttered Shannon; then, with a scarcely audible sigh: 'Bring two more and bring a dinner card.' And, turning to the older man: 'You're dining, Harrod?'

'If you like.'

A servant came and turned on an electric jet; Shannon scanned the card under the pale radiance, scribbled on the pad, and handed it to the servant.

'Did you put down my name?' asked Harrod curiously.

'No; you'll dine with me – if you don't mind.'

'I don't mind – for this last time.'

'Going away again?'

'Yes.'

Shannon signed the blank and glanced up at his friend. 'Are you well?' he asked abruptly.

Harrod, lying deep in his leather chair, nodded.

'Oh, you're rather white around the gills! We'll have another.'

'I thought you had cut that out, Shannon.'

'Cut what out?'

'Drinking.'

'Well, I haven't,' said Shannon sulkily, lifting his glass and throwing one knee over the other.

'The last time I saw you, you said you would cut it,' observed Harrod.

'Well, what of it?'

'But you haven't?'

'No, my friend.'

'Can't you stop?'

'I could – now. Tomorrow – I don't know; but I know

well enough I couldn't day after tomorrow. And day after tomorrow I shall not care.'

A short silence and Harrod said: 'That's why I came back here.'

'What?'

'To stop you.'

Shannon regarded him in sullen amazement.

A servant announcing dinner brought them to their feet; together they walked out into the empty dining-room and seated themselves by an open window.

Presently Shannon looked up with an impatient laugh.

'For Heaven's sake let's be cheerful, Harrod. If you knew how the damned town had got on my nerves.'

'*That's* what I came back for, too,' said Harrod with his strange white smile. 'I knew the world was fighting you to the ropes.'

'It is; here I stay on, day after day, on the faint chance of something doing.' He shrugged his shoulders. 'Business is worse than dead; I can't hold on much longer. You're right; the world has hammered me to the ropes, and it will be down and out for me unless—'

'Unless you can borrow on your own terms?'

'Yes, but I can't.'

'You are mistaken.'

'Mistaken? Who will—'

'I will.'

'You! Why, man, do you know how much I need? Do you know for how long I shall need it? Do you know what the chances are of my making good? *You*! Why, Harrod, I'd swamp you! You can't afford—'

'I can afford anything – now.'

Shannon stared. 'You have struck something?'

'Something that puts me beyond want.' He fumbled in his breast pocket, drew out a portfolio, and from the flat leather case he produced a numbered check bearing his signature, but not filled out.

'Tell them to bring pen and ink,' he said.

Shannon, perplexed, signed to a waiter. When the ink was brought, Harrod motioned Shannon to take the pen. 'Before I went to Bar Harbor,' he said, 'I had a certain sum—' He hesitated, mentioned the sum in a low voice, and asked Shannon to fill in the check for that amount. 'Now blot it, pocket it, and use it,' he added listlessly, looking out into the lamp-lighted street.

Shannon, whiter than his friend, stared at the bit of perforated yellow paper. 'I can't take it,' he stammered; 'my security is rotten. I tell you—'

'I want no security; I – I am beyond want,' said Harrod. 'Take it; I came back here for this – partly for this.'

'Came back here to – to – help *me*!'

'To help you. Shannon, I had been a lonely man in life; I think you never realized how much your friendship has been to me. I had nobody – no intimacies. You never understood – you with all your friends – that I cared more for our casual companionship than for anything in the world.'

Shannon bent his head. 'I did not know it,' he said.

Harrod raised his eyes and looked up at the starless sky; Shannon ate in silence; into his young face, already marred by dissipation, a strange light had come. And little by little order began to emerge from his whirling senses; he saw across an abyss a bridge glittering, and beyond that, beckoning to him through a white glory, all that his heart desired.

'I was at the ropes,' he muttered; 'how *could* you know it, Harrod? I – I never whined—'

'I know more than I did – yesterday,' said Harrod, resting his pale face on one thin hand.

Shannon, nerves on edge, all aquiver, the blood racing through every vein, began to speak excitedly: 'It's like a dream – one of the blessed sort – Harrod! Harrod! – the dreams I've had this last year! And I try – I try to understand what has happened – what you have done for me. I can't – I'm shaking all over, and I suppose I'm sitting here eating and drinking, but—'

He touched his glass blindly; it tipped and crashed to the floor, the breaking froth of the wine hissing on the cloth.

'Harrod! Harrod! What sort of a man am I to deserve this of you? What can I do—'

'Keep your nerve – for one thing.'

'I will! – you mean *that*!' touching the stem of the new glass, which the waiter had brought and was filling. He struck the glass till it rang out a clear, thrilling, crystalline note, then struck it more sharply. It splintered with a soft splashing crash. 'Is *that* all?' he laughed.

'No, not all.'

'What more will you let me do?'

'One thing more. Tell them to serve coffee below.'

So they passed out of the dining-room, through the deserted corridors, and descended the stairway to the lounging room. It was unlighted and empty; Shannon stepped back and the elder man passed him and took the corner chair by the window – the same seat where Shannon had first seen him sitting ten years before, and where he always looked to find him after the ending of a business day. And continuing his thoughts, the younger man spoke aloud impulsively: 'I remember perfectly well how we met. Do you? You had just come back to town from Bar Harbor, and I saw you stroll in and seat yourself in that corner, and, because I was sitting next to you, you asked if you might include me in your order – do you remember?'

'Yes, I remember.'

'And I told you I was a new member here, and you pointed out the portraits of all those dead governors of the club, and told me what good fellows they had been. I found out later that you yourself were a governor of the club.'

'Yes – I was.'

Harrod's shadowy face swerved toward the window, his eyes resting on the familiar avenue, empty now save for the policeman opposite, and the ragged children of the poor. In August the high tide from the slums washes Fifth Avenue, stranding a gasping flotsam at the thresholds of the absent.

'And I remember, too, what you told me,' continued Shannon.

'What?' said Harrod, turning noiselessly to confront his friend.

'About that child. Do you remember? That beautiful child you saw? Don't you remember that you told me how she used to leave her governess and talk to you on the rocks—'

'Yes,' said Harrod. '*That* too, is why I came back here to tell you the rest. For the evil days have come to her, Shannon, and the years draw nigh. Listen to me.'

There was a silence; Shannon, mute and perplexed, set his coffee on the window sill and leaned back, flicking the ashes from his cigar; Harrod passed his hands slowly over his hollow temples: 'Her parents are dead; she is not yet twenty; she is not equipped to support herself in life; and – she is beautiful. What chance has she, Shannon?'

The other was silent.

'What chance?' repeated Harrod. 'And, when I tell you that she is unsuspicious, and that she reasons only with her heart, answer me – what chance has she with a man? For you know of men, and so do I, Shannon, so do I.'

'Who is she, Harrod?'

'The victim of divorced parents – awarded to her mother. Let her parents answer; they are answering now, Shannon. But their plea is no concern of yours. What concerns you is the living. The child, grown to womanhood, is here, advertising for employment – here in New York, asking for a chance. What chance has she?'

'When did you learn this?' asked Shannon soberly.

'I learned it tonight – everything concerning her – tonight – an hour before I – I met you. *That* is why I returned. Shannon, listen to me attentively; listen to every word I say. Do you remember a passing fancy you had this spring for a

blue-eyed girl you met every morning on your way downtown? Do you remember that, as the days went on, little
by little she came to return your glance? – then your smile?
– then, at last, your greeting? And do you remember, once,
that you told me about it in a moment of depression – told
me that you were close to infatuation, that you believed her
to be everything sweet and innocent, that you dared not
drift any farther, knowing the chances and knowing the end
– bitter unhappiness either way, whether in guilt or innocence—'

'I remember,' said Shannon hoarsely. 'But that is not – it
cannot be—'

'That is the girl.'

'Not the child you told me of—'

'Yes.'

'How – when did you know—'

'Tonight. I know more than that, Shannon. You will learn
it later. Now ask me again, what it is that you may do.'

'I ask it,' said Shannon under his breath. 'What am I to
do?'

For a long while Harrod sat silent, staring out of the dark
window; then, 'It is time for us to go.'

'You wish to go out?'

'Yes; we will walk together for a little while – as we did
in the old days, Shannon – only a little while, for I must be
going back.'

'Where are you going, Harrod?'

But the elder man had already risen and moved toward
the door; and Shannon picked up his hat and followed him
out across the dusky lamplighted street.

Into the avenue they passed under the white, unsteady
radiance of arc lights which drooped like huge lilies from
stalks of bronze; here and there the front of some hotel lifted
like a cliff, its window-pierced façade pulsating with yellow
light, or a white marble mass, cold and burned out, spread
a sea of shadow over the glimmering asphalt. At times the
lighted lamps of cabs flashed in their faces; at times figures

passed like spectres; but into the street where they were now turning were neither lamps nor people nor sound, nor any light, save, far in the obscure vista, a dull hint of lightning edging the west.

Twice Shannon had stopped, peering at Harrod, who neither halted nor slackened his steady, noiseless pace; and the younger man, hesitating, moved on again, quickening his steps to his friend's side.

'Where are – are you going?'

'Do you not know?'

The color died out of Shannon's face; he spoke again, forming his words slowly with dry lips:

'Harrod, why – why do you come into this street – tonight? What do you know? *How* do you know? I tell you I – I cannot endure this – this tension—'

'*She* is enduring it.'

'Good God!'

'Yes, God is good,' said Harrod, turning his haggard face as they halted. 'Answer me, Shannon, where are we going?'

'To – her. You know it! Harrod! Harrod! How did you know? I – I did not know myself until an hour before I met you; I had not seen her in weeks – I had not dared to – for all trust in self was dead. Today, downtown, I faced the crash and saw across tomorrow the end of all. Then, in my journey hellward tonight, just at dusk, we passed each other, and before I understood what I had done we were side by side. And almost instantly – I don't know how – she seemed to sense the ruin before us both – for mine was heavy on my soul, Harrod, as I stood, measuring damnation with smiling eyes – at the brink of it, there. And she knew I was adrift at last.'

He looked up at the house before him. 'I said I would come. She neither assented nor denied me, nor asked a question. But in her eyes, Harrod, I saw what one sees in the eyes of children, and it stunned me . . . What shall I do?'

'Go to her and look again,' said Harrod. '*That* is what I have come back to ask of you. Goodbye.'

He turned, his shadowy face drooping, and Shannon followed to the avenue. There, in the white outbreak of electric lamps, he saw Harrod again as he had always known him, a hint of a smile in his worn eyes, the well-shaped mouth edged with laughter, and he was saying: 'It's all in a lifetime, Shannon – and more than you suspect – much more. You have not told me her name yet?'

'I do not know it.'

'Ah, she will tell you if you ask! Say to her that I remember her there on the sea rocks. Say to her that I have searched for her always, but that it was only tonight I knew what tomorrow she shall know – and you, Shannon, you, too, shall know. Goodbye.'

'Harrod! Wait. Don't – don't go—'

He turned and looked back at the younger man with that familiar gesture he knew so well.

It was final, and Shannon swung blindly on his heel and entered the street again, eyes raised to the high lighted window under which he had halted a moment before. Then he mounted the steps, groped in the vestibule for the illuminated number, and touched the electric knob. The door swung open noiselessly as he entered, closing behind him with a soft click.

Up he sped, mounting stair on stair, threading the narrow hallways, then upwards again, until of a sudden she stood confronting him, bent forward, white hands tightening on the banisters.

Neither spoke. She straightened slowly, fingers relaxing from the polished rail. Over her shoulders he saw a lamp-lighted room, and she turned and looked backward at the threshold and covered her face with both hands.

'What is it?' he whispered, bending close to her. 'Why do you tremble? You need not. There is nothing in all the world you need fear. Look into my eyes. Even a child may read them now.'

Her hands fell from her face and their eyes met, and what she read in his, and he in hers, God knows, for she swayed where she stood, lids closing: yielding hands and lips and throat and hair. She cried, too, later, her hands on his shoulders where he knelt beside her, holding him at arm's length from her fresh young face to search his for the menace she once had read there. But it was gone – that menace she had read and vaguely understood, and she cried a little more, one arm around his head pressed close to her side.

'From the very first – the first moment I saw you,' he said under his breath, answering the question aquiver on her lips – lips divinely merciful, repeating the lovers' creed and the confession of faith for which, perhaps, all souls in love are shriven in the end.

'Naida! Naida!' – for he had learned her name and could not have enough of it – 'all that the world holds for me of good is here, circled by my arms. Not mine the manhood to win out, alone – but there is a man who came to me tonight and stood sponsor for the falling soul within me.

'How he knew my peril and yours, God knows. But he came like Fate and held his buckler before me, and he led me here and set a flaming sword before your door – the door of the child he loved – there on the sea rocks ten years ago. Do you remember? He said you would. And he is no archangel – this man among men, this friend with whom, unknowing, I have this night wrestled face to face. His name is Harrod.'

'*My* name!' She stood up straight and pale, within the circle of his arms; he rose, too, speechless, uncertain – then faced her, white and appalled.

She said: 'He – he followed us to Bar Harbor. I was a child, I remember. I hid from my governess and talked with him on the rocks. Then we went away. I – I lost my father.' Staring at her, his stiffening lips formed a word, but no sound came.

'Bring him to me!' she whispered. 'How can he know I

am here and stay away! Does he think I have forgotten? Does he think shame of me? Bring him to me!'

She caught his hands in hers and kissed them passionately; she framed his face in her small hands of a child and looked deep, deep into his eyes: 'Oh, the happiness you have brought! I love you! You with whom I am to enter Paradise! Now bring him to me!'

Shaking, amazed, stunned in a whirl of happiness and doubt, he crept down the black stairway, feeling his way. The doors swung noiselessly; he was almost running when he turned into the avenue. The trail of white lights starred his path; the solitary street echoed his haste, and now he sprang into the wide doorway of the club, and as he passed, the desk clerk leaned forward, handing him a telegram. He took it, halted, breathing heavily, and asked for his friend.

'Mr Harrod?' repeated the clerk. 'Mr Harrod has not been here in a month, sir.'

'What? I dined with Mr Harrod here at eight o'clock!' he laughed.

'Sir? I – I beg your pardon, sir, but you dined here alone tonight—'

'Send for the steward!' broke in Shannon impatiently, slapping his open palm with the yellow envelope. The steward came, followed by the butler, and to a quick question from the desk clerk, replied: 'Mr Harrod has not been in the club for six weeks.'

'But I dined with Mr Harrod at eight! Wilkins, did you not serve us?'

'I served you, sir; you dined alone—' The butler hesitated, coughed discreetly; and the steward added: 'You ordered for two, sir—'

Something in the steward's troubled face silenced Shannon; the butler ventured: 'Beg pardon, sir, but we – the waiters thought you might be – ill, seeing how you talked to yourself and called for ink to write upon the cloth and broke two glasses, laughing like—'

Shannon staggered, turning a ghastly visage from one to

another. Then his dazed gaze centered upon the telegram crushed in his hand, and shaking from head to foot, he smoothed it out and opened the envelope.

But it was purely a matter of business; he was requested to come to Bar Harbor and identify a useless check, drawn to his order, and perhaps aid to identify the body of a drowned man in the morgue.

UN PEU D'AMOUR

When I returned to the plateau from my investigation of
the crater, I realized that I had descended the grassy pit as
far as any human being could descend. No living creature
could pass that barrier of flame and vapor. Of that I was
convinced.

Now, not only the crater but its steaming effluvia was
utterly unlike anything I had ever before beheld. There was
no trace of lava to be seen, or of pumice, ashes, or of volcanic
rejecta in any form whatever. There were no sulphuric odors,
no pungent fumes, nothing to teach the olfactory nerves
what might be the nature of the silvery steam rising from
the crater incessantly in a vast circle, ringing its circumference
halfway down the slope.

Under this thin curtain of steam a ring of pale yellow
flames played and sparkled, completely encircling the slope.

The crater was about half a mile deep; the sides sloped
gently to the bottom.

But the odd feature of the entire phenomenon was this:
the bottom of the crater seemed to be entirely free from fire
and vapor. It was disk-shaped, sandy, and flat, about a quarter
of a mile in diameter. Through my field-glasses I could see
patches of grass and wild flowers growing in the sand here
and there, and the sparkle of water, and a crow or two,
feeding and walking about.

I looked at the girl who was standing beside me, then
cast a glance around at the very unusual landscape.

We were standing on the summit of a mountain some two thousand feet high, looking into a cup-shaped depression or crater, on the edges of which we stood.

This low, flat-topped mountain, as I say, was grassy and quite treeless, although it rose like a truncated sugar-cone out of a wilderness of trees which stretched for miles below us, north, south, east, and west, bordered on the horizon by towering blue mountains, their distant ranges enclosing the forests as in a vast amphitheatre.

From the centre of this enormous green floor of foliage rose our grassy hill, and it appeared to be the only irregularity which broke the level wilderness as far as the base of the dim blue ranges encircling the horizon.

Except for the log bungalow of Mr Blythe on the eastern edge of this grassy plateau, there was not a human habitation in sight, nor a trace of man's devastating presence in the wilderness around us.

Again I looked questioningly at the girl beside me and she looked back at me rather seriously.

'Shall we seat ourselves here in the sun?' she asked.

I nodded.

Very gravely we settled down side by side on the thick green grass.

'Now,' she said, 'I shall tell you why I wrote you to come out here. Shall I?'

'By all means, Miss Blythe.'

Sitting cross-legged, she gathered her ankles into her hands, settling herself as snugly on the grass as a bird settles on its nest.

'The phenomena of nature,' she said, 'have always interested me intensely, not only from the artistic angle but from the scientific point of view.

'It is different with father. He is a painter; he cares only for the artistic aspects of nature. Phenomena of a scientific nature bore him. Also, you may have noticed that he is of a – a slightly impatient disposition.'

I had noticed it. He had been anything but civil to me

when I arrived the night before, after a five-hundred mile trip on a mule, from the nearest railroad – a journey performed entirely alone and by compass, there being no trail after the first fifty miles.

To characterize Blythe as slightly impatient was letting him down easy. He was a selfish, bad-tempered old pig.

'Yes,' I said, answering her, 'I did notice a negligible trace of impatience about your father.'

She flushed.

'You see I did not inform my father that I had written to you. He doesn't like strangers; he doesn't like scientists. I did not dare tell him that I had asked you to come out here. It was entirely my own idea. I felt that I *must* write you because I am positive that what is happening in this wilderness is of vital scientific importance.'

'How did you get a letter out of this distant and desolate place?' I asked.

'Every two months the storekeeper at Windflower Station sends in a man and a string of mules with staples for us. The man takes our further orders and our letters back to civilization.'

I nodded.

'He took my letter to you – among one or two others I sent—'

A charming color came into her cheeks. She was really extremely pretty. I liked that girl. When a girl blushes when she speaks to a man he immediately accepts her heightened color as a personal tribute. This is not vanity: it is merely a proper sense of personal worthiness.

She said thoughtfully:

'The mail bag which that man brought to us last week contained a letter which, had I received it earlier, would have made my invitation to you unnecessary. I am sorry I disturbed you.'

'*I* am not,' said I, looking into her beautiful eyes.

I twisted my mustache into two attractive points, shot my cuffs, and glanced at her again, receptively.

She had a far-away expression in her eyes. I straightened my necktie. A man, without being vain, ought to be conscious of his own worth.

'And now,' she continued, 'I am going to tell you the various reasons why I asked so celebrated a scientist as yourself to come here.'

I thanked her for her encomium.

'Ever since my father retired from Boston to purchase this hill and the wilderness surrounding it,' she went on, 'ever since he came here to live a hermit's life – a life devoted solely to painting landscapes – I also have lived here all alone with him.

'That is three years, now. And from the very beginning – from the very first day of our arrival, somehow or other I was conscious that there was something abnormal about this corner of the world.'

She bent forward, lowering her voice a trifle:

'Have you noticed,' she asked, 'that so many things seem to be *circular* out here?'

'Circular?' I repeated, surprised.

'Yes. That crater is circular; so is the bottom of it; so is this plateau, and the hill; and the forests surrounding us; and the mountain ranges on the horizon.'

'But all this is natural.'

'Perhaps. But in those woods, down there, there are, here and there, great circles of crumbling soil – *perfect* circles a mile in diameter.'

'Mounds built by prehistoric man, no doubt.'

She shook her head:

'These are not prehistoric mounds.'

'Why not?'

'Because they have been freshly made.'

'How do you know?'

'The earth is freshly upheaved; great trees, partly uprooted, slant at every angle from the sides of the enormous piles of newly upturned earth; sand and stones are still sliding from the raw ridges.'

She leaned nearer and dropped her voice still lower:

'More than that,' she said, 'my father and I both have seen one of these huge circles *in the making*!'

'What!' I exclaimed, incredulously.

'It is true. We have seen several. And it enrages father.'

'Enrages?'

'Yes, because it upsets the trees where he is painting landscapes, and tilts them in every direction. Which, of course, ruins his picture; and he is obliged to start another, which vexes him dreadfully.'

I think I must have gaped at her in sheer astonishment.

'But there is something more singular than that for you to investigate,' she said calmly. 'Look down at that circle of steam which makes a perfect ring around the bowl of the crater, halfway down. Do you see the flicker of fire under the vapor?'

'Yes.'

She leaned so near and spoke in such a low voice that her fragrant breath fell upon my cheek:

'In the fire, under the vapors, there are little animals.'

'What!'

'Little beasts live in the fire – slim, furry creatures, smaller than a weasel. I've seen them peep out of the fire and scurry back into it . . . *Now* are you sorry that I wrote you to come? And will you forgive me for bringing you out here?'

An indescribable excitement seized me, endowing me with a fluency and eloquence unusual:

'I thank you from the bottom of my heart!' I cried; '—from the depths of a heart the emotions of which are entirely and exclusively of scientific origin!'

In the impulse of the moment I held out my hand; she laid hers in it with charming diffidence.

'Yours is the discovery,' I said. 'Yours shall be the glory. Fame shall crown you; and perhaps if there remains any reflected light in the form of a by-product, some modest and negligible little ray may chance to illuminate me.'

Surprised and deeply moved by my eloquence, I bent over her hand and saluted it with my lips.

She thanked me. Her pretty face was rosy.

It appeared that she had three cows to milk, new-laid eggs to gather, and the construction of some fresh butter to be accomplished.

At the bars of the grassy pasture slope she dropped me a curtsey, declining very shyly to let me carry her lacteal paraphernalia.

So I continued on to the bungalow garden, where Blythe sat on a camp stool under a green umbrella, painting a picture of something or other.

'Mr Blythe!' I cried, striving to subdue my enthusiasm. 'The eyes of the scientific world are now open upon this house! The searchlight of Fame is about to be turned upon you—'

'I prefer privacy,' he interrupted. 'That's why I came here. I'll be obliged if you'll turn off that searchlight.'

'But, my dear Mr Blythe—'

'I want to be let alone,' he repeated irritably. 'I came out here to paint and to enjoy privately my own paintings.'

If what stood on his easel was a sample of his pictures, nobody was likely to share his enjoyment.

'Your work,' said I, politely, 'is – is—'

'Is what!' he snapped. '*What* is it – if you think you know?'

'It is entirely, so to speak, *per se* – by itself—'

'What the devil do you mean by that?'

I looked at his picture, appalled. The entire canvas was one monotonous vermilion conflagration. I examined it with my head on one side, then on the other side; I made a funnel with both hands and peered intently through it at the picture. A menacing murmuring sound came from him.

'Satisfying – exquisitely satisfying,' I concluded. 'I have often seen such sunsets—'

'What!'

'I mean such prairie fires—'

'Damnation!' he exclaimed. 'I'm painting a bowl of nasturtiums!'

'I was speaking purely in metaphor,' said I with a sickly

smile. 'To me a nasturtium by the river brink is more than a simple flower. It is a broader, grander, more magnificent, more stupendous symbol. It may mean anything, everything – such as sunsets and conflagrations and Götterdämmerungs! Or' – and my voice was subtly modulated to an appealing and persuasive softness – 'it may mean nothing at all – chaos, void, vacuum, negation, the exquisite annihilation of what has never even existed.'

He glared at me over his shoulder. If he was infected by Cubist tendencies he evidently had not understood what I said.

'If you won't talk about my pictures I don't mind your investigating this district,' he grunted, dabbing at his palette and plastering a wad of vermilion upon his canvas; 'but I object to any public invasion of my artistic privacy until I am ready for it.'

'When will that be?'

He pointed with one vermilion-soaked brush toward a long, low, log building.

'In that structure,' he said, 'are packed one thousand and ninety-five paintings – all signed by me. I have executed one or two every day since I came here. When I have painted exactly ten thousand pictures, no more, no less, I shall erect here a gallery large enough to contain them all.

'Only real lovers of art will ever come here to study them. It is five hundred miles from the railroad. Therefore, I shall never have to endure the praises of the dilettante, the patronage of the idler, the vapid rhapsodies of the vulgar. Only those who understand will care to make the pilgrimage.'

He waved his brushes at me:

'The conservation of national resources is all well enough – the setting aside of timber reserves, game preserves, bird refuges, all these projects are very good in a way. But I have dedicated this wilderness as a last and only refuge in all the world for true Art! Because true Art, except for my pictures, is, I believe, now practically extinct! . . . You're in my way. Would you mind getting out?'

I had sidled around between him and his bowl of nasturtiums, and I hastily stepped aside. He squinted at the flowers, mixed up a flamboyant mess of colour on his palette, and daubed away with unfeigned satisfaction, no longer noticing me until I started to go. Then:

'What is it you're here for, anyway?' he demanded abruptly. I said with dignity:

'I am here to investigate those huge rings of earth thrown up in the forest as by a gigantic mole.' He continued to paint for a few moments:

'Well, go and investigate 'em,' he snapped. 'I'm not infatuated with your society.'

'What do you think they are?' I asked, mildly ignoring his wretched manners.

'I don't know and I don't care, except, that sometimes when I begin to paint several trees, the very trees I'm painting are suddenly heaved up and tilted in every direction, and all my work goes for nothing. *That* makes me mad! Otherwise, the matter has no interest for me.'

'But what in the world could cause—'

'I don't know and I don't care!' he shouted, waving palette and brushes angrily. 'Maybe it's an army of moles working all together under the ground; maybe it's some species of circular earthquake. I don't know! I don't care! But it annoys me. And if you can devise any scientific means to stop it, I'll be much obliged to you. Otherwise, to be perfectly frank, you bore me.'

'The mission of Science,' said I solemnly, 'is to alleviate the inconveniences of mundane existence. Science, therefore, shall extend a helping hand to her frailer sister, Art—'

'Science can't patronize Art while I'm around!' he retorted. 'I won't have it!'

'But my dear Mr. Blythe—'

'I won't dispute with you, either! I don't like to dispute!' he shouted. 'Don't try to make me. Don't attempt to inveigle me into discussion! I know all I want to know. I don't want to know anything you want me to know, either!'

I looked at the old pig in haughty silence, nauseated by his conceit.

After he had plastered a few more tubes of vermilion over his canvas he quieted down, and presently gave me an oblique glance over his shoulder.

'Well,' he said, 'what else are you intending to investigate?'

'Those little animals that live in the crater fires,' I said bluntly.

'Yes,' he nodded, indifferently, 'there are creatures which live somewhere in the fires of that crater.'

'Do you realize what an astounding statement you are making?' I asked.

'It doesn't astound *me*. What do I care whether it astounds you or anybody else? Nothing interests me except Art.'

'But—'

'I tell you nothing interests me except Art!' he yelled. 'Don't dispute it! Don't answer me! Don't irritate me! I don't care whether anything lives in the fire or not! Let it live there!'

'But have you actually seen live creatures in the flames?'

'Plenty! *Plenty*! What of it! What about it? Let 'em live there, for all I care. I've painted pictures of 'em, too. That's all that interests me.'

'What do they look like, Mr Blythe?'

'Look like? *I* don't know! They look like weasels or rats or bats or cats or – stop asking me questions! It irritates me! It depresses me! Don't ask any more! Why don't you go in to lunch? And – tell my daughter to bring me a bowl of salad out here. *I've* no time to stuff myself. Some people have. *I* haven't. You'd better go in to lunch . . . And tell my daughter to bring me seven tubes of Chinese vermilion with my salad!'

'You don't mean to mix—' I began, then checked myself before his fury.

'I'd rather eat vermilion paint on my salad than sit here talking to *you*!' he shouted.

I cast a pitying glance at this impossible man, and went

into the house. After all, he was *her* father. I *had* to endure
him.

After Miss Blythe had carried to her father a large bucket of
lettuce leaves, she returned to the veranda of the bungalow.

A delightful luncheon awaited us; I seated her, then took
the chair opposite.

A delicious omelette, fresh biscuit, salad, and strawberry
preserves, and a tall tumbler of iced tea imbued me with a
sort of mild exhilaration.

Out of the corner of my eye I could see Blythe down in
the garden, munching his lettuce leaves like an ill-tempered
rabbit, and daubing away at his picture while he munched.

'Your father,' said I politely, 'is something of a genius.'

'I am so glad you think so,' she said gratefully. 'But don't
tell him so. He has been surfeited with praise in Boston.
That is why we came out here.'

'Art,' said I, 'is like science, or tobacco, or tooth-wash.
Every man to his own brand. Personally, I don't care for his
kind. But who can say which is the best kind of anything?
Only the consumer. Your father is his own consumer. He is
the best judge of what he likes. And that is the only true
test of art, or anything else.'

'How delightfully you reason!' she said. 'How logically,
how generously!'

'Reason is the handmaid of Science, Miss Blythe.'

She seemed to understand me. Her quick intelligence
surprised me, because I myself was not perfectly sure whether
I had emitted piffle or an epigram.

As we ate our strawberry preserves we discussed ways
and means of capturing a specimen of the little fire creatures
which, as she explained, so frequently peeped out at her
from the crater fires, and, at her slightest movement, scurried
back again into the flames. Of course I believed that this
was only her imagination. Yet, for years I had entertained
a theory that fire supported certain unknown forms of life.

'I have long believed,' said I, 'that fire is inhabited by

living organisms which require the elements and temperature of active combustion for their existence – microörganisms, but not,' I added smilingly, 'any higher type of life.'

'In the fireplace,' she ventured diffidently, 'I sometimes see curious things – dragons and snakes and creatures of grotesque and peculiar shapes.'

I smiled indulgently, charmed by this innocently offered contribution to science. Then she rose, and I rose and took her hand in mine, and we wandered over the grass toward the crater, while I explained to her the difference between what we imagine we see in the glowing coals of a grate fire and my own theory that fire is the abode of living animalculae.

On the grassy edge of the crater we paused and looked down the slope, where the circle of steam rose, partly veiling the pale flash of fire underneath.

'How near can we go?' I inquired.

'Quite near. Come; I'll guide you.'

Leading me by the hand, she stepped over the brink and we began to descend the easy grass slope together.

There was no difficulty about it at all. Down we went, nearer and nearer to the wall of steam, until at last, when but fifteen feet away from it, I felt the heat from the flames which sparkled below the wall of vapor.

Here we seated ourselves upon the grass, and I knitted my brows and fixed my eyes upon this curious phenomenon, striving to discover some reason for it.

Except for the vapor and the fires, there was nothing whatever volcanic about this spectacle, or in the surroundings.

From where I sat I could see that the bed of fire which encircled the crater, and the wall of vapor which crowned the flames, were about three hundred feet wide. Of course this barrier was absolutely impassable. There was no way of getting through it into the bottom of the crater.

A slight pressure from Miss Blythe's fingers engaged my attention; I turned toward her, and she said:

'There is one more thing about which I have not told you. I feel a little guilty, because *that* is the real reason I asked you to come here.'

'What is it?'

'I think there are emeralds on the floor of that crater.'

'Emeralds!'

'I *think* so.' She felt in the ruffled pocket of her apron, drew out a fragment of mineral, and passed it to me.

I screwed a jeweler's glass into my eye and examined it in astonished silence. It was an emerald; a fine, large, immensely valuable stone, if my experience counted for anything. One side of it was thickly coated with vermilion paint.

'Where did this come from?' I asked in an agitated voice.

'From the floor of the crater. Is it *really* an emerald?'

I lifted my head and stared at the girl incredulously.

'It happened this way,' she said excitedly. 'Father was painting a picture up there by the edge of the crater. He left his palette on the grass to go to the bungalow for some more tubes of color. While he was in the house, hunting for the colors which he wanted, I stepped out on the veranda, and I saw some crows alight near the palette and begin to stalk about in the grass. One bird walked right over his wet palette; I stepped out and waved my sun-bonnet to frighten him off, but he had both feet in a sticky mass of Chinese vermilion, and for a moment was unable to free himself.

'I almost caught him, but he flapped away over the edge of the crater, high above the wall of vapor, sailed down onto the crater floor, and alighted.

'But his feet bothered him; he kept hopping about on the bottom of the crater, half running, half flying; and finally he took wing and rose up over the hill.

'As he flew above me, and while I was looking up at his vermilion feet, something dropped from his claws and nearly struck me. It was that emerald.'

When I had recovered sufficient composure to speak steadily, I took her beautiful little hand in mine.

'This,' said I, 'is the most exciting locality I have ever visited for purposes of scientific research. Within this crater may lie millions of value in emeralds. You are probably, today, the wealthiest heiress upon the face of the globe!'

I gave her a winning glance. She smiled, shyly, and blushingly withdrew her hand.

For several exquisite minutes I sat there beside her in a sort of heavenly trance. How beautiful she was! How engaging – how sweet – how modestly appreciative of the man beside her, who had little beside his scientific learning, his fame, and a kind heart to appeal to such youth and loveliness as hers!

There was something about her that delicately appealed to me. Sometimes I pondered what this might be; sometimes I wondered how many emeralds lay on that floor of sandy gravel below us.

Yes, I loved her. I realised it now. I could even endure her father for her sake. I should make a good husband. I was quite certain of that.

I turned and gazed upon her, meltingly. But I did not wish to startle her, so I remained silent, permitting the chaste language of my eyes to interpret for her what my lips had not yet murmured. It was a brief but beautiful moment in my life.

'The way to do,' said I, 'is to trap several dozen crows, smear their feet with glue, tie a ball of Indian twine to the ankle of every bird, then liberate them. Some are certain to fly into the crater and try to scrape the glue off in the sand. Then,' I added, triumphantly, 'all we have to do is to haul in our birds and detach the wealth of Midas from their sticky claws!'

'That is an excellent suggestion,' she said gratefully, 'but I can do that after you have gone. All I wanted you to tell me was whether the stone is a genuine emerald.'

I gazed at her blankly.

'You are here for purposes of scientific investigation,' she added, sweetly. 'I should not think of taking your time for the mere sake of accumulating wealth for my father and me.'

There didn't seem to be anything for me to say at that moment. Chilled, I gazed at the flashing ring of fire.

And, as I gazed, suddenly I became aware of a little, pointed muzzle, two pricked-up ears, and two ruby-red eyes gazing intently out at me from the mass of flames.

The girl beside me saw it, too.

'Don't move!' she whispered. 'That is one of the flame creatures. It may venture out if you keep perfectly still.'

Rigid with amazement, I sat like a stone image, staring at the most astonishing sight I had ever beheld.

For several minutes the ferret-like creature never stirred from where it crouched in the crater fire; the alert head remained pointed toward us; I could even see that its thick fur must have possessed the qualities of asbestos, because here and there a hair or two glimmered incandescent; and its eyes, nose, and whiskers glowed and glowed as the flames pulsated around it.

After a long while it began to move out of the fire, slowly, cautiously, cunning eyes fixed on us – a small, slim, wiry, weasel-like creature on which the sunlight fell with a vitreous glitter as it crept forward into the grass.

Then, from the fire behind, another creature of the same sort appeared, another, others, then dozens of eager, lithe, little animals appeared everywhere from the flames and began to frisk and play and run about in the grass and nibble the fresh, green, succulent herbage with a snipping sound quite audible to us.

One came so near my feet that I could examine it minutely.

Its fur and whiskers seemed heavy and dense and like asbestos fibre, yet so fine as to appear silky. Its eyes, nose, and claws were scarlet, and seemed to possess a glassy surface.

I waited my opportunity, and when the little thing came nosing along within reach, I seized it. Instantly it emitted a bewildering series of whistling shrieks, and twisted around to bite me. Its body was icy.

'Don't let it bite!' cried the girl. 'Be careful, Mr Smith!'

But its jaws were toothless; only soft, cold gums pinched me, and I held it twisting and writhing, while the icy temperature of its body began to benumb my fingers and creep up my wrist, paralyzing my arm; and its incessant and piercing shrieks deafened me.

In vain I transferred it to the other hand, and then passed it from one hand to the other, as one shifts a lump of ice or a hot potato, in an attempt to endure the temperature: it shrieked and squirmed and doubled, and finally wriggled out of my stiffened and useless hands, and scuttled away into the fire.

It was an overwhelming disappointment. For a moment it seemed unendurable.

'Never mind,' I said huskily, 'if I caught one in my hands, I can surely catch another in a trap.'

'I am so sorry for your disappointment,' she said, pitifully.

'Do *you* care, Miss Blythe?' I asked.

She blushed. 'Of course I care,' she murmured.

My hands were too badly frost-nipped to become eloquent. I merely sighed and thrust them into my pockets. Even my arm was too stiff to encircle her shapeful waist. Devotion to Science had temporarily crippled me. Love must wait. But, as we ascended the grassy slope together, I promised myself that I would make her a good husband, and that I should spend at least part of every day of my life in trapping crows and smearing their claws with glue.

That evening I was seated on the veranda beside Wilna – Miss Blythe's name was Wilna – and what with gazing at her and fitting together some of the folding box-traps which I always carried with me – and what with trying to realise the pecuniary magnificence of our future existence together, I was exceedingly busy when Blythe came in to display, as I supposed, his most recent daub to me.

The canvas he carried presented a series of crimson speckles, out of which burst an eruption of green streaks – and it made me think of stepping on a caterpillar.

My instinct was to placate this impossible man. He was *her* father. I meant to honor him if I had to assault him to do it.

'Supremely satisfying!' I nodded, chary of naming the subject. 'It is a stride beyond the art of the future: it is a flying leap out of the Not Yet into the Possibly Perhaps! I thank you for enlightening me, Mr Blythe. I am your debtor.'

He fairly snarled at me:

'What are *you* talking about!' he demanded.

I remained modestly mute.

To Wilna he said, pointing passionately at his canvas:

'The crows have been walking all over it again! I'm going to paint in the woods after this, earthquakes or no earthquakes. Have the trees been heaved up anywhere recently?'

'Not since last week,' she said, soothingly. 'It usually happens after a rain.'

'I think I'll risk it then – although it did rain early this morning. I'll do a moonlight down there this evening.' And, turning to me: 'If you know as much about science as you do about art you won't have to remain here long – I trust.'

'What?' said I, very red.

He laughed a highly disagreeable laugh, and marched into the house. Presently he bawled for dinner, and Wilna went away. For her sake I had remained calm and dignified, but presently I went out and kicked up the turf two or three times; and, having foozled my wrath, I went back to dinner, realising that I might as well begin to accustom myself to my future father-in-law.

It seemed that he had a mania for prunes, and that's all he permitted anybody to have for dinner.

Disgusted, I attempted to swallow the loathly stewed fruit, watching Blythe askance as he hurriedly stuffed himself, using a tablespoon, with every symptom of relish.

'Now,' he cried, shoving back his chair, 'I'm going to paint a moonlight by moonlight. Wilna, if Billy arrives, make him comfortable, and tell him I'll return by midnight.' And without taking the trouble to notice me at all, he strode away toward the veranda, chewing vigorously upon his last prune.

'Your father,' said I, 'is eccentric. Genius usually is. But he is a most interesting and estimable man. I revere him.'

'It is kind of you to say so,' said the girl, in a low voice.

I thought deeply for a few moments, then:

'Who is "Billy"?' I inquired, casually.

I couldn't tell whether it was a sudden gleam of sunset light on her face, or whether she blushed.

'Billy,' she said softly, 'is a friend of father's. His name is William Green.'

'Oh.'

'He is coming out here to visit – father – I believe.'

'Oh. An artist; and doubtless of mature years.'

'He is a mineralogist by profession,' she said, '—and somewhat young.'

'Oh.'

'Twenty-four years old,' she added. Upon her pretty face was an absent expression, vaguely pleasant. Her blue eyes became dreamy and exquisitely remote.

I pondered deeply for a while:

'Wilna?' I said.

'Yes, Mr Smith?' as though aroused from agreeable meditation.

But I didn't know exactly what to say, and I remained uneasily silent, thinking about that man Green and his twenty-four years, and his profession, and the bottom of the crater, and Wilna – and striving to satisfy myself that there was no logical connection between any of these.

'I think,' said I, 'that I'll take a bucket of salad to your father.'

Why I should have so suddenly determined to ingratiate myself with the old grouch I scarcely understood: for the construction of a salad was my very best accomplishment.

Wilna looked at me in a peculiar manner, almost as though she were controlling a sudden and not unpleasant inward desire to laugh.

Evidently the finer and more delicate instincts of a woman were divining my motive and sympathizing with my mental and sentimental perplexity.

So when she said: 'I don't think you had better go near my father,' I was convinced of her gentle solicitude in my behalf.

'With a bucket of salad,' I whispered softly, 'much may be accomplished, Wilna.' And I took her little hand and pressed it gently and respectfully. 'Trust all to me,' I murmured.

She stood with her head turned away from me, her slim hand resting limply in mine. From the slight tremor of her shoulders I became aware how deeply her emotion was now swaying her. Evidently she was nearly ready to become mine.

But I remained calm and alert. The time was not yet. Her father had had his prunes, in which he delighted. And when pleasantly approached with a bucket of salad he could not listen otherwise than politely to what I had to say to him. Quick action was necessary – quick but diplomatic action – in view of the imminence of this young man Green, who evidently was *persona grata* at the bungalow of this irritable old dodo.

Tenderly pressing the pretty hand which I held, and saluting the finger-tips with a gesture which was, perhaps, not wholly ungraceful, I stepped into the kitchen, washed out several heads of lettuce, deftly chopped up some youthful onions, constructed a seductive French dressing, and, stirring together the crisp ingredients, set the savoury masterpiece away in the ice-box, after tasting it. It was delicious enough to draw sobs from any pig.

When I went out to the veranda, Wilna had disappeared. So I unfolded and set up some more box-traps, determined to lose no time.

Sunset still lingered beyond the chain of western mountains as I went out across the grassy plateau to the cornfield.

Here I set and baited several dozen aluminum crow-traps,

padding the jaws so that no injury could be done to the birds when the springs snapped on their legs.

Then I went over to the crater and descended its gentle, grassy slope. And there, all along the borders of the vapoury wall, I set box-traps for the lithe little denizens of the fire, baiting every trap with a handful of fresh, sweet clover which I had pulled up from the pasture beyond the cornfield.

My task ended, I ascended the slope again, and for a while stood there immersed in pleasurable premonitions.

Everything had been accomplished swiftly and methodically within the few hours in which I had first set eyes upon this extraordinary place – everything! – love at first sight, the delightfully lightning-like wooing and winning of an incomparable maiden and heiress; the discovery of the fire creatures; the solving of the emerald problem.

And now everything was ready, crow-traps, fire-traps, a bucket of irresistible salad for Blythe, a modest and tremulous avowal for Wilna as soon as her father tasted the salad and I had pleasantly notified him of my intentions concerning his lovely offspring.

Daylight faded from rose to lilac; already the mountains were growing fairy-like under that vague, diffuse lustre which heralds the rise of the full moon. It rose, enormous, yellow, unreal, becoming imperceptibly silvery as it climbed the sky and hung aloft like a stupendous arc-light flooding the world with a radiance so white and clear that I could very easily have written verses by it, if I wrote verses.

Down on the edge of the forest I could see Blythe on his camp-stool, madly besmearing his moonlit canvas, but I could not see Wilna anywhere. Maybe she had shyly retired somewhere by herself to think of me.

So I went back to the house, filled a bucket with my salad, and started toward the edge of the woods, singing happily as I sped on feet so light and frolicsome that they seemed to skim the ground. How wonderful is the power of love!

When I approached Blythe he heard me coming and turned around.

'What the devil do *you* want?' he asked with characteristic civility.

'I have brought you,' said I gaily, 'a bucket of salad.'

'I don't want any salad!'

'W-what?'

'I never eat it at night.'

I said confidently:

'Mr Blythe, if you will taste this salad I am sure you will not regret it.' And with hideous cunning I set the bucket beside him on the grass and seated myself near it. The old dodo grunted and continued to daub the canvas; but presently, as though forgetfully, and from sheer instinct, he reached down into the bucket, pulled out a leaf of lettuce, and shoved it into his mouth.

My heart leaped exultantly. I had him!

'Mr Blythe,' I began in a winningly modulated voice, and, at the same instant, he sprang from his camp-chair, his face distorted.

'There are onions in this salad!' he yelled. 'What the devil do you mean! Are you trying to poison me! What are you following me about for, anyway? Why are you running about under foot every minute!'

'My dear Mr Blythe,' I protested – but he barked at me, kicked over the bucket of salad, and began to dance with rage.

'What's the matter with you, anyway!' he bawled. 'Why are you trying to feed me? What do you mean by trying to be attentive to me!'

'I – I admire and revere you—'

'No, you don't!' he shouted. 'I don't want you to admire me! I don't desire to be revered! I don't like attention and politeness! Do you hear! It's artificial – out of date – ridiculous! The only thing that recommends a man to me is his bad manners, bad temper, and violent habits. There's some meaning to such a man, none at all to men like you!'

He ran at the salad bucket and kicked it again.

'They all fawned on me in Boston!' he panted. 'They ran

about under foot! They bought my pictures! And they made me sick! I came out here to be rid of 'em!'

I rose from the grass, pale and determined.

'You listen to me, you old grouch!' I hissed. 'I'll go. But before I go I'll tell you why I've been civil to you. There's only one reason in the world: I want to marry your daughter! And I'm going to do it!'

I stepped nearer him, menacing him with outstretched hand:

'As for you, you pitiable old dodo, with your bad manners and your worse pictures, and your degraded mania for prunes, you are a necessary evil that's all, and I haven't the slightest respect for either you or your art!'

'Is that true?' he said in an altered voice.

'True?' I laughed bitterly. 'Of course it's true, you miserable dauber!'

'D-dauber!' he stammered.

'Certainly! I *said* "dauber" and I mean it. Why, your work would shame the pictures on a child's slate!'

'Smith,' he said unsteadily, 'I believe I have utterly misjudged you. I believe you are a good deal of a man, after all—'

'I'm man enough,' said I, fiercely, 'to go back, saddle my mule, kidnap your daughter, and start for home. And I'm going to do it!'

'Wait!' he cried. 'I don't want you to go. If you'll remain I'll be very glad. I'll do anything you like. I'll quarrel with you, and you can insult my pictures. It will agreeably stimulate us both. Don't go, Smith—'

'If I stay, may I marry Wilna?'

'If you ask me I won't let you!'

'Very well!' I retorted, angrily. 'Then I'll marry her anyway!'

'That's the way to talk! Don't go, Smith. I'm really beginning to like you. And when Billy Green arrives you and he will have a delightfully violent scene—'

'What!'

He rubbed his hands gleefully.

'He's in love with Wilna. You and he won't get on. It is going to be very stimulating for me – I can see that! You and he are going to behave most disagreeably to each other. And I shall be exceedingly unpleasant to you both! Come, Smith, promise me that you'll stay!'

Profoundly worried, I stood staring at him in the moonlight, gnawing my mustache.

'Very well,' I said, 'I'll remain if—'

Something checked me, I did not quite know what for a moment. Blythe, too, was staring at me in an odd, apprehensive way. Suddenly I realised that under my feet the ground was stirring.

'Look out!' I cried; but speech froze on my lips as beneath me the solid earth began to rock and crack and billow up into a high, crumbling ridge, moving continually, as the sod cracks, heaves up, and crumbles above the subterranean progress of a mole.

Up into the air we were slowly pushed on the ever-growing ridge; and with us were carried rocks and bushes and sod, and even forest trees.

I could hear their tap-roots part with pistol-like reports; see great pines and hemlocks and oaks moving, slanting, settling, tilting crazily in every direction as they were heaved upward in this gigantic disturbance.

Blythe caught me by the arm; we clutched each other, balancing on the crest of the steadily rising mound.

'W-what is it?' he stammered. 'Look! It's circular. The woods are rising in a huge circle. What's happening? Do you know?'

Over me crept a horrible certainty that *something living* was moving under us through the depths of the earth – something that, as it progressed, was heaping up the surface of the world above its unseen and burrowing course – something dreadful, enormous, sinister, and *alive*!

'Look out!' screamed Blythe; and at the same instant the crumbling summit of the ridge opened under our feet and a fissure hundreds of yards long yawned ahead of us.

And along it, shining slimily in the moonlight, a vast, viscous, ringed surface was moving, retracting, undulating, elongating, writhing, squirming, shuddering.

'It's a worm!' shrieked Blythe. 'Oh, God! It's a mile long!'

As in a nightmare we clutched each other, struggling frantically to avoid the fissure; but the soft earth slid and gave way under us, and we fell heavily upon that ghastly, living surface.

Instantly a violent convulsion hurled us upward; we fell on it again, rebounding from the rubbery thing, strove to regain our feet and scramble up the edges of the fissure, strove madly while the mammoth worm slid more rapidly through the rocking forests, carrying us forward with a speed increasing.

Through the forest we tore, reeling about on the slippery back of the thing, as though riding on a plowshare, while trees clashed and tilted and fell from the enormous furrow on every side; then, suddenly out of the woods into the moonlight, far ahead of us we could see the grassy upland heave up, cake, break, and crumble above the burrowing course of the monster.

'It's making for the crater!' gasped Blythe; and horror spurred us on, and we scrambled and slipped and clawed the billowing sides of the furrow until we gained the heaving top of it.

As one runs in a bad dream, heavily, half-paralyzed, so ran Blythe and I, toiling over the undulating, tumbling upheaval until, half-fainting, we fell and rolled down the shifting slope onto solid and unvexed sod on the very edges of the crater.

Below us we saw, with sickened eyes, the entire circumference of the crater agitated, saw it rise and fall as avalanches of rock and earth slid into it, tons and thousands of tons rushing down the slope, blotting from our sight the flickering ring of flame, and extinguishing the last filmy jet of vapor.

Suddenly the entire crater caved in and filled up under my anguished eyes, quenching for all eternity the vapour wall, the fire, and burying the little denizens of the flames, and perhaps a billion dollars' worth of emeralds under as many billion tons of earth.

Quieter and quieter grew the earth as the gigantic worm bored straight down into the depths immeasurable. And at last the moon shone upon a world that lay without a tremor in its milky lustre.

'I shall name it *Verma gigantica*,' said I, with a hysterical sob; 'but nobody will ever believe me when I tell this story!'

Still terribly shaken, we turned toward the house. And, as we approached the lamplit veranda, I saw a horse standing there and a young man hastily dismounting.

And then a terrible thing occurred; for, before I could even shriek, Wilna had put both arms around that young man's neck, and both of his arms were clasping her waist.

Blythe was kind to me. He took me around the back way and put me to bed.

And there I lay through the most awful night I ever experienced, listening to the piano below, where Wilna and William Green were singing, 'Un Peu d'Amour'.

GREY MAGIC

In our first extract from The Slayer of Souls, *Victor Cleves meets Tressa Norne for the first time, unaware that she will become his wife . . .*

To Victor Cleves came the following telegram in code:

Washington,
April 14th, 1919.

Investigation ordered by the State Department as the result of frequent mention in despatches of Chinese troops operating with the Russian Bolsheviki forces has disclosed that the Bolsheviki are actually raising a Chinese division of 30,000 men recruited in Central Asia. This division has been guilty of the greatest cruelties. A strange rumour prevails among the Allied forces at Archangel that this Chinese division is led by Yezidee and Hassani officers belonging to the sect of devil-worshipers and that they employ black arts and magic in battle.

From information so far gathered by the several branches of the United States Secret Service operating throughout the world, it appears possible that the various revolutionary forces of disorder, in Europe and Asia, which now are violently threatening the peace and security, of all established civilization on earth, may have had a common origin. This origin, it is now suspected, may date back to a very remote epoch; the wide-spread forces of violence and merciless destruction may have had their beginning among some ancient and predatory race whose existence was maintained solely by robbery and murder.

Anarchists, terrorists, Bolshevists, Reds of all shades and degrees, are now believed to represent in modern times what perhaps once was a tribe of Assassins – a sect whose religion was founded upon a common predilection for crimes of violence.

On this theory then, for the present, the United States Government will proceed with this investigation of Bolshevism; and the Secret Service will continue to pay particular attention to all Orientals in the United States and other countries. You personally are formally instructed to keep in touch with XLY-371 (Alek Selden) and ZB-303 (James Benton), and to employ every possible means to become friendly with the girl Tressa Norne, win her confidence, and, if possible, enlist her actively in the Government Service as your particular aid and comrade.

It is equally important that the movements of the Oriental, called Sanang, be carefully observed in order to discover the identity and whereabouts of his companions. However, until further instructions he is not to be taken into custody. M.H. 2479.

(Signed)
JOHN RECKLOW

The long despatch from John Recklow made Cleves's duty plain enough.

For months, now, Selden and Benton had been watching Tressa Norne. And they had learned practically nothing about her.

And now the girl had come within Cleves's sphere of operation. She had been in New York for two weeks.

Telegrams from Benton in Chicago, and from Selden in Buffalo, had prepared him for her arrival.

He had his men watching her boarding-house on West Twenty-eighth Street, men to follow her, men to keep their eyes on her at the theatre, where every evening, at 10:45, her *entr'acte* was staged. He knew where to get her. But he, himself, had been on the watch for the man Sanang; and had failed to find the slightest trace of him in New York, although warned that he had arrived.

So, for that evening, he left the hunt for Sanang to others, put on his evening clothes, and dined with fashionable friends at the Patrons' Club, who never for an instant suspected that young Victor Cleves was in the Service of the United States Government. About half-past nine he strolled around to the theatre, desiring to miss as much as possible of the popular show without being too late to see the curious little *entr'acte* in which this girl, Tressa Norne, appeared alone.

He had secured an aisle seat near the stage at an outrageous price; the main show was still thundering and fizzing and glittering as he entered the theatre; so he stood in the rear behind the orchestra until the descending curtain extinguished the outrageous glare and din.

Then he went down the aisle, and as he seated himself Tressa Norne stepped from the wings and stood before the lowered curtain facing an expectant but oddly undemonstrative audience.

The girl worked rapidly, seriously, and in silence. She seemed a mere child there behind the footlights, not more than sixteen anyway – her winsome eyes and wistful lips unspoiled by the world's wisdom.

Yet once or twice the mouth drooped for a second and the winning eyes darkened to a remoter blue – the brooding iris hue of far horizons.

She wore the characteristic tabard of stiff golden tissue and the gold pagoda-shaped headpiece of a Yezidee temple girl. Her flat, slipper-shaped footgear was of stiff gold, too, and curled upward at the toes.

All this accentuated her apparent youth. For in face and throat no firmer contours had as yet modified the soft fullness of immaturity; her limbs were boyish and frail, and her bosom more undecided still, so that the embroidered breadth of gold fell flat and straight from her chest to a few inches above the ankles.

She seemed to have no stock of paraphernalia with which to aid the performance; no assistant, no orchestral diversion, nor did she serve herself with any magician's patter. She did her work close to the footlights.

Behind her loomed a black curtain; the strip of stage in front was bare even of carpet; the orchestra remained mute.

But when she needed anything – a little table, for example – well, it was suddenly there where she required it – a tripod, for instance, evidently fitted to hold the big iridescent bubble of glass in which swarmed little tropical fishes – and which arrived neatly from nowhere. She merely placed her hands before her as though ready to support something weighty which she expected and – suddenly, the huge crystal bubble was visible, resting between her hands. And when she tired of holding it, she set it upon the empty air and let go of it; and instead of crashing to the stage with its finny rainbow swarm of swimmers, out of thin air appeared a tripod to support it.

Applause followed, not very enthusiastic, for the sort of audience which sustains the shows of which her performance was merely an *entr'acte* is an audience responsive only to the obvious.

Nobody ever before had seen that sort of magic in America. People scarcely knew whether or not they quite liked it. The lightning of innovation stupefies the dull; ignorance is always suspicious of innovation – always afraid to put itself on record until its mind is made up by somebody else.

So in this typical New York audience approbation was cautious, but every fascinated eye remained focused on this young girl who continued to do incredible things, which seemed to resemble 'putting something over' on them; a thing which no uneducated American conglomeration ever quite forgives.

The girl's silence, too, perplexed them; they were accustomed to gabble, to noise, to jazz, vocal and instrumental, to that incessant metropolitan clamor which fills every second with sound in a city whose only distinction is its din. Stage, press, art, letters, social existence unless noisy mean nothing in Gotham; reticence, leisure, repose are the three lost arts. The megaphone is the city's symbol; its chiefest crime, silence.

The girl having finished with the big glass bubble full of tiny fish, picked it up and tossed it aside. For a moment it apparently floated there in space like a soap-bubble. Changing rainbow tints waxed and waned on the surface, growing deeper and more gorgeous until the floating globe glowed scarlet, then suddenly burst into flame and vanished. And only a strange, sweet perfume lingered in the air.

But she gave her perplexed audience no time to wonder; she had seated herself on the stage and was already swiftly busy unfolding a white veil with which she presently covered herself, draping it over her like a tent.

The veil seemed to be translucent; she was apparently visible seated beneath it. But the veil turned into smoke, rising into the air in a thin white cloud; and there, where she had been seated, was a statue of white stone the image of herself! – in all the frail springtide of early adolescence – a white statue, cold, opaque, exquisite in its sculptured immobility.

There came, the next moment, a sound of distant thunder; flashes lighted the blank curtain; and suddenly a vein of lightning and a sharper peal shattered the statue to fragments.

There they lay, broken bits of her own sculptured body, glistening in a heap behind the footlights. Then each fragment began to shiver with a rosy internal light of its own, until the pile of broken marble glowed like living coals under thickening and reddening vapors. And, presently, dimly perceptible, there she was in the flesh again, seated in the fiery center of the conflagration, stretching her arms luxuriously, yawning, seemingly awakening from refreshing slumber, her eyes unclosing to rest with a sort of confused apology upon her astounded audience.

As she rose to her feet nothing except herself remained on the stage – no débris, not a shred of smoke, not a spark.

She came down, then, across an inclined plank into the orchestra among the audience.

In the aisle seat nearest her sat Victor Cleves. His business was to be there that evening. But she didn't know that, knew nothing about him – had never before set eyes on him.

At her gesture of invitation he made a cup of both his hands. Into these she poured a double handful of unset diamonds – or what appeared to be diamonds – pressed her own hands above his for a second – and the diamonds in his palms had become pearls.

These were passed around to people in the vicinity, and finally returned to Mr Cleves, who, at her request, covered the heap of pearls with both his hands, hiding them entirely from view.

At her nod he uncovered them. The pearls had become emeralds. Again, while he held them, and without even touching him, she changed them into rubies. Then she turned away from him, apparently forgetting that he still held the gems, and he sat very still, one cupped hand over the other, while she poured silver coins into a woman's gloved hands, turned them into gold coins, then flung each coin into the air, where it changed to a living, fragrant rose and fell among the audience.

Presently she seemed to remember Cleves, came back down the aisle, and under his close and intent gaze drew from his cupped hands, one by one, a score of brilliant little living birds, which continually flew about her and finally perched, twittering, on her golden headdress – a rainbow-crest of living jewels.

As she drew the last warm, breathing little feathered miracle from Cleves's hands and released it, he said rapidly under his breath: 'I want a word with you later. Where?'

She let her clear eyes rest on him for a moment, then with a shrug so slight that it was perceptible, perhaps, only to him, she moved on along the inclined way, stepped daintily over the footlights, caught fire, apparently, nodded to a badly rattled audience, and sauntered off, burning from head to foot.

What applause there was became merged in a dissonant instrumental outburst from the orchestra; the great god Jazz, resumed direction, the mindless audience breathed freely again as the curtain rose upon a familiar, yelling turbulence, including all that Gotham really understands and cares for – legs and noise.

Victor Cleves glanced up at the stage, then continued to study the name of the girl on the programme. It was featured in rather pathetic solitude under 'Entr'acte'. And he read further: 'During the *entr'acte* Miss Tressa Norne will entertain you with several phases of Black Magic. This strange knowledge was acquired by Miss Norne from the Yezidees, among which almost unknown people still remain descendants of that notorious and formidable historic personage known in the twelfth century as The Old Man of the Mountain – or The Old Man of Mount Alamout.

'The pleasant profession of this historic individual was assassination; and some historians now believe that genuine occult power played a part in his dreadful record – a record which terminated only when the infantry of Genghis Khan took Mount Alamout by storm and hanged the Old Man of the Mountain and burned his body under a boulder of You-Stone.

'For Miss Norne's performance there appears to be no plausible, practical or scientific explanation.

'During her performance the curtain will remain lowered for fifteen minutes and will then rise on the last act of "You Betcha Life".'

The noisy show continued while Cleves, paying it scant attention, brooded over the program. And ever his keen, grey eyes reverted to her name, Tressa Norne.

SAMARIS

I

On the thirteenth day of March, 1906, Kerns received the following cable from an old friend:

> Is there anybody in New York who can find two criminals for me? I don't want to call in the police.
>
> J.T. BURKE.

To which Kerns replied promptly:

> Wire Keen, Tracer of Lost Persons, N.Y.

And a day or two later, being on his honeymoon, he forgot all about his old friend Jack Burke.

On the fifteenth day of March, 1906, Mr Keen, Tracer of Lost Persons, received the following cablegram from Alexandria, Egypt:

> *Keen, Tracer, New York*: – Locate Joram Smiles, forty, stout, lame, red hair, ragged red mustache, cast in left eye, pallid skin; carries one crutch; supposed to have arrived in America per S. S. *Scythian Queen*, with man known as Emanuel Gandon, swarthy, short, fat, light bluish eyes, Eurasian type.
>
> I will call on you at your office as soon as my steamer,

Empress of Babylon, arrives. If you discover my men, keep them under surveillance, but on no account call in police. Spare no expense. Dundas, Gray & Co. are my bankers and reference.

JOHN TEMPLETON BURKE.

On Monday, April 2nd, a few minutes after eight o'clock in the morning, the card of Mr John Templeton Burke was brought to Mr Keen, Tracer of Lost Persons, and a moment later a well-built, wiry, sun-scorched young man was ushered into Mr Keen's private office by a stenographer prepared to take minutes of the interview.

The first thing that the Tracer of Lost Persons noted in his visitor was his mouth; the next his eyes. Both were unmistakably good – the eyes which his Creator had given him looked people squarely in the face at every word; the mouth, which a man's own character fashions agreeably or mars, was pleasant, but firm when the trace of the smile lurking in the corners died out.

There were dozens of other external characteristics which Mr Keen always looked for in his clients; and now the rapid exchange of preliminary glances appeared to satisfy both men, for they advanced toward each other and exchanged a formal hand clasp.

'Have you any news for me?' asked Burke.

'I have,' said the Tracer. 'There are cigars on the table beside you – matches in that silver case. No, I never smoke; but I like the aroma – and I like to watch men smoke. Do you know, Mr Burke, that no two men smoke in the same fashion? There is as much character in the manner of holding a cigar as there is difference in the technique of artists.'

Burke nodded, amused, but, catching sight of the busy stenographer, his bronzed features became serious, and he looked at Mr Keen inquiringly.

'It is my custom,' said the Tracer. 'Do you object to my stenographer?'

Burke looked at the slim young girl in her black gown and white collar and cuffs. Then, very simply, he asked her pardon for objecting to her presence, but said that he could not discuss his case if she remained. So she rose, with a humorous glance at Mr Keen; and the two men stood up until she had vanished, then reseated themselves *vis-à-vis*. Mr Keen calmly dropped his elbow on the concealed button which prepared a hidden phonograph for the reception of every word that passed between them.

'What news have you for me, Mr Keen?' asked the younger man with that same directness which the Tracer had already been prepared for, and which only corroborated the frankness of eyes and voice.

'My news is brief,' he said. 'I have both your men under observation.'

'Already?' exclaimed Burke, plainly unprepared. 'Do you actually mean that I can see these men whenever I desire to do so? Are these scoundrels in this town – within pistol shot?'

His youthful face hardened as he snapped out his last word, like the crack of a whip.

'I don't know how far your pistol carries,' said Mr Keen. 'Do you wish to swear out a warrant?'

'No, I do not. I merely wish their addresses. You have not used the police in this matter, have you, Mr Keen?'

'No. Your cable was explicit,' said the Tracer. 'Had you permitted me to use the police it would have been much less expensive for you.'

'I can't help that,' said the young man. 'Besides, in a matter of this sort, a man cannot decently consider expense.'

'A matter of what sort?' asked the Tracer blandly.

'Of *this* sort.'

'Oh! Yet even now I do not understand. You must remember, Mr Burke, that you have not told me anything concerning the reasons for your quest of these two men, Joram Smiles and Emanuel Gandon. Besides, this is the first time you have mentioned pistol range.'

Burke, smoking steadily, looked at the Tracer through the blue fog of his cigar.

'No,' he said, 'I have not told you anything about them.'

Mr Keen waited a moment; then, smiling quietly to himself, he wrote down the present addresses of Joram Smiles and Emanuel Gandon, and, tearing off the leaf, handed it to the younger man, saying: 'I omit the pistol range, Mr Burke.'

'I am very grateful to you,' said Burke. 'The efficiency of your system is too famous for me to venture to praise it. All I can say is "Thank you"; all I can do in gratitude is to write my check – if you will be kind enough to suggest the figures.'

'Are you sure that my services are ended?'

'Thank you, quite sure.'

So the Tracer of Lost Persons named the figures, and his client produced a check book and filled in a check for the amount. This was presented and received with pleasant formality. Burke rose, prepared to take his leave, but the Tracer was apparently busy with the combination lock of a safe, and the young man lingered a moment to make his adieus.

As he stood waiting for the Tracer to turn around he studied the writing on the sheet of paper which he held toward the light:

Joram Smiles, no profession, 613 West 24th Street. Emanuel Gandon, no profession, same address. Very dangerous men.

It occurred to him that these three lines of pencil-writing had cost him a thousand dollars – and at the same instant he flushed with shame at the idea of measuring the money value of anything in such a quest as this.

And yet – and yet he had already spent a great deal of money in his brief quest, and – *was* he any nearer the goal – even with the penciled addresses of these two men in his possession? Even with these men almost within pistol shot!

Pondering there, immersed in frowning retrospection, the room, the Tracer, the city seemed to fade from his view. He saw the red sand blowing in the desert; he heard the sickly squealing of camels at the El Teb Wells; he saw the sun strike fire from the rippling waters of Saïs; he saw the plain, and the ruins high above it; and the odor of the Long Bazaar smote him like a blow, and he heard the far call to prayer from the minarets of Sa-el-Hagar, once Saïs, the mysterious – Saïs of the million lanterns, Saïs of that splendid festival where the Great Triad's worship swayed dynasty after dynasty, and where, through the hot centuries, Isis, veiled, impassive, looked out upon the hundredth king of kings, Meris, the Builder of Gardens, dragged dead at the chariot of Upper and Lower Egypt.

Slowly the visions faded; into his remote eyes crept the consciousness of the twentieth century again; he heard the river whistles blowing, and the far dissonance of the streets – that iron undertone vibrating through the metropolis of the West from river to river and from the Palisades to the sea.

His gaze wandered about the room, from telephone desk to bookcase, from the table to the huge steel safe, door ajar, swung outward like the polished breech of a twelve-inch gun.

Then his vacant eyes met the eyes of the Tracer of Lost Persons, almost helplessly. And for the first time the full significance of this quest he had undertaken came over him like despair – this strange, hopeless, fantastic quest, blindly, savagely pursued from the sand wastes of Saïs to the wastes of this vast arid city of iron and masonry, ringing to the sky with the menacing clamor of its five monstrous boroughs.

Curiously weary of a sudden, he sat down, resting his head on one hand. The Tracer watched him, bent partly over his desk. From moment to moment he tore minute pieces from the blotter, or drew imaginary circles and arabesques on his pad with an inkless pen.

'Perhaps I could help you, after all – if you'd let me try,' he said quietly.

'Do you mean – *me*?' asked Burke, without raising his head.

'If you like – yes, you – or any man in trouble – in perplexity – in the uncertain deductions which arise from an attempt at self-analysis.'

'It is true; I am trying to analyze myself. I believe that I don't know how. All has been mere impulse – so far. No, I don't know how to analyze it all.'

'I do,' said the Tracer.

Burke raised his level, unbelieving eyes.

'You are in love,' said the Tracer.

After a long time Burke looked up again. 'Do you think so?'

'Yes. Can I help you?' asked the Tracer pleasantly.

The young man sat silent, frowning into space; then:

'I tell you plainly enough that I have come here to argue with two men at the end of a pistol; and – you tell me I'm in love. By what logic—'

'It is written in your face, Mr Burke – in your eyes, in every feature, every muscle's contraction, every modulation of your voice. My tables, containing six hundred classified superficial phenomena peculiar to all human emotions, have been compiled and scientifically arranged according to Bertillon's system. It is an absolutely accurate key to every phase of human emotion, from hate, through all its amazingly paradoxical phenomena, to love, with all its genera under the suborder – all its species, subspecies, and varieties.'

He leaned back, surveying the young man with kindly amusement.

'You talk of pistol range, but you are thinking of something more fatal than bullets, Mr Burke. You are thinking of love – of the first, great, absorbing, unreasoning passion that has ever shaken you, blinded you, seized you and dragged you out of the ordered path of life, to push you violently into the strange and unexplored! That is what stares out on the world through those haunted eyes of yours, when the smile dies out and you are off your guard; that is what is hardening those flat, clean bands of muscle in jaw and cheek; that is what those hints of shadow mean beneath the eye, that new and delicate pinch to the nostril, that refining, almost to sharpness, of the nose, that sensitive edging to the lips, and the lean delicacy of the chin.'

He bent slightly forward in his chair.

'There is all that there, Mr Burke, and something else – the glimmering dawn of desperation.'

'Yes,' said the other, 'that is there. I am desperate.'

'*Ex*actly. Also you wear two revolvers in a light, leather harness strapped up under your armpits,' said the Tracer, laughing. 'Take them off, Mr Burke. There is nothing to be gained in shooting up Mr Smiles or converting Mr Gandon into nitrates.

'If it is a matter where one man can help another,' the Tracer added simply, 'it would give me pleasure to place my resources at your command – without recompense—'

'Mr Keen!' said Burke, astonished.

'Yes?'

'You are very amiable; I had not wished – had not expected anything except professional interest from you.'

'Why not? I like you, Mr Burke.'

The utter disarming candor of this quiet, elderly gentleman silenced the younger man with a suddenness born of emotions long crushed, long relentlessly mastered, and which now, in revolt, shook him fiercely in every fiber. All at once he felt very young, very helpless in the world – that same world through which, until within a few weeks, he had roved so confidently, so arrogantly, challenging man and the gods themselves in the pride of his strength and youth.

But now, halting, bewildered, lost amid the strange maze of byways whither impulse had lured and abandoned him, he looked out into a world of wilderness and unfamiliar stars and shadow shapes undreamed of, and he knew not which way to turn – not even how to return along the ways his impetuous feet had trodden in this strange and hopeless quest of his.

'How can you help me?' he said bluntly, while the quivering undertone rang in spite of him. 'Yes, I am in love; but how can any living man help me?'

'Are you in love with the dead?' asked the Tracer gravely. 'For that only is hopeless. Are you in love with one who is not living?'

'Yes.'

'You love one whom you know to be dead?'

'Yes; dead.'

'How do you know that she is dead?'

'That is not the question. I knew that when I fell in love with her. It is not that which appals me; I ask nothing more than to live my life out loving the dead. I – I ask very little.'

He passed his unsteady hand across his dry lips, across his eyes and forehead, then laid his clinched fist on the table.

'Some men remain constant to a memory; some to a picture – sane, wholesome, normal men. Some men, with a fixed ideal, never encounter its facsimile, and so never love. There is nothing strange, after all, in this; nothing abnormal, nothing unwholesome. Grünwald loved the marble head and shoulders of the lovely Amazon in the Munich Museum; he died unmarried, leaving the charities and good deeds of a blameless life to justify him. Sir Henry Guest, the great surgeon who worked among the poor without recompense, loved Gainsborough's "Lady Wilton". The portrait hangs above his tomb in St Clement's Hundreds. D'Epernay loved Mlle Jean Vacaresco, who died before he was born. And I – I love in my own fashion.'

His low voice rang with the repressed undertone of excitement; he opened and closed his clinched hand as though controlling the lever of his emotions.

'What can you do for a man who loves the shadow of Life?' he asked.

'If you love the shadow because the substance has passed away – if you love the soul because the dust has returned to the earth as it was—'

'It has *not*!' said the younger man.

The Tracer said very gravely: 'It is written that whenever "the Silver Cord" is loosed, "then shall the dust return unto the earth as it was, and the spirit shall return unto Him who gave it".'

'The spirit – yes; *that* has taken its splendid flight—'

His voice choked up, died out; he strove to speak again, but could not. The Tracer let him alone, and bent again over his desk, drawing imaginary circles on the stained blotter, while moment after moment passed under the tension of that fiercest of all struggles, when a man sits throttling his own soul into silence.

And, after a long time, Burke lifted a haggard face from the cradle of his crossed arms and shook his shoulders, drawing a deep, steady breath.

'Listen to *me*!' he said in an altered voice.

And the Tracer of Lost Persons nodded.

II

'When I left the Point I was assigned to the colored cavalry. They are good men; we went up Kettle Hill together. Then came the Philippine troubles, then that Chinese affair. Then I did staff duty, and could not stand the inactivity and resigned. They had no use for me in Manchuria; I tired of waiting, and went to Venezuela. The prospects for service there were absurd; I heard of the Moorish troubles and went to Morocco. Others of my sort swarmed there; matters dragged and dragged, and the Kaiser never meant business, anyway.

'Being independent, and my means permitting me, I got some shooting in the back country. This all degenerated into the merest nomadic wandering – nothing but sand, camels, ruins, tents, white walls, and blue skies. And at last I came to the town of Sa-el-Hagar.'

His voice died out; his restless, haunted eyes became fixed.

'Sa-el-Hagar, once ancient Saïs,' repeated the Tracer quietly; and the young man looked at him.

'You know *that*?'

'Yes,' said the Tracer.

For a while Burke remained silent, preoccupied, then, resting his chin on his hand and speaking in a curiously monotonous voice, as though repeating to himself by rote, he went on:

'The town is on the heights – have you a pencil? Thank you. Here is the town of Sa-el-Hagar, here are the ruins, here is the wall, and somewhere hereabouts should be the buried temple of Neith, which nobody has found.' He shifted his pencil. 'Here is the lake of Saïs; here, standing all alone on the plain, are those great monolithic pillars stretching away into perspective – four hundred of them in all – a hundred and nine still upright. There were one hundred and ten when I arrived at El Teb Wells.'

He looked across at the Tracer, repeating: 'One hundred and ten – when I arrived. One fell the first night – a distant pillar far away on the horizon. Four thousand years had it stood there. And it fell – the first night of my arrival. I heard it; the nights are cold at El Teb Wells, and I was lying awake, all a-shiver, counting the stars to make me sleep. And very, very far away in the desert I heard and felt the shock of its fall – the fall of forty centuries under the Egyptian stars.'

His eyes grew dreamy; a slight glow had stained his face.

'Did you ever halt suddenly in the Northern forests, listening, as though a distant voice had hailed you? Then you understand why that far, dull sound from the dark horizon brought me to my feet, bewildered, listening, as though my own name had been spoken.

'I heard the wind in the tents and the stir of camels; I heard the reeds whispering on Saïs Lake and the yap-yap of a shivering jackal; and always, always, the hushed echo in my ears of my own name called across the star-lit waste.

'At dawn I had forgotten. An Arab told me that a pillar had fallen; it was all the same to me, to him, to the others, too. The sun came out hot. I like heat. My men sprawled in the tents; some watered, some went up to the town to gossip in the bazaar. I mounted and cast bridle on neck –

you see how much I cared where I went! In two hours we had completed a circle – like a ruddy hawk above El Teb. And my horse halted beside the fallen pillar.'

As he spoke his language had become very simple, very direct, almost without accent, and he spoke slowly, picking his way with that lack of inflection, of emotion characteristic of a child reading a new reader.

'The column had fallen from its base, eastward, and with its base it had upheaved another buried base, laying bare a sort of cellar and a flight of stone steps descending into darkness.

'Into this excavation the sand was still running in tiny rivulets. Listening, I could hear it pattering far, far down into the shadows.

'Sitting there in the saddle, the thing explained itself as I looked. The fallen pillar had been built upon older ruins; all Egypt is that way, ruin founded on the ruin of ruins – like human hopes.

'The stone steps, descending into the shadow of remote ages, invited me. I dismounted, walked to the edge of the excavation, and, kneeling, peered downward. And I saw a wall and the lotus-carved rim of a vast stone-framed pool; and as I looked I heard the tinkle of water. For the pillar, falling, had unbottled the ancient spring, and now the stone-framed lagoon was slowly filling after its drought of centuries.

'There was light enough to see by, but, not knowing how far I might penetrate, I returned to my horse, pocketed matches and candles from the saddlebags, and, returning, started straight down the steps of stone.

'Fountain, wall, lagoon, steps, terraces half buried – all showed what the place had been: a water garden of ancient Egypt – probably royal – because, although I am not able to decipher hieroglyphics, I have heard somewhere that these picture inscriptions, when inclosed in a cartouch like this'
– he drew rapidly –

'or this

indicate that the subject of the inscription was once a king.

'And on every wall, every column, I saw the insignia of ancient royalty, and I saw strange hawk-headed figures bearing symbols engraved on stone – beasts, birds, fishes, unknown signs and symbols; and everywhere the lotus carved in stone – the bud, the blossom half-inclosed, the perfect flower.'

His dreamy eyes met the gaze of the Tracer, unseeing; he rested his sunburned face between both palms, speaking in the same vague monotone:

'Everywhere dust, ashes, decay, the death of life, the utter annihilation of the living – save only the sparkle of reborn waters slowly covering the baked bed of the stone-edged pool – strange, luminous water, lacking the vital sky tint, enameled with a film of dust, yet, for all that, quickening with imprisoned brilliancy like an opal.

'The slow filling of the pool fascinated me; I stood I know not how long watching the thin film of water spreading away into the dimness beyond. At last I turned and passed curiously along the wall where, at its base, mounds of dust marked what may have been trees. Into these I probed with my riding crop, but discovered nothing except the depths of the dust.

'When I had penetrated the ghost of this ancient garden for a thousand yards the light from the opening was no longer of any service. I lighted a candle; and its yellow rays fell upon a square portal into which led another flight of steps. And I went down.

'There were eighteen steps descending into a square stone room. Strange gleams and glimmers from wall and ceiling flashed dimly in my eyes under the wavering flame of the candle. Then the flame grew still – still as death – and Death lay at my feet – there on the stone floor – a man, square shouldered, hairless, the cobwebs of his tunic mantling him, lying face downward, arms outflung.

'After a moment I stooped and touched him, and the entire prostrate figure dissolved into dust where it lay, leaving at my feet a shadow shape in thin silhouette against the pavement – merely a gray layer of finest dust shaped like a man, a tracery of impalpable powder on the stones.

'Upward and around me I passed the burning candle; vast figures in blue and red and gold grew out of the darkness; the painted walls sparkled; the shadows that had slept through all those centuries trembled and shrank away into distant corners.

'And then – and then I saw the gold edges of her sandals sparkle in the darkness, and the clasped girdle of virgin gold around her slender waist glimmered like purest flame!'

Burke, leaning far across the table, interlocked hands tightening, stared and stared into space. A smile edged his mouth; his voice grew wonderfully gentle:

'Why, she was scarcely eighteen – this child – lying there so motionless, so lifelike, with the sandals edging her little upturned feet, and the small hands of her folded between the breasts. It was as though she had just stretched herself out there – scarcely sound asleep as yet, and her thick, silky hair – cut as they cut children's hair in these days, you know – cradled her head and cheeks.

'So marvelous the mimicry of life, so absolute the deception of breathing sleep, that I scarce dared move, fearing to awaken her.

'When I did move I forgot the dusty shape of the dead at my feet, and left, full across his neck, the imprint of a spurred riding boot. It gave me my first shudder; I turned, feeling beneath my foot the soft, yielding powder, and stood aghast. Then – it is absurd! – but I felt as a man feels who has trodden inadvertently upon another's foot – and in an impulse of reparation I stooped hastily and attempted to smooth out the mortal dust which bore the imprint of my heel. But the fine powder flaked my glove, and, looking about for something to compose the ashes with, I picked up a papyrus scroll. Perhaps he himself had written on it; nobody can ever know, and I used it as a sort of hoe to scrape him together and smooth him out on the stones.'

The young man drew a yellowish roll of paper-like substance from his pocket and laid it on the table.

'This is the same papyrus,' he said. 'I had forgotten that I carried it away with me until I found it in my shooting coat while packing to sail for New York.'

The Tracer of Lost Persons reached over and picked up the scroll. It was flexible still, but brittle; he opened it with great care, considered the strange figures upon it for a while, then turned almost sharply on his visitor.

'Go on,' he said.

And Burke went on:

'The candle was burning low; I lighted two more, placing them at her head and feet on the edges of the stone couch. Then, lighting a third candle, I stood beside the couch and looked down at the dead girl under her veil-like robe, set with golden stars.'

He passed his hand wearily over his hair and forehead.

'I do not know what the accepted meaning of beauty may be if it was not there under my eyes. Flawless as palest amber ivory and rose, the smooth-glowing contours melted into exquisite symmetry; lashes like darkest velvet rested on the pure curve of the cheeks; the closed lids, the mouth still faintly stained with color, the delicate nose, the full, childish lips, sensitive, sweet, resting softly upon each other – if these were not all parts of but one lovely miracle, then there is no beauty save in a dream of Paradise . . .

'A gold band of linked scarabs bound her short, thick hair straight across the forehead; thin scales of gold fell from a neck-lace, clothing her breasts in brilliant discolored metal, through which ivory-tinted skin showed. A belt of pure, soft gold clasped her body at the waist; gold-edged sandals clung to her little feet.

'At first, when the stunned surprise had subsided, I thought that I was looking upon some miracle of ancient embalming, hitherto unknown. Yet, in the smooth skin there was no slit to prove it, no opening in any vein or artery, no mutilation of this sculptured masterpiece of the Most High, no cerements, no bandages, no gilded carven case with painted face to stare open eyed through the waiting cycles.

'This was the image of sleep – of life unconscious – not of death. Yet it was death – death that had come upon her centuries and centuries ago; for the gold had turned iridescent and magnificently discolored; the sandal straps fell into dust as I bent above them, leaving the sandals clinging to her feet only by the wired silver core of the thongs. And, as I touched it fearfully, the veil-like garment covering her, vanished into thin air, its metal stars twinkling in a shower around her on the stone floor.'

The Tracer, motionless, intent, scarcely breathed; the younger man moved restlessly in his chair, the dazed light in his eyes clearing to sullen consciousness.

'What more is there to tell?' he said. 'And to what purpose? All this is time wasted. I have my work cut out for me. What more is there to tell?'

'What you have left untold,' said the Tracer, with the slightest ring of authority in his quiet voice.

And, as though he had added 'Obey!' the younger man sank back in his chair, his hands contracting nervously.

'I went back to El Teb,' he said; 'I walked like a dreaming man. My sleep was haunted by her beauty; night after night, when at last I fell asleep, instantly I saw her face, and her dark eyes opening into mine in childish bewilderment; day after day I rode out to the fallen pillar and descended to that dark chamber where she lay alone. Then there came a time when I could not endure the thought of her lying there alone. I had never dared to touch her. Horror of what might happen had held me aloof lest she crumble at my touch to that awful powder which I had trodden on.

'I did not know what to do; my Arabs had begun to whisper among themselves, suspicious of my absences, impatient to break camp, perhaps, and roam on once more. Perhaps they believed I had discovered treasure somewhere; I am not sure. At any rate, dread of their following me, determination to take my dead away with me, drove me into action; and that day when I reached her silent chamber I lighted my candle, and, leaning above her for one last look, I touched her shoulder with my finger tip.

'It was a strange sensation. Prepared for a dreadful dissolution, utterly unprepared for cool, yielding flesh, I almost dropped where I stood. For her body was neither cold nor warm, neither dust-dry nor moist; neither the skin of the living nor the dead. It was firm, almost stiff, yet not absolutely without a certain hint of flexibility.

'The appalling wonder of it consumed me; fear, incredulity, terror, apathy succeeded each other; then slowly a fierce shrinking happiness swept me in every fiber.

'This marvelous death, this triumph of beauty over death, was mine. Never again should she lie here alone through the solitudes of night and day; never again should the dignity of Death lack the tribute demanded of Life. Here was the appointed watcher – I, who had found her alone in the wastes of the world – all alone on the outermost edges of the world – a child, dead and unguarded. And standing there beside her I knew that I should never love again.'

He straightened up, stretching out his arm: 'I did not intend to carry her away to what is known as Christian burial. How could I consign her to darkness again, with all its dreadful mockery of marble, all its awful emblems?

'This lovely stranger was to be my guest forever. The living should be near her while she slept so sweetly her slumber through the centuries; she should have warmth, and soft hangings and sunlight and flowers; and her unconscious ears should be filled with the pleasant stir of living things . . . I have a house in the country, a very old house among meadows and young woodlands. And I – I had dreamed of giving this child a home—'

His voice broke; he buried his head in his hands a moment; but when he lifted it again his features were hard as steel.

'There was already talk in the bazaar about me. I was probably followed, but I did not know it. Then one of my men

disappeared. For a week I hesitated to trust my Arabs; but there was no other way. I told them there was a mummy which I desired to carry to some port and smuggle out of the country without consulting the Government. I knew perfectly well that the Government would never forego its claim to such a relic of Egyptian antiquity. I offered my men too much, perhaps. I don't know. They hesitated for a week, trying by every artifice to see the treasure, but I never let them out of my sight.

'Then one day two white men came into camp; and with them came a government escort to arrest me for looting an Egyptian tomb. The white men were Joram Smiles and that Eurasian, Emanuel Gandon, who was partly white, I suppose. I didn't comprehend what they were up to at first. They escorted me forty miles to confront the official at Shen-Bak. When, after a stormy week, I was permitted to return to Saïs, my Arabs and the white men were gone. And the stone chamber under the water garden wall was empty as the hand I hold out to you!'

He opened his palm and rose, his narrowing eyes clear and dangerous.

'At the bazaar I learned enough to know what had been done. I traced the white men to the coast. They sailed on the *Scythian Queen*, taking with them all that I care for on earth or in heaven! And you ask me why I measure their distance from me by a bullet's flight!'

The Tracer also rose, pale and grave.

'Wait!' he said. 'There are other things to be done before you prepare to face a jury for double murder.'

'It is for them to choose,' said Burke. 'They shall have the choice of returning to me my dead, or of going to hell full of lead.'

'*Ex*actly, my dear sir. That part is not difficult,' said the Tracer quietly. 'There will be no occasion for violence, I assure you. Kindly leave such details to me. I know what is to be done. You are outwardly very calm, Mr Burke – even dangerously placid; but though you maintain an admirable command over yourself superficially, you are laboring under terrible excitement. Therefore it is my duty to say to you at once that there is no cause for your excitement, no cause for your apprehension as to results. I feel exceedingly confident that you will, in due time, regain possession of all that you care for most – quietly, quietly, my dear sir! You are not yet ready to meet these men, nor am I ready to go with you. I beg you to continue your habit of self-command for a little while. There is no haste – that is to say, there is every reason to make haste slowly. And the quickest method is to seat yourself. Thank you. And I shall sit here beside you and spread out this papyrus scroll for your inspection.'

Burke stared at the Tracer, then at the scroll.

'What has that inscription to do with the matter in hand?' he demanded impatiently.

'I leave you to judge,' said the Tracer. A dull tint of excitement flushed his lean cheeks; he twisted his gray mustache and bent over the unrolled scroll which was now held flat by weights at the four corners.

'Can you understand any of these symbols, Mr Burke?' he asked.

'No.'

'Curious,' mused the Tracer. 'Do you know it was fortunate that you put this bit of papyrus in the pocket of your shooting coat – so fortunate that, in a way, it approaches the miraculous?'

'What do you mean? Is there anything in that scroll bearing on this matter?'

'Yes.'

'And you can read it? Are you versed in such learning, Mr Keen?'

'I am an Egyptologist – among other details,' said the Tracer calmly.

The young man gazed at him, astonished. The Tracer of Lost Persons picked up a pencil, laid a sheet of paper on the table beside the papyrus, and slowly began to copy the first symbol:

III

'The ancient Egyptian word for the personal pronoun "I" was *anuk*,' said the Tracer placidly. 'The phonetic for *a* was the hieroglyph

q

a reed; for *n* the water symbol

⌇⌇⌇⌇

for *u* the symbols

🐦 , ℂ

for *k*

⟁

Therefore this hieroglyphic inscription begins with the personal pronoun

q ⌇⌇⌇ 🐦 , ℂ ⟁

or *I*. That is very easy, of course.

'Now, the most ancient of Egyptian inscriptions read vertically in columns; there are only two columns in this papyrus, so we'll try it vertically and pass downward to the next symbol, which is inclosed in a sort of frame or cartouch. That immediately signifies that royalty is mentioned; therefore, we have already translated as much as "I, the king (or queen)". Do you see?'

'Yes,' said Burke, staring.

'Very well. Now this symbol, number two,

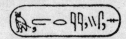

spells out the word "*Meris*," in this way: M (pronounced *me*) is phonetically symbolized by the characters

r by

○

(a mouth) and the comma

,

and the hieroglyph

⊂

i by two reeds

𐦀𐦀

and two oblique strokes

\\

and *s* by

⌐,—

'This gives us Meris, the name of that deposed and fugitive king of Egypt who, after a last raid on the summer palace of Mer-Shen, usurping ruler of Egypt, was followed and tracked to Saïs, where, with an arrow through his back, he crawled to El Teb and finally died there of his wound. All this Egyptologists are perfectly familiar with in the translations of the boastful tablets and inscriptions erected near Saïs by Mer-Shen, the three hundred and twelfth sovereign after Queen Nitocris.'

He looked up at Burke, smiling. 'Therefore,' he said, 'this papyrus scroll was written by Meris, ex-king, a speculative thousands of years before Christ. And it begins: "I, Meris the King".'

'How does all this bear upon what concerns me?' demanded Burke.

'Wait!'

Something in the quiet significance of the Tracer's brief command sent a curious thrill through the younger man. He leaned stiffly forward, studying the scroll, every faculty concentrated on the symbol which the Tracer had now touched with the carefully sharpened point of his pencil:

'That,' said Mr Keen, 'is the ancient Egyptian word for "little," "*Ket*." The next, below, written in two lines, is "Samaris," a proper name – the name of a woman. Under that, again, is the symbol for the number 18; the decimal sign,

∩

and eight vertical strokes,

||||||||

Under that, again, is a hieroglyph of another sort, an ideograph representing a girl with a harp; and, beneath that, the symbol which always represented a dancing girl and also the royal symbol inclosed in a cartouch,

which means literally "the Ruler of Upper and Lower Egypt".
Under that is the significant symbol

representing an arm and a hand holding a stick. This
always means *force* – to take forcibly or to use violence.
Therefore, so far, we have the following literal translation:
"I, Meris the King, little Samaris, eighteen, a harpist,
dancing girl, the Ruler of Upper and Lower Egypt, to take
by violence—"'

'What does that make?' broke in Burke impatiently.

'*Wait*! Wait until we have translated everything literally.
And, Mr Burke, it might make it easier for us both if you
would remember that I have had the pleasure of deciphering
many hundreds of papyri before you had ever heard that
there were such things.'

'I beg your pardon,' said the young man in a low voice.

'I beg yours for my impatience,' said the Tracer pleasantly.
'This deciphering always did affect my nerves and shorten
my temper. And, no doubt, it is quite hard on you. Shall
we go on, Mr Burke?'

'If you please, Mr Keen.'

So the Tracer laid his pencil point on the next symbol

'That is the symbol for night,' he said; 'and that

is the water symbol again, as you know, and that

is the ideograph, meaning a ship. The five reversed crescents

record the number of days voyage; the sign

means a house, and is also the letter H in the Egyptian alphabet.

'Under it, again, we have a repetition of the first symbol meaning *I*, and a repetition of the second symbol, meaning "Meris, the King". Then, below that cartouch, comes a new symbol,

which is the feminine personal pronoun, *sentus*, meaning "*she*"; and the first column is completed with the symbol for the ancient Egyptian verb, *nehes*, "to awake",

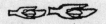

'And now we take the second column, which begins with the jackal ideograph expressing slyness or cleverness. Under it is the hieroglyph meaning "to run away", "to escape". And under that, Mr Burke, is one of the rarest of all Egyptian symbols; a symbol seldom seen on stone or papyrus, except in rare references to the mysteries of Isis. The meaning of it, so long in dispute, has finally been practically determined through a new discovery in the cuneiform inscriptions. It is the symbol of two hands holding two *closed* eyes; and it signifies power.'

'You mean that those ancients understood hypnotism?' asked Burke, astonished.

'Evidently their priests did; evidently hypnotism was understood and employed in certain mysteries. And there is the symbol of it; and under it the hieroglyphs

meaning "a day and a night", with the symbol

as usual present to signify force or strength employed. Under that, again, is a human figure stretched upon a typical Egyptian couch. And now, Mr Burke, *note carefully* three modifying signs; first, that it is a *couch* or *bed* on which the figure is stretched, not the funeral couch, not the embalming slab; second, there is no mummy mask covering the face, and no mummy case covering the body; third, that under the recumbent figure is pictured an *open* mouth, not a *closed* one.

'All these modify the ideograph, apparently representing death. But the sleep symbol is not present. Therefore it is a sound inference that all this simply confirms the symbol of hypnotism.'

Burke, intensely absorbed, stared steadily at the scroll.

'Now,' continued Mr Keen, 'we note the symbol of force again, always present; and, continuing horizontally, a cartouch quite empty except for the midday sun. That is simply translated; the midday sun illuminates nothing. Meris, deposed, is king only in name; and the sun no longer shines on him as "Ruler of Upper and Lower Egypt". Under that despairing symbol, "King of Nothing", we have

the phonetics which spell *sha*, the word for garden. And, just beyond this, horizontally, the modifying ideograph meaning "a *water* garden";

a design of lotus and tree alternating on a terrace. Under that is the symbol for the word "*aneb*",

a "wall". Beyond that, horizontally, is the symbol for "house". It should be placed under the wall symbol, but the Egyptians were very apt to fill up spaces instead of continuing their vertical columns. Now, beneath, we find the imperative command

"arise!" And the Egyptian personal pronoun "*entuten*",

which means "you" or "thou".
   'Under that is the symbol

which means "priest", or, literally, "priest man". Then comes the imperative "awake to life!"

After that, our first symbol again, meaning "*I*", followed horizontally by the symbol

signifying "to go".

'Then comes a very important drawing – you see? – the picture of a man with a jackal's head, not a dog's head. It is not accompanied by the phonetic in a cartouch, as it should be. Probably the writer was in desperate haste at the end. But, nevertheless, it is easy to translate that symbol of the man with a jackal's head. It is a picture of the Egyptian god, Anubis, who was supposed to linger at the side of the dying to conduct their souls. Anubis, the jackal-headed, is the courier, the personal escort of departing souls. And this is he.

'And now the creed ends with the cry "Pray for me!"

the last symbol on this strange scroll – this missive written by a deposed, wounded, and dying king to an unnamed priest. Here is the literal translation in columns.

I	cunning
Meris the King	escape
little	hypnotize
Samaris	King of Nothing ⎫
eighteen	place forcibly ⎭
a harpist	garden ⎫
a dancing girl—Ruler of	water garden ⎭

Upper and Lower Egypt	wall
took forcibly—night	house
by water	Arise. Do
five days	Thou
ship	Priest Man
house	Awake
I	to life
Meris the King	I go
she	Anubis
awake	Pray

'And this is what that letter, thousands of years old, means in this language of ours, hundreds of years young: "I, Meris the King, seized little Samaris, a harpist and a dancing girl, eighteen years of age, belonging to the King of Upper and Lower Egypt, and carried her away at night on shipboard – a voyage of five days – to my house. I, Meris the King, lest she lie awake watching cunningly for a chance to escape, hypnotized her (or had her hypnotized) so that she lay like one dead or asleep, but breathing, and I, King no longer of Upper and Lower Egypt, took her and placed her in my house under the wall of the water garden. Arise! therefore, O thou priest; (go) and awaken her to life. I am dying (I go with Anubis!). Pray for me!"'

IV

For a full minute the two men sat there without moving or speaking. Then the Tracer laid aside his pencil.

'To sum up,' he said, opening the palm of his left hand and placing the forefinger of his right across it, 'the excavation made by the falling pillar raised in triumph above the water garden of the deposed king, Meris, by his rival, was the subterranean house of Meris. The prostrate figure which crumbled to powder at your touch may have been the very priest to whom this letter or papyrus was written. Perhaps the bearer of the scroll was a traitor and stabbed the priest as he was reading the missive. Who can tell how that priest died? He either died or betrayed his trust, for he never aroused the little Samaris from her suspended animation. And the water garden fell into ruins and she slept; and the Ruler of Upper and Lower Egypt raised his columns, lotus crowned, above the ruins; and she slept on. Then – *you* came.'

Burke stared like one stupefied.

'I do not know,' said the Tracer gravely, 'what balm there may be in a suspension of sensation, perhaps a vitality, to protect the human body from corruption after death. I do not know how soon suspended animation or the state of hypnotic coma, undisturbed, changes into death – whether it comes gradually, imperceptibly freeing the soul; whether the soul hides there, asleep, until suddenly the flame of vitality is extinguished. I do not know how long she lay there with life in her.'

He leaned back and touched an electric bell, then, turning to Burke:

'Speaking of pistol range,' he said, 'unstrap those weapons and pass them over, if you please.'

And the young man obeyed as in a trance.

'Thank you. There are four men coming into this room. You will keep your seat, if you please, Mr Burke.'

After a moment the door opened noiselessly. Two men handcuffed together entered the room; two men, hands in their pockets, sauntered carelessly behind the prisoners and leaned back against the closed door.

'That short, red-haired, lame man with the cast in his eye – do you recognize him?' asked the Tracer quietly.

Burke, grasping the arms of his chair, had started to rise, fury fairly blazing from his eyes; but, at the sound of the Tracer's calm, even voice, he sank back into his chair.

'That is Joram Smiles? You recognize him?' continued Mr Keen.

Burke nodded.

'*Ex*actly – alias Limpy, alias Red Jo, alias Big Stick Joram, alias Pinky; swindler, international confidence man, fence, burglar, gambler; convicted in 1887, and sent to Sing Sing for forgery; convicted in 1898, and sent to Auburn for swindling; arrested by my men on board the S.S. *Scythian Queen*, at the cabled request of John T. Burke, Esquire, and held to explain the nature of his luggage, which consisted of the contents of an Egyptian vault or underground ruin, declared at the customhouse as a mummy, and passed as such.'

The quiet, monotonous voice of the Tracer halted, then, as he glanced at the second prisoner, grew harder:

'Emanuel Gandon, general international criminal, with over half a hundred aliases, arrested in company with Smiles and held until Mr Burke's arrival.'

Turning to Burke, the Tracer continued: 'Fortunately, the *Scythian Queen* broke down off Brindisi. It gave us time to act on your cable; we found these men aboard when she was signaled off the Hook. I went out with the pilot myself, Mr Burke.'

Smiles shot a wicked look at Burke; Gandon scowled at the floor.

'Now,' said the Tracer pleasantly, meeting the venomous glare of Smiles, 'I'll get you that warrant you have been demanding to have exhibited to you. Here it is – charging you and your amiable friend Gandon with breaking into and robbing the Metropolitan Museum of ancient Egyptian gold ornaments, in March, 1903, and taking them to France, where they were sold to collectors. It seems that you found the business good enough to go prowling about Egypt on a hunt for something to sell here. A great mistake, my friends – a very great mistake, because, after the Museum has finished with you, the Egyptian Government desires to extradite you. And I rather suspect you'll have to go.'

He nodded to the two quiet men leaning against the door.

'Come, Joram,' said one of them pleasantly.

But Smiles turned furiously on the Tracer. 'You lie, you old gray rat!' he cried. 'That ain't no mummy; that's a plain dead girl! And there ain't no extrydition for body snatchin', so I guess them niggers at Cairo won't get us, after all!'

'Perhaps,' said the Tracer, looking at Burke, who had risen, pale and astounded. 'Sit down, Mr Burke! There is no need to question these men; no need to demand what they robbed you of. For,' he added slowly, 'what they took from the garden grotto of Saïs, and from you, I have under my own protection.'

The Tracer rose, locked the door through which the prisoners and their escorts had departed; then, turning gravely on Burke, he continued:

'That panel, there, is a door. There is a room beyond – a room facing to the south, bright with sunshine, flowers, soft rugs, and draperies of the East. *She* is there – like a child asleep!'

Burke reeled, steadying himself against the wall; the Tracer stared at space, speaking very slowly:

'Such death I have never before heard of. From the moment she came under my protection I have dared to doubt – many things. And an hour ago you brought me a papyrus scroll confirming my doubts. I doubt still – Heaven knows what! Who can say how long the flame of life may flicker within suspended animation? A week? A month? A year? Longer than that? Yes; the Hindoos have proved it. How long? The span of a normal life? Or longer? Can the flame burn indefinitely when the functions are absolutely suspended – generation after generation, century after century—?'

Burke, ghastly white, straightened up, quivering in every limb; the Tracer, as pale as he, laid his hand on the secret panel.

'If – if you dare say it – the phrase is this: "*O Ket Samaris, Nehes!*" – "O Little Samaris, awake!"'

'I – dare. In Heaven's name, open that door!'

Then, averting his head, the Tracer of Lost Persons swung open the panel.

A flood of sunshine flashed on Burke's face; he entered; and the paneled door closed behind him without a sound.

Minute after minute passed; the Tracer stood as though turned to stone, gray head bent.

Then he heard Burke's voice ring out unsteadily:

'O Ket Samaris – Samaris! O Ket Samaris – *Nehes!*'

And again: 'Samaris! Samaris! O beloved, awake!'

And once more: 'Nehes! O Samaris!'

Silence, broken by a strange, sweet, drowsy plaint – like a child awakened at midnight by a dazzling light.

'Samaris!'

Then, through the stillness, a little laugh, and a softly tremulous voice.

'*Ari un aha, O Entuk sen!*'

IN SEARCH OF THE GREAT AUK

I

Because it all seems so improbable – so horribly impossible to me now, sitting here safe and sane in my own library – I hesitate to record an episode which already appears to me less horrible than grotesque. Yet, unless this story is written now, I know I shall never have the courage to tell the truth about the matter – not from fear of ridicule, but because I myself shall soon cease to credit what I now know to be true. Yet scarcely a month has elapsed since I heard the stealthy purring of what I believed to be the shoaling undertow – scarcely a month ago, with my own eyes, I saw that which, even now, I am beginning to believe never existed. As for the harbour-master – and the blow I am now striking at the old order of things— But of that I shall not speak now, or later; I shall try to tell the story simply and truthfully, and let my friends testify as to my probity and the publishers of this book corroborate them.

On the 29th of February I resigned my position under the government and left Washington to accept an offer from Professor Farrago – whose name he kindly permits me to use – and on the first day of April I entered upon my new and congenial duties as general superintendent of the water-fowl department connected with the Zoological Gardens then in course of erection at Bronx Park, New York.

For a week I followed the routine, examining the new

foundations, studying the architect's plans, following the surveyors through the Bronx thickets, suggesting arrangements for water-courses and pools destined to be included in the enclosures for swans, geese, pelicans, herons, and such of the waders and swimmers as we might expect to acclimatise in Bronx Park.

It was at that time the policy of the trustees and officers of the Zoological Gardens neither to employ collectors nor to send out expeditions in search of specimens. The society decided to depend upon voluntary contributions, and I was always busy, part of the day, in dictating answers to correspondents who wrote offering their services as hunters of big game, collectors of all sorts of fauna, trappers, snarers, and also to those who offered specimens for sale, usually at exorbitant rates.

To the proprietors of five-legged kittens, mangy lynxes, moth-eaten coyotes, and dancing bears I returned courteous but uncompromising refusals – of course, first submitting all such letters together with my replies, to Professor Farrago.

One day, towards the end of May, however, just as I was leaving Bronx Park to return to town, Professor Lesard, of the reptilian department, called out to me that Professor Farrago wanted to see me a moment; so I put my pipe into my pocket again and retraced my steps to the temporary wooden building occupied by Professor Farrago, general superintendent of the Zoological Gardens. The professor, who was sitting at his desk before a pile of letters and replies, submitted for approval by me, pushed his glasses down and looked over them at me with a whimsical smile that suggested amusement, impatience, annoyance, and perhaps a faint trace of apology.

'Now, here's a letter,' he said, with a deliberate gesture towards a sheet of paper impaled on a file – 'a letter that I suppose you remember.' He disengaged the sheet of paper and handed it to me.

'Oh, yes,' I replied, with a shrug; 'of course, the man is mistaken – or—'

'Or what?' demanded Professor Farrago tranquilly, wiping his glasses.

'Or a liar,' I replied.

After a silence he leaned back in his chair and bade me read the letter to him again, and I did so with a contemptuous tolerance for the writer, who must have been either a very innocent victim or a very stupid swindler. I said as much to Professor Farrago, but, to my surprise, he appeared to waver.

'I suppose,' he said, with his near-sighted, embarrassed smile, 'that nine hundred and ninety-nine men in a thousand would throw that letter aside and condemn the writer as a liar or a fool?'

'In my opinion,' said I, 'he's one or the other.'

'He isn't – in mine,' said the professor placidly.

'What!' I exclaimed. 'Here is a man living all alone on a strip of rock and sand between the wilderness and the sea, who wants you to send somebody to take charge of a bird that doesn't exist!'

'How do you know,' asked Professor Farrago, 'that the bird in question does not exist?'

'It is generally accepted,' I replied sarcastically, 'that the great auk has been extinct for years. Therefore I may be pardoned for doubting that our correspondent possesses a pair of them alive.'

'Oh, you young fellows,' said the professor, smiling wearily, 'you embark on a theory for destinations that don't exist.'

He leaned back in his chair, his amused eyes searching space for the imagery that made him smile.

'Like swimming squirrels, you navigate with the help of Heaven and a stiff breeze, but you never land where you hope to – do you?'

Rather red in the face, I said: 'Don't you believe the great auk to be extinct?'

'Audubon saw the great auk.'

'Who has seen a single specimen since?'

'Nobody – except our correspondent here,' he replied, laughing.

I laughed too, considering the interview at an end, but the professor went on coolly—

'Whatever it is that our correspondent has – and I am daring to believe that it *is* the great auk itself – I want you to secure it for the society.'

When my astonishment subsided my first conscious sentiment was one of pity. Clearly, Professor Farrago was on the verge of dotage – ah, what a loss to the world!

I believe now that Professor Farrago perfectly interpreted my thoughts, but he betrayed neither resentment nor impatience. I drew a chair up beside his desk – there was nothing to do but to obey, and this fool's errand was none of my conceiving.

Together we made out a list of articles necessary for me and itemized the expenses I might incur, and I set a date for my return, allowing no margin for a successful termination to the expedition.

'Never mind that,' said the professor. 'What I want you to do is to get those birds here safely. Now, how many men will you take?'

'None,' I replied bluntly; 'it's a useless expense, unless there is something to bring back. If there is I'll wire you, you may be sure.'

'Very well,' said Professor Farrago good-humouredly, 'you shall have all the assistance you may require. Can you leave tonight?'

The old gentleman was certainly prompt. I nodded half-sulkily, aware of his amusement.

'So,' I said, picking up my hat, 'I am to start north to find a place called Black Harbor, where there is a man named Halyard who possesses, among other household utensils, two extinct great auks—'

We were both laughing by this time. I asked him why on earth he credited the assertion of a man he had never before heard of.

'I suppose,' he replied, with the same half-apologetic, half-humorous smile, 'it is instinct. I feel, somehow, that this man Halyard *has* got an auk – perhaps two. I can't get away from the idea that we are on the eve of acquiring the rarest of living creatures. It's odd for a scientist to talk as I do; doubtless you're shocked – admit it, now!'

But I was not shocked; on the contrary, I was conscious that the same strange hope that Professor Farrago cherished was beginning, in spite of me, to stir my pulses too.

'If he has—' I began, then stopped.

The professor and I looked hard at each other in silence.

'Go on,' he said, encouragingly.

But I had nothing more to say, for the prospect of beholding with my own eyes a living specimen of the great auk produced a series of conflicting emotions within me which rendered speech profanely superfluous.

As I took my leave Professor Farrago came to the door of the temporary wooden office and handed me the letter written by the man Halyard. I folded it and put it into my pocket, as Halyard might require it for my own identification.

'How much does he want for the pair?' I asked.

'Ten thousand dollars. Don't demur – if the birds are really—'

'I know,' I said hastily, not daring to hope too much.

'One thing more,' said Professor Farrago gravely; 'you know, in that last paragraph of his letter, Halyard speaks of something else in the way of specimens – an undiscovered species of amphibious biped. Just read that paragraph again, will you?'

I drew the letter from my pocket and read as he directed –

'When you have seen the two living specimens of the great auk, and have satisfied yourself that I tell the truth, you may be wise enough to listen without prejudice to a statement I shall make concerning the existence of the strangest creature ever fashioned. I

will merely say, at this time, that the creature referred
to is an amphibious biped, and inhabits the ocean near
this coast. More I cannot say, for I personally have not
seen the animal, but I have a witness who has, and
there are many who affirm that they have seen the
creature. You will naturally say that my statement
amounts to nothing; but when your representative
arrives, if he be free from prejudice, I expect his reports
to you concerning this sea-biped will confirm the
solemn statements of a witness I *know* to be unimpeachable.

'Yours truly,

'BURTON HALYARD.
'BLACK HARBOR.'

'Well,' I said, after a moment's thought, 'here goes for the
wild-goose chase.'

'Wild auk, you mean,' said Professor Farrago, shaking
hands with me. 'You will start to-night, won't you?'

'Yes, but Heaven knows how I'm ever going to land in
this man Halyard's door-yard. Good-bye!'

'About that sea-biped—' began Professor Farrago shyly.

'Oh, don't!' I said; 'I can swallow the auks, feathers and
claws, but if this fellow Halyard is hinting he's seen an
amphibious creature resembling a man—'

'Or a woman,' said the professor cautiously.

I retired disgusted, my faith shaken in the mental vigour
of Professor Farrago.

II

The three days' voyage by boat and rail was irksome. I
bought my kit at Sainte Croix, on the Central Pacific Railroad,
and on June 1 I began the last stage of my journey *via* the
Sainte Isole broad-gauge, arriving in the wilderness by
daylight. A tedious forced march by blazed trail, freshly
spotted on the wrong side, of course, brought me to the

northern terminus of the rusty, narrow-gauge lumber railway which runs from the heart of the hushed pine wilderness to the sea.

Already a long train of battered flat-cars, piled with sluice-props and roughly hewn sleepers, was moving slowly off into the brooding forest gloom, when I came in sight of the track; but I developed a gratifying and unexpected burst of speed, shouting all the while. The train stopped; I swung myself aboard the last car, where a pleasant young fellow was sitting on the rear brake, chewing spruce and reading a letter.

'Come aboard, sir,' he said, looking up with a smile; 'I guess you're the man in a hurry.'

'I'm looking for a man named Halyard,' I said, dropping rifle and knapsack on the fresh-cut, fragrant pile of pine. 'Are you Halyard?'

'No, I'm Francis Lee, bossing the mica pit at Port-of-Waves,' he replied, 'but this letter is from Halyard, asking me to look out for a man in a hurry from Bronx Park, New York.'

'I'm that man,' said I, filling my pipe and offering him a share of the weed of peace, and we sat side by side smoking very amiably, until a signal from the locomotive sent him forward and I was left alone, lounging at ease, head pillowed on both arms, watching the blue sky fly through the branches overhead.

Long before we came in sight of the ocean I smelled it; the fresh, salt aroma stole into my senses, drowsy with the heated odour of pine and hemlock, and I sat up, peering ahead into the dusky sea of pines.

Fresher and fresher came the wind from the sea, in puffs, in mild, sweet breezes, in steady, freshening currents, blowing the feathery crowns of the pines, setting the balsam's blue tufts rocking.

Lee wandered back over the long line of flats, balancing himself nonchalantly as the cars swung around a sharp curve, where water dripped from a newly propped sluice that suddenly emerged from the depths of the forest to run parallel to the railroad track.

'Built it this spring,' he said, surveying his handiwork, which seemed to undulate as the cars swept past. 'It runs to the cove – or ought to—' He stopped abruptly with a thoughtful glance at me. 'So you're going over to Halyard's?' he continued, as though answering a question asked by himself.

I nodded.

'You've never been there – of course?'

'No,' I said, 'and I'm not likely to go again.'

I would have told him why I was going if I had not already begun to feel ashamed of my idiotic errand.

'I guess you're going to look at those birds of his,' continued Lee placidly.

'I guess I am,' I said sulkily, glancing askance to see whether he was smiling.

But he only asked me, quite seriously, whether a great auk was really a very rare bird; and I told him that the last one ever seen had been found dead off Labrador in January 1870. Then I asked him whether these birds of Halyard's were really great auks, and he replied, somewhat indifferently, that he supposed they were – at least, nobody had ever before seen such birds near Port-of-Waves.

'There's something else,' he said, running a pine-sliver through his pipe-stem – 'something that interests us all here more than auks, big or little. I suppose I might as well speak of it, as you are bound to hear about it sooner or later.'

He hesitated, and I could see that he was embarrassed, searching for the exact words to convey his meaning.

'If,' said I, 'you have anything in this region more important to science than the great auk, I should be very glad to know about it.'

Perhaps there was the faintest tinge of sarcasm in my voice, for he shot a sharp glance at me and then turned slightly. After a moment, however, he put his pipe into his pocket, laid hold of the brake with both hands, vaulted to his perch aloft, and glanced down at me.

'Did you ever hear of the harbor-master?' he asked maliciously.

'Which harbor-master?' I inquired.

'You'll know before long,' he observed, with a satisfied glance into perspective.

This rather extraordinary observation puzzled me. I waited for him to resume, and, as he did not, I asked him what he meant.

'If I knew,' he said, 'I'd tell you. But, come to think of it, I'd be a fool to go into details with a scientific man. You'll hear about the harbor-master – perhaps you will see the harbor-master. In that event I should be glad to converse with you on the subject.'

I could not help laughing at his prim and precise manner, and, after a moment, he also laughed, saying—

'It hurts a man's vanity to know he knows a thing that somebody else knows he doesn't know. I'm damned if I say another word about the harbor-master until you've been to Halyard's!'

'A harbor-master,' I persisted, 'is an official who superintends the mooring of ships – isn't he?'

But he refused to be tempted into conversation, and we lounged silently on the lumber until a long, thin whistle from the locomotive and a rush of stinging salt-wind brought us to our feet. Through the trees I could see the bluish-black ocean, stretching out beyond black headlands to meet the clouds; a great wind was roaring among the trees as the train slowly came to a stand-still on the edge of the primeval forest.

Lee jumped to the ground and aided me with my rifle and pack, and then the train began to back away along a curved side-track which, Lee said, led to the mica pit and company stores.

'Now what will you do?' he asked pleasantly. 'I can give you a good dinner and a decent bed tonight, if you like; and

I'm sure Mrs Lee would be very glad to have you stop with us as long as you choose.'

I thanked him, but said that I was anxious to reach Halyard's before dark, and he very kindly led me along the cliffs and pointed out the path.

'This man Halyard,' he said, 'is an invalid. He lives at a cove called Black Harbor, and all his truck goes through to him over the company's road. We receive it here, and send a pack-mule through once a month. I've met him; he's a bad-tempered hypochondriac, a cynic at heart, and a man whose word is never doubted. If he says he has a great auk, you may be satisfied he has.'

My heart was beating with excitement at the prospect; I looked out across the wooded headlands and tangled stretches of dune and hollow, trying to realize what it might mean to me, to Professor Farrago, to the world, if I should lead back to New York a live auk.

'He's a crank,' said Lee; 'frankly, I don't like him. If you find it unpleasant there, come back to us.'

'Does Halyard live alone?' I asked.

'Yes – except for a professional trained nurse – poor thing!'

'A man?'

'No,' said Lee disgustedly.

Presently he gave me a peculiar glance; hesitated, and finally said: 'Ask Halyard to tell you about his nurse and – the harbor-master. Goodbye; I'm due at the quarry. Come and stay with us whenever you care to; you will find a welcome at Port-of-Waves.'

We shook hands and parted on the cliff, he turning back into the forest along the railway, I starting northward, pack slung, rifle over my shoulder. Once I met a group of quarrymen, faces burned brick-red, scarred hands swinging as they walked. And, as I passed them with a nod, turning, I saw that they also had turned to look after me, and I caught a word or two of their conversation, whirled back to me on the sea-wind.

They were speaking of the harbor-master.

III

Towards sunset I came out on a sheer granite cliff where the sea-birds were whirling and clamoring, and the great breakers dashed, rolling in double-thundered reverberations on the sun-dyed, crimson sands below the rock.

Across the half-moon of beach towered another cliff, and, behind this, I saw a column of smoke rising in the still air. It certainly came from Halyard's chimney, although the opposite cliff prevented me from seeing the house itself.

I rested a moment to refill my pipe, then resumed rifle and pack, and cautiously started to skirt the cliffs. I had descended half-way towards the beach, and was examining the cliff opposite, when something on the very top of the rock arrested my attention – a man darkly outlined against the sky. The next moment, however, I knew it could not be a man, for the object suddenly glided over the face of the cliff and slid down the sheer, smooth face like a lizard. Before I could get a square look at it, the thing crawled into the surf – or, at least, it seemed to – but the whole episode occurred so suddenly, so unexpectedly, that I was not sure I had seen anything at all.

However, I was curious enough to climb the cliff on the land side and make my way towards the spot where I imagined I saw the man. Of course, there was nothing there – not a trace of a human being, I mean. Something *had* been there – a sea otter, possibly – for the remains of a freshly killed fish lay on the rock, eaten to the back-bone and tail.

The next moment, below me, I saw the house, a freshly painted, trim, flimsy structure, modern, and very much out of harmony with the splendid savagery surrounding it. It struck a nasty, cheap note in the noble, grey monotony of headland and sea.

The descent was easy enough. I crossed the crescent beach, hard as pink marble, and found a little trodden path among the rocks, that led to the front porch of the house.

There were two people on the porch – I heard their voices

before I saw them – and when I set my foot upon the wooden steps, I saw one of them, a woman, rise from her chair and step hastily towards me.

'Come back!' cried the other, a man with a smooth-shaven, deeply lined face, and a pair of angry blue eyes; and the woman stepped back quietly, acknowledging my lifted hat with a silent inclination.

The man, who was reclining in an invalid's rolling-chair, clapped both large, pale hands to the wheels and pushed himself out along the porch. He had shawls pinned about him, an untidy, drab-colored hat on his head, and, when he looked down at me, he scowled.

'I know who you are,' he said in his acid voice; 'you're one of the Zoological men from Bronx Park. You look it, anyway.'

'It is easy to recognize you from your reputation,' I replied, irritated at his discourtesy.

'Really,' he replied, with something between a sneer and a laugh, 'I'm obliged for your frankness. You're after my great auks, are you not?'

'Nothing else would have tempted me into this place,' I replied sincerely.

'Thank Heaven for that,' he said. 'Sit down a moment; you've interrupted us.' Then turning to the young woman, who wore the neat gown and tiny cap of a professional nurse, he bade her resume what she had been saying. She did so, with a deprecating glance at me, which made the old man sneer again.

'It happened so suddenly,' she said, in her low voice, 'that I had no chance to get back. The boat was drifting in the cove; I sat in the stern reading, both oars shipped, and the tiller swinging. Then I heard a scratching under the boat, but thought it might be seaweed – and, next moment, came those soft thumpings, like the sound of a big fish rubbing its nose against a float.'

Halyard clutched the wheels of his chair and stared at the girl in grim displeasure.

'Didn't you know enough to be frightened?' he demanded.

'No – not then,' she said, coloring faintly; 'but when, after a few moments, I looked up and saw the harbor-master running up and down the beach, I was horribly frightened.'

'Really?' said Halyard sarcastically; 'it was about time.' Then, turning to me, he rasped out: 'And that young lady was obliged to row all the way to Port-of-Waves and call to Lee's quarrymen to take her boat in.'

Completely mystified, I looked from Halyard to the girl, not in the least comprehending what all this meant.

'That will do,' said Halyard ungraciously, which curt phrase was apparently the usual dismissal for the nurse.

She rose and I rose, and she passed me with an inclination, stepping noiselessly into the house.

'I want beef-tea!' bawled Halyard after her; then he gave me an unamiable glance.

'I was a well-bred man,' he sneered; 'I'm a Harvard graduate, too, but I live as I like, and I do what I like, and I say what I like.'

'You certainly are not reticent,' I said, disgusted.

'Why should I be?' he rasped; 'I pay that young woman for my irritability; it's a bargain between us.'

'In your domestic affairs,' I said, 'there is nothing that interests me. I came to see those auks.'

'You probably believe them to be razor-billed auks,' he said contemptuously. 'But they're not; they're great auks.'

I suggested that he permit me to examine them, and he replied indifferently that they were in a pen in his backyard, and that I was free to step around the house when I cared to.

I laid my rifle and pack on the verandah, and hastened off with mixed emotions, among which hope no longer predominated. No man in his senses would keep two such precious prizes in a pen in his backyard, I argued, and I was perfectly prepared to find anything from a puffin to a penguin in that pen.

I shall never forget, as long as I live, my stupor of amazement

when I came to the wire-covered enclosure. Not only were
there two great auks in the pen, alive, breathing, squatting in
bulky majesty on their seaweed bed, but one of them was
gravely contemplating two newly hatched chicks, all bill and
feet, which nestled sedately at the edge of a puddle of salt-
water, where some small fish were swimming.

For a while excitement blinded, nay, deafened me. I tried
to realize that I was gazing upon the last individuals of an
all but extinct race – the sole survivors of the gigantic auk,
which, for thirty years, has been accounted an extinct creature.

I believe that I did not move muscle nor limb until the
sun had gone down and the crowding darkness blurred my
straining eyes and blotted the great, silent, bright-eyed birds
from sight.

Even then I could not tear myself away from the enclosure; I listened to the strange, drowsy note of the male bird,
the fainter responses of the female, the thin plaints of the
chicks, huddling under her breast; I heard their flipper-like,
embryotic wings beating sleepily as the birds stretched and
yawned their beaks and clacked them, preparing for slumber.

'If you please,' came a soft voice from the door, 'Mr
Halyard awaits your company to dinner.'

IV

I dined well – or, rather, I might have enjoyed my dinner if
Mr Halyard had been eliminated; and the feast consisted
exclusively of a joint of beef, the pretty nurse, and myself.
She was exceedingly attractive – with a disturbing fashion of
lowering her head and raising her dark eyes when spoken to.

As for Halyard, he was unspeakable, bundled up in his
snuffy shawls, and making uncouth noises over his gruel.
But it is only just to say that his table was worth sitting
down to and his wine was sound as a bell.

'Yah!' he snapped, 'I'm sick of this cursed soup – and I'll
trouble you to fill my glass—'

'It is pretty dangerous for you to touch claret,' said the pretty nurse.

'I might as well die at dinner as anywhere,' he observed.

'Certainly,' said I, cheerfully passing the decanter, but he did not appear overpleased with the attention.

'I can't smoke, either,' he snarled, hitching the shawls around until he looked like Richard the Third.

However, he was good enough to shove a box of cigars at me, and I took one and stood up, as the pretty nurse slipped past and vanished into the little parlor beyond.

We sat there for a while without speaking. He picked irritably at the bread-crumbs on the cloth, never glancing in my direction; and I, tired from my long foot-tour, lay back in my chair, silently appreciating one of the best cigars I ever smoked.

'Well,' he rasped out at length, 'what do you think of my auks – and my veracity?'

I told him that both were unimpeachable.

'Didn't they call me a swindler down there at your museum?' he demanded.

I admitted that I had heard the term applied. Then I made a clean breast of the matter, telling him that it was I who had doubted; that my chief, Professor Farrago, had sent me against my will, and that I was ready and glad to admit that he, Mr Halyard, was a benefactor of the human race.

'Bosh!' he said. 'What good does a confounded wobbly, bandy-toed bird do to the human race?'

But he was pleased, nevertheless; and presently he asked me, not unamiably, to punish his claret again.

'I'm done for,' he said; 'good things to eat and drink are no good to me. Some day I'll get mad enough to have a fit, and then—'

He paused to yawn.

'Then,' he continued, 'that little nurse of mine will drink up my claret and go back to civilization, where people are polite.'

Somehow or other, in spite of the fact that Halyard was

an old pig, what he said touched me. There was certainly not much left in life for him – as he regarded life.

'I'm going to leave her this house,' he said, arranging his shawls. 'She doesn't know it. I'm going to leave her my money, too. She doesn't know that. Good Lord! What kind of a woman can she be to stand my bad temper for a few dollars a month!'

'I think,' said I, 'that it's partly because she's poor, partly because she's sorry for you.'

He looked up with a ghastly smile.

'You think she really is sorry?'

Before I could answer he went on: 'I'm no mawkish sentimentalist, and I won't allow anybody to be sorry for me – do you hear?'

'Oh, I'm not sorry for you!' I said hastily, and, for the first time since I had seen him, he laughed heartily, without a sneer.

We both seemed to feel better after that; I drank his wine and smoked his cigars, and he appeared to take a certain grim pleasure in watching me.

'There's no fool like a young fool' he observed, presently.

As I had no doubt he referred to me, I paid him no attention. After fidgeting with his shawls, he gave me an oblique scowl and asked me my age.

'Twenty-four,' I replied.

'Sort of a tadpole, aren't you?' he said.

As I took no offence, he repeated his remark.

'Oh, come,' said I, 'there's no use in trying to irritate me. I see through you; a row acts like a cocktail on you – but you'll have to stick to gruel in my company.'

'I call that impudence!' he rasped out wrathfully.

'I don't care what you call it,' I replied, undisturbed. 'I am not going to be worried by you. Anyway,' I ended, 'it is my opinion that you could be very good company if you chose.'

The proposition appeared to take his breath away – at least, he said nothing more; and I finished my cigar in peace and tossed the stump into a saucer.

'Now,' said I, 'what price do you set upon your birds, Mr Halyard?'

'Ten thousand dollars,' he snapped, with an evil smile.

'You will receive a certified cheque when the birds are delivered,' I said quietly.

'You don't mean to say you agree to that outrageous bargain – and I won't take a cent less, either – Good Lord! haven't you any spirit left?' he cried, half rising from his pile of shawls.

His piteous eagerness for a dispute sent me into laughter impossible to control, and he eyed me, mouth open, animosity rising visibly.

Then he seized the wheels of his invalid chair and trundled away, too mad to speak; and I strolled out into the parlor, still laughing.

The pretty nurse was there, sewing under a hanging lamp.

'If I am not indiscreet—' I began.

'Indiscretion is the better part of valor,' said she, dropping her head but raising her eyes.

So I sat down with a frivolous smile peculiar to the appreciated.

'Doubtless,' said I, 'you are hemming a kerchief.'

'Doubtless I am not,' she said; 'this is a night-cap for Mr Halyard.'

A mental vision of Halyard in a night-cap, very mad, nearly set me to laughing again.

'Like the King of Yvetot, he wears his crown in bed,' I said flippantly.

'The King of Yvetot might have made that remark,' she observed, re-threading her needle.

It is unpleasant to be reproved. How large and red and hot a man's ears feel.

To cool them, I strolled out to the porch; and after a while, the pretty nurse came out too, and sat down in a chair not far away. She probably regretted her lost opportunity to be flirted with.

'I have so little company – it is a great relief to see somebody from the world,' she said. 'If you can be agreeable, I wish you would.'

The idea that she had come out to see me was so agreeable that I remained speechless until she said: 'Do tell me what people are doing in New York.'

So I seated myself on the steps and talked about the portion of the world inhabited by me, while she sat sewing in the dull light that straggled out from the parlor windows.

She had a certain coquetry of her own, using the usual methods with an individuality that was certainly fetching. For instance, when she lost her needle – and, another time, when we both, on hands and knees, hunted for her thimble.

However, directions for these pastimes may be found in contemporary classics.

I was as entertaining as I could be – perhaps not quite as entertaining as a young man usually thinks he is. However, we got on very well together until I asked her tenderly who the harbor-master might be, whom they all discussed so mysteriously.

'I do not care to speak about it,' she said, with a primness of which I had not suspected her capable.

Of course I could scarcely pursue the subject after that – and, indeed, I did not intend to – so I began to tell her how I fancied I had seen a man on the cliff that afternoon, and how the creature slid over the sheer rock like a snake.

To my amazement, she asked me kindly to discontinue the account of my adventures, in an icy tone, which left no room for protest.

'It was only a sea-otter,' I tried to explain, thinking perhaps she did not care for snake stories.

But the explanation did not appear to interest her, and I was mortified to observe that my impression upon her was anything but pleasant.

'She doesn't seem to like me and my stories,' thought I, 'but she is too young, perhaps, to appreciate them.'

So I forgave her – for she was even prettier than I had

thought her at first – and I took my leave, saying that Mr
Halyard would doubtless direct me to my room.

Halyard was in his library, cleaning a revolver, when I
entered.

'Your room is next to mine,' he said; 'pleasant dreams,
and kindly refrain from snoring.'

'May I venture an absurd hope that you will do the same!'
I replied politely.

That maddened him, so I hastily withdrew.

I had been asleep for at least two hours when a movement
by my bedside and a light in my eyes awakened me. I sat
bolt upright in bed, blinking at Halyard, who, clad in a
dressing-gown and wearing a night-cap, had wheeled himself
into my room with one hand, while with the other he
solemnly waved a candle over my head.

'I'm so cursed lonely,' he said – 'come, there's a good
fellow, talk to me in your own original, impudent way.'

I objected strenuously, but he looked so worn and thin,
so lonely and bad-tempered, so lovelessly grotesque, that I
got out of bed and passed a spongeful of cold water over
my head.

Then I returned to bed and propped the pillows up for a
back-rest, ready to quarrel with him if it might bring some
little pleasure into his morbid existence.

'No,' he said amiably, 'I'm too worried to quarrel, but I'm
much obliged for your kindly offer. I want to tell you something.'

'What?' I asked suspiciously.

'I want to ask you if you ever saw a man with gills like
a fish?'

'Gills?' I repeated.

'Yes, gills! Did you?'

'No,' I replied angrily, 'and neither did you.'

'No, I never did,' he said, in a curiously placid voice, 'but
there's a man with gills like a fish who lives in the ocean
out there. Oh, you needn't look that way – nobody ever
thinks of doubting my word, and I tell you that there's a

man – or a thing that looks like a man – as big as you are
too, all slate-coloured, with nasty red gills like a fish! And
I've a witness to prove what I say!'

'Who?' I asked sarcastically.

'The witness? My nurse.'

'Oh! She saw a slate-coloured man with gills?'

'Yes, she did. So did Francis Lee, superintendent of the
mica Quarry Company at Port-of-Waves. So have a dozen
men who work in the quarry. Oh, you needn't laugh, young
man. It's an old story here, and anybody can tell you about
the harbor-master.'

'The harbor-master!' I exclaimed.

'Yes, that slate-colored thing with gills, that looks like a
man – and, by Heaven! is a man – that's the harbor-master.
Ask any quarryman at Port-of-Waves what it is that comes
purring around their boats at the wharf and unties painters
and changes the mooring of every cat-boat in the cove at
night! Ask Francis Lee what it was he saw running and
leaping up and down the shoal at sunset last Friday! Ask
anybody along the coast what sort of a thing moves about
the cliffs like a man and slides over them into the sea like
an otter—'

'I saw it do that!' I burst out.

'Oh, did you? Well, *what was it*?'

Something kept me silent, although a dozen explanations
flew to my lips.

After a pause, Halyard said: 'You saw the harbor-master,
that's what you saw!'

I looked at him without a word.

'Don't mistake me,' he said pettishly; 'I don't think that
the harbor-master is a spirit or a sprite or a hobgoblin, or
any sort of damned rot. Neither do I believe it to be an
optical illusion.'

'What do you think it is?' I asked.

'I think it's a man – I think it's a branch of the human
race – that's what I think. Let me tell you something: the
deepest spot in the Atlantic Ocean is a trifle over five miles

deep, and I suppose you know that this place lies only about a quarter of a mile off this headland. The British exploring vessel, *Gull*, Captain Marotte, discovered and sounded it, I believe. Anyway, it's there, and it's my belief that the profound depths are inhabited by the remnants of the last race of amphibious human beings!'

This was childish; I did not bother to reply.

'Believe it or not, as you will,' he said angrily; 'one thing I know, and that is this: the harbor-master has taken to hanging around my cove, and he is attracted by my nurse! I won't have it! I'll blow his fishy gills out of his head if I ever get a shot at him! I don't care whether it's homicide or not – anyway, it's a new kind of murder, and it attracts me!'

I gazed at him incredulously, but he was working himself into a passion, and I did not choose to say what I thought.

'Yes, this slate-colored thing with gills goes purring and grinning and spitting about after my nurse – when she walks, when she rows, when she sits on the beach! Gad! It drives me nearly frantic. I won't tolerate it, I tell you!'

'No,' said I, 'I wouldn't either.' And I rolled over in bed convulsed with laughter.

The next moment I heard my door slam. I smothered my mirth and rose to close the window, for the land-wind blew cold from the forest, and a drizzle was sweeping the carpet as far as my bed.

That luminous glare which sometimes lingers after the stars go out threw a trembling, nebulous radiance over sand and cove. I heard the seething currents under the breakers' softened thunder – louder than I ever heard it. Then, as I closed my window, lingering for a last look at the crawling tide, I saw a man standing, ankle-deep, in the surf, all alone there in the night. But – was it a man? For the figure began suddenly running over the beach on all fours like a beetle, waving its limbs like feelers. Before I could throw open the window again it darted into the surf, and, when I leaned out into the chilling drizzle, I saw nothing save the flat ebb crawling on the coast – I heard nothing save the purring of bubbles on seething sands.

V

It took me a week to perfect my arrangements for transporting the great auks, by water, to Port-of-Waves, where a lumber schooner was to be sent from Petite Sainte Isole, chartered by me for voyage to New York.

I had constructed a cage made of osiers, in which my auks were to squat until they arrived at Bronx Park. My telegrams to Professor Farrago were brief. One merely said 'Victory!' Another explained that I wanted no assistance; a third read: 'Schooner chartered. Arrive New York July 1. Send furniture-van to foot of Bluff Street.'

My week as a guest of Mr Halyard proved interesting. I wrangled with that invalid to his heart's content, I worked all day on my osier cage, I hunted the thimble in the moonlight with the pretty nurse. We sometimes found it.

As for the thing they called the harbor-master I saw it a dozen times, but always either at night or so far away and so close to the sea that of course no trace of it remained when I reached the spot, rifle in hand.

I had quite made up my mind that the so-called harbor-master was a demented darky – wandered from, Heaven knows where – perhaps shipwrecked and gone mad from his sufferings. Still, it was far from pleasant to know that the creature was strongly attracted by the pretty nurse.

She, however, persisted in regarding the harbor-master as a sea creature; she earnestly affirmed that it had gills, like fish's gills, that it had a soft, fleshy hole for a mouth, and its eyes were luminous and lidless and fixed.

'Besides,' she said, with a shudder, 'it's all slate-color, like a porpoise, and it looks as wet as a sheet of india-rubber in a dissecting room.'

The day before I was to set sail with my auks in a cat-boat

bound for Port-of-Waves, Halyard trundled up to me in his chair and announced his intention of going with me.

'Going where?' I asked.

'To Port-of-Waves and then to New York,' he replied tranquilly.

I was doubtful, and my lack of cordiality hurt his feelings.

'Oh, of course, if you need the sea-voyage,' I began.

'I don't; I need you,' he said savagely; 'I need the stimulus of our daily quarrel. I never disagreed so pleasantly with anybody in my life; it agrees with me; I am a hundred per cent better than I was last week.'

I was inclined to resent this, but something in the deep-lined face of the invalid softened me. Besides, I had taken a hearty liking to the old pig.

'I don't want any mawkish sentiment about it,' he said, observing me closely; 'I won't permit anybody to feel sorry for me – do you understand?'

'I'll trouble you to use a different tone in addressing me,' I replied hotly; 'I'll feel sorry for you if I choose to!' And our usual quarrel proceeded, to his deep satisfaction.

By six o'clock next evening I had Halyard's luggage stowed away in the cat-boat and the pretty nurse's effects corded down, with the newly-hatched auk-chicks in a hat-box on top. She and I placed the osier cage aboard, securing it firmly, and then, throwing table-cloths over the auks' heads, we led those simple and dignified birds down the path and across the plank at the little wooden pier. Together we locked up the house, while Halyard stormed at us both and wheeled himself furiously up and down the beach below. At the last moment she forgot her thimble. But we found it, I forget where.

'Come on!' shouted Halyard, waving his shawls furiously; 'what the devil are you about up there?'

He received our explanation with a sniff, and we trundled him aboard without further ceremony.

'Don't run me across the plank like a steamer trunk!' he shouted, as I shot him dexterously into the cock-pit. But the wind was dying away and I had no time to dispute with him then.

The sun was setting above the pine-clad ridge as our sail flapped and partly filled, and I cast off and began a long tack, east by south, to avoid the spouting rocks on our starboard bow.

The sea-birds rose in clouds as we swung across the shoal, the black surf-ducks scattered out to sea, the gulls tossed their sun-tipped wings in the ocean, riding the rollers like bits of froth.

Already we were sailing slowly out across that great hole in the ocean, five miles deep, the most profound sounding ever taken in the Atlantic. The presence of some heights or great depths seen or unseen, always impresses the human mind – perhaps oppresses it. We were very silent; the sunlight stain on cliff and beach deepened to crimson, then faded into somber purple bloom that lingered long after the rose-tint died out in the zenith.

Our progress was slow; at times, although the sail filled with the rising land-breeze, we scarcely seemed to move at all.

'Of course,' said the pretty nurse, 'we couldn't be aground in the deepest hole in the Atlantic.'

'Scarcely,' said Halyard sarcastically, 'unless we're grounded on a whale.'

'What's that soft thumping?' I asked. 'Have we run afoul of a barrel or log?'

It was almost too dark to see, but I leaned over the rail and swept the water with my hand.

Instantly something smooth glided under it, like the back of a great fish, and I jerked my hand back to the tiller. At the same moment the whole surface of the water seemed to begin to purr, with a sound like the breaking of froth in a champagne-glass.

'What's the matter with you?' asked Halyard sharply.

'A fish came up under my hand,' I said; 'a porpoise or something—'

With a low cry, the pretty nurse clasped my arm in both her hands.

'Listen!' she whispered. 'It's purring around the boat.'

'What the devil's purring?' shouted Halyard. 'I won't have anything purring around me!'

At that moment, to my amazement, I saw that the boat had stopped entirely, although the sail was full and the small pennant fluttered from the mast-head. Something, too, was tugging at the rudder, twisting and jerking it until the tiller strained and creaked in my hand. All at once it snapped; the tiller swung useless and the boat whirled round, heeling in the stiffening wind, and drove shoreward.

It was then that I, ducking to escape the boom, caught a glimpse of something ahead – something that a sudden wave seemed to toss on deck and leave there, wet and flapping – a man with round, fixed, fishy eyes, and soft, slaty skin.

But the horror of the thing were the two gills that swelled and released spasmodically, emitting a rasping, purring sound – two gasping, blood-red gills, all fluted and scolloped and distended.

Frozen with amazement and repugnance, I stared at the creature; I felt the hair stirring on my head and the icy sweat on my forehead.

'It's the harbor-master!' screamed Halyard.

The harbor-master had gathered himself into a wet lump, squatting motionless in the bows under the mast; his lidless eyes were phosphorescent like the eyes of living codfish. After a while I felt that either fright or disgust was going to strangle me where I sat, but it was only the arms of the pretty nurse clasped around me in a frenzy of terror.

There was not a firearm aboard that we could get at. Halyard's hand crept backwards where a steel-shod boat-hook lay, and I also made a clutch at it. The next moment I had it in my hand, and staggered forward, but the boat was already tumbling shoreward among the breakers, and the next I knew the harbor-master ran at me like a colossal rat, just as the boat rolled over and over through the surf, spilling freight and passengers among the seaweed covered rocks.

When I came to myself I was thrashing about knee-deep in a rocky pool, blinded by the water and half suffocated, while under my feet, like a stranded porpoise, the harbor-master made the water boil in his efforts to upset me. But his limbs seemed soft and boneless; he had no nails, no teeth, and he bounced and thumped and flapped and splashed like a fish, while I rained blows on him with the boat-hook that sounded like blows on a football. And all the while his gills were blowing out and frothing, and purring, and his lidless eyes looked into mine, until, nauseated and trembling, I dragged myself back to the beach, where already the pretty nurse alternately wrung her hands and her petti-coats in ornamental despair.

Beyond the cove, Halyard was bobbing up and down, afloat in his invalid's chair, trying to steer shoreward. He was the maddest man I ever saw.

'Have you killed that rubber-headed thing yet?' he roared.

'I can't kill it,' I shouted breathlessly. 'I might as well try to kill a football!'

'Can't you punch a hole in it?' he bawled. 'If I can only get at him—'

His words were drowned in a thunderous splashing, a roar of great, broad flippers beating the sea, and I saw the gigantic forms of my two great auks, followed by their chicks, blundering past, in a shower of spray, driving headlong out into the ocean.

'Oh, Lord!' I said. 'I can't stand that,' and, for the first time in my life, I fainted peacefully – and appropriately – at the feet of the pretty nurse.

It is within the range of possibility that this story may be doubted. It doesn't matter; nothing can add to the despair of a man who has lost two great auks.

As for Halyard, nothing affects him – except his involun-tary sea-bath, and that did him so much good that he writes me from the South that he's going on a walking-tour through Switzerland – if I'll join him. I might have joined him if he had not married the pretty nurse. I wonder whether— But, of course, this is no place for speculation.

In regard to the harbor-master, you may believe it or not, as you choose. But if you hear of any great auks being found, kindly throw a tablecloth over their heads and notify the authorities at the Zoological Gardens in Bronx Park, New York. The reward is ten thousand dollars.

THE DEATH OF YARGHOUZ KHAN

In our second extract from The Slayer of Souls, *Victor Cleves and his wife Tressa, the West's last hope against the Yezidee, are in Florida, on the run from the Yezidee assassins sent to kill Tressa. A sinister man in white is shadowing them, who has in his possession a stolen phial of Lewisite, the deadliest poison known to man . . .*

The night grew sweet with the scent of orange bloom, and all the perfumed darkness was vibrant with the feathery whirr of hawk-moths' wings.

Tressa had taken her moon-lute to the hammock, but her fingers rested motionless on the strings.

Cleves and Recklow, shoulder to shoulder, paced the moonlit path along the hedges of oleander and hibiscus which divided garden from jungle.

And they moved cautiously on the white-shell road, not too near the shadow line. For in the cypress swamp the bloated gray death was awake and watching under the moon; and in the scrub palmetto the diamond-dotted death moved lithely.

And somewhere within the dark evil of the jungle a man in white might be watching.

So Recklow's pistol swung lightly in his right hand and Cleves's weapon lay in his side-pocket, and they strolled leisurely around the drive and up and down the white-shell walks, passing Tressa at regular intervals, where she sat in her hammock with the moon-lute across her knees.

Once Cleves paused to place two pink hibiscus blossoms in her hair above her ears; and the girl smiled gravely at him in the light.

Again, pausing beside her hammock on one of their tours of the garden, Recklow said in a low voice: 'If the beast would only show himself, Mrs Cleves, we'd not miss him. Have you caught a glimpse of anything white in the woods?'

'Only the night mist rising from the branch and a white ibis stealing through it.'

Cleves came nearer: 'Do you think the Yezidee is in the woods watching us, Tressa?'

'Yes, he is there,' she said calmly.

'You *know* it?'

'Yes.'

Recklow stared at the woods. 'We can't go in to hunt for him,' he said. 'That fellow would get us with his Lewisite gas before we could discover and destroy him.'

'Suppose he waits for a west wind and squirts his gas in this direction?' whispered Cleves.

'There is no wind,' said Tressa tranquilly. 'He has been waiting for it, I think. The Yezidee is very patient. And he is a Shaman sorcerer.'

'My God!' breathed Recklow. 'What sort of hellish things has the Old World been dumping into America for the last fifty years? An ordinary anarchist is bad enough, but this new breed of devil – these Yezidees – this sect of Assassins—'

'Hush!' whispered Tressa.

All three listened to the great cat-owl howling from the jungle. But Tressa had heard another sound – the vague stir of leaves in the live-oaks. Was it a passing breeze? Was a night wind rising? She listened. But heard no brittle clatter from the palm-fronds.

'Victor,' she said.

'Yes, Tressa.'

'If a wind comes, we must hunt him. That will be necessary.'

'Either we hunt him and get him, or he kills us here with his gas,' said Recklow quietly.

'If the night wind comes,' said Tressa, 'we must hunt the darkness for the Yezidee.' She spoke coolly.

'If he'd only show himself,' muttered Recklow, staring into the darkness.

The girl picked up her lute, caught Cleves's worried eyes fixed on her, suddenly comprehended that his anxiety was on her account, and blushed brightly in the moonlight. And he saw her teeth catch at her underlip; saw her look up again at him, confused.

'If I dared leave you,' he said, 'I'd go into the hammock and start that reptile. This won't do – this standing pat while he comes to some deadly decision in the woods there.'

'What else is there to do?' growled Recklow.

'Watch,' said the girl. 'Out-watch the Yezidee. If there is no night-wind he may tire of waiting. Then you must shoot fast – very, very fast and straight. But if the night-wind comes, then we must hunt him in darkness.'

Recklow, pistol in hand, stood straight and sturdy in the moonlight, gazing fixedly at the forest. Cleves sat down at his wife's feet.

She touched her moon-lute tranquilly and sang in her childish voice:

'Ring, ring, Buddha bells,
Gilded gods are listening.
Swing, swing, lily bells,
In my garden glistening.
Now I hear the Shaman drum;
Now the scarlet horsemen come;
      Ding-dong!
      Ding-dong!
Through the chanting of the throng
Thunders now the temple gong.
      Boom-boom!
      Ding-dong!

'Let the gold gods listen!
In my garden; what care I
Where my lily bells hang mute!
   Snowy-sweet they glisten
Where I'm singing to my lute.
In my garden; what care I
Who is dead and who shall die?
Let the gold gods save or slay
Scented lilies bloom in May.
   Boom, boom, temple gong!
      Ding-dong!
      Ding-dong!'

'What are you singing?' whispered Cleves.

'"The Bells of Yian".'

'Is it old?'

'Of the thirteenth century. There were few Buddhist bells in Yian then. It is Lamaism that has destroyed the Mongols and that has permitted the creed of the Assassins to spread – the devil worship of Erlik.'

He looked at her, not understanding. And she, pale, slim prophetess, in the moonlight, gazed at him out of lost eyes – eyes which saw, perhaps, the bloody age of men when mankind took the devil by the throat and all Mount Alamout went up in smoking ruin; and the Eight Towers were dark as death and as silent before the blast of the silver clarions of Ghenghis Khan.

'Something is stirring in the forest,' whispered Tressa, her fingers on her lips.

'Damnation,' muttered Recklow, 'it's the wind!'

They listened. Far in the forest they heard the clatter of palm-fronds. They waited. The ominous warning grew faint, then rose again – a long, low rattle of palm-fronds which became a steady monotone.

'We hunt,' said Recklow bluntly. 'Come on!'

But the girl sprang from the hammock and caught her husband's arm and drew Recklow back from the hibiscus hedge.

'Use me,' she said. 'You could never find the Yezidee. Let me do the hunting; and then shoot very, very fast.'

'We've got to take her,' said Recklow. 'We dare not leave her.'

'I can't let her lead the way into those black woods,' muttered Cleves.

'The wind is blowing in my face,' insisted Recklow. 'We'd better hurry.'

Tressa laid one hand on her husband's arm.

'I can find the Yezidee, I think. You never could find him before he finds you! Victor, let me use my own *knowledge*! Let me find the way. Please let me lead! Please, Victor. Because, if you don't, I'm afraid we'll all die here in the garden where we stand.'

Cleves cast a haggard glance at Recklow, then looked at his wife.

'All right,' he said.

The girl opened the hedge gate. Both men followed with pistols lifted.

The moon silvered the forest. There was no mist, but a night-wind blew mournfully through palm and cypress, carrying with it the strange, disturbing pungency of the jungle – wild, unfamiliar perfumes – the acrid aroma of swamp and rotting mould.

'What about snakes?' muttered Recklow, knee deep in wild phlox.

But there was a deadlier snake to find and destroy, somewhere in the blotched shadows of the forest.

The first sentinel trees were very near, now; and Tressa was running across a ghostly tangle, where once had been an orange grove, and where aged and dying citrus stumps rose stark amid the riot of encroaching jungle.

'She's circling to get the wind at our backs,' breathed Recklow, running forward beside Cleves. 'That's our only chance to kill the dirty rat – catch him with the wind at our backs!'

Once, traversing a dry hammock where streaks of moonlight

alternated with velvet-black shadow a rattlesnake sprang his goblin alarm.

They could not locate the reptile. They shrank together and moved warily, chilled with fear.

Once, too, clear in the moonlight, the Grey Death reared up from bloated folds and stood swaying rhythmically in a horrible shadow dance before them. And Cleves threw one arm around his wife and crept past, giving death a wide berth there in the checkered moonlight.

Now, under foot, the dry hammock lay everywhere and the night wind blew on their backs.

Then Tressa turned and halted the two men with a gesture. And went to her husband where he stood in the palm forest, and laid her hands on his shoulders, looking him very wistfully in the eyes.

Under her searching gaze he seemed oddly to comprehend her appeal.

'You are going to use – to use your *knowledge*,' he said mechanically. 'You are going to find the man in white.'

'Yes.'

'You are going to find him in a way we don't understand,' he continued, dully.

'Yes . . . You will not hold me in – in horror – will you?'

Recklow came up, making no sound on the spongy palm litter underfoot.

'Can you find this devil?' he whispered.

'I – think so.'

'Does your super-instinct – finer sense – knowledge – whatever it is – give you any inkling as to his whereabouts, Mrs Cleves?'

'I think he is here in this hammock. Only—' she turned again, with swift impulse, to her husband, '—only if you – if *you* do not hold me in – in horror – because of what I do—'

There was a silence; then:

'What are you about to do?' he asked hoarsely.

'Slay this man.'

'We'll do that,' said Cleves with a shudder. 'Only show him to us and we'll shoot the dirty reptile to slivers—'

'Suppose we hit the jar of gas,' said Recklow.

After a silence, Tressa said:

'I have got to give him back to Satan. There is no other way. I understood that from the first. He can not die by your pistols, though you shoot very fast and straight. No!'

After another silence, Recklow said:

'You had better find him before the wind changes. We hunt down wind or – we die here together.'

She looked at her husband.

'Show him to us in your own way,' he said, 'and deal with him as he must be dealt with.'

A gleam passed across her pale face and she tried to smile at her husband.

Then, turning down the hammock to the east, she walked noiselessly forward over the fibrous litter, the men on either side of her, their pistols poised.

They had halted on the edge of an open glade, ringed with young pines in fullest plumage.

Tressa was standing very straight and still in a strange, supple, agonised attitude, her left forearm across her eyes, her right hand clenched, her slender body slightly twisted to the left.

The men gazed pallidly at her with tense, set faces, knowing that the girl was in terrible mental conflict against another mind – a powerful, sinister mind which was seeking to grasp her thoughts and control them.

Minute after minute sped: the girl never moved, locked in her psychic duel with this other brutal mind – beating back its terrible thought-waves which were attacking her, fighting for mental supremacy, struggling in silence with an unseen adversary whose mental dominance meant death.

Suddenly her cry rang out sharply in the moonlight, and then, all at once, a man in white stood there in the lustre of the moon – a young, graceful man dressed in white flannels and carrying on his right arm what seemed to be a long white cloak.

Instantly the girl was transformed from a living statue into a lithe, supple, lightly moving thing that passed swiftly to the west of the glade, keeping the young man in white facing the wind, which was blowing and tossing the plumy young pines.

'So it is *you*, young man, with whom I have been wrestling here under the moon of the only God!' she said in a strange little voice, all vibrant and metallic with menacing laughter.

'It is I, Keuke Mongol,' replied the young man in white, tranquilly; yet his words came as though he were tired and out of breath, and the hand he raised to touch his small black moustache trembled as if from physical exhaustion.

'Yarghouz!' she exclaimed. 'Why did I not know you there on the golf links, Assassin of the Seventh Tower? And why do you come here with your shroud over your arm and hidden under it, in your right hand, a flask full of death?'

He said, smiling:

'I come because you are to die, Heavenly-Azure Eyes. I bring you your shroud.' And he moved warily westward around the open circle of young pines.

Instantly the girl flung her right arm straight upward.

'Yarghouz!'

'I hear thee, Heavenly Azure.'

'Another step to the west and I shatter thy flask of gas.'

'With what?' he demanded; but stood discreetly motionless.

'With what I grasp in an empty palm. Thou knowest, Yarghouz.'

'I have heard,' he said with smiling uncertainty, 'but to hear of force that can be hurled out of an empty palm is one thing, and to see it and feel it is another. I think you lie, Heavenly Azure.'

'So thought Gutchlug. And died of a yellow snake.'

The young man seemed to reflect. Then he looked up at her in his frank, smiling way.

'Wilt thou listen, Heavenly Eyes?'

'I hear thee, Yarghouz.'

'Listen then, Keuke Mongol. Take life from us as we offer it. Life is sweet. Erlik, like a spider, waits in darkness for lost souls that flutter to his net.'

'You think my soul was lost there in the temple, Yarghouz?'

'Unutterably lost, little temple girl of Yian. Therefore, live. Take life as a gift!'

'Whose gift?'

'Sanang's.'

'It is written,' she said gravely, 'that we belong to God and we return to him. Now then, Yezidee, do your duty as I do mine! Kai!'

At the sound of the formula always uttered by the sect of Assassins when about to do murder, the young man started and shrank back. The west wind blew fresh in his startled eyes.

'Sorceress,' he said less firmly, 'you leave your Yiort to come all alone into this forest and seek me. Why then have you come, if not to submit! – if not to take the gift of life – if not to turn away from your seducers who are hunting me, and who have corrupted you?'

'Yarghouz, I come to slay you,' she said quietly.

Suddenly the man snarled at her, flung the shroud at her feet and crept deliberately to the left.

'Be careful!' she cried sharply; 'look what you're about! Stand still, son of a dog! May your mother bewail your death!'

Yarghouz edged toward the west, clasping in his right hand the flask of gas.

'Sorceress,' he laughed, 'a witch of Thibet prophesied with a drum that the three purities, the nine perfections, and the nine times nine felicities shall be lodged in him who slays the treacherous temple girl, Keuke Mongol! There is more magic in this bottle which I grasp than in thy mind and body. Heavenly Eyes! I pray God to be merciful to this soul I send to Erlik!'

All the time he was advancing, edging cautiously around the circle of little plumy pines; and already the wind struck his left cheek.

'Yarghouz Khan!' cried the girl in her clear voice. 'Take up your shroud and repeat the fatha!'

'Backward!' laughed the young man, '—as do you, Keuke Mongol!'

'Heretic!' she retorted. 'Do you also refuse to name the ten Imaums in your prayers? Dog! Toad! Spittle of Erlik! May all your cattle die and all your horses take the glanders and all your dogs the mange!'

'Silence, sorceress!' he shouted, pale with fear and fury. 'Witch! Mud worm! May Erlik seize you! May your skin be covered with putrefying sores! May all the demons torment you! May God remember you in hell!'

'Yarghouz! Stand still!'

'Is your word then the Rampart of Gog and Magog, you young witch of Yian, that a Khan of the Seventh Tower need fear you!' he sneered, stealing stealthily westward through the feathery pines.

'I give thee thy last chance, Yarghouz Khan,' she said in an excited voice that trembled. 'Recite thy prayer naming the ten, because with their holy names upon thy lips thou mayest escape damnation. For I am here to slay thee, Yarghouz! Take up thy shroud and pray!'

The young man felt the west wind at the back of his left ear. Then he began to laugh.

'Heavenly Eyes,' he said, 'thy end is come – together with the two police who hide in the pines yonder behind thee! Behold the bottle magic of Yarghouz Khan!'

And he lifted the glass flask in the moonlight as though he were about to smash it at her feet.

Then a terrible thing occurred. The entire flask glowed red hot in his grasp; and the man screamed and strove convulsively to fling the bottle; but it stuck to his hand, melted into the smoking flesh.

Then he screamed again – or tried to – but his entire

lower jaw came off and he stood there with the awful orifice gaping in the moonlight – stood, reeled a moment – and then – and *then* – his whole face slid off, leaving nothing but a bony mask out of which burst shriek after shriek—

Keuke Mongol had fainted dead away. Cleves took her into his arms.

Recklow, trembling and deathly white, went over to the thing that lay among the young pines and forced himself to bend over it.

The glass flask still stuck to one charred hand, but it was no longer hot. And Recklow rolled the unspeakable thing into the white shroud and pushed it into the swamp.

An evil ooze took it, slowly sucked it under and engulfed it. A few stinking bubbles broke.

Recklow went back to the little glade among the pines.

A young girl lay sobbing convulsively in her husband's arms, asking God's pardon and his for the justice she had done upon an enemy of all mankind.

THE SIGN OF VENUS

In the card-room the game, which had started from a chance suggestion, bid fair to develop into an all-night séance: the young foreign diplomat had shed his coat and lighted a fresh cigar; somebody threw a handkerchief over the face of the clock, and a sleepy club-servant took reserve orders for two dozen siphons and other details.

'That lets me out,' said Hetherford, rising from his chair with a nod at the dealer. He tossed his cards on the table, settled side obligations with the man on his left, yawned, and put on his hat.

Somebody remonstrated. 'It's only two o'clock, Hetherford; you have no white man's burden sitting up for you at home.'

But Hetherford shook his head, smiling.

So a servant removed his chair, another man cut in, the dealer dealt cards all around. Presently from somewhere in the smoke haze came a voice, 'Hearts.' And a quiet voice retorted, 'I double it.'

Hetherford lingered a moment, then turned on his heel, sauntered out across the hallway and down the stairs into the court, refusing with a sign the offered cab.

Breathing deeply, yawning once or twice, he looked up at the stars. The night air refreshed him; he stood a moment, thoughtfully contemplating his half-smoked cigar, then tossed it away and stepped out into the street.

The street was quiet and deserted; darkened brownstone mansions stared at him through sombre windows as he

passed; his footsteps echoed across the pavement like the
sound of footsteps following him.

His progress was leisurely; the dreary monotony of the
house fronts soothed him. He whistled a few bars of a
commonplace tune, crossed the deserted avenue under the
electric lamps, and entered the dimly lighted street beyond.

Here all was silence; the doors of many houses were
boarded up – sign that their tenants had migrated to the
country. No shadowy cat fled along the iron railings at his
approach; no night-watchman prowled in deserted dooryards
or peered at him from obscurity.

Strolling at ease, thoughts nowhere, he had traversed half
the block, when an opening door and a glimmer of light
across the sidewalk attracted his attention.

As he approached the house whence the light came, a
figure suddenly appeared on the stoop – a girl in a white
ball-gown – hastily descending the stone steps. Gaslight from
the doorway tinted her bared arms and shoulders. She bent
her graceful head and gazed earnestly at Hetherford.

'I beg your pardon,' she almost whispered, 'might I ask
you to please help me?'

Hetherford stopped and wheeled short.

'I – I really beg your pardon,' she said, 'but I am in such
distress. Could I ask you to find me a cab?'

'A cab!' he repeated, uncertainly; 'why, yes – I will with
pleasure—' he turned and looked up and down the deserted
street, slowly lifting his hand to his short mustache. 'If you
are in a hurry,' he said, 'I had better go to the nearest
stables—'

'But there is something more,' she said, in a tremulous
voice. 'Could you get me a wrap – a cloak – anything to
throw over my gown?'

He looked up at her, bewildered. 'Why, I don't believe
I—' he began, then fell silent before her troubled gaze. 'I'll
do anything I can for you,' he said, abruptly. 'I have a rain-
coat at the club – if your need is urgent—'

'It is urgent; but there is something else – something more

urgent – more difficult for me to ask you. I must go to Willow Brook – I must go now, tonight! And I – I have no money.'

'Do you mean Willow Brook in Westchester?' he asked, astonished. 'There is no train at this hour of the morning!'

'Then – then what am I to do?' she faltered. 'I cannot stay another moment in that house.'

After a silence he said, 'Are you afraid of anybody in that house?'

'There is nobody in the house,' she said, with a shudder; 'my mother is in Westchester; all the household are there. I – I came back – a few moments ago – unexpectedly—' She stammered, and winced under his keen scrutiny; then the pallor of utter despair came into her cheeks, and she hid her white face in her hands.

Hetherford watched her for a moment.

'I don't exactly understand,' he said, gently, 'but I'll do anything I can for you. I'll go to the club and get my rain-coat; I'll go to the stables and get a cab; I haven't any money with me, but it would take only a few minutes for me to drive to the club and get some . . . Please don't be distressed; I'll do anything you desire.'

She dropped her arms with a hopeless gesture.

'But you say there is no train!'

'You could drive to the house of some of your friends—'

'No, no! Oh, my friends must never know of this!'

'I see,' he said, gravely.

'No, you don't see,' she said, unsteadily. 'The truth is that I am almost frightened to death.'

'Can you not tell me what has frightened you so?'

'If I tried to tell you, you would think me mad – you would indeed—'

'Try,' he said, soothingly.

'Why – why, it startled me to find myself in this house,' she began. 'You see, I didn't expect to come here; I didn't really want to come here,' she added, piteously. 'Oh, it is simply dreadful to come – like this!' She glanced fearfully over her shoulder at the lighted doorway above, then turned to Hetherford as though dazed.

'Tell me,' he said, in a quiet voice.

'Yes – I'll tell you. At first it was all dark – but I must have known I was in my own room, for I felt around on the dresser for the matches and lighted a candle. And when I saw that it was truly my own room, and when I caught sight of my own face in the mirror, it terrified me—' She pressed her fingers to her cheeks with a shudder. 'Then I ran downstairs and lighted the gas in the hall and peered into the mirror; and I saw a face there – a face like my own—'

Pale, voiceless, she leaned on the bronze balustrade, fair head dropping, lids closed.

Presently, eyes still closed, she said. 'You will not leave me alone here – will you—' Her voice died to a whisper.

'No – of course not,' he replied, slowly.

There was an interval of silence; she passed her hand across her eyes and raised her head, looking up at the stars.

'You see,' she murmured, 'I dare not be alone; I *dare* not lose touch with the living. I suppose you think me mad, but I am not; I am only stunned. Please stay with me.'

'Of course,' he said, in a soothing voice. 'Everything will come out all right.'

'Are you sure?'

'Perfectly. I don't quite know what to say – how to reassure you and offer you any help—'

He fell silent, standing there on the sidewalk, worrying his short mustache. The situation was a new one to him.

'Suppose,' he suggested, 'that you try to take a little rest. I'll sit down on the steps—'

She looked at him in wide-eyed alarm. 'Do you mean that I should go into that house – alone!'

'Well – you oughtn't to stand on the steps all night. It is nearly three o'clock. You are frightened and nervous. Really you must go in and—'

'Then you must come too,' she said, desperately. 'This

nightmare is more than I can endure alone. I'm not a coward; none of my race are. But I need a living being near me. Will you come?'

He bowed. She turned, hastily gathering her filmy gown, and mounted the shadowy steps without a sound; and he followed, leisurely, even perhaps warily, every sense alert.

He was prepared to see the end of this encounter – see it through to an explanation if it took all summer. Of the situation, however, and of her, he had so far ventured no theory. The type of woman and the situation were perfectly new to him. He was aware that anything might happen in New York, and, closing the heavy front door, he was ready for it.

The hall gas-jets were burning brightly, and in the darkened drawing-room he could distinguish the heavy outlines of furniture cased in dust-coverings.

She asked him to strike a match and light the sconces in the drawing-room, and he did so, his curiosity now thoroughly aroused.

As the gas flared up, shrouded pictures and furniture sprang into view surrounding him, and in the dusk of the room beyond he saw a ray of light glimmering on the foliated carving of a gilded harp.

Slowly he turned to the girl beside him. A warm shadow dimmed her delicate features, yet they were the loveliest he had ever looked upon.

Suddenly he understood the mute message of her eyes: 'My imprudence places me at your mercy.'

'Your helplessness places me at yours,' he said, aloud, scarcely conscious that he had spoken.

At that a bright flush transfigured her. 'I trusted you the moment I saw you,' she said, impulsively. 'Do you mind sitting there opposite me? I shall take this chair – rather near you—'

She sank into an armchair; and, touched and a trifle amused, he seated himself, at a little nod from her, awaiting her further pleasure.

She lay there for a minute or two without speaking, rounded arms resting on the gilt arms of the chair, eyes thoughtfully studying him.

'I've simply got to tell you everything,' she said, at length.

'It can do no harm, I think,' he replied, pleasantly.

'No; no harm. The harm has been done. Yet, with you sitting there so near me, I am not frightened now. It is curious,' she mused, 'that I should feel no apprehension now. And yet – and yet—'

She leaned toward him, dropping her linked fingers in her lap.

'Tell me, did you ever hear of the Sign of Venus? – the *Signum Veneris*?' she asked.

'I've heard of it – yes,' he replied, surprised. And as she said nothing, he went on: 'The distinguished gentleman who occupies the chair of Applied Psychics at the university lectures on the Sign of Venus, I believe.'

'Did you attend the lectures?' she asked, calmly.

He said he had not, smiling a trifle.

'I did.'

'They were probably amusing,' he ventured.

'Not very. Psychic phenomena bored me; I went during Lent. Psychic phenomena—' She hesitated, embarrassed at his amusement. 'I suppose you laugh at that sort of thing.'

'No, I don't laugh at it. Queer things occur, they say. All I know is that I myself have never seen anything happen that could not be explained by natural laws.'

'I have,' she said.

He bent his head in polite acquiescence.

'I went to the lectures,' she said. 'I am not very intellectual; nothing he said interested me very much – which was, of course, suitable for a lenten amusement.'

She leaned a little nearer, small hands tightly interlaced on her knee.

'His lecture on the Sign of Venus was the last.' She lifted a white finger, drawing the imaginary *Signum Veneris* in the air. Hetherford nodded gravely.

'The lecture,' she continued, 'ended with an explanation of the Sign of Venus – how, contemplating it by starlight, one might pass into that physical unconsciousness which leaves the mind free to control the soul.'

She held out her left hand toward him. On a stretched finger a ring glistened, mounted with the Sign of Venus blazing in brilliants.

'I had this made specially,' she said; 'not that I had any particular desire to test it – no curiosity. It never occurred to me that here in New York one could – could—'

'What?' asked Hetherford, dryly.

'—could leave one's own body at will.'

'I don't believe it could be accomplished in New York,' he said, with great gravity. 'And that's a pretty safe conclusion to come to, is it not?'

She dropped her eyes, silent for a moment, resting her delicate chin on the palm of her hand. Then she lifted her eyes to him calmly, and the direct beauty of her gaze disturbed him.

'No, it is not a safe conclusion to come to. Listen to me. Last night they gave a dance at the Willow Brook Hunt. It was nearly two o'clock this morning when I left the club-house and started home across the lawn with my mother and the maid—'

'But how on earth could—' he began, then begged her pardon and waited.

She continued, serenely: 'The night was warm and lovely, and it was clear starlight. When I entered my room I sent the maid away and sat down by the open window. The scent of the flowers and the beauty of the night made me restless; I went downstairs, unbolted the door, and slipped out through the garden to the pergola. My hammock hung there, and I lay down in it, looking out at the stars.'

She drew the ring from her finger, holding it out for him to see.

'The starlight caught the gems on the Sign of Venus,' she said, under her breath; 'that was the beginning. And then

– I don't know why – as I lay there idly turning the ring on my finger, I found myself saying, "I must go to New York: I must leave my body here asleep in the hammock and go to my own room in Fifty-eighth Street."'

A curious little chill passed over Hetherford.

'I said it again and again – I don't know why. I remember the ring glittered; I remember it grew brighter and brighter. And then – and then! I found myself upstairs in the dark, groping over the dresser for the matches.'

Again that faint little chill touched Hetherford.

'I was stupefied for a moment,' she said, tremulously; 'then I suspected what I had done, and it frightened me. And when I lighted the candle, and saw it was truly my own room – and when I caught sight of my own face in the mirror – terror seized me – it was like a glimpse of something taken unawares. For, do you know that although in the glass I saw my own face, the face was not looking back at me.' She dropped her head, crushing the ring in both hands. 'The reflected face was far lovelier than mine; and it was mine, I think, yet it was not looking at me, and it moved when I did not move. I wonder – I wonder—'

The tension was too much. 'If that be so,' he said, steadying his voice, 'if you saw a face in your mirror, the face was your own.' He made an impatient gesture, rising to his feet at the same moment. 'All that you have told me can be explained,' he said.

'How can it? At this very moment I am asleep in my hammock.'

'We will deal with that later,' he said, smiling down at her. 'Where is there a looking-glass?'

'There is one in the hallway.' She rose, slipping the ring on her finger, and led the way to where an oval gilt mirror hung partly covered with dust-cloths.

He cast aside the coverings. 'Now look into the glass,' he said, gayly.

She raised her head and faced the mirror for an instant.

'Come here,' she whispered; and he stepped behind her, looking over her shoulder.

In the glass, as though reflected, he saw her face, but *the face was in profile*!

A shiver passed over him from head to foot.

'Did I not tell you?' she whispered. 'Look! See the other face is moving while I am still!'

'There's something wrong about the glass, of course,' he muttered, 'it's defective.'

'But who is that in the glass?'

'It is you – your profile. I don't exactly understand. Good Lord! It's turning away from us!'

She shrank against the wall, wide-eyed, breathing rapidly.

'There is no use in our being frightened,' he said, scarcely knowing what he uttered. 'This is Fifty-eighth Street, New York, 1903.' He shook his shoulders, squaring them, and forced a smile. 'Don't be frightened; there's an explanation for all this. You are not asleep in Westchester; you are here in your own house. You mustn't tremble so. Give me your hand a moment.'

She laid her hand in his obediently; it shook like a leaf. He held it firmly, touching the fluttering pulse.

'You are certainly no spirit,' he said, smiling; 'your hand is warm and yielding. Ghosts don't have hands like that, you know.'

Her fingers lay in his, quite passive now, but the pulse quickened.

'The explanation of it all is this,' he said: 'You have had a temporary suspension of consciousness, during which time you, without being aware of what you were doing, came to town from Willow Brook. You believe you went to the dance at the Hunt Club, but probably you did not. Instead, during a lapse of consciousness, you went to the station, took a train to town, came straight to your own house—' He hesitated.

'Yes,' she said, 'I have a key to the door. Here it is.' She drew it from the bosom of her gown; Heatherford took it triumphantly.

'You simply awoke to consciousness while you were groping for the matches. That is all there is to it; and you need not be frightened at all!' he announced.

'No, not frightened,' she said, shaking her head, 'only – only I wonder how I can get back. I've tried to fix my mind on my ring – on the Sign of Venus – I cannot seem to—'

'But that's nonsense!' he protested, cheerfully. 'That ring has nothing to do with the matter.'

'But it brought me here! Truly I am asleep in my hammock. Won't you believe it?'

'No; and you mustn't, either,' he said, impatiently. 'Why, just now I explained to you—'

'I know,' she said, looking down at the ring on her hand, 'but you are wrong – truly you are.'

'I am not wrong,' he said, laughing. 'It was only a dream – the dance, the return, the hammock – all these were parts of a dream so intensely real that you cannot shake it off at once.'

'Then – then *who* was that we saw in the mirror?'

'Let us try it again,' he said, confidently. She suffered him to lead her again to the mirror; again they peered into its glimmering depths, heads close together.

A second's breathless silence, then she caught his hand in both of hers with a low cry; for the strange profile was slowly turning toward them a face of amazing beauty – her own face transfigured, radiantly glorified.

'My soul!' she gasped, and would have fallen at his feet had he not held her and supported her to the stairs, where she sank down, hiding her face in her arms.

As for him, he was terribly shaken; he strove to speak, to reason with her, with himself, but a stupor chained body and mind, and he only leaned there on the newel-post, vaguely aware of his own helplessness.

Far away in the night the bells of a church began striking the hour – one, two, three, four. Presently the distant rattle of a wagon sounded. The city stirred in its slumbers.

He found himself bending beside her, her passive hands

in his once more, and he was saying: 'As a matter of fact, all this is quite capable of an explanation. Don't be distressed – please don't be frightened or sad. We've both had some sort of hallucination, that's all – really that is all.'

'I am not frightened now,' she said, dreamily. 'I am quite sure that – that I am not dead. I am only asleep in my hammock. When I awake—'

Again, in spite of himself, he shivered.

'Will you do one more thing for me?' she asked.

'Yes – a million.'

'Only one. It is unreasonable, it is perhaps silly – and I have no right to ask—'

'Ask it,' he begged.

'Then – then, will you go to Willow Brook? Now?'

'Now?' he repeated, blankly.

'Yes.' She looked down at him with the shadow of a smile touching lips and eyes. 'I am asleep in the hammock; I sleep very, very soundly – and very, very late into the morning. They may not find me there for a long while. So would you mind going to Willow Brook to awaken me?'

'I – I – but you do not expect me to leave you here and find you in Westchester!' he stammered.

'You need not go,' she said, quietly.

'No,' he said, 'I will go – I will go anywhere on earth for you.'

'Thank you,' she said, sweetly. 'When you awake me, give me this.' She held out the *Signum Veneris*; and he took it, and bending his head slowly, raised it to his lips.

It was almost morning when he entered his own house. In a dull trance he dressed, turned again to the stairs, and crept out into the shadowy street.

People began to pass him; an early electric tram whizzed up Forty-second Street as he entered the railway station. Presently he found himself in a car, clutching his ticket in one hand, her ring in the other.

'It is I who am mad, not she,' he muttered as the train glided from the station, through the long yard, dim in morning mist, where green and crimson lanterns still sparkled faintly.

Again he pressed the *Signum Veneris* to his lips. 'It is I who am mad – love-mad!' he whispered as the far treble warning of the whistle aroused him and sent him stumbling out into the soft fresh morning air.

The rising sun smote him full in the eyes as he came in sight of the clubhouse among the still green trees, and the dew on the lawn flashed like the gems of the *Signum Veneris* on the ring he held so tightly.

Across the clubhouse lawn stood another house, circled with gardens in full bloom; and to the left, among young trees, the white columns of a pergola glistened.

There was not a soul astir as he crossed the lawn and entered the garden.

Suddenly, at a turn in the path, he came upon the pergola, and saw a brilliant hammock hanging in the shadow.

Over the hammock's fringe something light and fluffy fell in folds like the billowy frills of a ball gown. He stumbled forward, dazed, incredulous.

Then, speechless, he sank down beside her, and dropped the ring into the palm of her half-closed and unconscious hand.

A ray of sunlight fell across her hair; slowly her blue eyes unclosed. And in her partly open palm the Sign of Venus glimmered like dew.

THE THIRD EYE

Although the man's back was turned towards me, I was uncomfortably conscious that he was watching me. How he could possibly be watching me while I stood directly behind him, I did not ask myself; yet, nevertheless, instinct warned me that I was being inspected; that somehow or other the man was staring at me as steadily as though he and I had been face to face and his faded, sea-green eyes were focused upon me.

It was an odd sensation which persisted in spite of logic, and of which I could not rid myself. Yet the little waitress did not seem to share it. Perhaps she was not under his glassy inspection. But then, of course, I could not be either.

No doubt the nervous tension incident to the expedition was making me supersensitive and even morbid.

Our sailboat rode the shallow turquoise-tinted waters at anchor, rocking gently just off the snowy coral reef on which we were now camping. The youthful waitress who, for economy's sake, wore her cap, apron, collar and cuffs over her dainty print dress, was seated by the signal fire writing in her diary. Sometimes she thoughtfully touched her pencil point with the tip of her tongue; sometimes she replenished the fire from a pile of dead mangrove branches heaped up on the coral reef beside her. Whatever she did she accomplished gracefully.

As for the man, Grue, his back remained turned towards

us both and he continued, apparently, to scan the horizon for the sail which we all expected. And all the time I could not rid myself of the unpleasant idea that somehow or other he was looking at me, watching attentively the expression of my features and noting my every movement.

The smoke of our fire blew across leagues of shallow, sparkling water, or, when the wind veered, whirled back into our faces across the reef, curling and eddying among the standing mangroves like fog drifting.

Seated there near the fire, from time to time I swept the horizon with my marine glasses; but there was no sign of Kemper; no sail broke the far sweep of sky and water; nothing moved out there save when a wild duck took wing amid the dark raft of its companions to circle low above the ocean and settle at random, invisible again except when, at intervals, its white breast flashed in the sunshine.

Meanwhile the waitress had ceased to write in her diary and now sat with the closed book on her knees and her pencil resting against her lips, gazing thoughtfully at the back of Grue's head.

It was a ratty head of straight black hair, and looked greasy. The rest of him struck me as equally unkempt and dingy – a youngish man, lean, deeply bitten by the sun of the semi-tropics to a mahogany hue, and unusually hairy.

I don't mind a brawny, hairy man, but the hair on Grue's arms and chest was a rusty red, and like a chimpanzee's in texture, and sometimes a wildly absurd idea possessed me that the man needed it when he went about in the palm forests without his clothes.

But he was only a 'poor white' – a 'cracker' recruited from one of the reefs near Pelican Light, where he lived alone by fishing and selling his fish to the hotels at Heliatrope City. The sailboat was his; he figured as our official guide on this expedition – an expedition which already had begun to worry me a great deal.

For it was, perhaps, the wildest goose chase and the most

absurdly hopeless enterprise ever undertaken in the interest of science by the Bronx Park authorities.

Nothing is more dreaded by scientists than ridicule; and it was in spite of this terror of ridicule that I summoned sufficient courage to organise an exploring party and start in search of something so extraordinary, so hitherto unheard of, that I had not dared reveal to Kemper by letter the object of my quest.

No, I did not care to commit myself to writing just yet; I had merely sent Kemper a letter to join me on Stingray Key.

He telegraphed me from Tampa that he would join me at the rendezvous; and I started directly from Bronx Park for Heliatrope City; arrived there in three days; found the waitress all ready to start with me; enquired about a guide and discovered the man Grue in his hut off Pelican Light; made my bargain with him; and set sail for Stingray Key, the most excited and the most nervous young man who ever had dared disaster in the sacred cause of science.

Everything was now at stake, my honour, reputation, career, fortune. For, as chief of the Anthropological Field Survey Department of the great Bronx Park Zoological Society, I was perfectly aware that no scientific reputation can survive ridicule.

Nevertheless, the die had been cast, the Rubicon crossed in a sailboat containing one beachcombing cracker, one hotel waitress, a pile of camping kit and special utensils, and myself!

How was I going to tell Kemper? How was I going to confess to him that I was staking my reputation as an anthropologist upon a letter or two and a personal interview with a young girl – a waitress at the Hotel Gardenia in Heliatrope City?

I lowered my sea-glasses and glanced sideways at the waitress. She was still chewing the end of her pencil, reflectively.

She was a pretty girl, one Evelyn Grey, and had been a country schoolteacher in Massachusetts until her health broke.

Florida was what she required; but that healing climate was possible to her only if she could find there a self-supporting position.

Also she had nourished an ambition for a post-graduate education, with further aspirations to a government appointment in the Smithsonian Institute.

All very worthy, no doubt – in fact, particularly commendable because the wages she saved as waitress in a Florida hotel during the winter were her only means of support while studying for college examinations during the summer in Boston, where she lived.

Yet, although she was an inmate of Massachusetts, her face and figure would have ornamented any light-opera stage. I never looked at her but I thought so; and her cuffs and apron merely accentuated the delusion. Such ankles are seldom seen when the curtain rises after the overture. Odd that frivolous thoughts could flit through an intellect dedicated only to science!

The man, Grue, had not stirred from his survey of the Atlantic Ocean. He had a somewhat disturbing capacity for remaining motionless – like a stealthy and predatory bird which depends on immobility for aggressive and defensive existence.

The sea-wind fluttered his cotton shirt and trousers and the tattered brim of his straw hat. And always I felt as though he were watching me out of the back of his ratty head, through the raveled straw brim that sagged over his neck.

The pretty waitress had now chewed the end of her pencil to a satisfactory pulp, and she was writing again in her diary, very intently, so that my cautious touch on her arm seemed to startle her.

Meeting her inquiring eyes I said in a low voice:

'I am not sure why, but I don't seem to care very much for that man, Grue. Do you?'

She glanced at the water's edge, where Grue stood, immovable, his back still turned to us.

'I never liked him,' she said under her breath.

'Why?' I asked cautiously.

She merely shrugged her shoulders. She did it gracefully. I said:

'Have you any particular reason for disliking him?'

'He's dirty.'

'He *looks* dirty, yet every day he goes into the sea and swims about. He ought to be clean enough.'

She thought for a moment, then:

'He seems, somehow, to be fundamentally unclean – I don't mean that he doesn't wash himself. But there are certain sorts of animals and birds and other creatures from which one instinctively shrinks – not, perhaps, because they are materially unclean—'

'I understand,' I said. After a silence I added: 'Well, there's no chance now of sending him back, even if I were inclined to do so. He appears to be familiar with these latitudes. I don't suppose we could find a better man for our purpose. Do you?'

'No. He was a sponge fisher once, I believe.'

'Did he tell you so?'

'No. But yesterday, when you took the boat and cruised to the south, I sat writing here and keeping up the fire. And I saw Grue climbing about among the mangroves over the water in a most uncanny way; and two snake-birds sat watching him, and they never moved.

'He didn't seem to see them; his back was towards them. And than, all at once, he leaped backward at them where they sat on a mangrove, and he got one of them by the neck—'

'What!'

The girl nodded.

'By the neck,' she repeated, 'and down they went into the water. And what do you suppose happened?'

'I can't imagine,' said I with a grimace.

'Well, Grue went under, still clutching the squirming, flapping bird; and he *stayed* under.'

'Stayed under the *water?*'

'Yes, longer than any sponge diver I ever heard of. And I was becoming frightened when the bloody bubbles and feathers began to come up—'

'*What* was he doing under water?'

'He must have been tearing the bird to pieces. Oh, it was quite unpleasant, I assure you, Mr Smith. And when he came up and looked at me out of those very vitreous eyes he resembled something horridly amphibious . . . And I felt rather sick and dizzy.'

'He's got to stop that sort of thing!' I said angrily. 'Snakebirds are harmless and I won't have him killing them in that barbarous fashion. I've warned him already to let birds alone. I don't know how he catches them or why he kills them. But he seems to have a mania for doing it—'

I was interrupted by Grue's soft and rather pleasant voice from the water's edge, announcing a sail on the horizon. He did not turn when speaking.

The next moment I made out the sail and focussed my glasses on it.

'It's Professor Kemper,' I announced presently.

'I'm so glad,' remarked Evelyn Grey.

I don't know why it should have suddenly occurred to me, apropos of nothing, that Billy Kemper was unusually handsome. Or why I should have turned and looked at the pretty waitress – except that she was, perhaps, worth gazing upon from a purely non-scientific point of view. In fact, to a man not entirely absorbed in scientific research and not passionately and irrevocably wedded to his profession, her violet-blue eyes and rather sweet mouth might have proved disturbing.

As I was thinking about this she looked up at me and smiled.

'It's a good thing,' I thought to myself, 'that I am irrevocably wedded to my profession.' And I gazed fixedly across the Atlantic Ocean.

There was scarcely sufficient breeze of a steady character to bring Kemper to Stingray Key; but he got out his sweeps when I hailed him and came in at a lively clip, anchoring alongside of our boat and leaping ashore with that unnecessary dash and abandon which women find pleasing.

Glancing sideways at my waitress through my spectacles, I found her looking into a small hand mirror and patting her hair with one slim and sun-tanned hand.

When Professor Kemper landed on the coral he shot a curious look at Grue, and then came striding across the reef to me.

'Hello, Smithy!' he said, holding out his hand. 'Here I am, you see! Now what's up—'

Just then Evelyn Grey got up from her seat beside the fire; and Kemper turned and gazed at her with every symptom of unfeigned approbation.

I introduced him. Evelyn Grey seemed a trifle indifferent. A good-looking man doesn't last long with a clever woman. I smiled to myself, polishing my spectacles gleefully. Yet, I had no idea why I was smiling.

We three people turned and walked towards the comb of the reef. A solitary palm represented the island's vegetation, except, of course, for the water-growing mangroves.

I asked Miss Grey to precede us and wait for us under the palm; and she went forward in that light-footed way of hers which, to any non-scientific man, might have been a trifle disturbing. It had no effect upon me. Besides, I was looking at Grue, who had gone to the fire and was evidently preparing to fry our evening meal of fish and rice. I didn't like to have him cook, but I wasn't going to do it myself; and my pretty waitress didn't know how to cook anything more complicated than beans. We had no beans.

Kemper said to me:

'Why on earth did you bring a waitress?'

'Not to wait on table,' I replied, amused. 'I'll explain her later. Meanwhile, I merely want to say that you need not remain with this expedition if you don't want to. It's optional with you.'

'That's a funny thing to say!'

'No, not funny; sad. The truth is that if I fail I'll be driven into obscurity by the ridicule of my brother scientists the world over. I had to tell them at the Bronx what I was going after. Every man connected with the society attempted to dissuade me, saying that the whole thing was absurd and that my reputation would suffer if I engaged in such a ridiculous quest. So when you hear what the girl and I are after out here in the semi-tropics, and when you are in possession of the only evidence I have to justify my credulity, if you want to go home, go. Because I don't wish to risk *your* reputation as a scientist unless you choose to risk it yourself.'

He regarded me curiously, then his eyes strayed towards the palm-tree which Evelyn Grey was now approaching.

'All right,' he said briefly, 'let's hear what's up.'

So we moved forward to rejoin the girl, who had already seated herself under the tree.

She looked very attractive in her neat cuffs, tiny cap, and pink print gown, as we approached her.

'Why does she dress that way?' asked Kemper, uneasily.

'Economy. She desires to use up the habiliments of a service which there will be no necessity for her to re-enter if this expedition proves successful.'

'Oh. But Smithy—'

'What?'

'Was it – moral – to bring a waitress?'

'Perfectly,' I replied sharply. 'Science knows no sex!'

'I don't understand how a waitress can be scientific,' he muttered, 'and there seems to be no question about her possessing plenty of sex—'

'If that girl's conclusions are warranted,' I interrupted coldly, 'she is a most intelligent and clever person. *I* think they are warranted. If you don't, you may go home as soon as you like.'

I glanced at him; he was smiling at her with that strained politeness which alters the natural expression of men in the imminence of a conversation with a new and pretty woman.

I often wonder what particular combination of facial

muscles are brought into play when that politely receptive expression transforms the normal and masculine features into a fixed simper.

When Kemper and I had seated ourselves, I calmly cut short the small talk in which he was already indulging, and to which, I am sorry to say, my pretty waitress was beginning to respond. I had scarcely thought it of her – but that's neither here nor there – and I invited her to reca- pitulate the circumstances which had resulted in our present foregathering here on this strip of coral in the Atlantic Ocean.

She did so very modestly and without embarrassment, stating the case and reviewing the evidence so clearly and so simply that I could see how every word she uttered was not only amazing but also convincing Kemper.

When she had ended he asked a few questions very seri- ously:

'Granted,' he said, 'that the pituitary gland represents what we assume it represents, how much faith is to be placed in the testimony of a Seminole Indian?'

'A Seminole Indian,' she replied, 'has seldom or never been known to lie. And where a whole tribe testify alike the truth of what they assert can not be questioned.'

'How did you make them talk? They are a sullen, suspi- cious people, haughty, uncommunicative, seldom even replying to an ordinary question for a white man.'

'They consider me one of them.'

'Why?' he asked in surprise.

'I'll tell you why. It came about through a mere accident. I was waitress at the hotel; it happened to be my afternoon off; so I went down to the coquina dock to study. I study in my leisure moments, because I wish to fit myself for a college examination.'

Her charming face became serious; she picked up the hem of her apron and continued to pleat it slowly and with precision as she talked:

'There was a Seminole named Tiger-tail sitting there, his

feet dangling above his moored canoe, evidently waiting for
the tide to turn before he went out to spear crayfish. I merely
noticed he was sitting there in the sunshine, that's all. And
then I opened my mythology book and turned to the story
of Argus, on which I was reading up.

'And this is what happened: there was a picture of the
death of Argus, facing the printed page which I was reading
– the well-known picture where Juno is holding the head
of the decapitated monster – and I had read scarcely a dozen
words in the book before the Seminole beside me leaned
over and placed his forefinger squarely upon the head of
Argus.

'"Who?" he demanded.

'I looked around good-humouredly and was surprised at
the evident excitement of the Indian. They're not excitable,
you know.

'"That," said I, "is a Greek gentleman named Argus." I
suppose he thought I meant a Minorcan, for he nodded.
Then, without further comment, he placed his finger on
Juno.

'"*Who*?" he inquired emphatically.

'I said flippantly: "Oh, that's only my aunt, Juno."

'"Aunty of you?"

'"Yes."

'"She kill 'um Three-eye?"

'Argus had been depicted with three eyes.

'"Yes," I said, "my Aunt Juno had Argus killed."

'"Why kill 'um?"

'"Well, Aunty needed his eyes to set in the tails of the
peacocks which drew her automobile. So when they cut off
the head of Argus my aunt had the eyes taken out; and
that's a picture of how she set them into the peacock."

'"Aunty of *you*?" he repeated.

'"Certainly," I said gravely; "I am a direct descendant of
the Goddess of Wisdom. That's why I'm always studying
when you see me down on the dock here."

'"*You Seminole*!" he said emphatically.

'"Seminole," I repeated, puzzled.

'"You Seminole! Aunty Seminole – *you* Seminole!"

'"Why, Tiger-tail?"

'"Seminole hunt Three-eye long time – hundred, hundred year – hunt 'um Three-eye, kill 'um Three-eye."

'"You say that for hundreds of years the Seminoles have hunted a creature with three eyes?"

'"Sure! Hunt 'um now!"

'"*Now*?"

'"Sure!"

'"But, Tiger-tail, if the legends of your people tell you that the Seminoles hunted a creature with three eyes hundreds of years ago, certainly no such three-eyed creatures remain today?"

'"Some."

'"What! Where?"

'"Black Bayou."

'"Do you mean to tell me that a living creature with three eyes still inhabits the forests of Black Bayou?"

'"Sure. Me see 'um. Me kill 'um three-eye man."

'"You have killed a man who had *three eyes*?"

'"Sure."

'"A man? *With three eyes*?"

'"Sure."'

The pretty waitress, excitedly engrossed in her story, was unconsciously acting out the thrilling scene of her dialogue with the Indian, even imitating his voice and gestures. And Kemper and I listened and watched her breathlessly, fascinated by her lithe and supple grace as well as by the astounding story she was so frankly unfolding with the consummate artlessness of a natural actress.

She turned her flushed face to us:

'I made up my mind,' she said, 'that Tiger-tail's story was worth investigating. It was perfectly easy for me to secure corroboration, because the Seminole went back to his Everglade camp and told every one of his people that I was a white Seminole because my ancestors also hunted the three-eyed man and nobody except a Seminole could know that such a thing as a three-eyed man existed.

'So, the next afternoon off, I embarked in Tiger-tail's canoe and he took me to his camp. And there I talked to his people, men and women, questioning, listening, putting this and that together, trying to discover some foundation for their persistent statements concerning men, still living in the jungles of Black Bayou, who had three eyes instead of two.

'All told the same story; all asserted that since the time their records ran the Seminoles had hunted and slain every three-eyed man they could catch; and that as long as the Seminoles had lived in the Everglades the three-eyed men had lived in the forests beyond Black Bayou.'

She paused, dramatically, cooling her cheeks in her palms and looking from Kemper to me with eyes made starry by excitement.

'And *what* do you think!' she continued, under her breath. 'To prove what they said they brought for my inspection a skull. And then two more skulls like the first one.

'Every skull had been painted with Spanish red; the coarse black hair still stuck to the scalps. And, behind, just over where the pituitary gland is situated, was a hollow, bony orbit – unmistakably the socket of a *third eye*!'

'W-where are those skulls?' demanded Kemper, in a voice not entirely under control.

'They wouldn't part with one of them. I tried every possible persuasion. On my own responsibility, and even before I communicated with Mr Smith' – turning towards me – 'I offered them twenty thousand dollars for a single skull, staking my word of honor that the Bronx Museum would pay that sum.

'It was useless. Not only do the Seminoles refuse to part with one of those skulls, but I have also learned that I am the first person with a white skin who has ever even heard of their existence – so profoundly have these red men of the Everglades guarded their secret through the centuries.'

After a silence Kemper, rather pale, remarked:

'This is a most astonishing business, Miss Grey.'

'What do you think about it?' I demanded. 'Is it not worth while for us to explore Black Bayou?'

He nodded in a dazed sort of way, but his gaze remained riveted on the girl. Presently he said:

'Why does Miss Grey go?'

She turned in surprise:

'Why am I going? But it is *my* discovery – *my* contribution to science, isn't it?'

'Certainly!' we exclaimed warmly and in unison. And Kemper added: 'I was only thinking of the dangers and hardships. Mr Smith and I could do the actual work—'

'Oh!' she cried in quick protest, 'I wouldn't miss one moment of the excitement, one pain, one pang! I *love* it! It would simply break my heart not to share every chance, hazard, danger of this expedition – every atom of hope, excitement, despair, uncertainty – and the ultimate success – the unsurpassable thrill of exultation in the final instant of triumph!'

She sprang to her feet in a flash of uncontrollable enthusiasm, and stood there, aglow with courage and resolution, making a highly agreeable picture in her apron and cuffs, the sea wind fluttering the bright tendrils of her hair under her dainty cap.

We got to our feet much impressed; and now absolutely convinced that there did exist, somewhere, descendants of prehistoric men in whom the third eye – placed in the back of the head for purposes of defensive observation – had not become obsolete and reduced to the traces which we know only as the pituitary body or pituitary gland.

Kemper and I were, of course, aware that in the insect world the ocelli served the same purpose that the degenerate pituitary body once served in the occiput of man.

As we three walked slowly back to the campfire, where our evening meal was now ready, Evelyn Grey, who walked between us, told us what she knew about the hunting of these three-eyed men by the Seminoles – how intense was the hatred of the Indians for these people, how murderously they behaved towards any one of them whom they could track down and catch.

'Tiger-tail told me,' she went on, 'that in all probability the strange race was nearing extinction, but that all had not yet been exterminated because now and then, when hunting along Black Bayou, traces of living three-eyed men were still found by him and his people.

'No later than last week Tiger-tail himself had startled one of these strange denizens of Black Bayou from a meal of fish; and had heard him leap through the bushes and plunge into the water. It appears that centuries of persecution have made these three-eyed men partly amphibious – that is, capable of filling their lungs with air and remaining under water almost as long as a turtle.'

'That's impossible!' said Kemper bluntly.

'I thought so myself,' she said with a smile, 'until Tiger-tail told me a little more about them. He says that they can breathe through the pores of their skins; that their bodies are covered with a thick, silky hair, and that when they dive they carry down with them enough air to form a sort of skin over them, so that under water their bodies appear to be silver-plated.'

'Good Lord!' faltered Kemper. 'That is a little too much!'

'Yet,' said I, 'that is exactly what air-breathing water beetles do. The globules of air, clinging to the body-hairs, appear to silver-plate them; and they can remain below indefinitely, breathing through spiracles. Doubtless the skin pores of these men have taken on the character of spiracles.'

'You know,' he said in a curious, flat voice, which sounded like the tones of a partly stupefied man, 'this whole business is so grotesque – apparently so wildly absurd – that it's having a sort of nightmare effect on me.' And, dropping his voice to a whisper close to my ear: 'Good heavens!' he said. 'Can you reconcile such a creature as we are starting to hunt, with anything living known to science?'

'No,' I replied in guarded tones. 'And there are moments, Kemper, since I have come into possession of Miss Grey's story, when I find myself seriously doubting my own sanity.'

'I'm doubting mine, now,' he whispered, 'only that girl is so fresh and wholesome and human and sane—'

'She is a very clever girl,' I said.

'And really beautiful!'

'She is intelligent,' I remarked. There was a chill in my tone which doubtless discouraged Kemper, for he ventured nothing further concerning her superficially personal attractions.

After all, if any questions of priority were to arise, the pretty waitress was *my* discovery. And in the scientific world it is an inflexible rule that he who first discovers any particular specimen of any species whatever is first entitled to describe and comment upon that specimen without interference or unsolicited advice from anybody.

Maybe there was in my eye something that expressed as much. For when Kemper caught my cold gaze fixed upon him he winced and looked away like a reproved setter dog who knew better. Which also, for the moment, put an end to the rather gay and frivolous line of small talk which he had again begun with the pretty waitress.

I was exceedingly surprised at Professor William Henry Kemper, D.F.

As we approached the campfire the loathsome odour of frying mullet saluted my nostrils.

Kemper, glancing at Grue, said aside to me:

'That's an odd-looking fellow. What is he? Minorcan?'

'Oh, just a beachcomber. I don't know what he is. He strikes me as dirty – though he can't be so, physically. I don't like him and I don't know why. And I wish we'd engaged somebody else to guide us.'

Towards dawn something awoke me and I sat up in my blanket under the moon. But my leg had not been pulled.

Kemper snored at my side. In her little dog-tent the pretty

waitress probably was fast asleep. I knew it because the string she had tied to one of her ornamental ankles still lay across the ground convenient to my hand. In any emergency I had only to pull it to awake her.

A similar string, tied to my ankle, ran parallel to hers and disappeared under the flap of her tent. This was for her to pull if she liked. She had never yet pulled it. Nor I the other. Nevertheless I truly felt that these humble strings were, in a subtler sense, ties that bound us together. No wonder Kemper's behavior had slightly irritated me.

I looked up at the silver moon; I glanced at Kemper's unlovely bulk, swathed in a blanket; I contemplated the dog-tent with, perhaps, that slight trace of sentiment which a semi-tropical moon is likely to inspire even in a jellyfish. And suddenly I remembered Grue and looked for him.

He was accustomed to sleep in his boat, but I did not see him in either of the boats. Here and there were a few lumpy shadows in the moonlight, but none of them was Grue lying prone on the ground. Where the devil had he gone?

Cautiously I untied my ankle string, rose in my pyjamas, stepped into my slippers, and walked out through the moon-light.

There was nothing to hide Grue, no rocks or vegetation except the solitary palm on the back-bone of the reef.

I walked as far as the tree and looked up into the arching fronds. Nobody was up there. I could see the moonlit sky through the fronds. Nor was Grue lying asleep anywhere on the other side of the coral ridge.

And suddenly I became aware of all my latent distrust and dislike for the man. And the vigour of my sentiments surprised me because I really had not understood how deep and thorough my dislike had been.

Also, his utter disappearance struck me as uncanny. Both boats were there; and there were many leagues of sea to the nearest coast.

Troubled and puzzled I turned and walked back to the

dead embers of the fire. Kemper had merely changed the timbre of his snore to a whistling aria, which at any other time would have enraged me. Now, somehow, it almost comforted me.

Seated on the shore I looked out to sea, racking my brains for an explanation of Grue's disappearance. And while I sat there racking them, far out on the water a little flock of ducks suddenly scattered and rose with frightened quackings and furiously beating wings.

For a moment I thought I saw a round, dark object on the waves where the flock had been.

And while I sat there watching, up out of the sea along the reef to my right crawled a naked, dripping figure holding a dead duck in his mouth.

Fascinated, I watched it, recognising Grue with his ratty black hair all plastered over his face.

Whether he caught sight of me or not, I don't know; but he suddenly dropped the dead duck from his mouth, turned, and dived under water.

It was a grim and horrid species of sport or pastime, this amphibious business of his, catching wild birds and dragging them about as though he were an animal.

Evidently he was ashamed of himself, for he had dropped the duck. I watched it floating by on the waves, its head under water. Suddenly something jerked it under, a fish perhaps, for it did not come up and float again, as far as I could see.

When I went back to camp Grue lay apparently asleep on the north side of the fire. I glanced at him in disgust and crawled into my tent.

The next day Evelyn Grey awoke with a headache and kept to her tent. I had all I could do to prevent Kemper from prescribing for her. I did that myself, sitting beside her and testing her pulse for hours at a time, while Kemper took one of Grue's grains and went off into the mangroves and speared grunt and eels for a chowder which he said he knew how to concoct.

Towards afternoon the pretty waitress felt much better, and I warned Kemper and Grue that we should sail for Black Bayou after dinner.

Dinner was a mess, as usual, consisting of fried mullet and rice, and a sort of chowder in which the only ingredients I recognised were sections of crayfish.

After we had finished and had withdrawn from the fire, Grue scraped every remaining shred of food into a kettle and went for it. To see him feed made me sick, so I rejoined Miss Grey and Kemper, who had found a green coconut and were alternately deriving nourishment from the milk inside it.

Somehow or other there seemed to me a certain levity about that performance, and it made me uncomfortable; but I managed to smile a rather sickly smile when they offered me a draught, and I took a pull at the milk – I don't exactly know why, because I don't like it. But the moon was up over the sea, now, and the dusk was languorously balmy, and I didn't care to leave those two drinking milk out of the same coconut under a tropic moon.

Not that my interest in Evelyn Grey was other than scientific. But after all it was I who had discovered her.

We sailed as soon as Grue, gobbling and snuffling, had cleaned up the last crumb of food. Kemper blandly offered to take Miss Grey into his boat, saying that he feared my boat was overcrowded, what with the paraphernalia, the folding cages, Grue, Miss Grey and myself.

I sat on that suggestion, but offered to take my own tiller and lend him Grue. He couldn't wriggle out of it, seeing that his alleged motive had been the overcrowding of my boat, but he looked rather sick when Grue went aboard his boat.

As for me, I hoisted sail with something so near a chuckle that it surprised me; and I looked at Evelyn Grey to see whether she had noticed the unseemly symptom.

Apparently she had not. She sat forward, her eyes fixed

soulfully upon the moon. Had I been dedicated to any profession except a scientific one – but let that pass.

Grue in Kemper's sailboat led, and my boat followed out into the silvery and purple dusk, now all sparkling under the high lustre of the moon. Dimly I saw vast rafts of wild duck part and swim leisurely away to port and starboard, leaving a glittering lane of water for us to sail through; into the scintillant night from the sea sprang mullet, silvery, quivering, falling back into the wash with a splash.

Here and there in the moonlight steered ominous black triangles, circling us, leading us, sheering across bow and flashing wake, all phosphorescent with lambent sea-fire – the fins of great sharks.

'You need have no fear,' said I to the pretty waitress.

She said nothing.

'Of course if you *are* afraid,' I added, 'perhaps you might care to change your seat.'

There was room in the stern where I sat.

'Do you think there is any danger?' she asked.

'From sharks?'

'Yes.'

'Reaching up and biting you?'

'Yes.'

'Oh, I don't really suppose there is,' I said, managing to convey the idea, I am ashamed to say, that the catastrophe was a possibility.

She came over and seated herself beside me. I was very much ashamed of myself, but I could not repress a triumphant glance ahead at the other boat, where Kemper sat huddled forward, evidently bored to extinction.

Every now and then I could see him turn and crane his neck as though in an effort to distinguish what was going on in our boat.

There was nothing going on, absolutely nothing. The moon was magnificent; and I think the pretty waitress must have been a little tired, for her head dropped and nodded at moments, even while I was talking to her about a specimen of *Euplectilla speciosa* on which I had written a monograph. So she must have been really tired, for the subject was interesting.

'You won't incommode my operations with sheet and tiller,' I said to her kindly, 'if you care to rest your head against my shoulder.'

Evidently she was very tired, for she did so, and closed her eyes.

After a while, fearing that she might fall over backward into the sea – but let that pass . . . I don't know whether or not Kemper could distinguish anything aboard our boat. He craned his head enough to twist it off his neck.

To be so utterly, so blindly devoted to science is a great safeguard for a man. Single-mindedness, however, need not induce atrophy of every human impulse. I drew the pretty waitress closer – not that the night was cold, but it might become so. Changes in the tropics come swiftly. It is well to be prepared.

Her cheek felt very soft against my shoulder. There seemed to be a faint perfume about her hair. It really was odd how subtly fragrant she seemed to be – almost, perhaps, a matter of scientific interest.

Her hands did not seem to be chilled; they did seem unusually smooth and soft.

I said to her: 'When at home, I suppose your mother tucks you in; doesn't she?'

'Yes,' she nodded sleepily.

'And what does she do then?' said I, with something of that ponderous playfulness with which I make scientific jokes at a meeting of the Bronx Anthropological Association, when I preside.

'She kisses me and turns out the light,' said Evelyn Grey, innocently.

I don't know how much Kemper could distinguish. He kept dodging about and twisting his head until I really thought it would come off, unless it had been screwed on like the top of a piano stool.

A few minutes later he fired his pistol twice; and Evelyn sat up. I never knew why he fired; he never offered any explanation.

Towards midnight I could hear the roar of breakers on our starboard bow. Evelyn heard them, too, and sat up enquiringly.

'Grue has found the inlet to Black Bayou, I suppose,' said I.

And it proved to be the case, for, with the surf thundering on either hand, we sailed into a smoothly flowing inlet through which the flood tide was running between high dunes all sparkling in the moonlight and crowned with shadowy palms.

Occasionally I heard noises ahead of us from the other boat, as though Kemper was trying to converse with us, but as his apropos was as unintelligible as it was inopportune, I pretended not to hear him. Besides, I had all I could do to maneuver the tiller and prevent Evelyn Grey from falling off backward into the bayou. Besides, it is not customary to converse with the man at the helm.

After a while – during which I seemed to distinguish in Kemper's voice a quality that rhymes with his name – his tones varied through phases all the way from irony to exasperation. After a while he gave it up and took to singing.

There was a moon, and I suppose he thought he had a voice. It didn't strike me so. After several somewhat melancholy songs, he let off his pistol two or three times and then subsided into silence.

I didn't care; neither his songs nor his shots interrupted – but let that pass, also.

We were now sailing into the forest through pool after pool of interminable lagoons, startling into unseen and clattering flight hundreds of water-fowl. I could feel the wind from their whistling wings in the darkness, as they drove by us out to sea. It seemed to startle the pretty waitress. It is a solemn thing to be responsible for a pretty girl's peace of mind. I reassured her continually, perhaps a trifle nervously.

But there were no more pistol shots. Perhaps Kemper had used up his cartridges.

We were still drifting along under drooping sails, borne inland almost entirely by the tide, when the first pale, watery, gray light streaked the east. When it grew a little lighter, Evelyn sat up; all danger of sharks being over. Also, I could begin to see what was going on in the other boat. Which was nothing remarkable; Kemper slumped against the mast, his head turned in our direction; Grue sat at the helm, motionless, his tattered straw hat sagging on his neck.

When the sun rose, I called out cheerily to Kemper, asking him how he had passed the night. Evelyn also raised her head, pausing while bringing her disordered hair under discipline, to listen to his reply.

But he merely mumbled something. Perhaps he was still sleepy.

As for me, I felt exceedingly well; and when Grue turned his craft in shore, I did so, too; and when, under the overhanging foliage of the forest, the nose of my boat grated on the sand, I rose and crossed the deck with a step distinctly frolicsome.

Kemper seemed distant and glum; Evelyn Grey spoke to him shyly now and then, and I noticed she looked at him only when he was gazing elsewhere than her. She had a funny, conciliatory air with him, half ashamed, partly humorous and amused, as though something about Kemper's sulky ill-humor was continually making tiny in-roads on her gravity.

Some mullet had jumped into the two boats – half a dozen during our moonlight voyage – and these were now being fried with rice for us by Grue. Lord! How I hated to eat them!

After we had finished breakfast, Grue, as usual, did everything to the remainder except to get into the fry-pan with both feet; and as usual he sickened me.

When he'd cleaned up everything, I sent him off into the

forest to find a dry shell-mound for camping purposes; then I made fast both boats, and Kemper and I carried ashore our paraphernalia, spare *batterie-de-cuisine*, firearms, fishing tackle, spears, harpoons, grains, oars, sails, spars, folding cage – everything with which a strictly scientific expedition is usually burdened.

Evelyn was washing her face in the crystal waters of a branch that flowed into the lagoon from under the live-oaks. She looked very pretty doing it, like a naiad or dryad scrubbing away at her forest toilet.

It was, in fact, such a pretty spectacle that I was going over to sit beside her while she did it, but Kemper started just when I was going to, and I turned away. Some men invariably do the wrong thing. But a handsome man doesn't last long with a pretty girl.

I was thinking of this as I stood contemplating an alligator slide, when Grue came back saying that the shore on which we had landed was the termination of a shell-mound, and that it was the only dry place he had found.

So I bade him pitch our tents a few feet back from the shore; and stood watching him while he did so, one eye reverting occasionally to Evelyn Grey and Kemper. They both were seated cross-legged beside the branch, and they seemed to be talking a great deal and rather earnestly. I couldn't quite understand what they found to talk about so earnestly and volubly all of a sudden, inasmuch as they had heretofore exchanged very few observations during a most brief and formal acquaintance, dating only from sundown the day before.

Grue set up our three tents, carried the luggage inland, and then hung about for a while until the vast shadow of a vulture swept across the trees.

I never saw such an indescribable expression on a human face as I saw on Grue's as he looked up at the huge, unclean bird. His vitreous eyes fairly glittered; the corners of his mouth quivered and grew wet; and to my astonishment he seemed to emit a low, mewing noise.

'What the devil are you doing?' I said impulsively, in my amazement and disgust.

He looked at me, his eyes still glittering, the corners of his mouth still wet; but the curious sounds had ceased.

'What?' he asked.

'Nothing. I thought you spoke.' I didn't know what else to say.

He made no reply. Once, when I had partly turned my head, I was aware that he was warily turning his to look at the vulture, which had alighted heavily on the ground near the entrails and heads of the mullet, where he had cast them on the dead leaves.

I walked over to where Evelyn Grey and Kemper sat so busily conversing; and their volubility ceased as they glanced up and saw me approaching. Which phenomenon both perplexed and displeased me.

I said:

'This is Black Bayou forest, and we have the most serious business of our lives before us. Suppose you and I start out, Kemper, and see if there are any traces of what we are after in the neighborhood of our camp.'

'Do you think it safe to leave Miss Grey alone in camp?' he asked gravely.

I hadn't thought of that:

'No, of course not,' I said. 'Grue can stay.'

'I don't need anybody,' she said quickly. 'Anyway, I'm rather afraid of Grue.'

'Afraid of Grue?' I repeated.

'Not exactly afraid. But he's – unpleasant.'

'I'll remain with Miss Grey,' said Kemper politely.

'Oh,' she exclaimed, 'I couldn't ask that. It is true that I felt a little tired and nervous, but I can go with you and Mr Smith and Grue—'

I surveyed Kemper in cold perplexity. As chief of the expedition, I couldn't very well offer to remain with Evelyn Grey, but I didn't propose that Kemper should, either.

'Take Grue,' he suggested, 'and look about the woods for

a while. Perhaps after dinner Miss Grey may feel sufficiently
rested to join us.'

'I am sure,' she said, 'that a few hours' rest in camp will
set me on my feet. All I need is rest. I didn't sleep very
soundly last night.'

I felt myself growing red, and looked away from them
both.

'Oh,' said Kemper, in apparent surprise, 'I thought you
had slept soundly all night long.'

'Nobody,' said I, 'could have slept very pleasantly during
that musical performance of yours.'

'Were you singing?' she asked innocently of Kemper.

'He was singing when he wasn't firing off his pistol,' I
remarked. 'No wonder you couldn't sleep with any satisfaction to yourself.'

Grue had disappeared into the forest; I stood watching
for him to come out again. After a few minutes I heard a
furious but distant noise of flapping; the others also heard
it; and we listened in silence, wondering what it was.

'It's Grue killing something,' faltered Evelyn Grey, turning
a trifle pale.

'Confound it!' I exclaimed. 'I'm going to stop that right
now.'

Kemper rose and followed me as I started for the woods;
but as we passed the beached boats Grue appeared from
among the trees.

'Where have you been?' I demanded.

'In the woods.'

'Doing what?'

'Nothing.'

There was a bit of down here and there clinging to his
cotton shirt and trousers, and one had caught and stuck at
the corner of his mouth.

'See here, Grue,' I said, 'I don't want you to kill any birds
except for camp purposes. Why do you try to catch and kill
birds?'

'I don't.'

I stared at the man and he stared back at me out of his glassy eyes.

'You mean to say that you don't, somehow or other, manage to catch and kill birds?'

'No, I don't.'

There was nothing further for me to say unless I gave him the lie. I didn't care to do that, needing his services.

Evelyn Grey had come up to join us; there was a brief silence; we all stood looking at Grue; and he looked back at us out of his pale, washed-out, and unblinking eyes.

'Grue,' I said, 'I haven't yet explained to you the object of this expedition to Black Bayou. Now, I'll tell you what I want. But first let me ask you a question or two. You know the Black Bayou forests, don't you?'

'Yes.'

'Did you ever see anything unusual in these forests?'

'No.'

'Are you sure?'

The man stared at us, one after another. Then he said:

'What are you looking for in Black Bayou?'

'Something very curious, very strange, very unusual. So strange and unusual, in fact, that the great Zoological Society of the Bronx in New York has sent me down here at the head of this expedition to search the forests of Black Bayou.'

'For what?' he demanded, in a dull, accentless voice.

'For a totally new species of human being, Grue. I wish to catch one and take it back to New York in that folding cage.'

His green eyes had grown narrow as though sun-dazzled. Kemper had stepped behind us into the woods and was now busy setting up the folding cage. Grue remained motionless.

'I am going to offer you,' I said, 'the sum of one thousand dollars in gold if you can guide us to a spot where we may see this hitherto unknown species – a creature which is apparently a man but which has, in the back of his head, *a third eye—*'

I paused in amazement: Grue's cheeks had suddenly puffed

out and were quivering; and from the corners of his slitted mouth he was emitting a whimpering sound like the noise made by a low-circling pigeon.

'Grue!' I cried. 'What's the matter with you?'

'What is *he* doing?' screamed Grue, quivering from head to foot, but not turning around.

'Who?' I cried.

'The man behind me!'

'Professor Kemper? He's setting up the folding cage—'

With a screech that raised my hair, Grue whipped out his murderous knife and *hurled himself backwards* at Kemper, but the latter shrank aside behind the partly erected cage, and Grue whirled around, snarling, hacking and even biting at the wood frame and steel bars.

And then occurred a thing so horrid that it sickened me to the pit of my stomach; for the man's sagging straw hat had fallen off, and there, in the back of his head, through the coarse, black, ratty hair, I saw a glassy eye glaring at me.

'Kemper!' I shouted. 'He's got a third eye! He's one of them! Knock him flat with your rifle-stock!' And I seized a shotgun from the top of the baggage bundle on the ground beside me, and leaped at Grue, aiming a terrific blow at him.

But the glassy eye in the back of his head was watching me between the clotted strands of hair, and he dodged both Kemper and me, swinging his heavy knife in circles and glaring at us both out of the front and back of his head.

Kemper seized him by his arm, but Grue's shirt came off, and I saw his entire body was as furry as an ape's. And all the while he was snapping at us and leaping hither and thither to avoid our blows; and from the corners of his puffed cheeks he whined and whimpered and mewed through the saliva foam.

'Keep him from the water!' I panted, following him with clubbed shotgun; and as I advanced I almost stepped on a soiled heap of foulness – the dead buzzard which he had caught and worried to death with his teeth.

Suddenly he threw his knife at my head, hurling it

backward; dodged, screeched, and bounded by me towards the shore of the lagoon, where the pretty waitress was standing, petrified.

For one moment I thought he had her, but she picked up her skirts, ran for the nearest boat, and seized a harpoon; and in his fierce eagerness to catch her he leaped clear over the boat and fell with a splash into the lagoon.

As Kemper and I sprang aboard and looked over into the water, we could see him going down out of reach of a harpoon; and his body seemed to be silver-plated, flashing and glittering like a burnished eel, so completely did the skin of air envelop him, held there by the fur that covered him.

And, as he rested for a moment on the bottom, deep down through the clear waters of the lagoon where he lay prone, I could see, as the current stirred his long, black hair, the third eye looking up at us, glassy, unwinking, horrible.

A bubble or two, like globules of quicksilver, were detached from the burnished skin of air that clothed him, and came glittering upward.

Suddenly there was a flash; a flurrying cloud of blue mud; and Grue was gone.

After a long while I turned around in the muteness of my despair. And slowly froze.

For the pretty waitress, becomingly pale, was gathered in Kemper's arms, her cheek against his shoulder. Neither seemed to be aware of me.

'Darling,' he said, in the imbecile voice of a man in love, 'why do you tremble so when I am here to protect you? Don't you love and trust me?'

'Oo—h—yes,' she sighed, pressing her cheek closer to his shoulder.

I shoved my hands into my pockets, passed them without noticing them, and stepped ashore.

And there I sat down under a tree, with my back towards

them, all alone and face to face with the greatest grief of my life.

But which it was – the loss of her or the loss of Grue, I had not yet made up my mind.

THE SEAL OF SOLOMON

I

The news of Gatewood's fate filled Kerns with a pleasure bordering upon melancholy. It was his work; he had done it; it was good for Gatewood too – time for him to stop his irresponsible cruise through life, lower sail, heave to, set his signals, and turn over matters to this charming pilot.

And now they would come into port together and anchor somewhere east of Fifth Avenue – which, Kerns reflected, was far more proper a place for Gatewood than somewhere east of Suez, where young men so often sail.

And yet, and yet there was something melancholy in the pleasure he experienced. Gatewood was practically lost to him. He knew what might be expected from engaged men and newly married men. Gatewood's club life was ended – for a while; and there was no other man with whom he cared to embark for those brightly lighted harbours twinkling east of Suez across the metropolitan wastes.

'It's very generous of me to get him married,' he said frequently to himself, rather sadly. 'I did it pretty well, too. It only shows that women have no particular monopoly in the realms of diplomacy and finesse; in fact, if a man really chooses to put his mind to such matters, he can make it no trumps and win out behind a bum ace and a guarded knave.'

He was pleased with himself. He followed Gatewood about explaining how good he had been to him. An enthusiasm for marrying off his friends began to germinate within him; he tried it on Darrell, on Barnes, on Yates, but was turned down and severely stung.

Then one day Harren of the Philippine Scouts turned up at the club, and they held a determined reunion until daylight, and they told each other all about it all and what upper-cuts life had handed out to them since the troopship sailed.

And after the rosy glow had deepened to a more gorgeous hue in the room, and the electric lights had turned into silver pinwheels; and after they had told each other the story of their lives, and the last siphon fizzed impotently when urged beyond its capacity, Kerns arose and extended his hand, and Harren took it. And they executed a song resembling 'Auld Lang Syne'.

'Ole man,' said Kerns reproachfully, 'there's one thing you have been deuced careful *not* to mention, and that is about what happened to you three years ago—'

'Steady!' said Harren; 'there is nothing to tell, Tommy.'

'Nothing?'

'Nothing. I never saw her again. I never shall.'

Kerns looked long and unsteadily upon his friend; then very gravely fumbled in his pocket and drew forth the business card of Westrel Keen, Tracer of Lost Persons.

'That,' he said, 'will be about all.' And he bestowed the card upon Harren with magnificent condescension.

And about five o'clock the following afternoon Harren found the card among various effects of his, scattered over his dresser.

It took him several days to make up his mind to pay any attention to the card or the suggestion it contained. He scarcely considered it seriously even when, passing along Fifth Avenue one sunny afternoon, he chanced to glance up and see the sign

KEEN & CO.
TRACERS OF LOST PERSONS

staring him in the face.

He continued his stroll, but that evening, upon mere impulse, he sat down and wrote a letter to Mr Keen.

The next morning's mail brought a reply and an appointment for an interview on Wednesday week. Harren tossed the letter aside, satisfied to let the matter go, because his leave expired on Tuesday, and the appointment was impossible.

On Sunday, however, the melancholy of the deserted club affected his spirits. A curious desire to see this Tracer of Lost Persons seized him with a persistence unaccountable. He slept poorly, haunted with visions.

On Monday he went to see Mr Keen. It could do no harm; it was too late to do either harm or good, for his leave expired the next day at noon.

The business of Keen & Co., Tracers of Lost Persons, had grown to enormous proportions; appointments for a personal interview with Mr Keen were now made a week in advance, so when young Harren sent his card, the gayly liveried Negro servant came back presently, threading his way through the waiting throng with pomp and circumstance, and returned the card to Barren with the date of appointment rewritten in ink across the top. The day named was Wednesday. On Tuesday Harren's leave expired.

'That won't do,' said the young man brusquely; 'I must see Mr Keen today. I wrote last week for an appointment.'

The liveried Negro was polite but obdurate.

'Dis here am de 'pintment, suh,' he explained persuasively.

'But I want to see Mr Keen at once,' insisted Harren.

'Hit ain't no use, suh,' said the servant respectfully; 'dey's mi'ions an' mi'ions ob gemmen jess a-settin' roun' an' waitin' foh Mistuh Keen. In dis here perfeshion, suh, de fustest gemman dat has a 'pintment is de fustest gemman dat kin see Mistuh Keen. You is a military gemman yohse'f, Cap'm Harren, an' you is aware dat precedence am de rigger.'

The bronzed young man smiled, glanced at the date of appointment written on his card, which also bore his own name followed by the letters U.S.A., then his amused gray eyes darkened and he glanced leisurely around the room, where a dozen or more assorted people sat waiting their turns to interview Mr Keen: all sorts and conditions of people

– smartly gowned women, an anxious-browed businessman or two, a fat German truck driver, his greasy cap on his knees, a surly policeman, and an old Irishwoman, wearing a shawl and an ancient straw bonnet. Harren's eyes reverted to the Negro servant.

'You will explain to Mr Keen,' he said, 'that I am an army officer on leave, and that I am obliged to start for Manila tomorrow. This is my excuse for asking an immediate interview; and if it's not a good enough excuse I must cancel this appointment, that is all.'

The servant stood, irresolute, inclined to argue, but something in the steel-gray eyes of the man set him in involuntary motion, and he went away once more with the young man's message. Harren turned and walked back to his seat. The old woman with the faded shawl was explaining volubly to a handsomely gowned woman beside her that she was looking for her boy, Danny; that her name was Mrs Regan, and that she washed for the aristocracy of Hunter's Point at a liberal price per dozen, using no deleterious substances in the suds as Heaven was her witness.

The German truck driver, moved by this confidence, was stirred to begin an endless account of his domestic misfortunes, and old Mrs Regan, becoming impatient, had already begun to interrupt with an account of Regan's recent hoisting on the wings of a premature petard, when the dark servant reappeared.

'Mistuh Keen will receive you, suh,' he whispered, leading the way into a large room where dozens of attractive young girls sat very busily engaged at typewriting machines. Door after door they passed, all numbered on the ground-glass panes, then swung to the right, where the servant bowed him into a big, handsomely furnished room flooded with the morning sun. A tall, gray man, faultlessly dressed in a gray frock suit and wearing white spats, turned from the breezy, open window to inspect him; the lean, well groomed, rather lank type of gentleman suggesting a retired colonel of cavalry; unmistakably well bred from the ends of his drooping gray mustache to the last button on his immaculate spats.

'Captain Harren?' he said pleasantly.

'Mr Keen?'

They bowed. Young Harren drew from his pocket a card. It was the business card of Keen & Co., and, glancing up at Mr Keen, he read it aloud, carefully:

KEEN & CO.
TRACERS OF LOST PERSONS
Keen & Co. are prepared to locate the
whereabouts of anybody on earth.
No charges will be made unless
the person searched for
is found.
Blanks on Application.
WESTREL KEEN, Manager.

Harren raised his clear, gray eyes. 'I assume this statement to be correct, Mr Keen?'

'You may safely assume so,' said Mr Keen, smiling.

'Does this statement include *all* that you are prepared to undertake?'

The Tracer of Lost Persons inspected him coolly. 'What more is there, Captain Harren? I undertake to find lost people. I even undertake to find the undiscovered ideals of young people who have failed to meet them. What further field would you suggest?' Harren glanced at the card which he held in his gloved hand; then, very slowly, he re-read, 'the whereabouts of anybody *on earth*,' accenting the last two words deliberately as he encountered Keen's piercing gaze again.

'Well?' asked Mr Keen laughingly, 'is not that sufficient? Our clients could scarcely expect us to invade heaven in our search for the vanished.'

'There are other regions,' said Harren.

'*Ex*actly. Sit down, sir. There is a row of bookcases for your amusement. Please help yourself while I clear decks for action.'

Harren stood fingering the card, his gray eyes lost in retrospection; then he sauntered over to the bookcases, scanning the titles. The Searcher for Lost Persons studied him for a moment or two, turned, and began to pace the room. After a moment or two he touched a bell. A sweet-faced young girl entered; she was gowned in black and wore a white collar, and cuffs turned back over her hands.

'Take this memorandum,' he said. The girl picked up a pencil and pad, and Mr Keen, still pacing the room, dictated in a quiet voice as he walked to and fro:

'Mrs Regan's Danny is doing six months in Butte, Montana. Break it to her as mercifully as possible. He is a bad one. We make no charge. The truck driver, Becker, can find his wife at her mother's house, Leonia, New Jersey. Tell him to be less pig-headed or she'll go for good some day. Ten dollars. Mrs M., No. 36001, can find her missing butler in service at 79 Vine Street, Hartford, Connecticut. She may notify the police whenever she wishes. His portrait is No. 170529, Rogues' Gallery. Five hundred dollars. Miss K. (No. 3679) may send her letter, care of Cisneros & Co., Rio, where the person she is seeking has gone into the coffee business. If she decides that she really does love him, he'll come back fast enough. Two hundred and fifty dollars. Mr W. (No. 3620) must go to the morgue for further information. His repentance is too late; but he can see that there is a decent burial. The charge: one thousand dollars to the Florence Mission. You may add that we possess his full record.'

The Tracer paused and waited for the stenographer to finish. When she looked up: 'Who else is waiting?' he asked.

The girl read over the initials and numbers.

'Tell that policeman that Kid Conroy sails on the *Carania* tomorrow. Fifty dollars. There is nothing definite in the other cases. Report progress and send out a general alarm for the cashier inquired for by No. 3608. You will find details in vol. xxxix under B.'

'Is that all, Mr Keen?'

'Yes. I'm going to be very busy with' – turning slowly

toward Harren – 'with Captain Harren, of the Philippine Scouts, until tomorrow – a very complicated case, Miss Borrow, involving cipher codes and photography—'

II

Harren started, then walked slowly to the center of the room as the pretty stenographer passed out with a curious level glance at him.

'Why do you say that photography plays a part in my case?' he asked.

'Doesn't it?'

'Yes. But how—'

'Oh, I only guessed it,' said Keen with a smile. 'I made another guess that your case involved a cipher code. Does it?'

'Y-es,' said the young man, astonished, 'but I don't see—'

'It also involves the occult,' observed Keen calmly. 'We may need Miss Borrow to help us.'

Almost staggered, Harren stared at the Tracer out of his astonished gray eyes until that gentleman laughed outright and seated himself, motioning Harren to do likewise.

'Don't be surprised, Captain Harren,' he said. 'I suppose you have no conception of our business, no realization of its scope – its network of information bureaus all over the civilized world, its myriad sources of information, the immensity of its delicate machinery, the endless data and the infinitesimal details we have at our command. You, of course, have no idea of the number of people of every sort and condition who are in our employ, of the ceaseless yet inoffensive surveillance we maintain. For example, when your letter came last week I called up the person who has charge of the army list. There you were, Kenneth Harren, Captain Philippine Scouts, with the date of your graduation from West Point. Then I called up a certain department devoted to personal detail, and in five minutes I knew your entire history. I then touched another electric button, and in a minute I had before me the date of your arrival in New York, your present address, and' – he looked up quizzically at Harren – 'and several items of general information, such as your peculiar use of your camera, and the list of books on Psychical Phenomena and Cryptograms which you have been buying—'

Harren flushed up. 'Do you mean to say that I have been spied upon, Mr Keen?'

'No more than anybody else who comes to us as a client. There was nothing offensive in the surveillance.' He shrugged his shoulders and made a deprecating gesture. 'Ours is a business, my dear sir, like any other. We, of course, are obliged to know about people who call on us. Last week you wrote me, and I immediately set every wheel in motion; in other words, I had you under observation from the day I received your letter to this very moment.'

'You learned much concerning me?' asked Harren quietly.

'*Ex*actly, my dear sir.'

'But,' continued Harren with a touch of malice, 'you didn't learn that my leave is up tomorrow, did you?'

'Yes, I learned that, too.'

'Then why did you give me an appointment for the day after tomorrow?' demanded the young man bluntly.

The Tracer looked him squarely in the eye. 'Your leave is to be extended,' he said.

'What?'

'*Ex*actly. It has been extended one week.'

'How do you know that?'

'You applied for extension, did you not?'

'Yes,' said Harren, turning red, 'but I don't see how you knew that I—'

'By cable?'

'Y-yes.'

'There's a cablegram in your rooms at this very moment,' said the Tracer carelessly. 'You have the extension you desired. And now, Captain Harren,' with a singularly pleasant smile, 'what can I do to help you to a pursuit of that true happiness which is guaranteed for all good citizens under our Constitution?'

Captain Harren crossed his long legs, dropping one knee over the other, and deliberately surveyed his interrogator.

'I really have no right to come to you,' he said slowly. 'Your prospectus distinctly states that Keen & Co. undertake to find *live* people, and I don't know whether the person I am seeking is alive or – or—'

His steady voice faltered; the Tracer watched him curiously.

'Of course, that is important,' he said. 'If she *is* dead—'

'*She!*'

'Didn't you say "she," Captain?'

'No, I did not.'

'I beg your pardon, then, for anticipating you,' said the Tracer carelessly.

'Anticipating? *How* do you know it is not a man I am in search of?' demanded Harren.

'Captain Harren, you are unmarried and have no son; you have no father, no brother, no sister. Therefore I infer – several things – for example, that you are in love.'

'I? In love?'

'Desperately, Captain.'

'Your inferences seem to satisfy you, at least,' said Harren almost sullenly, 'but they don't satisfy me – clever as they appear to be.'

'*Ex*actly. Then you are *not* in love?'

'I don't know whether I am or not.'

'I do,' said the Tracer of Lost Persons.

'Then you know more than I,' retorted Harren sharply.

'But that is my business – to know more than you do,' returned Mr Keen patiently. 'Else why are you here to consult me?' And as Harren made no reply: 'I have seen thousands and thousands of people in love. I have reduced the superficial muscular phenomena and facial symptomatic aspect of such people to an exact science founded upon a schedule approximating the Bertillon system of records. And,' he added, smiling, 'out of the twenty-seven known vocal variations your voice betrays twenty-five unmistakable symptoms; and out of the sixteen reflex muscular symptoms your face has furnished six, your hands three, your limbs and feet six. Then there are other superficial symptoms—'

'Good heavens!' broke in Harren; 'how can you prove a man to be in love when he himself doesn't know whether he is or not? If a man isn't in love no Bertillon system can make him so; and if a man doesn't know whether or not he is in love, who can tell him the truth?'

'I can,' said the Tracer calmly.

'What! When I tell you I myself don't know?'

'*That*,' said the Tracer, smiling, 'is the final and convincing symptom. *You* don't know. *I* know because you *don't* know. That is the easiest way to be sure that you are in love, Captain Harren, because you always are when you are not sure. You'd know if you were *not* in love. Now, my dear sir, you may lay your case confidently before me.'

Harren, unconvinced, sat frowning and biting his lip and twisting his short, crisp mustache which the tropical sun had turned straw color and curly.

'I feel like a fool to tell you,' he said. 'I'm not an imaginative man, Mr Keen; I'm not fanciful, not sentimental. I'm perfectly healthy, perfectly normal – a very busy man in my profession, with no time and no inclination to fall in love.'

'Just the sort of man who does it,' commented Keen. 'Continue.'

Harren fidgeted about in his chair, looked out of the window, squinted at the ceiling, then straightened up, folding his arms with sudden determination.

'I'd rather be boloed than tell you,' he said. 'Perhaps, after all, I *am* a lunatic; perhaps I've had a touch of the Luzon sun and don't know it.'

'I'll be the judge,' said the Tracer, smiling.

'Very well, sir. Then I'll begin by telling you that I've seen a ghost.'

'There are such things,' observed Keen quietly.

'Oh, I don't mean one of those fabled sheeted creatures

that float about at night; I mean a phantom – a real phantom – in the sunlight – standing before my very eyes in broad day! . . . Now do you feel inclined to go on with my case, Mr Keen?'

'Certainly,' replied the Tracer gravely. 'Please continue, Captain Harren.'

'All right, then. Here's the beginning of it: three years ago, here in New York, drifting along Fifth Avenue with the crowd, I looked up to encounter the most wonderful pair of eyes that I ever beheld – that any living man ever beheld! The most – wonderfully – beautiful—'

He sat so long immersed in retrospection that the Tracer said: 'I am listening, Captain,' and the Captain woke up with a start.

'What was I saying? How far had I proceeded?'

'Only to the eyes.'

'Oh, I see! The eyes were dark, sir, dark and lovely beyond any power of description. The hair was also dark – very soft and thick and – er – wavy and dark. The face was extremely youthful, and ornamental to the uttermost verges of a beauty so exquisite that, were I to attempt to formulate for you its individual attractions, I should, I fear, transgress the strictly rigid bounds of that reticence which becomes a gentleman in complete possession of his sense.'

'*Ex*actly,' mused the Tracer.

'Also,' continued Captain Harren, with growing animation, 'to attempt to describe her figure would be utterly useless, because I am a practical man and not a poet, nor do I read poetry or indulge in futile novels or romances of any description. Therefore I can only add that it was a figure, a poise, absolutely faultless, youthful, beautiful, erect, wholesome, gracious, graceful, charmingly buoyant and – well, I cannot describe her figure, and I shall not try.'

'*Ex*actly; don't try.'

'No,' said Harren mournfully, 'it is useless'; and he relapsed into enchanted retrospection.

'Who was she?' asked Mr Keen softly.

'I don't know.'

'You never again saw her?'

'Mr Keen, I – I am not ill-bred, but I simply could not help following her. She was so b-b-beautiful that it hurt; and I only wanted to look at her; I didn't mind being hurt. So I walked on and on, and sometimes I'd pass her and sometimes I'd let her pass me, and when she wasn't looking I'd look – not offensively, but just because I *couldn't* help it. And all the time my senses were humming like a top and my heart kept jumping to get into my throat, and I hadn't a notion where I was going or what time it was or what day of the week. She didn't see me; she didn't dream that I was looking at her; she didn't know me from any of the thousand silk-hatted, frock-coated men who passed and repassed her on Fifth Avenue. And when she went into St Berold's Church, I went, too, and I stood where I could see her and where she couldn't see me. It was like a touch of the Luzon sun, Mr Keen. And then she came out and got into a Fifth Avenue stage, and I got it, too. And whenever she looked away I looked at her – without the slightest offence, Mr Keen, until, once, she caught my eye—'

He passed an unsteady hand over his forehead.

'For a moment we looked full at one another,' he continued. 'I got red, sir; I felt it, and I couldn't look away. And when I turned color like a blooming beet, she began to turn pink like a rosebud, and she looked full into my eyes with such a wonderful purity, such exquisite innocence, that I – I never felt so near – er – heaven in my life! No, sir, not even when they ambushed us at Manoa Wells – but that's another thing – only it is part of this business.'

He tightened his clasped hands over his knee until the knuckles whitened.

'*That's* my story, Mr Keen,' he said crisply.

'All of it?'

Harren looked at the floor, then at Keen: 'No, not all. You'll think me a lunatic if I tell you all.'

'Oh, you saw her again?'

'N-never! That is—'

'Never?'

'Not in – in the flesh.'

'Oh, in dreams?'

Harren stirred uneasily. 'I don't know what you call them. I have seen her since – in the sunlight, in the open, in my quarters in Manila, standing there perfectly distinct, looking at me with such strange, beautiful eyes—'

'Go on,' said the Tracer, nodding.

'What else is there to say?' muttered Harren.

'You saw her – or a phantom which resembled her. Did she speak?'

'No.'

'Did you speak to her?'

'N-no. Once I held out my – my arms.'

'What happened?'

'She wasn't there,' said Harren simply.

'She vanished?'

'No – I don't know. I – I didn't see her any more.'

'Didn't she fade?'

'No. I can't explain. She – there was only myself in the room.'

'How many times has she appeared to you?'

'A great many times.'

'In your room?'

'Yes. And in the road under a vertical sun; in the forest, in the paddy fields. I have seen her passing through the hallway of a friend's house – turning on the stair to look back at me! I saw her standing just back of the firing-line at Manoa Wells when we were preparing to rush the forts, and it scared me so that I jumped forward to draw her back. But – she wasn't there, Mr Keen . . .

'On the transport she stood facing me on deck one moonlit evening for five minutes. I saw her in 'Frisco; she sat in the Pullman twice between Denver and this city. Twice in my room at the Vice-Regent she has sat opposite me at midday, so clear, so beautiful, so real that – that I could scarcely believe she was only a – a—' He hesitated.

'The apparition of her own subconscious self,' said the Tracer quietly. 'Science has been forced to admit such things, and, as you know, we are on the verge of understanding the alphabet of some of the unknown forces which we must some day reckon with.'

Harren, tense, a trifle pale, gazed at him earnestly.

'Do *you* believe in such things?'

'How can I avoid believing?' said the Tracer. 'Every day, in my profession, we have proof of the existence of forces for which we have as yet no explanation – or, at best, a very crude one. I have had case after case of premonition; case after case of dual and even multiple personality; case after case where apparitions played a vital part in the plot which was brought to me to investigate. I'll tell you this, Captain: I, personally, never saw an apparition, never was obsessed by premonitions, never received any communications from the outer void. But I have had to do with those who undoubtedly did. Therefore I listen with all seriousness and respect to what you tell me.'

'Suppose,' said Harren, growing suddenly red, 'that I should tell you I have succeeded in photographing this phantom.'

The Tracer sat silent. He was astounded, but he did not betray it.

'You have that photograph, Captain Harren?'

'Yes.'

'Where is it?'

'In my rooms.'

'You wish me to see it?'

Harren hesitated. 'I – there is – seems to be – something almost sacred to me in that photograph . . . You understand me, do you not? Yet, if it will help you in finding her—'

'Oh,' said the Tracer in guileless astonishment, 'you desire to find this young lady. Why?'

Harren stared. 'Why? Why do I want to find her? Man, I – I can't live without her!'

'I thought you were not certain whether you really could be in love.'

The hot color in the Captain's bronzed cheeks mounted to his hair.

'*Ex*actly,' purred the Tracer, looking out of the window. 'Suppose we walk around to your rooms after luncheon. Shall we?'

Harren picked up his hat and gloves, hesitating, lingering on the threshold. 'You *don't* think she is – a – dead?' he asked unsteadily.

'No,' said Mr Keen, 'I don't.'

'Because,' said Harren wistfully, 'her apparition is so superbly healthy and – and glowing with youth and life—'

'That is probably what sent it half the world over to confront you,' said the Tracer gravely; 'youth and life aglow with spiritual health. I think, Captain, that she has been seeing you, too, during these three years, but probably only in her dreams – memories of your encounters with her subconscious self floating over continents and oceans in a quest of which her waking intelligence is innocently unaware.'

The Captain colored like a schoolboy, lingering at the door, hat in hand. Then he straightened up to the full height of his slim but powerful figure.

'At three?' he inquired bluntly.

'At three o'clock in your room, Hotel Vice-Regent. Good morning, Captain.'

'Good morning,' said Harren dreamily, and walked away, head bent, gray eyes lost in retrospection, and on his lean, bronzed, attractive face an afterglow of color wholly becoming.

III

When the Tracer of Lost Persons entered Captain Harren's room at the Hotel Vice-Regent that afternoon he found the young man standing at a center table, pencil in hand, studying a sheet of paper which was covered with letters and figures.

The two men eyed one another in silence for a moment, then Harren pointed grimly to the confusion of letters and figures covering dozens of scattered sheets lying on the table.

'That's part of my madness,' he said with a short laugh. 'Can you make anything of such lunatic work?'

The Tracer picked up a sheet of paper covered with letters of the alphabet and Roman and Arabic numerals. He dropped it presently and picked up another comparatively blank sheet, on which were the following figures:

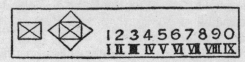

He studied it for a while, then glanced interrogatively at Harren.

'It's nothing,' said Harren. 'I've been groping for three years – but it's no use. That's lunatics' work.' He wheeled squarely on his heels, looking straight at the Tracer. '*Do* you think I've had a touch of the sun?'

'No,' said Mr Keen, drawing a chair to the table. 'Saner men than you or I have spent a lifetime over this so-called Seal of Solomon.' He laid his finger on the two symbols—

Then, looking across the table at Harren: 'What,' he asked, 'has the Seal of Solomon to do with your case?'

'*She*—' muttered Harren, and fell silent.

The Tracer waited; Harren said nothing.

'Where is the photograph?'

Harren unlocked a drawer in the table, hesitated, looked strangely at the Tracer.

'Mr Keen,' he said, 'there is nothing on earth I hold more sacred than this. There is only one thing in the world that could justify me in showing it to a living soul – my – my desire to find – her—'

'No,' said Keen coolly, 'that is not enough to justify you – the mere desire to find the living original of this apparition.

Nothing could justify your showing it unless you love her.'

Harren held the picture tightly, staring full at the Tracer. A dull flush mounted to his forehead, and very slowly he laid the picture before the Tracer of Lost Persons.

Minute after minute sped while the Tracer bent above the photograph, his finely modelled features absolutely devoid of expression. Harren had drawn his chair beside him, and now sat leaning forward, bronzed cheek resting in his hand, staring fixedly at the picture.

'When was this – this photograph taken?' asked the Tracer quietly.

'The day after I arrived in New York. I was here, alone, smoking my pipe and glancing over the evening paper just before dressing for dinner. It was growing rather dark in the room; I had not turned on the electric light. My camera lay on the table – there it is! – that Kodak. I had taken a few snapshots on shipboard; there was one film left.'

He leaned more heavily on his elbow, eyes fixed upon the picture.

'It was almost dark,' he repeated. 'I laid aside the evening paper and stood up, thinking about dressing for dinner, when my eyes happened to fall on the camera. It occurred to me that I might as well unload it, let the unused film go, and send the roll to be developed and printed; and I picked up the camera—'

'Yes,' said the Tracer softly.

'I picked it up and was starting toward the window where there remained enough daylight to see by—'

The Tracer nodded gently.

'Then I saw *her*!' said Harren under his breath.

'Where?'

'There – standing by that window. You can see the window and curtain in the photograph.'

The Tracer gazed intently at the picture.

'She looked at me,' said Harren, steadying his voice. 'She was as real as you are, and she stood there, smiling faintly, her dark, lovely eyes meeting mine.'

'Did you speak?'

'No.'

'How long did she remain there?'

'I don't know – time seemed to stop – the world – everything grew still . . . Then, little by little, something began to stir under my stunned senses – that germ of misgiving, that dreadful doubt of my own sanity . . . I scarcely knew what I was doing when I took the photograph; besides, it had grown quite dark, and I could scarcely see her.' He drew himself erect with a nervous movement. 'How on earth could I have obtained that photograph of her in the darkness?' he demanded.

'N-rays,' said the Tracer coolly. 'It has been done in France.'

'Yes, from living people, but—'

'What the N-ray is in living organisms, we must call, for lack of a better term, the subaura in the phantom.'

They bent over the photograph together. Presently the Tracer said: 'She is very, very beautiful?'

Harren's dry lips unclosed, but he uttered no sound.

'She is beautiful, is she not?' repeated the Tracer, turning to look at the young man.

'Can you not see she is?' he asked impatiently.

'No,' said the Tracer.

Harren stared at him.

'Captain Harren,' continued the Tracer, 'I can see nothing upon this bit of paper that resembles in the remotest degree a human face or figure.'

Harren turned white.

'Not that I doubt that *you* can see it,' pursued the Tracer calmly. 'I simply repeat that I see absolutely nothing on this paper except a part of a curtain, a window pane, and – and—'

'What! for God's sake!' cried Harren hoarsely.

'I don't know yet. Wait; let me study it.'

'Can you not see her face, her eyes? *Don't* you see that exquisite slim figure standing there by the curtain?' demanded Harren, laying his shaking finger on the photograph. 'Why, man, it is as clear, as clean cut, as distinct as though the picture had been taken in sunlight! Do you mean to say that there is nothing there – that I am crazy?'

'No. Wait.'

'Wait! How can I wait when you sit staring at her picture and telling me that you can't see it, but that it is doubtless there? Are you deceiving me, Mr Keen? Are you trying to humour me, trying to be kind to me, knowing all the while that I'm crazy—'

'Wait, man! You are no more crazy than I am. I tell you that I can see something on the window pane—'

He suddenly sprang up and walked to the window, leaning close and examining the glass. Harren followed and laid his hand lightly over the pane.

'Do you see any marks on the glass?' demanded Keen.

Harren shook his head.

'Have you a magnifying glass?' asked the Tracer.

Harren pointed back to the table, and they returned to the photograph, the Tracer bending over it and examining it through the glass.

'All I see,' he said, still studying the photograph, 'is a corner of a curtain and a window on which certain figures seem to have been cut . . . Look, Captain Harren, can you see them?'

'I see some marks – some squares.'

'You can't see anything written on that pane – as though cut by a diamond?'

'Nothing distinct.'

'But you see *her*?'

'Perfectly.'

'In minute detail?'

'Yes.'

The Tracer thought a moment: 'Does she wear a ring?'

'Yes; can't you see?'

'Draw it for me.'

They seated themselves side by side, and Harren drew a rough sketch of the ring which he insisted was so plainly visible on her hand:

'Oh,' observed the Tracer, 'she wears the Seal of Solomon on her ring.'

Harren looked up at him. 'That symbol has haunted me persistently for three years,' he said. 'I have found it everywhere – on articles that I buy, on house furniture, on the belts of dead ladrones, on the hilts of creeses, on the funnels of steamers, on the headstalls of horses. If they put a laundry mark on my linen it's certain to be this!

If I buy a box of matches the sign is on it. Why, I've even seen it on the brilliant wings of tropical insects. It's got on my nerves. I dream about it.'

'And you buy books about it and try to work out its mystical meaning?' suggested the Tracer, smiling.

But Harren's gray eyes were serious. He said: '*She* never comes to me without that symbol somewhere about her . . . I told you she never spoke to me. That is true; yet once, in a vivid dream of her, she did speak. I – I was almost ashamed to tell you of that.'

'Tell me.'

'A – a dream? Do you wish to know what I dreamed?'

'Yes – if it was a dream.'

'It was. I was asleep on the deck of the *Mindinao*, dead tired after a fruitless hike. I dreamed she came toward me through a young woodland all lighted by the sun, and in her hands she held masses of that wild flower we call Solomon's Seal. And she said – in the voice I know must be like hers: "If you could only read! If you would only understand the message I send you! It is everywhere on earth for you to read, if you only would!"

'I said: "Is the message in the seal? Is that the key to it?"

'She nodded, laughing, burying her face in the flowers, and said:

'"Perhaps I can write it more plainly for you some day; I will try very, very hard."

'And after that she went away – not swiftly – for I saw her at moments far away in the woods; but I must have confused her with the glimmering shafts of sunlight, and in a little while the woodland grew dark and I woke with the racket of a Colt's automatic in my ears.'

He passed his sun-bronzed hand over his face, hesitated, then leaned over the photograph once more, which the Tracer was studying intently through the magnifying glass.

'There is something on that window in the photograph which I'm going to copy,' he said. 'Please shove a pad and pencil toward me.'

Still examining the photograph through the glass which he held in his right hand, Mr Keen picked up the pencil and, feeling for the pad, began very slowly to form the following series of symbols:

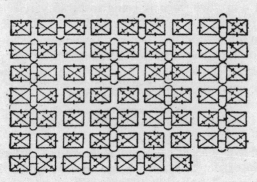

'What on earth are you doing?' muttered Captain Harren, twisting his short mustache in perplexity.

'I am copying what I see through this magnifying glass written on the window pane in the photograph,' said the Tracer calmly. 'Can't you see those marks?'

'I – I do now; I never noticed them before particularly – only that there were scratches there.'

When at length the Tracer had finished his work he sat, chin on hand, examining it in silence. Presently he turned toward Harren, smiling.

'Well?' inquired the younger man impatiently; 'do those scratches representing Solomon's Seal mean anything?'

'It's the strangest cipher I ever encountered,' said Mr Keen – 'the strangest I ever heard of. I have seen hundreds of ciphers – hundreds – secret codes of the State Department, secret military codes, elaborate Oriental ciphers, symbols used in commercial transactions, symbols used by criminals and every species of malefactor. And every one of them can be solved with time and patience and a little knowledge of the subject. But this' – he sat looking at it with eyes half closed – 'this is *too* simple.'

'Simple!'

'Very. It's so simple that it's baffling.'

'Do you mean to say you are going to be able to find a meaning in squares and crosses?'

'I – I don't believe it is going to be so very difficult to translate them.'

'Great guns!' said the Captain. 'Do you mean to say that you can ultimately translate that cipher?'

The Tracer smiled. 'Let's examine it for repetitions first. Here we have this symbol

repeated five times. It's likely to be the letter E. I think—' His voice ceased; for a quarter of an hour he pored over the symbols, pencil in hand, checking off some, substituting a letter here and there.

'No,' he said; 'the usual doesn't work in this case. It's an absurdly simple cipher. I have a notion that numbers play a part in it – you see where these crossed squares are bracketed – those must be numbers requiring two figures—'

He fell silent again, and for another quarter of an hour he remained motionless, immersed in the problem before him, Harren frowning at the paper over his shoulder.

IV

'Come!' said the Tracer suddenly; 'this won't do. There are too few symbols to give us a key; too few repetitions to furnish us with any key basis. Come, Captain, let us use our intellects; let us talk it over with that paper lying there between us. It's a simple cipher – a childishly simple one if we use our wits. Now, sir, what I see repeated before us on this sheet of paper is merely one of the forms of a symbol known as Solomon's Seal. The symbol is, as we see, repeated a great many times. Every seal

has been dotted or crossed on some one of the lines composing it; some seals are coupled with brackets and armatures.'

'What of it?' inquired Harren vacantly.

'Well, sir, in the first place, that symbol

is supposed to represent the spiritual and material, as you know. What else do you know about it?'

'Nothing. I bought a book about it, but made nothing of it.'

'Isn't it supposed,' asked Mr Keen, 'to contain within itself the nine numerals, 1, 2, 3, 4, 5, 6, 7, 8, 9, and even the zero symbol?'

'I believe so.'

'*Ex*actly. Here's the seal

Now I'll mark the one, two, and three by crossing the lines, like this: one,

one,   two,   three,

Now, eliminating all lines not crossed there remains the one,

the one,   **1**   the two,   **Z**   the three,   **3**

And here is the entire series: **1 Z 3 4 5 6 7 8 9**

and the zero— **▷**

A sudden excitement stirred Harren; he leaned over the paper, gazing earnestly at the cipher; the Tracer rose and glanced around the room as though in search of something.

'Is there a telephone here?' he asked.

'For Heaven's sake, don't give this up just yet,' exclaimed Harren. 'These things mean numbers; don't you see? Look at that!' pointing to a linked pair of seals,

'That means the number nineteen! You can form it by using only the crossed lines of the seal

† ⅌

Don't you see, Mr Keen?'

'Yes, Captain Harren, the cipher is, as you say, very plain; quite as easy to read as so much handwriting. That is why I wish to use your telephone – at once, if you please.'

'It's in my bedroom; you don't mind if I go on working out this cipher while you're telephoning?'

'Not in the least,' said the Tracer blandly. He walked into the Captain's bedroom, closing the door behind him; then he stepped over to the telephone, unhooked the receiver, and called up his own headquarters.

'Hello. This is Mr Keen. I want to speak to Miss Borrow.'

In a few moments Miss Borrow answered: 'I am here, Mr Keen.'

'Good. Look up the name Inwood. Try New York first – Edith Inwood is the name. Look sharp, please; I am holding the wire.'

He held it for ten full minutes; then Miss Borrow's low voice called him over the wire.

'Go ahead,' said the Tracer quietly.

'There is only one Edith Inwood in New York, Mr Keen – Miss Edith Inwood, graduate of Barnard, 1902 – left an orphan 1903 and obliged to support herself – became an assistant to Professor Boggs of the Museum of Inscriptions. Is considered an authority upon Arabian cryptograms. Has written a monograph on the Herati symbol – a short treatise on the Swastika. She is twenty-four years of age. Do you require further details?'

'No,' said the Tracer; 'please ring off.'

Then he called up General Information. 'I want the Museum of Inscriptions. Get me their number, please.' After a moment: 'Is this the Museum of Inscriptions?'

. . . . .

'Is Professor Boggs there?'

. . . . .

'Is this Professor Boggs?'

. . . . .

'Could you find time to decipher an inscription for me at once?'

. . . . .

'Of course I know you are extremely busy, but have you no assistant who could do it?'

. . . . .

'What did you say her name is? Miss Inwood?'

. . . . .

'Oh! And will the young lady translate the inscription at once if I send a copy of it to her by messenger?'

. . . . .

'Thank you very much, Professor. I will send a messenger to Miss Inwood with a copy of the inscription. Goodbye.'

He hung up the receiver, turned thoughtfully, opened the door again, and walked into the sunlit living-room.

'Look here!' cried the Captain in a high state of excitement. 'I've got a lot of numbers out of it already.'

'Wonderful!' murmured the Tracer, looking over the young man's broad shoulders at a sheet of paper bearing these numbers:

9–14–5–22–5–18–19–1–23–25–15–21–2–21–20–15–14 –3–5–9–12–15–22–5–25–15–21–5–4–9–20–8–9–14–23–15–15–4.

'Marvellous!' repeated the Tracer, smiling. 'Now what *do* you suppose those numbers can stand for?'

'Letters!' announced the Captain triumphantly. 'Take the number nine, for example. The ninth letter in the alphabet is I! Mr Keen, suppose we try writing down the letters according to that system!'

'Suppose we do,' agreed the Tracer gravely.

So, counting under his breath, the young man set down the letters in the following order, not attempting to group them into words:

INEVERSAWYOUBUTONCEILOVEYOUEDITHINWOOD.

Then he leaned back, excited, triumphant.

'There you are!' he said; 'only, of course, it makes no sense.' He examined it in silence, and gradually a hopeless expression effaced the animation. 'How the deuce am I going to separate that mass of letters into words?' he muttered.

'This way,' said the Tracer, smilingly taking the pencil

from his fingers, and he wrote: I-NEVER-SAW-YOU-BUT-ONCE. I-LOVE-YOU. EDITH INWOOD.

Then he laid the pencil on the table and walked to the window.

Once or twice he fancied that he heard incoherent sounds behind him. And after a while he turned, retracing his steps leisurely. Captain Harren, extremely pink, stood tugging at his short mustache and studying the papers on the desk.

'Well?' inquired the Tracer, amused.

The young man pointed to the translation with unsteady finger. 'W-what on earth does that mean?' he demanded shakily. 'Who is Edith Inwood? W-what on earth does that cryptogram mean on the window pane in the photograph? How did it come there? It isn't on my window pane, you see!'

The Tracer said quietly: 'That is not a photograph of your window.'

'What!'

'No, Captain. Here! Look at it closely through this glass. There are sixteen small panes in that sash; now count the panes in your window – eight! Besides, look at that curtain. It is made of some figured stuff like chintz. Now, look at your own curtain yonder! It is of plain velour.'

'But – but I took that photograph! She stood there – there by that very window!'

The Tracer leaned over the photograph, examining it through the glass. And, studying it, he said: 'Do you still see *her* in this photograph, Captain Harren?'

'Certainly. Can you not see her?'

'No,' murmured the Tracer, 'but I see the window which she really stood by when her phantom came here seeking you. And this is sufficient. Come, Captain Harren, we are going out together.'

The Captain looked at him earnestly; something in Mr Keen's eyes seemed to fascinate him.

'You think that – that it's likely we are g-going to see – *her*!' he faltered.

'If I were you,' mused the Tracer of Lost Persons, joining

the tips of his lean fingers meditatively – 'If I were you I should wear a silk hat and a frock coat. It's – it's afternoon, anyhow,' he added deprecatingly, 'and we are liable to make a call.'

Captain Harren turned like a man in a dream and entered his bedroom. And when he emerged he was dressed and groomed with pathetic precision.

'Mr Keen,' he said, 'I – I don't know why I am d-daring to hope for all s-sorts of things. Nothing you have said really warrants it. But somehow I'm venturing to cherish an absurd notion that I may s-see her.'

'Perhaps,' said the Tracer, smiling.

'Mr Keen! You wouldn't say that if – if there was no chance, would you? You wouldn't dash a fellow's hopes—'

'No, I wouldn't,' said Mr Keen. 'I tell you frankly that I expect to find her.'

'Today?'

'We'll see,' said Mr Keen guardedly. 'Come, Captain, don't look that way! Courage, sir! We are about to execute a turning movement; but you look like a Russian general on his way to the south front.'

Harren managed to laugh; they went out, side by side, descended the elevator, and found a cab at the *porte-cochère*. Mr Keen gave the directions and followed the Captain into the cab.

'Now,' he said, as they wheeled south, 'we are first going to visit the Museum of Inscriptions and have this cipher translation verified. Here is the cipher as I copied it. Hold it tightly, Captain; we've only a few blocks to drive.'

Indeed they were already nearly there. The hansom drew up in front of a plain granite building wedged in between some rather elaborate private dwelling-houses. Over the door were letters of dull bronze:

AMERICAN MUSEUM OF INSCRIPTIONS

and the two men descended and entered a wide marble hall lined with glass-covered cabinets containing plaster casts of various ancient inscriptions and a few bronze and marble originals. Several female frumps were nosing the exhibits.

An attendant in livery stood in the middle distance. The Tracer walked over to him. 'I have an appointment to consult Miss Inwood,' he whispered.

'This way, sir,' nodded the attendant, and the Tracer signalled the Captain to follow.

They climbed several marble stairways, crossed a rotunda, and entered a room – a sort of library. Beyond was a door which bore the inscription:

ASSISTANT CURATOR

'Now,' said the Tracer of Lost Persons in a low voice to Captain Harren, 'I am going to ask you to sit here for a few minutes while I interview the assistant curator. You don't mind, do you?'

'No, I don't mind,' said Harren wearily, 'only, when are we going to begin to search for – *her*?'

'Very soon – I may say extremely soon,' said Mr Keen gravely. 'By the way, I think I'll take that sheet of paper on which I copied the cipher. Thank you. I won't be long.'

The attendant had vanished. Captain Harren sat down by a window and gazed out into the late afternoon sunshine. The Tracer of Lost Persons, treading softly across the carpeted floor, approached the sanctuary, turned the handle, and walked in, carefully closing the door behind him.

There was a young girl seated at a desk by an open window; she looked up quietly as he entered, then rose leisurely.

'Miss Inwood?'

'Yes.'

She was slender, dark-eyed, dark-haired – a lovely, wholesome young creature, gracious and graceful. And that was all – for the Tracer of Lost Persons could not see through the eyes of Captain Harren, and perhaps that is why he was not able to discern a miracle of beauty in the pretty girl who

confronted him – no' magic and matchless marvel of
transcendent loveliness – only a quiet, sweet-faced, dark-eyed
young girl whose features and figure were attractive in the
manner that youth is always attractive. But then it is a gift
of the gods to see through eyes anointed by the gods.

The Tracer touched his gray mustache and bowed; the
girl bowed very sweetly.

'You are Mr Keen,' she said; 'you have an inscription for
me to translate.'

'A mystery for young eyes to interpret,' he said, smiling.
'May I sit here – and tell my story before I show you my
inscription?'

'Please do,' she said, seating herself at her desk and facing
him, one slender white hand supporting the oval of her face.

The Tracer drew his chair a little forward. 'It is a curious
matter,' he said. 'May I give you a brief outline of the details?'

'By all means, Mr Keen.'

'Then let me begin by saying that the inscription of which
I have a copy was probably scratched upon a window pane
by means of a diamond.'

'Oh! Then – then it is not an ancient inscription, Mr Keen.'

'The theme is ancient – the oldest theme in the world –
love! The cipher is old – as old as King Solomon.' She looked
up quickly. The Tracer, apparently engrossed in his own
story, went on with it. 'Three years ago the young girl who
wrote this inscription upon the window pane of her – her
bedroom, I think it was – fell in love. Do you follow me,
Miss Inwood?'

Miss Inwood sat very still – wide, dark eyes fixed on him.

'Fell in love,' repeated the Tracer musingly, 'not in the
ordinary way. That is the point, you see. No, she fell in love
at first sight; fell in love with a young man whom she never
before had seen, never again beheld – and never forgot him.
I am not sure, but I think she sometimes dreamed of him.
She dreamed of him awake, too. Once she inscribed a
message to him, cutting it with the diamond in her ring on
the window pane—'

A slight sound escaped from Miss Inwood's lips. 'I beg your pardon,' said the Tracer, 'did you say something?'

The girl had risen, pale, astounded, incredulous.

'Who are you?' she faltered. 'What has this – this story to do with me?'

'Child,' said the Tracer of Lost Persons, 'the Seal of Solomon is a splendid mystery. All of heaven and earth are included within its symbol. And more, more than you dream of, more than I dare fathom; and I am an old man, my child – old, alone, with nobody to fear for, nothing to dread, not even the end of all – because I am ready for that, too. Yet I, having nothing on earth to dread, dare not fathom what that symbol may mean, nor what vast powers it may exert on life. God knows. It may be the very signet of Fate itself; the sign manual of Destiny.'

He drew the paper from his pocket, unrolled it, and spread it out under her frightened eyes.

'*That*!' she whispered, steadying herself blindly against the arm he offered. She stood a moment so, then, shuddering, covered her eyes with both hands. The Tracer of Lost Persons looked at her, turned and opened the door.

'Captain Harren!' he called quietly. Harren, pacing the anteroom, turned and came forward. As he entered the door he caught sight of the girl crouching by the window, her face hidden in her hands, and at the same moment she dropped her hands and looked straight at him.

'*You*!' she gasped.

The Tracer of Lost Persons stepped out, closing the door. For a moment he stood there, tall, gaunt, gray, staring vacantly into space.

'She *was* beautiful – when she looked at him,' he muttered.

For another minute he stood there, hesitating, glancing backward at the closed door. Then he went away, stooping slightly, his top hat held close against the breast of his tightly buttoned frock coat.

THE BRIDAL PAIR

'If I were you,' said the elder man, 'I should take three months' solid rest.'

'A month is enough,' said the younger man. 'Ozone will do it; the first brace of grouse I bag will do it—' He broke off abruptly, staring at the line of dimly lighted cars, where Negro porters stood by the vestibuled sleepers, directing passengers to staterooms and berths.

'Dog all right, doctor?' inquired the elder man pleasantly.

'All right, doctor,' replied the younger; 'I spoke to the baggage master.'

There was a silence; the elder man chewed an unlighted cigar reflectively, watching his companion with keen narrowing eyes.

The younger physician stood full in the white electric light, lean head lowered, apparently preoccupied with a study of his own shadow swimming and quivering on the asphalt at his feet.

'So you fear I may break down?' he observed, without raising his head.

'I think you're tired out,' said the other.

'That's a more agreeable way of expressing it,' said the young fellow. 'I hear' – he hesitated, with a faint trace of irritation – 'I understand that Forbes Stanly thinks me mentally unsound.'

'He probably suspects what you're up to,' said the elder man soberly.

'Well, what will he do when I announce my germ theory? Put me in a strait-jacket?'

'He'll say you're mad, until you prove it; every physician will agree with him – until your radium test shows us the microbe of insanity.'

'Doctor,' said the young man abruptly, 'I'm going to admit something – to *you*.'

'All right; go ahead and admit it.'

'Well, I *am* a bit worried about my own condition.'

'It's time you were,' observed the other.

'Yes – it's about time. Doctor, I am seriously affected.'

The elder man looked up sharply.

'Yes, I'm – in love.'

'Ah!' muttered the elder physician, amused and a trifle disgusted; 'so that's your malady, is it?'

'A malady – yes; not explainable by our germ theory – not affected by radio-activity. Doctor, I'm speaking lightly enough, but there's no happiness in it.'

'Never is,' commented the other, striking a match and lighting his ragged cigar. After a puff or two the cigar went out. 'All I have to say,' he added, 'is, don't do it just now. Show me a scale of pure radium and I'll give you leave to marry every spinster in New York. In the meantime go and shoot a few dozen harmless, happy grouse; they can't shoot back. But let love alone . . . By the way, who is she?'

'I don't know.'

'You know her name, I suppose?'

The younger fellow shook his head. 'I don't even know where she lives,' he said finally.

After a pause the elder man took him gently by the arm: 'Are you subject to this sort of thing? Are you susceptible?'

'No, not at all.'

'Ever before in love?'

'Yes – once.'

'When?'

'When I was about ten years old. Her name was Rosamund

– aged eight. I never had the courage to speak to her. She died recently, I believe.'

The reply was so quietly serious, so destitute of any suspicion of humor, that the elder man's smile faded; and again he cast one of his swift, keen glances at his companion.

'Won't you stay away three months?' he asked patiently.

But the other only shook his head, tracing with the point of his walking stick the outline of his own shadow on the asphalt.

A moment later he glanced at his watch, closed it with a snap, silently shook hands with his equally silent friend, and stepped aboard the sleeping car.

Neither had noticed the name of the sleeping car.

It happened to be the *Rosamund*.

Loungers and passengers on Wildwood station drew back from the platform's edge as the towering locomotive shot by them, stunning their ears with the clangor of its melancholy bell.

Slower, slower glided the dusty train, then stopped, jolting; eddying circles of humanity closed around the cars, through which descending passengers pushed.

'Wildwood! Wildwood!' cried the trainmen; trunks tumbling out of the forward car descended with a bang! – a yelping, wagging setter dog landed on the platform, hysterically grateful to be free; and at the same moment a young fellow in tweed shooting clothes, carrying gripsack and gun case, made his way forward toward the baggage master, who was being jerked all over the platform by the frantic dog.

'Much obliged; I'll take the dog,' he said, slipping a bit of silver into the official's hand, and receiving the dog's chain in return,

'Hope you'll have good sport,' replied the baggage master. 'There's a lot o' birds in this country, they tell me. You've got a good dog there.'

The young man smiled and nodded, released the chain

from his dog's collar, and started off up the dusty village street, followed by an urchin carrying his luggage.

The landlord of the Wildwood Inn stood on the veranda, prepared to receive guests. When a young man, a white setter dog, and a small boy loomed up, his speculative eyes became suffused with benevolence.

'How-de-do, sir?' he said cordially. 'Guess you was with us three year since – stayed to supper. Ain't that so?'

'It certainly is,' said his guest cheerfully. 'I am surprised that you remember me.'

'Be ye?' rejoined the landlord, gratified. 'Say! I can tell the name of every man, woman, an' child that has ever set down to eat with us. You was here with a pair o' red bird dawgs; shot a mess o' birds before dark, come back pegged out, an' took the ten-thirty to Noo York. Hey? Yaas, an' you was cussin' round because you couldn't stay an' shoot for a month.'

'I had to work hard in those days,' laughed the young man. 'You are right; it was three years ago this month.'

'Time's a flyer; it's fitted with triple screws these days,' said the landlord. 'Come right in an' make yourself to home. Ed! O Ed! Take this bag to 13! We're all full, sir. You ain't scared at No. 13, by ye? Say! If I ain't a liar you had 13 three years ago! Waal, now! – ain't that the dumbdest— But you can have what you want Monday. How long was you calkerlatin' to stay?'

'A month – if the shooting is good.'

'It's all right. Orrin Plummer come in last night with a mess o' pa'tridges. He says the woodcock is droppin' in to the birches south o' Sweetbrier Hill.'

The young man nodded, and began to remove his gun from the service-worn case of sole leather.

'Ain't startin' right off, be ye?' inquired his host, laughing.

'I can't begin too quickly,' said the young man, busy locking barrels to stock, while the dog looked on, thumping the veranda floor with his plumy tail.

The landlord admired the slim, polished weapon. 'That's the instrument!' he observed. 'That there's a slick bird dawg, too. Guess I'd better fill my ice box. Your limit's thirty of each – cock an' pa'tridge. After that there's ducks.'

'It's a good, sane law,' said the young man, dropping his gun under one arm.

The landlord scratched his ear reflectively. 'Lemme see,' he mused; 'wasn't you a doctor? I heard tell that you made up pieces for the papers about the idjits an' loonyticks of Rome an' Roosia an' furrin climes.'

'I have written a little on European and Asiatic insanity,' replied the doctor good-humoredly.

'Was you over to them parts?'

'For three years.' He whistled the dog in from the road, where several yellow curs were walking round and round him, every hair on end.

The landlord said: 'You look a little peaked yourself. Take it easy the fust, is my advice.'

His guest nodded abstractedly, lingering on the veranda, preoccupied with the beauty of the village street, which stretched away westward under tall elms. Autumn-tinted hills closed the vista; beyond them spread the blue sky.

'The cemetery lies that way, does it not?' inquired the young man.

'Straight ahead,' said the landlord. 'Take the road to the Holler.'

'Do you' – the doctor hesitated – 'do you recall a funeral there three years ago?'

'Whose?' asked his host bluntly.

'I don't know.'

'I'll ask my woman; she saves them funeral pieces an' make a album . . . Friend o' yours buried there?'

'No.'

The landlord sauntered toward the barroom, where two fellow taxpayers stood shuffling their feet impatiently.

'Waal, good luck, doc,' he said, without intentional offence; 'supper's at six. We'll try an' make you comfortable.'

'Thank you,' replied the doctor, stepping out into the road, and motioning the white setter to heel.

'I remember now,' he muttered, as he turned northward, where the road forked; 'the cemetery lies to the westward; there should be a lane at the next turning—'

He hesitated and stopped, then resumed his course, mumbling to himself: 'I can pass the cemetery later; she would not be there; I don't think I shall ever see her again . . . I – I wonder whether I am – perfectly – well—'

The words were suddenly lost in a sharp indrawn breath; his heart ceased beating, fluttered, then throbbed on violently; and he shook from head to foot.

There was a glimmer of a summer gown under the trees; a figure passed from shadow to sunshine, and again into the cool dusk of a leafy lane.

The pallor of the young fellow's face changed; a heavy flush spread from forehead to neck; he strode forward, dazed, deafened by the tumult of his drumming pulses. The dog, alert, suspicious, led the way, wheeling into the bramble-bordered lane, only to halt, turn back, and fall in behind his master again.

In the lane ahead the light summer gown fluttered under the foliage, bright in the sunlight, almost lost in the shadows. Then he saw her on the hill's breezy crest, poised for a moment against the sky.

When at length he reached the hill, he found her seated in the shade of a pine. She looked up serenely, as though she had expected him, and they faced each other. A moment later his dog left him, sneaking away without a sound.

When he strove to speak, his voice had an unknown tone to him. Her upturned face was his only answer. The breeze in the pinetops, which had been stirring lazily and monotonously, ceased.

Her delicate face was like a blossom lifted in the still air; her upward glance chained him to silence. The first breeze broke the spell: he spoke a word, then speech died on his lips; he stood twisting his shooting cap, confused, not daring to continue.

The girl leaned back, supporting her weight on one arm, fingers almost buried in the deep green moss.

'It is three years today,' he said, in the dull voice of one who dreams; 'three years today. May I not speak?'

In her lowered head and eyes he read acquiescence; in her silence, consent.

'Three years ago today,' he repeated; 'the anniversary has given me courage to speak to you. Surely you will not take offense; we have travelled so far together! – from the end of the world to the end of it, and back again, here – to this place of all places in the world! And now to find you here on this day of all days – here within a step of our first meeting place – three years ago today! And all the world we have travelled over since, never speaking, yet ever passing on paths parallel – paths which for thousands of miles ran almost within arm's distance—'

She raised her head slowly, looking out from the shadows of the pines into the sunshine. Her dreamy eyes rested on acres of golden-rod and hillside brambles quivering in the September heat; on fern-choked gullies edged with alder; on brown and purple grasses; on pine thickets where slim silver birches glimmered.

'Will you speak to me?' he asked. 'I have never even heard the sound of your voice.'

She turned and looked at him, touching with idle fingers the soft hair curling on her temples. Then she bent her head once more, the faintest shadow of a smile in her eyes.

'Because,' he said humbly, 'these long years of silent recognition count for something! And then the strangeness of it! – the fate of it – the quiet destiny that ruled our lives – that rules them now – now as I am speaking, weighting every second with its tiny burden of fate.'

She straightened up, lifting her half-buried hand from the moss; and he saw the imprint there where the palm and fingers had rested.

'Three years that end today – end with the new moon,' he said. 'Do you remember?'

'Yes,' she said.

He quivered at the sound of her voice. 'You were there, just beyond those oaks,' he said eagerly; 'we can see them from here. The road turns there—'

'Turns by the cemetery,' she murmured.

'Yes, yes, by the cemetery! You had been there, I think.'

'Do you remember that?' she asked.

'I have never forgotten – never!' he repeated, striving to hold her eyes to his own; 'it was not twilight; there was a glimmer of day in the west, but the woods were darkening, and the new moon lay in the sky, and the evening was very clear and still.'

Impulsively he dropped on one knee beside her to see her face; and as he spoke, curbing his emotion and impatience with that subtle deference which is inbred in men or never acquired, she stole a glance at him; and his worn visage brightened as though touched with sunlight.

'The second time I saw you was in New York,' he said – 'only a glimpse of your face in the crowd – but I knew you.'

'I saw you,' she mused.

'Did you?' he cried, enchanted. 'I dared not believe that you recognised me.'

'Yes, I knew you . . . Tell me more.'

The thrilling voice set him aflame; faint danger signals tinted her face and neck.

'In December,' he went on unsteadily, 'I saw you in Paris – I saw only you amid the thousand faces in the candlelight of Notre Dame.'

'And I saw you . . . And then?'

'And then two months of darkness . . . And at last a light – moonlight – and you on the terrace at Amara.'

'There was only a flower bed – a few spikes of white hyacinths between us,' she said dreamily.

He strove to speak coolly. 'Day and night have built many a wall between us; was that you who passed me in the starlight, so close that our shoulders touched, in that narrow street in Samarcand? And the dark figure with you—'

'Yes, it was I and my attendant.'

'And . . . you, there in the fog—'

'At Archangel? Yes, it was I.'

'On the Goryn?'

'It was I . . . And I am here at last – with you. It is our destiny.'

So, kneeling there beside her in the shadow of the pines, she absolved him in their dim confessional, holding him guiltless under the destiny that awaits us all.

Again that illumination touched his haggard face as though brightened by a sun ray stealing through the still foliage above. He grew younger under the level beauty of her gaze; care fell from him like a mask; the shadows that had haunted his eyes faded; youth awoke, transfiguring him and all his eyes beheld.

Made prisoner by love, adoring her, fearing her, he knelt beside her, knowing already that she had surrendered, though fearful yet by word or gesture or a glance to claim what destiny was holding for him – holding securely, inexorably, for him alone.

He spoke of her kindness in understanding him, and of his gratitude; of her generosity, of his wonder that she had ever noticed him on his way through the world.

'I cannot believe that we have never before spoken to each other,' he said; 'that I do not even know your name. Surely there was once a corner in the land of childhood where we sat together when the world was younger.'

She said, dreamily: 'Have you forgotten?'

'Forgotten?'

'That sunny corner in the land of childhood.'

'Had you been there, I should not have forgotten,' he replied, troubled.

'Look at me,' she said. Her lovely eyes met his; under the penetrating sweetness of her gaze his heart quickened and grew restless and his uneasy soul stirred, awaking memories.

'There was a child,' she said, 'years ago; a child at school.

You sometimes looked at her; you never spoke. Do you remember?'

He rose to his feet, staring down at her.

'Do you remember?' she asked again.

'Rosamund! Do you mean Rosamund? How should you know that?' he faltered.

The struggle for memory focused all his groping senses; his eyes seemed to look her through and through.

'How can you know?' he repeated unsteadily. 'You are not Rosamund . . . Are you? . . . She is dead. I heard that she was dead . . . *Are you Rosamund*?'

'Do you not know?'

'Yes; you are not Rosamund . . . What do you know of her?'

'I think she loved you.'

'Is she dead?'

The girl looked up at him, smiling, following with delicate perception the sequence of his thoughts; and already his thoughts were far from the child Rosamund, a sweetheart of a day long since immortal; already he had forgotten his question, though the question was of life or death.

Sadness and unrest and the passing of souls concerned not him; she knew that all his thoughts were centered on her; that he was already living over once more the last three years, with all their mystery and charm, savoring their fragrance anew in the exquisite enchantment of her presence.

Through the autumn silence the pines began to sway in a wind unfelt below. She raised her eyes and saw their green crests shimmering and swimming in a cool current; a thrilling sound stole out, and with it floated the pine perfume, exhaling in the sunshine. He heard the dreamy harmony above, looked up; then, troubled, somber, moved by he knew not what, he knelt once more in the shadow beside her – close beside her.

She did not stir. Their destiny was close upon them. It came in the guise of love.

He bent nearer. 'I love you,' he said. 'I loved you from the first. And shall forever. You knew it long ago.'

She did not move.

'You knew I loved you?'

'Yes, I knew it.'

The emotion in her voice, in every delicate contour of her face, pleaded for mercy. He gave her none, and she bent her head in silence, clasped hands tightening.

And when at last he had had his say, the burning words still rang in her ears through the silence. A curious faintness stole upon her, coming stealthily like a hateful thing. She strove to put it from her, to listen, to remember and understand the words he had spoken, but the dull confusion grew with the sound of the pines.

'Will you love me? Will you try to love me?'

'I love you,' she said; 'I have loved you so many, many years; I – I am Rosamund—'

She bowed her head and covered her face with both hands.

'Rosamund! Rosamund!' he breathed, enraptured.

She dropped her hands with a little cry; the frightened sweetness of her eyes held back his outstretched arms. 'Do not touch me,' she whispered; 'you will not touch me, will you? – not yet – not now. Wait till I understand!' She pressed her hands to her eyes, then again let them fall, staring straight at him. 'I loved you so!' she whispered. 'Why did you wait?'

'Rosamund! Rosamund!' he cried sorrowfully, 'what are you saying? I do not understand; I can understand nothing save that I worship you. May I not touch you? – touch your hand, Rosamund? I love you so.'

'And I love you. I beg you not to touch me – not yet. There is something – some reason why—'

'Tell me, sweetheart.'

'Do you not know?'

'By Heaven, I do not!' he said, troubled and amazed.

She cast one desperate, unhappy glance at him, then rose to her full height, gazing out over the hazy valleys to where the mountains began, piled up like dim sun-tipped clouds in the north.

The hill wind stirred her hair and fluttered the white ribbons at waist and shoulder. The golden-rod swayed in the sunshine. Below, amid yellow treetops, the roofs and chimneys of the village glimmered.

'Dear, do you not understand?' she said. 'How can I make you understand that I love you – too late?'

'Give yourself to me, Rosamund; let me touch you – let me take you—'

'Will you love me always?'

'In life, in death, which cannot part us. Will you marry me, Rosamund?'

She looked straight into his eyes. 'Dear, do you not understand? Have you forgotten? I died three years ago today.'

The unearthly sweetness of her white face startled him. A terrible light broke in on him; his heart stood still.

In his dull brain words were sounding – his own words, written years ago: 'When God takes the mind and leaves the body alive, there grows in it, sometimes, a beauty almost supernatural.'

He had seen it in his practice. A thrill of fright penetrated him, piercing every vein with its chill. He strove to speak; his lips seemed frozen; he stood there before her, a ghastly smile stamped on his face, and in his heart, terror.

'What do you mean, Rosamund?' he said at last.

'That I am dead, dear. Did you not understand that? I – I thought you knew it – when you first saw me at the cemetery, after all those years since childhood . . . Did you not know it?' she asked wistfully. 'I must wait for my bridal.'

Misery whitened his face as he raised his head and looked out across the sunlit world. Something had smeared and marred the fair earth; the sun grew gray as he stared.

Stupefied by the crash, the ruins of life around him, he stood mute, erect, facing the west.

She whispered, 'Do you understand?'

'Yes,' he said; 'we will wed later. You have been ill, dear; but it is all right now – and will always be – God help us! Love is stronger than all – stronger than death.'

'I know it is stronger than death,' she said, looking out dreamily over the misty valley.

He followed her gaze, calmly, serenely reviewing all that he must renounce, the happiness of wedlock, children – all that a man desires.

Suddenly instinct stirred, awaking man's only friend – hope. A lifetime for the battle! – for a cure! Hopeless? He laughed at his excitement. Despair? – when the cure lay almost within his grasp! – the work he had given his life to! A month more in the laboratory – two months – three – perhaps a year. What of it? It must surely come – how could he fail when the work of his life meant all in life for her?

The light of exaltation slowly faded from his face; ominous, foreboding thoughts crept in; fear laid a shaky hand on his head which fell heavily forward on his breast.

Science and man's cunning and the wisdom of the world!

'O God,' he groaned, 'for Him who cured by laying on His hands!' Now that he had learned her name, and that her father was alive, he stood mutely beside her, staring steadily at the chimneys and stately dormered roof almost hidden behind the crimson maple foliage across the valley – her home.

She had seated herself once more upon the moss, hands clasped upon one knee, looking out into the west with dreamy eyes.

'I shall not be long,' he said gently. 'Will you wait here for me? I will bring your father with me.'

'I will wait for you. But you must come before the new moon. Will you? I must go when the new moon lies in the west.'

'Go, dearest? Where?'

'I may not tell you,' she sighed, 'but you will know very soon – very soon now. And there will be no more sorrow, I think,' she added timidly.

'There will be no more sorrow,' he repeated quietly.

'For the former things are passing away,' she said.

He broke a heavy spray of golden-rod and laid it across

her knees; she held out a blossom to him – a blind gentian, blue as her eyes. He kissed it.

'Be with me when the new moon comes,' she whispered. 'It will be so sweet. I will teach you how divine is death, if you will come.'

'You shall teach me the sweetness of life,' he said tremulously.

'Yes – life. I did not know you called it by its truest name.'

So he went away, trudging sturdily down the lane, gun glistening on his shoulder.

Where the lane joins the shadowy village street his dog skulked up to him, sniffing at his heels.

A mill whistle was sounding; through the red rays of the setting sun people were passing. Along the row of village shops loungers followed him with vacant eyes. He saw nothing, heard nothing, though a kindly voice called after him, and a young girl smiled at him on her short journey through the world.

The landlord of the Wildwood Inn sat sunning himself in the red evening glow.

'Well, doctor,' he said, 'you look tired to death. Eh? What's that you say?'

The young man repeated his question in a low voice. The landlord shook his head.

'No, sir. The big house on the hill is empty – been empty these three years. No, sir, there ain't no family there now. The old gentleman moved away three years ago.'

'You are mistaken,' said the doctor; 'his daughter tells me he lives there.'

'His – his daughter?' repeated the landlord. 'Why, doctor, she's dead.' He turned to his wife, who sat sewing by the open window: 'Ain't it three years, Marthy?'

'Three years today,' said the woman, biting off her thread. 'She's buried in the family vault over the hill. She was a right pretty little thing, too.'

'Turned nineteen,' mused the landlord, folding his newspaper reflectively.

*

The great gray house on the hill was closed, windows and door boarded over, lawn, shrubbery, and hedges tangled with weeds. A few scarlet poppies glimmered above the brown grass. Save for these, and clumps of tall phlox, there were no blossoms among the weeds.

His dog, which had sneaked after him, cowered as he turned northward across the fields. Swifter and swifter he strode; and as he stumbled on, the long sunset clouds faded, the golden light in the west died out, leaving a calm, clear sky tinged with faintest green.

Pines hid the west as he crept toward the hill where she awaited him. As he climbed through dusky purple grasses, higher, higher, he saw the new moon's crescent tipping above the hills; and he crushed back the deathly fright that clutched at him and staggered on.

'Rosamund!'

The pines answered him.

'Rosamund!'

The pines replied, answering together. Then the wind died away, and there was no answer when he called.

East and south the darkening thickets, swaying, grew still. He saw the slim silver birches glimmering like the ghosts of young trees dead; he saw on the moss at his feet a broken stalk of golden-rod.

The new moon had drawn a veil across her face; sky and earth were very still.

While the moon lasted he lay, eyes open, listening, his face pillowed on the moss. It was long after sunrise when his dog came to him; later still when men came.

And at first they thought he was asleep.

IN SEARCH OF THE MAMMOTH

I

Before I proceed any further, common decency requires me to assure my readers concerning my intentions, which, Heaven knows, are far from flippant.

To separate fact from fancy has always been difficult for me, but now that I have had the honor to be chosen secretary of the Zoological Gardens in Bronx Park, I realize keenly that unless I give up writing fiction nobody will believe what I write about science. Therefore it is to a serious and unimaginative public that I shall hereafter address myself; and I do it in the modest confidence that I shall neither be distrusted nor doubted, although unfortunately I still write in that irrational style which suggests covert frivolity, and for which I am undergoing a course of treatment in English literature at Columbia College. No, having promised to avoid originality and confine myself to facts, I shall tell what I have to tell concerning the dingue, the mammoth and – *something else*.

For some weeks it had been rumored that Professor Farrago, president of the Bronx Park Zoological Society, would resign, to accept an enormous salary as manager of Barnum & Bailey's circus. He was now with the circus in London, and had promised to cable his decision before the day was over.

I hoped he would decide to remain with us. I was his secretary and particular favorite, and I viewed, without enthusiasm, the advent of a new president, who might shake us all out of our congenial and carefully excavated ruts. However, it was plain that the trustees of the society expected the resignation of Professor Farrago, for they had been in secret session all day, considering the names of possible candidates to fill Professor Farrago's large, old-fashioned shoes. These preparations worried me, for I could scarcely expect another chief as kind and considerate as Professor Leonidas Farrago.

That afternoon in June I left my office in the Administration Building in Bronx Park, and strolled out under the trees for a breath of air. But the heat of the sun soon drove me to seek shelter under a little square arbor, a shady retreat covered with purple wisteria and honeysuckle. As I entered the arbor I noticed that there were three other people seated there – an elderly lady with masculine features and short hair, a younger lady sitting beside her, and, farther away, a rough-looking young man reading a book.

For a moment I had an indistinct impression of having met the elder lady somewhere, and under circumstances not entirely agreeable, but beyond a stony and indifferent glance she paid no attention to me. As for the younger lady, she did not look at me at all. She was very young, with pretty eyes, a mass of silky brown hair, and a skin as fresh as a rose which had just been rained on.

With that delicacy peculiar to lonely scientific bachelors, I modestly sat down beside the rough young man, although there was more room beside the younger lady. 'Some lazy loafer reading a penny dreadful,' I thought, glancing at him, then at the title of his book. Hearing me beside him, he turned around and blinked over his shabby shoulder, and the movement uncovered the page he had been silently conning. The volume in his hands was Darwin's famous monograph on the monodactyl.

He noticed the astonishment on my face and smiled uneasily, shifting the short clay pipe in his mouth.

'I guess,' he observed, 'that this here book is too much for me, mister.'

'It's rather technical,' I replied, smiling.

'Yes,' he said, in vague admiration; 'it's fierce, ain't it?'

After a silence I asked him if he would tell me why he had chosen Darwin as a literary pastime.

'Well,' he said placidly, 'I was tryin' to read about anner-mals, but I'm up against a word-slinger this time all right. Now here's a gum-twister,' and he painfully spelled out m-o-n-o-d-a-c-t-y-l, breathing hard all the while.

'Monadactyl,' I said, 'means a single-toed creature.'

He turned the page with alacrity. 'Is that the beast he's talkin' about?' he asked.

The illustration he pointed out was a wood-cut representing Darwin's reconstruction of the dingue from the fossil bones in the British Museum. It was a well-executed wood-cut, showing a dingue in the foreground and, to give scale, a mammoth in the middle distance.

'Yes,' I replied, 'that is the dingue.'

'I've seen one,' he observed calmly.

I smiled and explained that the dingue had been extinct for some thousands of years.

'Oh, I guess not,' he replied, with cool optimism. Then he placed a grimy forefinger on the mammoth.

'I've seen them things too,' he remarked.

Again I pointed out his error, and suggested that he referred to the elephant.

'Elephant be blowed!' he replied scornfully. 'I guess I know what I seen. An' I seen that there thing you call a dingue, too.'

Not wishing to prolong a futile discussion, I remained silent. After a moment he wheeled around, removing his pipe from his hard mouth.

'Did you ever hear tell of Graham's Glacier?' he demanded.

'Certainly,' I replied, astonished; 'it's the southernmost glacier in British America.'

'Right,' he said. 'And did you ever hear tell of the Hudson Mountings, mister?'

'Yes,' I replied.

'What's behind 'em?' he snapped out.

'Nobody knows,' I answered. 'They are considered impass-able.'

'They ain't though,' he said doggedly; 'I've been behind 'em.'

'Really!' I replied, tiring of his yarn.

'Ya-as, reely,' he repeated sullenly. Then he began to fumble and search through the pages of his book until he found what he wanted.

'Mister,' he said, 'jest read that out loud, please.'

The passage he indicated was the famous chapter beginning:

Is the mammoth extinct? Is the dingue extinct? Probably. And yet the aborigines of British America maintain the contrary. Probably both the mammoth and the dingue are extinct; but until expeditions have penetrated and explored not only the unknown region in Alaska but also that hidden tableland beyond the Graham Glacier and the Hudson Mountains, it will not be possible to definitely announce the total extinction of either the mammoth or the dingue.

When I had read it, slowly, for his benefit, he brought his hand down smartly on one knee and nodded rapidly.

'Mister,' he said, 'that gent knows a thing or two, and don't you forget it!' Then he demanded, abruptly, how I knew he hadn't been behind the Graham Glacier.

I explained.

'Shucks!' he said; 'there's a road five mile wide inter that there tableland. Mister, I ain't been in New York long; I come inter port a week ago on the *Arctic Belle*, whaler. I was in the Hudson range when that there Graham Glacier bust up—'

'What!' I exclaimed.

'Didn't you know it?' he asked. 'Well, mebbe it ain't in the papers, but it busted all right – blowed up by an earth-quake an' volcano combine. An', mister, it was oreful. My, how I did run!'

'Do you mean to tell me that some convulsion of the earth has shattered the Graham Glacier?' I asked.

'Convulsions? Ya-as, an' fits too,' he said sulkily. 'The hull blame thing dropped inter a hole. An' say, mister, home an' mother is good enough fur me now.'

I stared at him stupidly.

'Once,' he said, 'I ketched pelts fur them sharps at Hudson Bay, like any yaller husky, but the things I seen arter that convulsion-fit – the *things I seen behind the Hudson Mountings* – don't make me hanker arter no life on the pe-rarie wild, lemme tell yer. I may be a Mother Carey's chicken, but this chicken has got enough.'

After a long silence I picked up his book again and pointed at a picture of the mammoth.

'What color is it?' I asked.

'Kinder red an' brown,' he answered promptly. 'It's woolly too.'

Astounded, I pointed to the dingue.

'One-toed,' he said quickly; 'makes a noise like a bell when scutterin' about.'

Intensely excited, I laid my hand on his arm.

'My society will give you a thousand dollars,' I said, 'if you pilot me inside the Hudson tableland and show me either a mammoth or a dingue!'

He looked me calmly in the eye.

'Mister,' he said slowly, 'have you got a million for to squander on me?'

'No,' I said suspiciously.

'Because,' he went on, 'it wouldn't be enough. Home an' mother suits me now.'

He picked up his book and rose. In vain I asked his name and address; in vain I begged him to dine with me – to become my honored guest.

'Nit,' he said shortly, and shambled off down the path.

But I was not going to lose him like that. I rose and deliberately started to stalk him. It was easy. He shuffled along, pulling at his pipe, and I after him.

It was growing a little dark, although the sun still reddened the tops of the maples. Afraid of losing him in the falling dusk, I once more approached him and laid my hand upon his ragged sleeve.

'Look here,' he cried, wheeling about, 'I want you to quit follerin' me. Don't I tell you money can't make me go back to them mountings!' And as I attempted to speak, he suddenly tore off his cap and pointed to his head. His hair was as white as snow.

'That's what come of monkeyin' inter your cursed mountings,' he shouted fiercely. 'There's things in there what no Christian oughter see. Lemme alone er I'll bust yer.'

He shambled on, doubled fists swinging by his side. The next moment, setting my teeth obstinately, I followed him and caught him by the park gate. At my hail he whirled around with a snarl, but I grabbed him by the throat and backed him violently against the park wall.

'You invaluable ruffian,' I said, 'now you listen to me. I live in that big stone building, and I'll give you a thousand dollars to take me behind the Graham Glacier. Think it over and call on me when you are in a pleasanter frame of mind. If you don't come by noon tomorrow I'll go to the Graham Glacier without you.'

He was attempting to kick me all the time, but I managed to avoid him, and when I had finished I gave him a shove which almost loosened his spinal column. He went reeling out across the side walk, and when he had recovered his breath and his balance he danced with displeasure and displayed a vocabulary that astonished me. However, he kept his distance.

As I turned back into the park, satisfied that he would not follow, the first person I saw was the elderly, stony-faced lady of the wisteria arbor advancing on tiptoe. Behind her came the younger lady with cheeks like a rose that had been rained on.

Instantly it occurred to me that they had followed us, and at the same moment I knew who the stony-faced lady was. Angry, but polite, I lifted my hat and saluted her, and she, probably furious at having being caught tiptoeing after me, cut me dead. The younger lady passed me with face averted, but even in the dusk I could see the tip of one little ear turn scarlet.

Walking on hurriedly, I entered the Administration Building, and found Professor Lesard, of the reptilian department, preparing to leave.

'Don't you do it,' I said sharply; 'I've got exciting news.'

'I'm only going to the theater,' he replied. 'It's a good show – Adam and Eve; there's a snake in it, you know. It's in my line.'

'I can't help it,' I said; and I told him briefly what had occurred in the arbor.

'But that's not all,' I continued savagely. 'Those women followed us, and who do you think one of them turned out to be? Well, it was Professor Smawl, of Barnard College, and I'll bet every pair of boots I own that she starts for the Graham Glacier within a week. Idiot that I was!' I exclaimed, smiting my head with both hands. 'I never recognised her until I saw her tiptoeing and craning her neck to listen. Now she knows about the glacier; she heard every word that young ruffian said, and she'll go to the glacier if it's only to forestall me.'

Professor Lesard looked anxious. He knew that Miss Smawl, professor of natural history at Barnard College, had long desired an appointment at the Bronx Park gardens. It was even said that she had a chance of succeeding Professor Farrago as president, but that, of course, must have been a joke. However, she haunted the gardens, annoying the keepers by persistently poking the animals with her umbrella. On one occasion she sent us word that she desired to enter the tigers' enclosure for the purpose of making experiments in hypnotism. Professor Farrago was absent, but I took it upon myself to send back word that I feared the tigers might injure her. The miserable small boy who took my message informed her that I was afraid she might injure the tigers, and the unpleasant incident almost cost me my position.

'I am quite convinced,' said I to Professor Lesard, 'that Miss Smawl is perfectly capable of abusing the information she overhead, and of starting herself to explore a region that, by all the laws of decency, justice, and prior claim, belongs to me.'

'Well,' said Lesard, with a peculiar laugh, 'it's not certain whether you can go at all.'

'Professor Farrago will authorise me,' I said confidently.

'Professor Farrago has resigned,' said Lesard. It was a bolt from a clear sky.

'Good Heavens!' I blurted out. 'What will become of the rest of us, then?'

'I don't know,' he replied. 'The trustees are holding a meeting over in the Administration Building to elect a new president for us. It depends on the new president what becomes of us.'

'Lesard,' I said hoarsely, 'you don't suppose that they could possibly elect Miss Smawl as our president, do you?'

He looked at me askance and bit his cigar.

'I'd be in a nice position, wouldn't I?' said I anxiously.

'The lady would probably make you walk the plank for that tiger business,' he replied.

'But I didn't do it,' I protested, with sickly eagerness. 'Besides, I explained to her.'

He said nothing, and I stared at him, appalled by the possibility of reporting to Professor Smawl for instructions next morning.

'See here, Lesard,' I said nervously, 'I wish you would step over to the Administration Building and ask the trustees if I may prepare for this expedition. Will you?'

He glanced at me sympathetically. It was quite natural for me to wish to secure my position before the new president was elected – especially as there was a chance of the new president being Miss Smawl.

'You are quite right,' he said; 'the Graham Glacier would be the safest place for you if our next president is to be the Lady of the Tigers.' And he started across the park puffing his cigar.

I sat down on the doorstep to wait for his return, not at all charmed with the prospect. It made me furious, too, to see my ambition nipped with the frost of a possible veto from Miss Smawl.

'If she is elected,' thought I, 'there is nothing for me but to resign – to avoid the inconvenience of being shown the door. Oh, I wish I had allowed her to hypnotise the tigers!'

Thoughts of crime flitted through my mind. Miss Smawl would not remain president – or anything else very long – if she persisted in her desire for the tigers. And then when she called for help I would pretend not to hear.

Aroused from criminal meditation by the return of Professor Lesard, I jumped up and peered into his perplexed eyes. 'They've elected a president,' he said, 'but they won't tell us who the president is until tomorrow.'

'You don't think—' I stammered.

'I don't know. But I know this: the new president sanctions the expedition to the Graham Glacier, and directs you to choose an assistant and begin preparations for four people.'

Overjoyed, I seized his hand and said, 'Hurray!' in a voice weak with emotion. 'The old dragon isn't elected this time,' I added triumphantly.

'By the way,' he said, 'who was the other dragon with her in the park this evening?'

I described her in a more modulated voice.

'Whew!' observed Professor Lesard, 'that must be her assistant, Professor Dorothy Van Twiller! She's the prettiest blue-stocking in town.'

With this curious remark my confrére followed me into my room and wrote down the list of articles I dictated to him. The list included a complete camping equipment for myself and three other men.

'Am I one of those other men?' inquired Lesard, with an unhappy smile.

Before I could reply my door was shoved open and a figure appeared at the threshold, cap in hand.

'What do you want?' I asked sternly; but my heart was beating high with triumph.

The figure shuffled; then came a subdued voice:

'Mister, I guess I'll go back to the Graham Glacier along with you. I'm Billy Spike, an' it kinder scares me to go back to them Hudson Mountains, but somehow, mister, when you choked me and kinder walked me off on my ear, why, mister, I kinder took to you, like.'

There was absolute silence for a minute; then he said:

'So if you go, I guess I'll go too, mister.'

'For a thousand dollars?'

'Fur nawthin',' he muttered, 'or what you like.'

'All right, Billy,' I said briskly; 'just look over those rifles and ammunition and see that everything's sound.'

He slowly lifted his tough young face and gave me a doglike glance. They were hard eyes, but there was gratitude in them.

'You'll get your throat slit,' whispered Lesard.

'Not while Billy's with me,' I replied cheerfully.

Late that night, as I was preparing for pleasant dreams, a knock came on my door and a telegraph-messenger handed me a note, which I read, shivering in my bare feet, although the thermometer marked eighty Fahrenheit:

You will immediately leave for the Hudson Mountains *via* Wellman Bay, Labrador, there to await further instructions. Equipment for yourself and one assistant will include following articles [here began a list of camping utensils, scientific paraphernalia, and provisions]. The steamer *Penguin* sails at five o'clock tomorrow morning. Kindly find yourself on board at that hour. Any excuse for not complying with these orders will be accepted as your resignation.

SUSAN SMAWL
President Bronx Zoological Society

'Lesard!' I shouted, trembling with fury.

He appeared at his door, chastely draped in pyjamas; and he read the insolent letter with terrified alacrity.

'What are you going to do – resign?' he asked, much frightened.

'Do!' I snarled, grinding my teeth; 'I'm going – that's what I'm going to do!'

'But – but you can't get ready and catch that steamer, too,' he stammered.

He did not know me.

II

And so it came about that one calm evening towards the end of June, William Spike and I went into camp under the southerly shelter of the vast granite wall called the Hudson Mountains, there to await the promised 'further instructions'.

It had been a tiresome trip by steamer to Anticosti, from there by schooner to Widgeon Bay, then down the coast and up the Cape Clear River to Port Borpoise. There we bought three pack-mules and started due north on the Great Fur Trail. The second day out we passed Fort Boise, the last outpost of civilisation, and on the sixth day we were travelling eastward under the granite mountain parapets.

On the evening of the sixth day out from Fort Boise we went into camp for the last time before entering the unknown land.

I could see it already through my field-glasses, and while William was building the fire I climbed up among the rocks above and sat down, glasses levelled, to study the prospect.

There was nothing either extraordinary or forbidding in the landscape which stretched out beyond; to the right the solid palisade of granite cut off the view; to the left the palisade continued, an endless barrier of sheer cliffs crowned with pine and hemlock. But the interesting section of the landscape lay almost directly in front of me – a rent in the mountain-wall through which appeared to run a level, arid plain, miles wide, and as smooth and even as a highroad.

There could be no doubt concerning the significance of that rent in the solid mountain-wall; and, moreover, it was exactly as William Spike had described it. However, I called to him, and he came up from the smoky camp-fire, ax on shoulder.

'Yep,' he said, squatting beside me; 'the Graham Glacier used to meander through that there hole, but somethin' went wrong with the earth's in'ards an' there was a bust-up.'

'And you saw it, William?' I said, with a sigh of envy.

'Hey? Seen it? Sure I seen it! I was to Spoutin' Springs, twenty-mile west, with a bale o' blue fox an' otter pelt. Fust I knew them geysers begun for to groan egregious like, an' I seen the caribou gallopin' hell-bent south. "This climate," sez I, "is too bracin' for me" so I struck a back trail an' landed on to a hill. Then them geysers blowed up, one arter the next, an' I heard somethin' kinder cave in between here an' China. I disremember things what happened. Somethin' throwed me down, but I couldn't stay there, for the blamed ground was runnin' like a river – all wavy-like, an' the sky hit me on the back o' me head.'

'And then?' I urged, in that new excitement which every repetition of the story revived. I had heard it all twenty times since we left New York, but mere repetition could not apparently satisfy me.

'Then,' continued William, 'the whole world kinder went off like a firecracker, an' I come to, an' ran like—'

'I know,' said I, cutting him short, for I had become wearied of the invariable profanity which lent a lurid ending to his narrative.

'After that,' I continued, 'you went through the rent in the mountains?'

'Sure.'

'And you saw a dingue and a creature that resembled a mammoth?'

'Sure,' he repeated sulkily.

'And you saw something else?' I always asked this question; it fascinated me to see the sullen fright flicker in William's eyes, and the mechanical backward glance, as though what he had seen might still be behind him.

He had never answered this third question but once, and

that time he fairly snarled in my face as he growled: 'I seen what no Christian oughter see.'

So when I repeated: 'And you saw something else, William?' he gave me a wicked, frightened leer, and shuffled off to feed the mules. Flattery, entreaties, threats left him unmoved; he never told me what the third thing was that he had seen behind the Hudson Mountains.

William had retired to mix up with his mules; I resumed my binoculars and my silent inspection of the great, smooth path left by the Graham Glacier when something or other exploded that vast mass of ice into vapor.

The arid plain wound out from the unknown country like a river, and I thought then, and think now, that when the glacier was blown into vapor the vapor descended in the most terrific rain the world has ever seen, and poured through the newly blasted mountain-gateway, sweeping the earth to bedrock. To corroborate this theory, miles to the southward I could see the *dèbris* winding out across the land towards Wellman Bay, but as the terminal moraine of the vanished glacier formerly ended there I could not be certain that my theory was correct. Owing to the formation of the mountains I could not see more than half a mile into the unknown country. What I could see appeared to be nothing but the continuation of the glacier's path, scored out by the cloud-burst, and swept as smooth as a floor.

Sitting there, my heart beating heavily with excitement, I looked through the evening glow at the endless, pine-crowned mountain-wall with its giant's gateway pierced for me! And I thought of all the explorers and the unknown heroes – trappers, Indians, humble naturalists, perhaps – who had attempted to scale that sheer barricade and had died there or failed, beaten back from those eternal cliffs. Eternal? No! For the Eternal Himself had struck the rock, and it had sprung asunder, thundering obedience.

In the still evening air the smoke from the fire below mounted in a straight, slender pillar, like the smoke from those ancient altars builded before the first blood had been shed on earth.

The evening wind stirred the pines; a tiny spring brook made thin harmony among the rocks; a murmur came from the quiet camp. It was William adjuring his mules. In the deepening twilight I descended the hillock, stepping cautiously among the rocks.

Then, suddenly, as I stood outside the reddening ring of firelight, far in the depths of the unknown country, far behind the mountain-wall, a sound grew on the quiet air. William heard it and turned his face to the mountains. The sound faded to a vibration which was felt, not heard. Then once more I began to divine a vibration in the air, gathering in distant volume until it became a sound, lasting the space of a spoken word, fading to vibration, then silence.

Was it a cry?

I looked at William inquiringly. He had quietly fainted away.

I got him to the little brook and poked his head into the icy water, and after a while he sat up pluckily.

To an indignant question he replied: 'Naw, I ain't a-cussin you. Lemme be or I'll have fits.'

'Was it that sound that scared you?' I asked.

'Ya-as,' he replied with a dauntless shiver.

'Was it the voice of a mammoth?' I persisted excitedly. 'Speak, William, or I'll drag you about and kick you!'

He replied that it was neither a mammoth nor a dingue, and added a strong request for privacy, which I was obliged to grant, as I could not torture another word out of him.

I slept little that night; the exciting proximity of the unknown land was too much for me. But although I lay awake for hours, I heard nothing except the tinkle of water among the rocks and the plover calling from some hidden marsh. At daybreak I shot a ptarmigan which had walked into camp, and the shot sent the echoes yelling among the mountains.

William, sullen and heavy-eyed, dressed the bird, and we broiled it for breakfast.

Neither he nor I alluded to the sound we had heard the night before; he boiled water and cleaned up the mess-kit, and I pottered about among the rocks for another ptarmigan. Wearying of this, I returned to the mules and William, and sat down for a smoke.

'It strikes me,' I said, 'that our instructions to "await further orders" are idiotic. How are we to receive "further orders" here?'

William did not know.

'You don't suppose,' said I, in sudden disgust, 'that Miss Smawl believes there is a summer hotel and daily mail service in the Hudson Mountains?'

William thought perhaps she did suppose something of the sort.

It irritated me beyond measure to find myself at last on the very border of the unknown country, and yet checked, held back, by the irresponsible orders of a maiden lady named Smawl. However, my salary depended upon the whim of that maiden lady, and although I fussed and fumed and glared at the mountains through my glasses, I realised that I could not stir without the permission of Miss Smawl. At times this grotesque situation became almost unbearable, and I often went away by myself and indulged in fantasies, firing my gun off and pretending I had hit Miss Smawl by mistake. At such moments I would imagine I was free at last to plunge into the strange country, and I would squat on a rock and dream of bagging my first mammoth.

The time passed heavily; the tension increased with each new day. I shot ptarmigan and kept our table supplied with brook-trout. William chopped wood, conversed with his mules, and cooked very badly.

'See here,' I said one morning; 'we have been in camp a week today, and I can't stand your cooking another minute!'

William, who was washing a saucepan, looked up and begged me sarcastically to accept the *cordon bleu*. But I know only how to cook eggs, and there were no eggs within some hundred miles.

To get the flavor of the breakfast out of my mouth I walked up to my favorite hillock and sat down for a smoke. The next moment, however, I was on my feet, cheering excitedly and shouting for William.

'Here come "further instructions" at last!' I cried, pointing to the southward, where two dots on the grassy plain were imperceptibly moving in our direction.

'People on mules,' said William, without enthusiasm.

'They must be messengers for us!' I cried, in chaste joy. 'Three cheers for the northward trail, William, and the mischief take Miss— Well, never mind now,' I added.

'On them approachin' mules,' observed William, 'there is wimmen.'

I stared at him for a second, then attempted to strike him. He dodged warily and repeated his incredible remark: 'Ya-as, there is – wimmen – two female ladies onto them there mules.'

'Bring me my glasses!' I said hoarsely; 'bring me those glasses, William, because I shall destroy you if you don't!'

Somewhat awed by my calm fury, he hastened back to camp and returned with the binoculars. It was a breathless moment. I adjusted the lenses with a steady hand and raised them.

Now, of all unexpected sights my fate may reserve for me in the future, I trust – nay, I know – that none can ever prove as unwelcome as the sight I perceived through my binoculars. For upon the backs of those distant mules were two women, and the first one was Miss Smawl!

Upon her head she wore a helmet, from which fluttered a green veil. Otherwise she was clothed in tweeds; and at moments she beat upon her mule with a thick umbrella.

Surfeited with the sickening spectacle, I sat down on the rock and tried to cry.

'I told yer so,' observed William; but I was too tired to attack him.

When the caravan rode into camp I was myself again, smilingly prepared for the worst, and I advanced, cap in hand, followed furtively by William.

'Welcome,' I said, violently injecting joy into my voice. 'Welcome, Professor Smawl, to the Hudson Mountains!'

'Kindly take my mule,' she said, climbing down to mother earth.

'William,' I said with dignity, 'take the lady's mule.'

Miss Smawl gave me a stolid glance, then made directly for the camp-fire, where a kettle of game broth simmered over the coals. The last I saw of her she was smelling of it, and I turned my back and advanced towards the second lady pilgrim, prepared to be civil until snubbed.

Now, it is quite certain that never before had William Spike or I beheld so much feminine loveliness in one human body on the back of a mule. She was clad in the daintiest of shooting-kilts, yet there was nothing mannish about her except the way she rode the mule, and that only accentuated her adorable femininity.

I remembered what Professor Lesard had said about blue stockings – but Miss Dorothy Van Twiller's were gray, turned over at the tops, and disappearing into canvas spats buckled across a pair of slim shooting-boots.

'Welcome,' said I, attempting to restrain a too violent cordiality. 'Welcome, Professor Van Twiller, to the Hudson Mountains.'

'Thank you,' she replied, accepting my assistance very sweetly; 'it is a pleasure to meet a human being again.'

I glanced at Miss Smawl. She was eating game broth, but she resembled a human being in a general way.

'I should very much like to wash my hands,' said Professor Van Twiller, drawing the buckskin gloves from her slim fingers.

I brought towels and soap and conducted her to the brook.

She called to Professor Smawl to join her, and her voice was crystalline; Professor Smawl declined, and her voice was batrachian.

'She is so hungry!' observed Miss Van Twiller. 'I am very thankful we are here at last, for we've had a horrid time. You see, neither of us knows how to cook.'

I wondered what they would say to William's cooking, but I held my peace and retired, leaving the little brook to mirror the sweetest face that ever was bathed in water.

III

That afternoon our expedition, in two sections, moved forward. The first section comprised myself and all the mules; the second section was commanded by Professor Smawl, followed by Professor Van Twiller, armed with a tiny shotgun. William, loaded down with the ladies' toilet articles, skulked in the rear. I say skulked; there was no other word for it.

'So you're a guide, are you?' observed Professor Smawl when William, cap in hand, had approached her with well-meant advice. 'The woods are full of lazy guides. Pick up those Gladstone bags! I'll do the guiding for this expedition.'

Made cautious by William's humiliation, I associated with the mules exclusively. Nevertheless, Professor Smawl had her hard eyes on me, and I realised she meant mischief.

The encounter took place just as I, driving the five mules, entered the great mountain gateway, thrilled with anticipation which almost amounted to foreboding. As I was about to set foot across the imaginary frontier which divided the world from the unknown land, Professor Smawl hailed me, and I halted until she came up.

'As commander of this expedition,' she said, somewhat out of breath, 'I desire to be the first living creature who has ever set foot behind the Graham Glacier. Kindly step aside, young sir!'

'Madam,' said I, rigid with disappointment, 'my guide, William Spike, entered that unknown land a year ago.'

'He *says* he did,' sneered Professor Smawl.

'As you like,' I replied; 'but it is scarcely generous to forestall the person whose stupidity gave you the clue to this unexplored region.'

'You mean yourself?' she asked, with a stony stare.

'I do,' said I firmly.

Her little, hard eyes grew harder, and she clutched her umbrella until the steel ribs crackled.

'Young man,' she said insolently, 'if I could have gotten rid of you I should have done so the day I was appointed president. But Professor Farrago refused to resign unless your position was assured, subject, of course, to your good behavior. Frankly, I don't like you, and I consider your views on science ridiculous, and if an opportunity presents itself, I will be most happy to request your resignation. Kindly collect your mules and follow me.'

Mortified beyond measure, I collected my mules and followed my president into the strange country behind the Hudson Mountains – I who had aspired to lead, compelled to follow in the rear, driving mules.

The journey was monotonous at first, but we shortly ascended a ridge from which we could see, stretching out below us, the wilderness where, save the feet of William Spike, no human feet had passed.

As for me, tingling with enthusiasm, I forgot my chagrin, I forgot my gross injustice, I forgot my mules. 'Excelsior!' I cried, running up and down the ridge in uncontrollable excitement at the sublime spectacle of forest, mountain, and valley all set with little lakes.

'Excelsior!' repeated an excited voice at my side, and Professor Van Twiller sprang to the ridge beside me, her eyes bright as stars.

Exalted, inspired by the mysterious beauty of the view, we clasped hands and ran up and down the grassy ridge.

'That will do,' said Professor Smawl coldly, as we raced about like a pair of distracted kittens. The chilly voice broke the spell: I dropped Professor Van Twiller's hand and sat down on a boulder, aching with wrath.

Late that afternoon we halted beside a tiny lake, deep in the unknown wilderness, where purple and scarlet bergamot choked the shores and the spruce-partridge strutted fearlessly under our very feet. Here we pitched our two tents. The afternoon sun slanted through the pines; the lake glittered; acres of golden brake perfumed the forest silence, broken only at rare intervals by the distant thunder of a partridge drumming.

Professor Smawl ate heavily and retired to her tent to lie torpid until evening. William drove the unloaded mules into an interval full of sun-cured, fragrant grasses; I sat down beside Professor Van Twiller.

The wilderness is electric. Once within the influence of its currents, human beings become positively or negatively charged, violently attracting or repelling each other.

'There is something the matter with this air,' said Professor Van Twiller. 'It makes me feel as though I were desperately enamored of the entire human race.'

She leaned back against a pine, smiling vaguely, and crossing one knee over the other.

Now, I am not bold by temperament, and, normally, I fear ladies. Therefore it surprised me to hear myself begin a frivolous *causerie*, replying to her pretty epigrams with epigrams of my own, advancing to the borderland of badinage, fearlessly conducting her and myself over that delicate frontage to meet upon the terrain of undisguised flirtation.

It was clear that she was out for a holiday. The seriousness and restraints of twenty-two years she had left behind her in the civilised world, and now, with a shrug of her young shoulders, she unloosened her burden of reticence, dignity, and responsibility, and let the whole load fall with a discreet thud.

'Even hares go mad in March,' she said seriously. 'I know you intend to flirt with me – and I don't care. Anyway, there's nothing else to do, is there?'

'Suppose,' said I solemnly, 'I should take you behind that big tree and attempt to kiss you!'

The prospect did not appear to appal her, so I looked around with that sneaking yet conciliatory caution peculiar to young men who are novices in the art. Before I had satisfied myself that neither William nor the mules were observing us, Professor Van Twiller rose to her feet and took a short step backward.

'Let's set traps for a dingue,' she said, 'will you?'

I looked at the big tree, undecided. 'Come on,' she said; 'I'll show you how.' And away we went into the woods, she leading, her kilts flashing through the golden half-light.

Now, I had not the faintest notion how to trap the dingue, but Professor Van Twiller asserted that it formerly fed on the tender tips of the spruce, quoting Darwin as her authority.

So we gathered a bushel of spruce-tips, piled them on the bank of a little stream, then built a miniature stockade around the bait, a foot high. I roofed this with hemlock, then laboriously whittled out and adjusted a swinging shutter for the entrance, setting it on springy twigs.

'The dingue, you know, was supposed to live in the water,' she said, kneeling beside me over our trap.

I took her little hand and thanked her for the information.

'Doubtless,' she said enthusiastically, 'a dingue will come out of the lake tonight to feed on our spruce-tips. Then,' she added, 'we've got him.'

'True!' I said earnestly, and pressed her fingers very gently.

Her face was turned a little away; I don't remember what she said; I don't remember that she said anything. A faint rose-tint stole over her cheek. A few moments later she said: 'You must not do that again.'

It was quite late when we strolled back to camp. Long before we came in sight of the twin tents we heard a deep voice bawling our names. It was Professor Smawl's and she pounced upon Dorothy and drove her ignominiously into the tent.

'As for you,' she said, in hollow tones, 'you may explain your conduct at once, or place your resignation at my disposal.'

But somehow or other I appeared to be temporarily lost to shame, and I only smiled at my infuriated president, and entered my own tent with a step that was distinctly frolicsome.

'Billy,' said I to William Spike, who regarded me morosely from the depths of the tent, 'I'm going out to bag a mammoth tomorrow, so kindly clean my elephant-gun and bring an ax to chop out the tusks.'

That night Professor Smawl complained bitterly of the cooking, but as neither Dorothy nor I know how to improve it, she revenged herself on us by eating everything on the table and retiring to bed, taking Dorothy with her.

I could not sleep very well; the mosquitoes were intrusive, and Professor Smawl dreamed she was a pack of wolves and yelped in her sleep.

'Bird, ain't she?' said William, roused from slumber by her weird noises.

Dorothy, much frightened, crawled out of her tent, where her blanket-mate still dreamed dyspeptically, and William and I made her comfortable by the campfire.

It takes a pretty girl to look pretty half asleep in a blanket.

'Are you sure you are quite well?' I asked her.

To make sure, I tested her pulse. For an hour it varied more or less, but without alarming either of us. Then she went back to bed and I sat alone by the camp-fire.

Towards midnight I suddenly began to feel that strange distant vibration that I had once before felt. As before, the vibration grew on the still air, increasing in volume until it became a sound, then died out into silence.

I rose and stole into my tent.

William, white as death, lay in his corner, weeping in his sleep.

I roused him remorselessly, and he sat up scowling, but refused to tell me what he had been dreaming.

'Was it about that third thing you saw—' I began. But he snarled up at me like a startled animal, and I was obliged to go to bed and toss about and speculate.

The next morning it rained. Dorothy and I visited our dingue-trap, but found nothing in it. We were inclined, however, to stay out in the rain behind a big tree, but Professor Smawl vetoed that proposition and sent me off to supply the larder with fresh meat.

I returned, mad and wet, with a dozen partridges and a white hare – brown at that season – and William cooked them vilely.

'I can taste the feathers!' said Professor Smawl indignantly.

'There's no accounting for taste,' I said, with a polite gesture of deprecation; 'personally, I find feathers unpalatable.'

'You may hand in your resignation this evening!' cried Professor Smawl, in hollow tones of passion.

I passed her the pancakes with a cheerful smile, and flippantly pressed the hand next to me. Unexpectedly it proved to be William's sticky fist, and Dorothy and I laughed until her tears ran into Professor Smawl's coffee cup – an accident which kindled her wrath to red heat, and she requested my resignation five times during the evening.

The next day it rained again, more or less. Professor Smawl complained of the cooking, demanded my resignation, and finally marched out to explore, lugging the reluctant William with her. Dorothy and I sat down behind the largest tree we could find.

I don't remember what we were saying when a peculiar sound interrupted us, and we listened earnestly.

It was like a bell in the woods, ding-dong! ding-dong! ding-dong! – a low, mellow, golden harmony, coming nearer, then stopping.

I clasped Dorothy in my arms in my excitement.

'It is the note of the dingue!' I whispered, 'that explains its name, handed down from remote ages along with the names of the behemoth and the coney. It was because of its bell-like cry that it was named! Darling!' I cried, forgetting our short acquaintance, 'we have made a discovery that the whole world will ring with!'

Hand in hand we tiptoed through the forest to our trap. There was something in it that took fright at our approach, and rushed panic-stricken round and round the interior of the trap, uttering its alarm-note, which sounded like the jangling of a whole string of bells.

I seized the strangely beautiful creature; it neither attempted to bite nor scratch, but crouched in my arms, trembling and eyeing me.

Delighted with the lovely, tame animal, we bore it tenderly back to the camp and placed it on my blanket. Hand in hand we stood before it, awed by the sight of this beast, so long believed to be extinct.

'It is too good to be true,' sighed Dorothy, clasping her white hands under her chin and gazing at the dingue in rapture.

'Yes,' said I solemnly, 'you and I, my child, are face to face with the fabled *dingue – Dingus solitarius*! Let us continue to gaze at it, reverently, prayerfully, humbly—'

Dorothy yawned – probably with excitement.

We were still mutely adoring the dingue when Professor Smawl burst into the tent at a hand-gallop, bawling hoarsely for her Kodak and notebook.

Dorothy seized her triumphantly by the arm and pointed at the dingue, which appeared to be frightened to death.

'What!' cried Professor Smawl scornfully, '*that* a dingue? Rubbish!'

'Madam,' I said firmly, 'it is a dingue! It's a monodactyl! See! It has but a single toe!'

'Bosh!' she retorted; 'it's got four!'

'Four!' I repeated blankly.

'Yes; one on each foot!'

'Of course,' I said; 'you didn't suppose a monodactyl meant a beast with one leg and one toe!'

But she laughed hatefully and declared it was a woodchuck.

We squabbled for a while until I saw the significance of her attitude. The unfortunate woman wished to find the dingue first and be accredited with the discovery.

I lifted the dingue in both hands and shook the creature gently, until the chiming ding-dong of its protestations filled our ears like sweet bells jangled out of tune.

Pale with rage at this final proof of the dingue's identity, she seized her camera and notebook.

'I haven't any time to waste over that musical woodchuck!' she shouted, and bounced out of the tent.

'What have you discovered, dear?' cried Dorothy, running after her.

'A mammoth!' bawled Professor Smawl triumphantly; 'and I'm going to photograph him!'

Neither Dorothy nor I believed her. We watched the flight of the infatuated woman in silence.

And now, at last, the tragic shadow falls over my paper as I write. I was never passionately attached to Professor Smawl, yet I would gladly refrain from chronicling the episode that must follow if, as I have hitherto attempted, I succeed in sticking to the unornamented truth.

I have said that neither Dorothy nor I believed her. I don't know why, unless it was that we had not yet made up our minds to believe that the mammoth still existed on earth. So, when Professor Smawl disappeared in the forest, scuttling through the underbush like a demoralised hen, we viewed her flight with unconcern. There was a large tree in the neighborhood – a pleasant shelter in case of rain. So we sat down behind it, although the sun was shining fiercely.

It was one of those peaceful afternoons in the wilderness when the whole forest dreams, and the shadows are asleep and every little leaflet takes a nap. Under the still tree-tops the dappled sunlight, motionless, soaked the sod; the forest-flies no longer whirled in circles, but sat sunning their wings on slender twig-tips.

The heat was sweet and spicy; the sun drew out the delicate essence of gum and sap, warming volatile juices until they exhaled through the aromatic bark.

The sun went down into the wilderness; the forest stirred in its sleep; a fish splashed in the lake. The spell was broken. Presently the wind began to rise somewhere far away in the unknown land. I heard it coming, nearer, nearer – a brisk wind that grew heavier and blew harder as it neared us – a gale that swept distant branches – a furious gale that set limbs clashing and cracking, nearer and nearer. Crack! and the gale grew to a hurricane, trampling trees like dead twigs! Crack! Crackle! Crash! Crash!

Was it the wind!

With the roaring in my ears I sprang up, staring into the forest vista, and at the same instant, out of the crashing forest sped Professor Smawl, skirts tucked up, thin legs flying like bicycle-spokes. I shouted, but the crashing drowned my voice. Then all at once the solid earth began to shake, and with the rush and roar of a tornado a gigantic living thing burst out of the forest before our eyes – a vast shadowy bulk that rocked and rolled along, mowing down trees in its course.

Two great crescents of ivory curved from its head; its back swept through the tossing tree-tops. Once it bellowed like a gun fired from a high bastion.

The apparition passed with the noise of thunder rolling on towards the ends of the earth. Crack! crash! went the trees, the tempest swept away in a rolling volley of reports, distant, more distant, until, long after the tumult had deadened, then ceased, the stunned forest echoed with the fall of mangled branches slowly dropping.

That evening an agitated young couple sat close together in the deserted camp, calling timidly at intervals for Professor Smawl and William Spike. I say timidly, because it is correct; we did not care to have a mammoth respond to our calls. The lurking echoes across the lake answered our cries; the full moon came up over the forest to look at us. We were not much to look at. Dorothy was moistening my shoulder with unfeigned tears, and I, afraid to light the fire, sat hunched up under the common blanket, wildly examining the darkness around us.

Chilled to the spinal marrow, I watched the gray lights whiten in the east. A single bird awoke in the wilderness. I saw the nearer tree looming in the mist, and the silver fog rolling on the lake.

All night long the darkness had vibrated with the strange monotone which I had heard the first night, camping at the gate of the unknown land. My brain seemed to echo that subtle harmony which rings in the auricular labyrinth after sound has ceased.

There are ghosts of sound which return to haunt long after sound is dead. It was these voiceless specters of a voice long dead that stirred the transparent silence, intoning tone-less tones.

I think I make myself clear.

It was an uncanny night; morning whitened the east; gray daylight stole into the woods, blotting the shadows to paler tints. It was nearly midday before the sun became visible through the fine-spun web of mist – a pale spot of gilt in the zenith.

By this pallid light I labored to strike the two empty tents, gather up our equipment and pack them on our five mules. Dorothy aided me bravely, whimpering when I spoke of Professor Smawl and William Spike, but abating nothing of her industry until we had the mules loaded and I was ready to drive them, Heaven knows whither.

'Where shall we go?' quavered Dorothy, sitting on a log with the dingue in her lap.

One thing was certain; this mammoth-ridden land was no place for women, and I told her so.

We placed the dingue in a basket and tied it around the leading mule's neck. Immediately the dingue, alarmed, began dingling like a cowbell. It acted like a charm on the other mules, and they gravely filed off after their leader, following the bell. Dorothy and I, hand in hand, brought up the rear.

I shall never forget the scene in the forest – the gray arch of the heavens swimming in mist through which the sun peered shiftily, the tall pines wavering through the fog, the preoccupied mules marching single file, the foggy bell-note of the gentle dingue in its swinging basket, and Dorothy, limp kilts dripping with dew, plodding through the white dusk.

We followed the terrible tornado-path which the mammoth had left in its wake, but there were no traces of its human victims – neither one jot of Professor Smawl nor one solitary tittle of William Spike.

And now I would be glad to end this chapter if I could;

I would gladly leave myself as I was, there in the misty forest, with an arm encircling the slender body of my little companion, and the mules moving in a monotonous line, and the dingue discreetly jingling – but again that menacing shadow falls across my page, and truth bids me tell all, and I, the slave of accuracy, must remember my vows as the dauntless disciple of truth.

Towards sunset – or that pale parody of sunset which set the forest swimming in a ghastly, colorless haze – the mammoth's trail of ruin brought us suddenly out of the trees to the shore of a great sheet of water.

It was a desolate spot; northward a chaos of somber peaks rose, piled up like thunder-clouds along the horizon; east and south the darkening wilderness spread like a pall. Westward, crawling out into the mist from our very feet, the gray waste of water moved under the dull sky, and flat waves slapped the squatting rocks, heavy with slime.

And now I understand why the trail of the mammoth continued straight into the lake, for on either hand black, filthy tamarack swamps lay under ghostly sheets of mist. I strove to creep out into the bog, seeking a footing, but the swamp quaked and the smooth surface trembled like jelly in a bowl. A stick thrust into the slime sank into unknown depths.

Vaguely alarmed, I gained the firm land again and looked around, believing there was no road open but the desolate trail we had traversed. But I was in error; already the leading mule was wading out into the water, and the others, one by one, followed.

How wide the lake might be we could not tell, because the band of fog hung across the water like a curtain. Yet out into this flat, shallow void our mules went steadily, slop! slop! slop! in single file. Already they were growing indistinct in the fog, so I bade Dorothy hasten and take off her shoes and stockings.

She was ready before I was, I having to unlace my shooting-boots, and she stepped out into the water, kilts fluttering, moving her white feet cautiously. In a moment I was beside her, and we waded forward, sounding the shallow water with our poles.

When the water had risen to Dorothy's knees I hesitated, alarmed. But when we attempted to retrace our steps we could not find the shore again, for the blank mist shrouded everything, and the water deepened at every step.

I halted and listened for the mules. Far away in the fog I heard a dull splashing, receding as I listened. After while all sound died away, and a slow horror stole over me – a horror that froze the little network of veins in every limb. A step to the right and the water rose to my knees; a step to the left and the cold, thin circle of the flood chilled my breast. Suddenly Dorothy screamed, and the next moment a far cry answered – a far, sweet cry that seemed to come from the sky, like the rushing harmony of the world's swift winds. Then the curtain of fog before us lighted up from behind; shadows moved on the misty screen, outlines of trees and grassy shores, and tiny birds flying. Thrown on the vapory curtain, in silhouette, a man and a woman passed under the lovely trees, arms about each other's necks; near them the shadows of five mules grazed peacefully; a dingue gambolled close by.

'It is a mirage!' I muttered, but my voice made no sound. Slowly the light behind the fog died out; the vapor around us turned to rose, then dissolved, while mile on mile of a limitless sea spread away till, like a quick line pencilled at a stroke, the horizon cut sky and sea in half, and before us lay an ocean from which towered a mountain of snow – or a gigantic berg of milky ice – for it was moving.

'Good Heavens,' I shrieked; 'it is alive!'

At the sound of my crazed cry the mountain of snow became a pillar, towering to the clouds, and a wave of golden glory drenched the figure to its knees! Figure? Yes – for a colossal arm shot across the sky, then curved back in exquisite grace to a head of awful beauty – a woman's head, with eyes like the blue lake of heaven – ay, a woman's splendid form, upright from the sky to the earth, knee-deep in the sea. The evening clouds drifted across her brow; her shimmering hair lighted the world beneath with sunset. Then, shading her white brow with one hand, she bent, and, with the other hand dipped in the sea, she sent a wave rolling at us. Straight out of the horizon it sped – a ripple that grew to a wave, then to a furious breaker which caught us up in a whirl of foam, bearing us onward, faster, faster, swiftly flying through leagues of spray until consciousness ceased and all was blank.

Yet ere my senses fled I heard again that strange cry – that sweet, thrilling harmony rushing out over the foaming waters, filling earth and sky with its soundless vibrations.

And I knew it was the hail of the Spirit of the North warning us back to life again.

Looking back, now, over the days that passed before we staggered into the Hudson Bay outpost at Gravel Cove, I am inclined to believe that neither Dorothy nor I was clothed entirely in our proper minds – or, if we were, our minds, no doubt, must have been in the same condition as our clothing. I remember shooting ptarmigan, and that we ate them; flashes of memory recall the steady downpour of rain through the endless twilight of shaggy forests; dim days on the foggy tundra, mud-holes from which the wild ducks rose in thousands; then the stunted hemlocks, then the forest again. And I do not even recall the moment when, at last, stumbling into the smooth path left by the Graham Glacier, we crawled through the mountain-wall, out of the unknown land, and once more into a world protected by the Lord Almighty.

A hunting party of Elbon Indians brought us in to the post, and everybody was most kind – that I remember, just before going into several weeks of unpleasant delirium mercifully mitigated with unconsciousness.

Curiously enough, Professor Van Twiller was not very much battered, physically, for I had carried her for days pickaback. But the awful experience had produced a shock which resulted in a nervous condition that lasted so long after she returned to New York that the wealthy and eminent specialist who attended her insisted upon taking her to the Riviera and marrying her. I sometimes wonder – but, as I have said, such reflections have no place in these austere pages.

However, anybody, I fancy, is at liberty to speculate upon the fate of the late Professor Smawl and William Spike, and upon the mules and the gentle dingue. Personally, I am convinced that the suggestive silhouettes I saw on that ghastly curtain of fog were cast by beatified beings in some earthly paradise – a mirage of bliss of which we caught but the colorless shadow-shapes floating 'twixt sea and sky.

At all events, neither Professor Smawl nor her William Spike ever returned; no exploring expedition has found a trace of a mule or lady, of William or the dingue. The new expedition to be organised by Barnard College may penetrate still farther. I suppose that, when the time comes, I shall be expected to volunteer. But Professor Van Twiller is married, and William and Professor Smawl ought to be, and altogether, considering the mammoth and that gigantic and splendid apparition that bent from the zenith to the ocean and sent a tidal-wave rolling from the palm of one white hand – I say, taking all these various matters under consideration, I think I shall decide to remain in New York and continue writing for the scientific periodicals.

DEATH TRAIL

Our final extract from The Slayer of Souls *finds the Cleves's joined by Sansa, one of Tressa's temple companions. Now in Chambers's familiar haunt of the Adirondacks, in New York State, they must track and kill another Yezidee assassin, who is making unholy magic in the woods . . .*

The way to Fool's Acre was under a tangled canopy of thorns, under rotting windfalls of grey mirch, through tunnel after tunnel of fallen debris woven solidly by millions of strands of tough cat-briers which cut the flesh like barbed wire.

There was blood on Tressa, where her flannel shirt had been pierced in a score of places. Cleves and Selden had been painfully slashed.

Silent, thread-like streams flowed darkling under the tangled mass that roofed them. Sometimes they could move upright; more often they were bent double; and there were long stretches where they had to creep forward on hands and knees through sparse wild grasses, soft, rotten soil, or paths of sphagnum which cooled their feverish skin in velvety, icy depths.

At noon they rested and ate, lying prone under the matted roof of their tunnel.

Cleves and Selden had their rifles. Tressa lay like a slender boy, her brier-torn hands empty.

And, as she lay there, her husband made a sponge of a

handful of sphagnum moss, and bathed her face and her arms, cleansing the dried blood from the skin, while the girl looked up at him out of grave, inscrutable eyes.

The sun hung low over the wilderness when they came to the woods of Fool's Acre. They crept cautiously out of the briers, among ferns and open spots carpeted with pine needles and dead leaves which were beginning to burn ruddy gold under the level rays of the sun.

Lying flat behind an enormous oak, they remained listening for a while. Selden pointed through the woods, eastward, whispering that the house stood there not far away.

'Don't you think we might risk the chance and use our rifles?' asked Cleves in a low voice.

'No. It is the Tchor-Dagh that confronts us. I wish to talk to Sansa,' she murmured.

A moment later Selden touched her arm.

'My God,' he breathed, 'who is that!'

'It is Sansa,' said Tressa calmly, and sat up among the ferns. And the next instant Sansa stepped daintily out of the red sunlight and seated herself among them without a sound.

Nobody spoke. The newcomer glanced at Selden, smiled slightly, blushed, then caught a glimpse of Cleves where he lay in the brake, and a mischievous glimmer came into her slanting eyes.

'Did I not tell my lord truths?' she inquired in a demure whisper. 'As surely as the sun is a dragon, and the flaming pearl burns between his claws, so surely burns the soul of Heart of Flame between thy guarding hands. There are as many words as there are demons, my lord, but it is written that *Niaz* is the greatest of all words save only the name of God.'

She laughed without any sound, sweetly malicious where she sat among the ferns.

'Heart of Flame,' she said to Tressa, 'you called me and I *made the effort.*'

'Darling,' said Tressa in her thrilling voice, 'the Yezidees

are making living things out of dust – as Sanang Noïane
made that thing in the Temple . . . And slew it before our
eyes.'

'The Tchor-Dagh,' said Sansa calmly.

'The Tchor-Dagh,' whispered Tressa.

Sansa's smooth little hands crept up to the collar of her
odd, blue tunic; grasped it.

'In the name of God the Merciful,' she said without tremor,
'listen to me, Heart of Flame, and may my soul be ransom
for yours!'

'I hear you, Sansa.'

Sansa said, her fingers still grasping the embroidered collar
of her tunic:

'Yonder, behind walls, two Tower Chiefs meddle with the
Tchor-Dagh, making living things out of the senseless dust
they scrape from the garden.'

Selden moistened his dry lips. Sansa said:

'The Yezidees who have come into this wilderness are
Arrak Sou-Sou, the Squirrel; and Tiyang Khan . . . May God
remember them in Hell!'

'May God remember them,' said Tressa mechanically.

'And those two Yezidee Sorcerers,' continued Sansa coolly,
'have advanced thus far in the Tchor-Dagh; for they now
roam these woods, digging like demons for the roots of
Ginseng; and thou knowest, O Heart of Flame, what that
indicates.'

'Does Ginseng grow in these woods!' exclaimed Tressa
with a new terror in her widening eyes.

'Ginseng grows here, little Rose-Heart, and the roots are as
perfect as human bodies. And Tiyang Khan squats in the walled
garden moulding the Ginseng roots in his unclean hands, while
Sou-Sou the Squirrel scratches among the dead leaves of the
woods for roots as perfect as a naked human body.

'All day long the Sou-Sou rummages among the trees; all
day long Tiyang pats and rubs and moulds the Ginseng roots
in his skinny fingers. It is the Tchor-Dagh, Heart of Flame.
And these Sorcerers must be destroyed.'

'Are their bodies here?'

'Arrak is in the body. And thus it shall be accomplished: listen attentively, Rose Heart Afire! – I shall remain here with—' she looked at Selden and flushed a trifle, '—with you, my lord. And when the Squirrel comes a-digging, so shall my lord slay him with a bullet . . . And when I hear his soul bidding his body farewell, then I shall make prisoner his soul . . . And send it to the Dark Star . . . And the rest shall be in the hands of Allah.'

She turned to Tressa and caught her hands in both of her own:

'It is written on the Iron Pages,' she whispered, 'that we belong to Erlik and we return to him. But in the Book of Gold it is written otherwise: "God preserve us from Satan who was stoned!" . . . Therefore, in the name of Allah! Now then, Heart of Flame, do your duty!'

A burning flush leaped over Tressa's features.

'Is my soul, then, my own!'

'It belongs to God,' said Sansa gravely.

'And – Sanang?'

'God is greatest.'

'But – was God there – at the Lake of the Ghosts?'

'God is everywhere. It is so written in the Book of Gold,' replied Sansa, pressing her hands tenderly.

'Recite the Fatha, Heart of Flame. Thy lips shall not stiffen; God listens.'

Tressa rose in the sunset glory and stood as though dazed, and all crimsoned in the last fiery bars of the declining sun.

Cleves also rose.

Sansa laughed noiselessly: 'My lord would go whither thou goest, Heart of Fire!' she whispered. 'And thy ways shall be his ways!'

Tressa's cheeks flamed and she turned and looked at Cleves.

Then Sansa rose and laid a hand on Tressa's arm and on her husband's:

'Listen attentively. Tiyang Khan must be destroyed. The

signal sounds when my lord's rifle-shot makes a loud noise here among these trees.'

'Can I prevail against the Tchor-Dagh?' asked Tressa, steadily.

'Is not that event already in God's hands, darling?' said Sansa softly. She smiled and resumed her seat beside Selden, amid the drooping fern fronds.

'Bid thy dear lord leave his rifle here,' she added quietly.

Cleves laid down his weapon. Selden pointed eastward in silence.

So they went together into the darkening woods.

In the dusk of heavy foliage overhanging the garden, Tressa lay flat as a lizard on the top of the wall. Beside her lay her husband.

In the garden below them flowers bloomed in scented thickets, bordered by walks of flat stone slabs split from boulders. A little lawn, very green, centered the garden.

And on this lawn, in the clear twilight still tinged with the somber fires of sundown, squatted a man dressed in a loose white garment.

Save for a twisted breadth of white cloth, his shaven head was bare. His sinewy feet were naked, too, the lean, brown toes buried in the grass.

Tressa's lips touched her husband's ear.

'Tiyang Khan,' she breathed. 'Watch what he does!'

Shoulder to shoulder they lay there, scarcely daring to breathe. Their eyes were fastened on the Mongol Sorcerer, who, squatted below on his haunches, grave and deliberate as a great gray ape, continued busy with the obscure business which so intently preoccupied him.

In a short semi-circle on the grass in front of him he had placed a dozen wild Ginseng roots. The roots were enormous, astoundingly shaped like the human body, almost repulsive in their weird symmetry.

The Yezidee had taken one of these roots into his hands. Squatting there in the semi-dusk, he began to massage it between his long, muscular fingers, rubbing, moulding, pressing the root with caressing deliberation.

His unhurried manipulation, for a few moments, seemed to produce no result. But presently the Ginseng root became lighter in colour and more supple, yielding to his fingers, growing ivory pale, sinuously limber in a newer and more delicate symmetry.

'Look!' gasped Cleves, grasping his wife's arm. '*What* is that man doing!'

'The Tchor-Dagh!' whispered Tressa. 'Do you see what lies twisting there in his hands!'

The Ginseng root had become the tiny naked body of a woman – a little ivory-white creature, struggling to escape between the hands that had created it – dark, powerful, masterly hands, opening leisurely now, and releasing the living being they had fashioned.

The thing scrambled between the fingers of the Sorcerer, leaped into the grass, ran a little way and hid, crouched down, panting, almost hidden by the long grass. The shocked watchers on the wall could still see the creature. Tressa felt Cleves's body trembling beside her. She rested a cool, steady hand on his.

'It is the Tchor-Dagh,' she breathed close to his face. 'The Mongol Sorcerer is becoming formidable.'

'Oh, God!' murmured Cleves, 'that thing he made is *alive*! I saw it. I can see it hiding there in the grass. It's frightened – breathing! It's alive!'

His pistol, clutched in his right hand, quivered. His wife laid her hand on it and cautiously shook her head.

'No,' she said, 'that is of no use.'

'But what that Yezidee is doing is – is blasphemous—'

'Watch him! His mind is stealthily feeling its way among the laws and secrets of the Tchor-Dagh. He has found a thread. He is following it through the maze into hell's own labyrinth! He has created a tiny thing in the image of the Creator. He will try to create a larger being now. Watch him with his Ginseng roots!'

Tiyang, looming ape-like on his haunches in the deepening dusk, moulded and massaged the Ginseng roots, one after another. And one after another, tiny naked creatures wriggled out of his palms between his fingers and scuttled away into the herbage.

Already the dim lawn was alive with them, crawling, scurrying through the grass, creeping in among the flower-beds, little, ghostly-white things that glimmered from shade into shadow like moonbeams.

Tressa's mouth touched her husband's ear:

'It is for the secret of Destruction that the Yezidee seeks. But first he must learn the secret of creation. He is learning . . . And he must learn no more than he has already learned.'

'That Yezidee is a living man. Shall I fire?'

'No.'

'I can kill him with the first shot.'

'Hark!' she whispered excitedly, her hand closing convulsively on her husband's arm.

The whip-crack of a rifle-shot still crackled in their ears.

Tiyang had leaped to his feet in the dusk, a Ginseng root, half-alive, hanging from one hand and beginning to squirm.

Suddenly the first moonbeam fell across the wall. And in its luster Tressa rose to her knees and flung up her right hand.

Then it was as though her palm caught and reflected the moon's ray, and hurled it in one blinding shaft straight into the dark visage of Tiyang Khan.

The Yezidee fell as though he had been pierced by a shaft of steel, and lay sprawling there on the grass in the ghastly glare.

And where his features had been there gaped only a hole into the head.

Then a dreadful thing occurred; for everywhere the grass swarmed with the little naked creatures he had made, running, scrambling, scuttling, darting into the black hole which had been the face of Tiyang Khan.

They poured into the awful orifice, crowding, jostling one

another so violently that the head jerked from side to side on the grass, a wabbling, inert, soggy mass in the moonlight.

And presently the body of Tiyang Khan, Warden of the Rampart of Gog and Magog, and Lord of the Seventh Tower, began to burn with white fire – a low, glimmering combustion that seemed to clothe the limbs like an incandescent mist.

On the wall knelt Tressa, the glare from her lifted hand streaming over the burning form below.

Cleves stood tall and shadowy beside his wife, the useless pistol hanging in his grasp.

Then, in the silence of the woods, and very near, they heard Sansa laughing. And Selden's anxious voice:

'Arrak is dead. The Sou-Sou hangs across a rock, head down, like a shot squirrel. Is all well with you?'

'Tiyang is on his way to his star,' said Tressa calmly. 'Somewhere in the world his body has bid its mind farewell . . . And so his body may live for a little, blind, in mental darkness, fed by others, and locked in all day, all night, until the end.'

THE CASE OF MR HELMER

He had really been too ill to go; the penetrating dampness of the studio, the nervous strain, the tireless application, all had told on him heavily. But the feverish discomfort in his head and lungs gave him no rest; it was impossible to lie there in bed and do nothing; besides, he did not care to disappoint his hostess. So he managed to crawl into his clothes, summon a cab, and depart. The raw night air cooled his head and throat; he opened the cab window and let the snow blow in on him.

When he arrived he did not feel much better, although Catharine was glad to see him. Somebody's wife was allotted to him to take in to dinner, and he executed the commission with that distinction of manner peculiar to men of his temperament.

When the women had withdrawn and the men had lighted cigars and cigarettes, and the conversation wavered between municipal reform and *contes drolatiques*, and the Boznovian attaché had begun an interminable story, and Count Fantozzi was emphasising his opinion of women by joining the tips of his overmanicured thumb and forefinger and wafting spectral kisses at an annoyed Englishman opposite, Helmer laid down his unlighted cigar and, leaning over, touched his host on the sleeve.

'Hello! what's up, Philip?' said his host cordially; and Helmer, dropping his voice a tone below the sustained pitch of conversation, asked him the question that had been burning his feverish lips since dinner began.

To which his host replied, 'What girl do you mean?' and bent nearer to listen.

'I mean the girl in the fluffy black gown, with shoulders and arms of ivory, and the eyes of Aphrodite.'

His host smiled. 'Where did she sit, this human wonder?'

'Beside Colonel Farrar.'

'Farrar? Let's see' – he knit his brows thoughtfully, then shook his head. 'I can't recollect; we're going in now and you can find her and I'll—'

His words were lost in the laughter and hum around them; he nodded an abstracted assurance at Helmer; others claimed his attention, and by the time he rose to signal departure he had forgotten the girl in black.

As the men drifted toward the drawing-rooms, Helmer moved with the throng. There were a number of people there whom he knew and spoke to, although through the increasing feverishness he could scarce hear himself speak. He was too ill to stay; he would find his hostess and ask the name of that girl in black, and go.

The white drawing-rooms were hot and over-thronged. Attempting to find his hostess, he encountered Colonel Farrar, and together they threaded their way aimlessly forward.

'Who is the girl in black, Colonel?' he asked; 'I mean the one that you took in to dinner.'

'A girl in black? I don't think I saw her.'

'She sat beside you!'

'Beside *me*?' The Colonel halted, and his inquiring gaze rested for a moment on the younger man, then swept the crowded rooms.

'Do you see her now?' he asked.

'No,' said Helmer, after a moment.

They stood silent for a little while, then parted to allow the Chinese minister thoroughfare – a suave gentleman, all antique silks, and a smile 'thousands of years old'. The minister passed, leaning on the arm of the general commanding at Governor's Island, who signalled Colonel

Farrar to join them; and Helmer drifted again, until a voice repeated his name insistently, and his hostess leaned forward from the brilliant group surrounding her, saying: 'What in the world is the matter, Philip? You look wretchedly ill.'

'It's a trifle close here – nothing's the matter.'

He stepped nearer, dropping his voice: 'Catharine, who was that girl in black?'

'What girl?'

'She sat beside Colonel Farrar at dinner – or I thought she did—'

'Do you mean Mrs Van Siclen? She is in white, silly!'

'No – the girl in black.'

His hostess bent her pretty head in perplexed silence, frowning a trifle with the effort to remember.

'There were so many,' she murmured; 'let me see it – it is certainly strange that I cannot recollect. Wait a moment! Are you sure she wore black? Are you *sure* she sat next to Colonel Farrar?'

'A moment ago I was certain—' he said, hesitating. 'Never mind, Catharine; I'll prowl about until I find her.'

His hostess, already partly occupied with the animated stir around her, nodded brightly; Helmer turned his fevered eyes and then his steps toward the cool darkness of the conservatories. But he found there a dozen people who greeted him by name, demanding not only his company but his immediate and undivided attention.

'Mr Helmer might be able to explain to us what his own work means,' said a young girl, laughing.

They had evidently been discussing his sculptured group, just completed for the new façade of the National Museum. Press and public had commented very freely on the work since the unveiling a week since; critics quarrelled concerning the significance of the strange composition in marble. The group was at the same time repellent and singularly beautiful; but nobody denied its technical perfection. This was the sculptured group: a vaquero, evidently dying, lay in a loose heap among some desert rocks. Beside him, chin on palm, sat an exquisite winged figure, calm eyes fixed on the dying man. It was plain that death was near; it was stamped on the ravaged visage, on the collapsed frame. And yet, in the dying boy's eyes there was nothing of agony, no fear, only an intense curiosity as the lovely winged figure gazed straight into the glazing eyes.

'It may be,' observed an attractive girl, 'that Mr Helmer will say with Mr Gilbert,

'"It is really very clever,
But I don't know what it means."'

Helmer laughed and started to move away. 'I think I'd better admit that at once,' he said, passing his hand over his aching eyes; but the tumult of protest blocked his retreat, and he was forced to find a chair under the palms and tree ferns. 'It was merely an idea of mine,' he protested, good-humoredly, 'an idea that has haunted me so persistently that, to save myself further annoyance, I locked it up in marble.'

'Demoniac obsession?' suggested a very young man, with a taste for morbid literature.

'Not at all,' protested Helmer, smiling; 'the idea annoyed me until I gave it expression. It doesn't bother me any more.'

'You said,' observed the attractive girl, 'that you were going to tell us all about it.'

'About the idea? Oh, no, I didn't promise that—'

'Please, Mr Helmer!'

A number of people had joined the circle; he could see others standing here and there among the palms, evidently pausing to listen.

'There is no logic in the idea,' he said, uneasily – 'nothing to attract your attention. I have only laid a ghost—'

He stopped short. The girl in black stood there among the others, intently watching him. When she caught his eye, she nodded with the friendliest little smile; and as he started to rise she shook her head and stepped back with a gesture for him to continue.

They looked steadily at one another for a moment.

'The idea that has always attracted me,' he began slowly, 'is purely instinctive and emotional, not logical. It is this: as long as I can remember I have taken it for granted that a person who is doomed to die, never dies utterly alone. We who die in our beds – or expect to – die surrounded by the living. So fall soldiers on the firing line; so end the great majority – never absolutely alone. Even in a murder, the murderer at least must be present. If not, something else is there.

'But how is it with those solitary souls isolated in the world – the lone herder who is found lifeless in some vast, waterless desert, the pioneer whose bones are stumbled over by the tardy pickets of civilisation – and even those nearer us – here in our city – who are found in silent houses, in deserted streets, in the solitude of salt meadows, in the miserable desolation of vacant lands beyond the suburbs?'

The girl in black stood motionless, watching him intently.

'I like to believe,' he went on, 'that no living creature dies absolutely and utterly alone. I have thought that, perhaps in the desert, for instance, when a man is doomed, and there is no chance that he could live to relate the miracle, some winged sentinel from the uttermost outpost of Eternity, putting off the armor of invisibility, drops through space to watch beside him so that he may not die alone.'

There was absolute quiet in the circle around him. Looking always at the girl in black, he said:

'Perhaps those doomed on dark mountains or in solitary deserts, or the last survivor at sea, drifting to certain destruction after the wreck has foundered, finds death no terror, being guided to it by those invisible to all save the surely doomed. That is really all that suggested the marble – quite illogical, you see.'

In the stillness, somebody drew a long, deep breath; the easy reaction followed; people moved, spoke together in low voices; a laugh rippled up out of the darkness. But Helmer had gone, making his way through the half light toward a figure that moved beyond through the deeper shadows of the foliage – moved slowly and more slowly. Once she looked back, and he followed, pushing forward and parting the heavy fronds of fern and palm and masses of moist blossoms. Suddenly he came upon her, standing there as though waiting for him.

'There is not a soul in this house charitable enough to present me,' he began.

'Then,' she answered laughingly, 'charity should begin at home. Take pity on yourself – and on me. I have waited for you.'

'Did you really care to know me?' he stammered.

'Why am I here alone with you?' she asked, bending above a scented mass of flowers. 'Indiscretion may be a part of valor, but it is the best part of – something else.'

That blue radiance which a starless sky sheds lighted her white shoulders; transparent shadow veiled the contour of neck and cheeks.

'At dinner,' he said, 'I did not mean to stare so – but I simply could not keep my eyes from yours—'

'A hint that mine were on yours, too?'

She laughed a little laugh so sweet that the sound seemed part of the twilight and the floating fragrance. She turned gracefully, holding out her hand.

'Let us be friends,' she said, 'after all these years.'

Her hand lay in his for an instant; then she withdrew it and dropped it caressingly upon a cluster of massed flowers.

'Forced bloom,' she said, looking down at them, where her fingers, white as the blossoms, lay half buried. Then, raising her head, 'You do not know me, do you?'

'Know you?' he faltered; 'how could I know you? Do you think for a moment that I could have forgotten you?'

'Ah, you have not forgotten me!' she said, still with her wide smiling eyes on his; 'you have not forgotten. There is a trace of me in the winged figure you cut in marble – not the features, not the massed hair, nor the rounded neck and limbs – but in the eyes. Who living, save yourself, can read those eyes?'

'Are you laughing at me?'

'Answer me; who alone in all the world can read the message in those sculptured eyes?'

'Can you?' he asked, curiously troubled.

'Yes; I, and the dying man in marble.'

'What do you read there?'

'Pardon for guilt. You have foreshadowed it unconsciously – the resurrection of the soul. That is what you have left in marble for the mercilessly just to ponder on; that alone is the meaning of your work.'

Through the throbbing silence he stood thinking, searching his clouded mind.

'The eyes of the dying man are your own,' she said. 'Is it not true?'

And still he stood there, groping, probing through dim and forgotten corridors of thought toward a faint memory scarcely perceptible in the wavering mirage of the past.

'Let us talk of your career,' she said, leaning back against the thick foliage – 'your success, and all that it means to you,' she added gayly.

He stood staring at the darkness. 'You have set the phantoms of forgotten things stirring and whispering together somewhere within me. Now tell me more; tell me the truth.'

'You are slowly reading it in my eyes,' she said, laughing sweetly. 'Read and remember.'

The fever in him seared his sight as he stood there, his confused gaze on hers.

'Is it a threat of hell you read in the marble?' he asked.

'No, nothing of destruction, only resurrection and hope of Paradise. Look at me closely.'

'Who are you?' he whispered, closing his eyes to steady his swimming senses. 'When have we met?'

'You were very young,' she said under her breath – 'and I was younger – and the rains had swollen the Canadian river so that it boiled amber at the fords; and I could not cross – alas!'

A moment of stunning silence, then her voice again: 'I said nothing, not a word even of thanks when you offered aid . . . I – was not too heavy in your arms, and the ford was soon passed – soon passed. That was very long ago.' Watching him from shadowy sweet eyes, she said:

'For a day you knew the language of my mouth and my arms around you, there in the white sun glare of the river. For every kiss taken and retaken, given and forgiven, we must account – for every one, even to the last.

'But you have set a monument for us both, preaching the resurrection of the soul. Love is such a little thing – and ours endured a whole day long! Do you remember? Yet He who created love, designed that it should last a lifetime. Only the lost outlive it.'

She leaned nearer:

'Tell me, you who have proclaimed the resurrection of dead souls, are you afraid to die?'

Her low voice ceased; lights broke out like stars through the foliage around them; the great glass doors of the ballroom were opening; the illuminated fountain flashed, a falling shower of silver. Through the outrush of music and laughter swelling around them, a clear far voice called 'Francoise!'

Again, close by, the voice range faintly, 'Francoise! Francoise!'

She slowly turned, staring into the brilliant glare beyond.

'Who called?' he asked hoarsely.

'My mother,' she said, listening intently. 'Will you wait for me?'

His ashen face glowed again like a dull ember. She bent nearer, and caught his fingers in hers.

'By the memory of our last kiss, wait for me!' she pleaded, her little hand tightening on his.

'Where?' he said, with dry lips. 'We cannot talk here! – we cannot say here the things that must be said.'

'In your studio,' she whispered. 'Wait for me.'

'Do you know the way?'

'I tell you I will come; truly I will! Only a moment with my mother – then I will be there!'

Their hands clung together an instant, then she slipped

away into the crowded rooms; and after a moment Helmer followed, head bent, blinded by the glare.

'You are ill, Philip,' said his host, as he took his leave. 'Your face is as ghastly as that dying vaquero's – by Heaven, man, you *look* like him!'

'Did you find your girl in black?' asked his hostess curiously.

'Yes,' he said; 'good night.'

The air was bitter as he stepped out – bitter as death. Scores of carriage lamps twinkled as he descended the snowy steps, and a faint gust of music swept out of the darkness, silenced as the heavy doors closed behind him.

He turned west, shivering. A long smear of light bounded his horizon as he pressed toward it and entered the sordid avenue beneath the iron arcade which was even now trembling under the shock of an oncoming train. It passed overhead with a roar; he raised his hot eyes and saw, through the tangled girders above, the illuminated disk of the clock tower – all distorted – for the fever in him was disturbing everything – even the cramped and twisted street into which he turned, fighting for breath like a man stabbed through and through.

'What folly!' he said aloud, stopping short in the darkness. 'This is fever – all this. She could not know where to come—'

Where two blind alleys cut the shabby block, worming their way inward from the avenue and from Tenth Street, he stopped again, his hands working at his coat.

'It is fever, fever!' he muttered. 'She was not there.'

There was no light in the street save for the red fire lamp burning on the corner, and a glimmer from the Old Grapevine Tavern across the way. Yet all around him the darkness was illuminated with pale unsteady flames, lighting him as he groped through the shadows of the street to the blind alley. Dark old silent houses peered across the paved lane at their aged counterparts, waiting for him.

And at last he found a door that yielded, and he stumbled

into the black passageway, always lighted on by the unsteady pallid flames which seemed to burn in infinite depths of night.

'She was not there – she was never there,' he gasped, bolting the door and sinking down upon the floor. And, as his mind wandered, he raised his eyes and saw the great bare room growing whiter and whiter under the uneasy flames.

'It will burn as I burn,' he said aloud – for the phantom flames had crept into his body. Suddenly he laughed, and the vast studio rang again.

'Hark!' he whispered, listening intently. 'Who knocked?'

There was someone at the door; he managed to raise himself and drag back the bolt.

'You!' he breathed, as she entered hastily, her hair disordered and her black skirts powdered with snow,

'Who but I?' she whispered, breathless. 'Listen! do you hear my mother calling me? It is too late; but she was with me to the end.'

Through the silence, from an infinite distance, came a desolate cry of grief – 'Francoise!'

He had fallen back into his chair again, and the little busy flames enveloped him so that the room began to whiten again into a restless glare. Through it he watched her.

The hour struck, passed, struck and passed again. Other hours grew, lengthening into night. She sat beside him with never a word or sigh or whisper of breathing; and dream after dream swept him, like burning winds. Then sleep immersed him so that he lay senseless, sightless eyes still fixed on her. Hour after hour – and the white glare died out, fading to a glimmer. In densest darkness, he stirred, awoke, his mind quite clear, and spoke her name in a low voice.

'Yes, I am here,' she answered gently.

'Is it death?' he asked, closing his eyes.

'Yes. Look at me, Philip.'

His eyes unclosed; into his altered face there crept an

intense curiosity. For he beheld a glimmering shape, wide-winged and deep-eyed, kneeling beside him, and looking him through and through.

BIBLIOGRAPHY

Stories in this volume come from these sources:

The King in Yellow (F. Tennyson Neely, 1895; British Edition: Chatto & Windus, 1895)
'The Yellow Sign'
'The Demoiselle d'Ys'
'The Mask'
'In the Court of the Dragon'

The Maker of Moons (G.P. Putnam's Sons, 1896)
'The Maker of Moons'
'A Pleasant Evening'

The Mystery of Choice (Appleton, 1897; British Edition: Harper, 1898)
'The Messenger'
'Passeur'
'The Key to Grief'

In Search of the Unknown (Harper Bros, 1904; British edition: A. Constable, 1905)
'In Search of the Great Auk'
'In Search of the Mammoth'

The Tracer of Lost Persons (D. Appleton & Co., 1906; British
edition: John Murray, 1907)
'Samaris'
'The Seal of Solomon'

The Tree of Heaven (D. Appleton & Co., 1907; British edition:
A. Constable, 1908)
'Out of the Depths'
'The Sign of Venus'
'The Bridal Pair'
'The Case of Mr Helmer'

Police!!! (D. Appleton & Co., 1915)
'Un Peu d'Amour'
'The Third Eye'

The Slayer of Souls (George H. Doran, 1920; British edition:
Hodder & Stoughton, 1920 – printed in America)
'Grey Magic'
'The Death of Yarghouz Khan'
'Death Trail'

ACKNOWLEDGEMENTS

Chambers has been one of my favourite authors for as long as I've been reading books in this genre, and the idea for a collection of his stories goes back as far as March 1989, and a long phone call with Mike Ashley. We were casting about for ideas for the much-lamented Equation Chillers series, and Chambers seemed an ideal candidate. Mike supplied valuable biographical and bibliographical information on Chambers, and when I revived the project after some years (it hadn't survived the Equation demise), he lent me E.F. Bleiler's splendid collection of Robert W. Chambers stories. So, first, thanks to Mike.

The late Richard Dalby supplied more information on the author, and showed me pictures of him (the first I'd ever seen of Robert W. Chambers). Thanks to Richard as well.

Larry Loc in California sent an invaluable e-mail about Broadalbin, and my very grateful thanks go to him for throwing light on an unfamiliar side of Chambers and his life.

And thanks once again to David Brawn at HarperCollins, who has brought Robert W. Chambers (and some other authors) back to the light again.

It would be churlish of me not to give grateful thanks to three researchers – Everett Bleiler, Sam Moskowitz and Lee Weinstein – whose brief articles on Robert W. Chambers have been so helpful for this book. Chambers is a strange biographical bird – there isn't much about him, particularly in Britain.

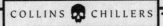
ALSO AVAILABLE

Acknowledged as one of the finest writers of Edwardian supernatural fiction, the name E. F. Benson is mentioned in the same breath as other greats such as M. R. James and H. R. Wakefield, but his success sadly overshadowed the work of his brothers in the ghost story genre. In fact, the Benson brothers – Arthur Christopher, Edward Frederic and Robert Hugh – were one of the most extraordinary and prolific literary families, between them writing more than 150 books.

Now the best supernatural tales of A. C. and R. H. Benson have been gathered into one volume by anthologist Hugh Lamb, whose introduction examines the lives and writings of these two complex and fascinating men. Originally published between 1903 and 1927, the stories include A. C. Benson's masterful 'Basil Netherby' and 'The Uttermost Farthing', and an intriguing article by R. H. Benson about real-life haunted houses.

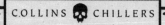
ALSO AVAILABLE

Emile Erckmann and Louis Alexandre Chatrian began
their writing partnership in the 1840s and continued
working together until Chatrian's death in 1890. At the
height of their powers they were known as 'the twins',
and their works proved popular translated into English,
but after their deaths they slipped into obscurity.

In *The Invisible Eye*, veteran horror anthologist Hugh
Lamb has collected together the finest weird tales by
Erckmann–Chatrian. Praised by successors including
M.R. James and H. P. Lovecraft, they wrote vividly of a
world of noblemen and peasants, enchanted castles and
mysterious woods, haunted by witches, monsters, curses
and spells. With an introduction by Hugh Lamb, this
collection will transport the reader to the darkest depths
of the nineteenth century: a time when anything could
happen – and occasionally did.

ALSO AVAILABLE

Edith Nesbit's natural gift for storytelling, exemplified by
The Railway Children and *Five Children and It*, has brought her
worldwide renown as a classic children's author. But beyond her
beloved children's stories lay a darker side to her imagination,
revealed here in her chilling tales of the supernatural. Haunted
by lifelong phobias which provoked, in her own words, 'nights
and nights of anguish and horror, long years of bitterest fear and
dread', Nesbit was inspired to pen terrifying stories of a twilight
world where the dead walked the earth.

All but forgotten for almost a hundred years until *In the Dark*
was first published 30 years ago, this collection finally restored
Nesbit's reputation as one of the most accomplished and
entertaining ghost-story writers of the Victorian age. With
seven extra newly-discovered stories now appearing for the first
time in paperback, this revised edition includes an introduction
by Hugh Lamb exploring the life of the woman behind these
tales and the events and experiences that contributed to her
fascination with the macabre.

ALSO AVAILABLE

Bernard Capes was celebrated as one of the most prolific authors of the late Victorian period, and his greatest acclaim came from penning some of the most terrifying ghost stories of the era. Yet following his death in 1918 his work all but slipped into oblivion until the 1980s, when veteran anthologist Hugh Lamb first collected Capes's tales of terror as *The Black Reaper*.

Every story bears the stamp of Capes's fertile and deeply pessimistic imagination, from werewolf priests and haunted typewriters to marble hands that come to life and plague-stricken villagers haunted by a scythe-wielding ghost. Now expanded with eleven further stories, a revised introduction and a new foreword by Capes's grandson, Ian Burns, this classic collection will thrill horror fans and restore Capes's reputation as one of the best writers in the horror genre.

ALSO AVAILABLE

Jerome K. Jerome's reputation as a humorist, renowned for his comic novel *Three Men in a Boat*, has thrown into undeserved obscurity his fine efforts in the ghost story genre. *Three Men in the Dark* collects Jerome's major horror stories, together with a selection from two of his friends with whom he founded the magazines *The Idler* and *Today* – the journalist Robert Barr and the humorist Barry Pain.

This new edition includes as an extra bonus the long-lost novelette, 'The Mystery of Black Rock Creek'. Written in five parts by Jerome K. Jerome, Barry Pain, Eden Phillpotts, E. F. Benson and Bram Stoker's brother-in-law Frank Frankfort Moore, it rounds off one of the most unusual and entertaining anthologies of the macabre of recent years.

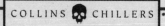
ALSO AVAILABLE

The most famous vampire novel of them all is Bram Stoker's *Dracula*, published in 1897. But it was not the first piece of fiction to describe the doings of the undead, and it was by no means the last.

In celebration of the 120th anniversary of the publication of *Dracula*, this unique anthology gathers together 24 rare vampire stories written by contemporaries of Bram Stoker between 1867 and 1940, including Sir Arthur Conan Doyle and M. R. James.

Dracula's Brood provides a veritable feast of pleasure for all lovers of supernatural and fantasy fiction. This new edition includes for the first time Barry Pain's 'The Tree of Death'.

ALSO AVAILABLE

In 1897, Bram Stoker's iconic *Dracula* redefined the horror genre and had a significant impact on the image of the vampire in popular culture. But encounters with the undead were nothing new: they had electrified readers of Gothic fiction since even before Victorian times.

Dracula's Brethren is a tribute to those early writers, a collation of 19 archetypal tales written between 1820 and 1910, many long forgotten, celebrating the vampire stories that both inspired and were inspired by Bram Stoker's iconic novel.

A companion to Richard Dalby's definitive anthology, *Dracula's Brood*, itself 30 years old, these rediscovered stories are a genuine treasure trove for classic thrill-seekers and all lovers of supernatural fiction.